About Steve Berry

Steve Berry is the *New York Times* bestselling author of *The Templar Legacy*, *The Third Secret* and *The Romanov Prophecy*. He lives on the Georgia coast, and is a lawyer who has travelled extensively throughout the Caribbean, Mexico, Europe and Russia. His books have been translated into over thirty languages. He is currently at work on his next thriller. Visit his website at www.steveberry.org.

Also by Steve Berry

The Romanov Prophecy
The Third Secret
The Templar Legacy

THE
AMBER
ROOM

STEVE BERRY

HODDER

Published by arrangement with Ballantine Books, an imprint of Random House
Publishing Group, a division of Random House, Inc.

First published in Great Britain in 2007 by Hodder & Stoughton
A division of Hodder Headline

A Hodder paperback

8

A CIP catalogue record for this title is available from the British Library

ISBN 978-0-340-92089-3

Printed and bound by
Clays Ltd, St Ives plc

Hodder Headline's policy is to use papers that are natural, renewable and
recyclable products and made from wood grown in sustainable forests. The
logging and manufacturing processes are expected to conform to the
environmental regulations of the country of origin.

Hodder & Stoughton Ltd
A division of Hodder Headline
338 Euston Road
London NW1 3BH

For my father,
who unknowingly kindled the fire decades ago,

and my mother,
who taught me the discipline to sustain the blaze

ACKNOWLEDGMENTS

I WAS ONCE TOLD THAT WRITING IS A LONELY ENDEAVOR AND the observation is correct. But a manuscript is never completed in a vacuum, especially one that is fortunate enough to be published, and in my case there are many who helped along the way.

First, Pam Ahearn, an extraordinary agent who rode out every storm into calm waters. Next, Mark Tavani, a remarkable editor who gave me a chance. Then there are Fran Downing, Nancy Pridgen, and Daiva Woodworth, three lovely women who made every Wednesday night special. I am honored to be "one of the girls." The novelists David Poyer and Lenore Hart not only provided practical lessons, but they led me to Frank Green, who took the time to teach me what I should know. Also, Arnold and Janelle James, my in-laws, who never voiced a discouraging word. Finally, there are all those who listened to me ramble, read my attempts, and offered their opinions. I'm afraid to list names in fear of forgetting someone. Please know that each of you is important and your thoughtful consideration, without question, moved the journey along.

Above all, though, are two special people who mean the most. My wife, Amy, and daughter, Elizabeth, who together make all things possible, including this.

For whatever cause a country is ravaged, we ought to spare those edifices which do honor to human society, and do not contribute to increase an enemy's strength—such as temples, tombs, public buildings, and all works of remarkable beauty. . . . It is declaring one's self to be an enemy of mankind, thus wantonly to deprive them of these wonders of art.
— EMMERICH DE VATTEL, *The Law of Nations,* 1758

I have studied in detail the state of the historic monuments in Peterhof, Tsarskoe Selo, and Pavlovsk, and in all three towns I have witnessed monstrous outrages against the integrity of these monuments. Moreover, the damage caused—a full inventory of which would be extremely difficult to give because it is so extensive—bears the marks of premeditation.
— Testimony of Iosif Orbeli, director of the Hermitage, before the Nürnberg tribunal, February 22, 1946

PROLOGUE

THE PRISONERS CALLED HIM EARS BECAUSE HE WAS THE ONLY Russian in Hut 8 who understood German. Nobody ever used his given name, Karol Borya. *Ýxo*—Ears—had been his label from the first day he entered the camp over a year ago. It was a tag he regarded with pride, a responsibility he took to heart.

"What do you hear?" one of the prisoners whispered to him through the dark.

He was cuddled close to the window, pressed against the frigid pane, his exhales faint as gossamer in the dry sullen air.

"Do they want more amusement?" another prisoner asked.

Two nights ago the guards came for a Russian in Hut 8. He was an infantryman from Rostov near the Black Sea, relatively new to the camp. His screams were heard all night, ending only after a burst of staccato gunfire, his bloodied body hung by the main gate the next morning for all to see.

He glanced quickly away from the pane. "Quiet. The wind makes it difficult to hear."

The lice-ridden bunks were three-tiered, each prisoner allocated less than one square meter of space. A hundred pairs of sunken eyes stared back at him.

All the men respected his command. None stirred, their fear long ago absorbed into the horror of Mauthausen. He suddenly turned from the window. "They're coming."

An instant later the hut's door was flung open. The frozen

night poured in behind Sergeant Humer, the attendant for
Prisoners' Hut 8.

"Achtung!"

Claus Humer was *Schutzstaffel,* SS. Two more armed SS
stood behind him. All the guards in Mauthausen were SS.
Humer carried no weapon. Never did. A six-foot frame and
beefy limbs were all the protection he needed.

"Volunteers are required," Humer said. "You, you, you,
and you."

Borya was the last selected. He wondered what was happening. Few prisoners died at night. The death chamber remained idle, the time used to flush the gas and wash the tiles
for the next day's slaughter. The guards tended to stay in
their barracks, huddled around iron stoves kept warm by
firewood prisoners died cutting. Likewise, the doctors and
their attendants slept, readying themselves for another day
of experiments in which inmates were used indiscriminately
as lab animals.

Humer looked straight at Borya. "You understand me,
don't you?"

He said nothing, staring back into the guard's black eyes.
A year of terror had taught him the value of silence.

"Nothing to say?" Humer asked in German. "Good. You
need to understand . . . with your mouth shut."

Another guard brushed past with four wool overcoats
draped across his outstretched arms.

"Coats?" muttered one of the Russians.

No prisoner wore a coat. A filthy burlap shirt and tattered
pants, more rags than clothing, were issued on arrival. At
death they were stripped off to be reissued, stinking and un-
washed, to the next arrival. The guard tossed the coats on the
floor.

Humer pointed. *"Mäntel anziehen."*

Borya reached down for one of the green bundles.
"The sergeant says to put them on," he explained in Russian.

The other three followed his lead.

The wool chafed his skin but felt good. It had been a long time since he was last even remotely warm.

"Outside," Humer said.

The three Russians looked at Borya and he motioned toward the door. They all walked into the night.

Humer led the file across the ice and snow toward the main grounds, a frigid wind howling between rows of low wooden huts. Eighty thousand people were crammed into the surrounding buildings, more than lived in Borya's entire home province in Belarus. He'd come to think that he would never see that place again. Time had almost become irrelevant, but for his sanity he tried to maintain some sense. It was late March. No. Early April. And still freezing. Why couldn't he just die or be killed? Hundreds met that fate every day. Was his destiny to survive this hell?

But for what?

At the main grounds Humer turned left and marched into an open expanse. More prisoners' huts stood on one side. The camp's kitchen, jail, and infirmary lined the other. At the far end was the roller, a ton of steel dragged across the frozen earth each day. He hoped their task did not involve that unpleasant chore.

Humer stopped before four tall stakes.

Two days ago a detail was taken into the surrounding forest, Borya one of ten prisoners chosen then, as well. They'd felled three aspens, one prisoner breaking an arm in the effort and shot on the spot. The branches were sheared and the logs quartered, then dragged back to camp and planted to the height of a man in the main grounds. But the stakes had remained bare the past couple of days. Now two armed guards watched them. Arc lights burned overhead and fogged the bitterly dry air.

"Wait here," Humer said.

The sergeant pounded up a short set of stairs and entered the jail. Light spilled out in a yellow rectangle from the open door. A moment later four naked men were led outside. Their blond heads were not shaved like the rest of the Russians,

Poles, and Jews who constituted the vast majority of the
camp's prisoners. No weak muscles or slow movements, either. No apathetic looks, or eyes sunk deep in their sockets, or
edema swelling emaciated frames. These men were stocky.
Soldiers. Germans. He'd seen their look before. Granite faces,
no emotion. Stone cold, like the night.

The four walked straight and defiant, arms at their sides,
none evidencing the unbearable cold their milky skin must
have been experiencing. Humer followed them out of the jail
and motioned to the stakes. "Over there."

The four naked Germans marched where directed.

Humer approached and tossed four coils of rope in the
snow. "Tie them to the stakes."

Borya's three companions looked at him. He bent down
and retrieved all four coils, handing them to the other three
and telling them what to do. They each approached a naked
German, the men standing at attention before the rough
aspen logs. What violation had provoked such madness? He
draped the rough hemp around his man's chest and strapped
the body to the wood.

"Tight," Humer yelled.

He knotted a loop and pulled the coarse fiber hard across
the German's bare chest. The man never winced. Humer
looked away at the other three. He took the opportunity to
whisper in German, "What did you do?"

No reply.

He pulled the rope tight. "They don't even do this to us."

"It is an honor to defy your captor," the German whispered.

Yes, he thought. It was.

Humer turned back. Borya knotted the last loop. "Over
there," Humer said.

He and the other three Russians trudged across fresh
snow, out of the way. To keep the cold at bay he stuffed
his hands into his armpits and shifted from foot to foot.
The coat felt wonderful. It was the first warmth he'd known
since being brought to the camp. It was then that his

identity had been completely stripped away, replaced by a number—10901—tattooed onto his right forearm. A triangle was stitched to the left breast of his tattered shirt. An R in his signified that he was Russian. Color was important, too. Red for political prisoners. Green for criminals. Yellow Star of David for Jews. Black and brown for prisoners of war.

Humer seemed to be waiting for something.

Borya glanced to his left.

More arc lights illuminated the parade ground all the way to the main gate. The road outside, leading to the quarry, faded into darkness. The command headquarters building just beyond the fence stood unlit. He watched as the main gate swung open and a solitary figure entered the camp. The man wore a greatcoat to his knees. Light trousers extended out the bottom to tan jackboots. A light-colored officer's hat covered his head. Outsize thighs hitched bowlegged in a determined gait, the man's portly belly leading the way. The lights revealed a sharp nose and clear eyes, the features not unpleasant.

And instantly recognizable.

Last commander of the Richthofen Squadron, Commander of the German Air Force, Speaker of the German Parliament, Prime Minister of Prussia, President of the Prussian State Council, Reichmaster of Forestry and Game, Chairman of the Reich Defense Council, Reichsmarschall of the Greater German Reich. The Führer's chosen successor.

Hermann Göring.

Borya had seen Göring once before. In 1939. Rome. Göring appeared then wearing a flashy gray suit, his fleshy neck wrapped in a scarlet cravat. Rubies had adorned his bulbous fingers, and a Nazi eagle studded with diamonds was pinned to the left lapel. He'd delivered a restrained speech urging Germany's place in the sun, asking, *Would you rather have guns or butter? Should you import lard or metal ore? Preparedness makes us powerful. Butter merely makes us fat.* Göring had finished that oratory in a flurry, promising Germany and Italy would march shoulder to shoulder in the coming struggle. He remembered listening intently and not being impressed.

"Gentlemen, I trust you are comfortable," Göring said in a calm voice to the four bound prisoners.

No one replied.

"What did he say, *Ỳxo*," whispered one of the Russians.

"He's ridiculing them."

"Shut up," Humer muttered. "Give your attention or you'll join them."

Göring positioned himself directly before the four naked men. "I ask each of you again. Anything to say?"

Only the wind replied.

Göring inched close to one of the shivering Germans. The one Borya had bound to the stake.

"Mathias, surely you don't want to die this way? You're a soldier, a loyal servant of the Führer."

"The—Führer—has nothing to do—with this," the German stammered, his body shivering in violet quakes.

"But everything we do is for his greater glory."

"Which is why I—choose to die."

Göring shrugged. A casual gesture, as someone would do if deciding whether to have another pastry. He motioned to Humer. The sergeant signaled two guards, who toted a large barrel toward the bound men. Another guard approached with four ladles and tossed them into the snow. Humer glared at the Russians. "Fill them with water, and go stand by one of those men."

He told the other three what to do and four ladles were picked up, then submerged.

"Spill nothing," Humer warned.

Borya was careful, but the wind buffeted a few drops out. No one noticed. He returned to the German he'd bound to the stake. The one called Mathias. Göring stood in the center, pulling off black leather gloves.

"See, Mathias," Göring said, "I'm removing my gloves so I can feel the cold, as your skin does."

Borya stood close enough to see the heavy silver ring wrapping the third finger of the man's right hand, a clutched mailed fist embossed on it. Göring stuffed his right hand into a trouser pocket and removed a stone. It was golden, like honey. Borya recognized it. Amber. Göring fingered the clump and said, "Water will be showered over you every five minutes until somebody tells me what I want to know, or you die. Either is acceptable to me. But, remember, whoever talks lives. Then one of these miserable Russians will take your place. You can then have your coat back and pour water on him until he dies. Imagine what fun that would be. All you have to do is tell me what I want to know. Now, anything to say?"

Silence.

Göring nodded to Humer.

"Gieße es," Humer said. *Pour it.*

Borya did, and the other three followed his lead. Water soaked into Mathias's blond mane, then trickled down his face and chest. Shivers accompanied the stream. The German uttered not a sound, other than the chatter of his teeth.

"Anything to say?" Göring asked again.

Nothing.

Five minutes later the process was repeated. Twenty minutes later, after four more dousings, hypothermia started setting in. Göring stood impassive and methodically massaged the amber. Just before another five minutes expired he approached Mathias.

"This is ridiculous. Tell me where *das Bernstein-zimmer* is hidden and stop your suffering. This is not worth dying for."

The shivering German only stared back, his defiance admirable. Borya almost hated being Göring's accomplice in killing him.

"Sie sind ein lügnerisch diebisch-schwein," Mathias managed in one breath. *You are a lying, thieving pig.* Then the German spat.

Göring reeled back, spittle splotching the front of his

greatcoat. He released the buttons and shook the stain away, then culled back the flaps, revealing a pearl gray uniform heavy with decorations. "I am your *Reichsmarschall.* Second only to the Führer. No one wears this uniform but me. How dare you think you can soil it so easily. You will tell me what I want to know, Mathias, or you will freeze to death. Slowly. Very slowly. It will not be pleasant."

The German spat again. This time on the uniform. Göring stayed surprisingly calm.

"Admirable, Mathias. Your loyalty is noted. But how much longer can you hold out? Look at you. Wouldn't you like to be warm? Pressing your body close to a big fire, your skin wrapped in a cozy wool blanket." Göring suddenly reached over and yanked Borya close to the bound German. Water splattered from the ladle onto the snow. "This coat would feel wonderful, would it not, Mathias? Are you going to allow this miserable cossack to be warm while you freeze?"

The German said nothing. Only shivered.

Göring shoved Borya away. "How about a little taste of warmth, Mathias?"

The *Reichsmarschall* unzipped his trousers. Hot urine arched out, steaming on impact, leaving yellow streaks on bare skin that raced down to the snow. Göring shook his organ dry, then zipped his trousers. "Feel better, Mathias?"

"Verrottet in der schweinshölle."

Borya agreed. *Rot in hell pig.*

Göring rushed forward and backhanded the soldier hard across the face, his silver ring ripping open the cheek. Blood oozed out.

"Pour!" Göring screamed.

Borya returned to the barrel and refilled his ladle.

The German named Mathias started shouting. *"Mein Führer. Mein Führer. Mein Führer."* His voice grew louder. The other three bound men joined in.

Water rained down.

Göring stood and watched, now furiously fingering the amber. Two hours later, Mathias died caked in ice. Within another hour the remaining three Germans succumbed. No one mentioned anything about *das Bernstein-zimmer.*

The Amber Room.

PART ONE

ONE

JUDGE RACHEL CUTLER GLANCED OVER THE TOP OF HER TOR-toiseshell glasses. The lawyer had said it again, and this time she wasn't going to let the comment drop. "Excuse me, counselor."

"I said the defendant moves for a mistrial."

"No. Before that. What did you say?"

"I said, 'Yes, sir.'"

"If you haven't noticed, I'm not a sir."

"Quite correct, Your Honor. I apologize."

"You've done that four times this morning. I made a note each time."

The lawyer shrugged. "It seems such a trivial matter. Why would Your Honor take the time to note my simple slip of the tongue?"

The impertinent bastard even smiled. She sat erect in her chair and glared down at him. But she immediately realized what T. Marcus Nettles was doing. So she said nothing.

"My client is on trial for aggravated assault, Judge. Yet the court seems more concerned with how I address you than with the issue of police misconduct."

She glanced over at the jury, then at the other counsel table. The Fulton County assistant district attorney sat impassive, apparently pleased that her opponent was digging his own grave. Obviously, the young lawyer didn't grasp what Nettles was attempting. But she did. "You're absolutely right, counselor. It is a trivial matter. Proceed."

She sat back in her chair and noticed the momentary look

of annoyance on Nettles's face. An expression that a hunter might give when his shot missed the mark.

"What of my motion for mistrial?" Nettles asked.

"Denied. Move on. Continue with your summation."

Rachel watched the jury foreman as he stood and pronounced a guilty verdict. Deliberations had taken only twenty minutes.

"Your Honor," Nettles said, coming to his feet. "I move for a presentence investigation prior to sentencing."

"Denied."

"I move that sentencing be delayed."

"Denied."

Nettles seemed to sense the mistake he'd made earlier. "I move for the court to recuse itself."

"On what grounds?"

"Bias."

"To whom or what?"

"To myself and my client."

"Explain."

"The court has shown prejudice."

"How?"

"With that display this morning about my inadvertent use of *sir.*"

"As I recall, counselor, I admitted it was a trivial matter."

"Yes, you did. But our conversation occurred with the jury present, and the damage was done."

"I don't recall an objection or a motion for mistrial concerning the conversation."

Nettles said nothing. She looked over at the assistant DA. "What's the State's position?"

"The State opposes the motion. The court has been fair."

She almost smiled. At least the young lawyer knew the right answer.

"Motion to recuse denied." She stared at the defendant, a young white male with scraggly hair and a pockmarked face. "The defendant shall rise." He did. "Barry King, you've been found guilty of the crime of aggravated assault. This court hereby remands you to the Department of Corrections for a period of twenty years. The bailiff will take the defendant into custody."

She rose and stepped toward an oak-paneled door that led to her chambers. "Mr. Nettles, could I see you a moment?" The assistant DA headed toward her, too. "Alone."

Nettles left his client, who was being cuffed, and followed her into the office.

"Close the door, please." She unzipped her robe but did not remove it. She stepped behind her desk. "Nice try, counselor."

"Which one?"

"Earlier, when you thought that jab about *sir* and *ma'am* would set me off. You were getting your butt chapped with that half-cocked defense, so you thought me losing my temper would get you a mistrial."

He shrugged. "You gotta do what you gotta do."

"What you have to do is show respect for the court and not call a female judge *sir.* Yet you kept on. Deliberately."

"You just sentenced my guy to twenty years without the benefit of a presentence hearing. If that isn't prejudice, what is?"

She sat down and did not offer the lawyer a seat. "I didn't need a hearing. I sentenced King to aggravated battery two years ago. Six months in, six months' probation. I remember. This time he took a baseball bat and fractured a man's skull. He's used up what little patience I have."

"You should have recused yourself. All that information clouded your judgment."

"Really? That presentence investigation you're screaming for would have revealed all that, anyway. I simply saved you the trouble of waiting for the inevitable."

"You're a fucking bitch."

"That's going to cost you a hundred dollars. Payable now. Along with another hundred for the stunt in the courtroom."

"I'm entitled to a hearing before you find me in contempt."

"True. But you don't want that. It'll do nothing for that chauvinistic image you go out of your way to portray."

He said nothing, and she could feel the fire building. Nettles was a heavyset, jowled man with a reputation for tenacity, surely unaccustomed to taking orders from a woman.

"And every time you show off that big ass of yours in my court, it's going to cost you a hundred dollars."

He stepped toward the desk and withdrew a wad of money, peeling off two one-hundred-dollar bills, crisp new ones with the swollen Ben Franklin. He slapped both on the desk, then unfolded three more.

"Fuck you."

One bill dropped.

"Fuck you."

The second bill fell.

"Fuck you."

The third Ben Franklin fluttered down.

TWO

RACHEL DONNED HER ROBE, STEPPED BACK INTO THE COURTroom, and climbed three steps to the oak dais she'd occupied for the past four years. The clock on the far wall read 1:45 P.M. She wondered how much longer she'd have the privilege of being a judge. It was an election year, qualifying had ended two weeks back, and she'd drawn two opponents for the July primary. There'd been talk of people getting into the race, but no one appeared until ten minutes before five on Friday to plunk down the nearly four-thousand-dollar fee needed to run. What could have been an easy uncontested election had now evolved into a long summer of fund-raisers and speeches. Neither of which was pleasurable.

At the moment she didn't need the added aggravation. Her dockets were jammed, with more cases being added by the day. Today's calendar, though, was shortened by a quick verdict in *State of Georgia v. Barry King*. Less than a half hour of deliberation was fast by any standard, the jurors obviously not impressed with T. Marcus Nettles's theatrics.

With the afternoon free, she decided to tend to a backlog of non-jury matters that had clogged over the past two weeks of jury trials. The trial time had been productive. Four convictions, six guilty pleas, and one acquittal. Eleven criminal cases out of the way, making room for the new batch her secretary said the scheduling clerk would deliver in the morning.

The *Fulton County Daily Report* rated all the local superior court judges annually. For the past three years she'd been ranked near the top, disposing of cases faster than most of her fellow judges, with a reversal rate in the appellate courts of only 2 percent. Not bad being right 98 percent of the time.

She settled behind the bench and watched the afternoon parade begin. Lawyers hustled in and out, some ferrying clients in need of a final divorce or a judge's signature, others looking for a resolution to pending motions in civil cases awaiting trial. About forty different matters in all. By the time she glanced again at the clock across the room, it was 4:15 and the docket had whittled down to two items. One was an adoption, a task she really enjoyed. The seven-year-old reminded her of Brent, her own seven-year-old. The last matter was a simple name change, the petitioner unrepresented by counsel. She'd specifically scheduled the case at the end, hoping the courtroom would be empty.

The clerk handed her the file.

She stared down at the old man dressed in a beige

tweed jacket and tan trousers who stood before the counsel table.

"Your full name?" she asked.

"Karl Bates." His tired voice carried an East European accent.

"How long have you lived in Fulton County?"

"Forty-six years."

"You were not born in this country?"

"No. I come from Belarus."

"And you are an American citizen?"

He nodded. "I'm an old man. Eighty-three. Almost half my life spent here."

The question and answer was not relevant to the petition, but neither the clerk nor the court reporter said anything. Their faces seemed to understand the moment.

"My parents, brothers, sisters—all slaughtered by Nazis. Many died in Belarus. We were White Russians. Very proud. After the war, not many of us were left when the Soviets annexed our land. Stalin was worse than Hitler. A madman. Butcher. Nothing remained there when he was through, so I leave. This country is the land of promise, right?"

"Were you a Russian citizen?"

"I believe correct designation was Soviet citizen." He shook his head. "But I never consider myself Soviet."

"Did you serve in the war?"

"Only of necessity. The Great Patriotic War, Stalin called it. I was lieutenant. Captured and sent to Mauthausen. Sixteen months in a concentration camp."

"What was your occupation here after immigrating?"

"Jeweler."

"You have petitioned this court for a change of name. Why do you wish to be known as Karol Borya?"

"It is my birth name. My father named me Karol. It means 'strong-willed.' I was youngest of six children and almost die at birth. When I immigrate to this country, I thought, must protect identity. I work for government commissions while in Soviet Union. I hated Communists. They ruin my homeland, and I speak out. Stalin sent many countrymen to Siberian camps. I thought harm would come to my family. Very few could leave then. But before my death, I want my heritage returned."

"Are you ill?"

"No. But I wonder how long this tired body will hold out."

She looked at the old man standing before her, his frame shrunken with age but still distinguished. The eyes were inscrutable and deep-set, hair stark white, voice gravelly and enigmatic. "You look marvelous for a man your age."

He smiled.

"Do you seek this change to defraud, evade prosecution, or hide from a creditor?"

"Never."

"Then I grant your petition. You shall be Karol Borya once again."

She signed the order attached to the petition and handed the file to the clerk. Stepping from the bench, she approached the old man. Tears slipped down his stubbled cheeks. Her eyes had reddened, as well. She hugged him and softly said, "I love you, Daddy."

THREE

4:50 P.M.

PAUL CUTLER STOOD FROM THE OAK ARMCHAIR AND ADDRESSED the court, his lawyerly patience wearing thin. "Your Honor, the estate does not contest movant's services. Instead, we merely challenge the amount he's attempting to charge. Twelve thousand three hundred dollars is a lot of money to paint a house."

"It was a big house," the creditor's lawyer said.

"I would hope," the probate judge added.

Paul said, "The house is two thousand square feet. Not a thing unusual about it. The paint job was routine. Movant is not entitled to the amount charged."

"Judge, the decedent contracted with my client for a complete house painting, which my client did."

"What the movant did, Judge, was take advantage of a seventy-three-year-old man. He did not render twelve thousand three hundred dollars' worth of services."

"The decedent promised my client a bonus if he finished within a week, and he did."

He couldn't believe the other lawyer was pressing the point with a straight face. "That's convenient, considering the only other person to contradict that promise is dead. The bottom line is that our firm is the named executor on the estate, and we cannot in good conscience pay this bill."

"You want a trial on it?" the crinkly judge asked the other side.

The creditor's lawyer bent down and whispered with the housepainter, a younger man noticeably uncomfortable in a tan polyester suit and tie. "No, sir. Perhaps a compromise. Seven thousand five hundred."

Paul never flinched. "One thousand two hundred and fifty. Not a dime more. We employed another painter to view the work. From what I've been told, we have a good suit for shoddy workmanship. The paint also appears to have been watered down. As far as I'm concerned, we'll let the jury decide." He looked at the other lawyer. "I get two hundred and twenty dollars an hour while we fight. So take your time, counselor."

The other lawyer never even consulted his client. "We don't have the resources to litigate this matter, so we have no choice but to accept the estate's offer."

"I bet. Bloody damn extortionist," Paul muttered, just loud enough for the other lawyer to hear, as he gathered his file.

"Draw an order, Mr. Cutler," the judge said.

Paul quickly left the hearing room and marched down the corridors of the Fulton County probate division. It was three floors down from the mélange of Superior Court and a world apart. No sensational murders, high-profile litigation, or contested divorces. Wills, trusts, and guardianships formed the extent of its limited jurisdiction—mundane, boring, with evidence usually amounting to diluted memories and tales of alliances both real and imagined. A recent state statute Paul helped draft allowed jury trials in certain instances, and occasionally a litigant would demand one. But, by and large, business was tended to by a stable of elder judges, themselves once advocates who roamed the same halls in search of letters testamentary.

Ever since the University of Georgia sent him out into the world with a juris doctorate, probate work had been Paul's specialty. He'd not gone right to law school from college, summarily rejected by the twenty-two schools he'd applied to. His father was devastated. For three years he labored at the Georgia Citizens Bank in the probate and trust department as a glorified clerk, the experience enough motivation for him to retake the law school admission exam and reapply. Three schools ultimately accepted him, and a third-year clerkship resulted in a job at Pridgen & Woodworth after graduation. Now, thirteen years later, he was a sharing-partner in the firm, senior enough in the probate and trust department to be next in line for full partnership and the department's managerial reins.

He turned a corner and zeroed in on double doors at the far end.

Today had been hectic. The painter's motion had been scheduled for over a week, but right after lunch his office received a call from another creditor's lawyer to hear a hastily arranged motion. Originally it was set for 4:30, but the lawyer on the other side failed to show. So he'd shot over to an adjacent hearing room and taken care of the house-painter's attempted thievery. He yanked open the wooden

doors and stalked down the center aisle of the deserted courtroom. "Heard from Marcus Nettles yet?" he asked the clerk
at the far end.

A smile creased the woman's face. "Sure did."

"It's nearly five. Where is he?"

"He's a guest of the sheriff's department. Last I heard,
they've got him in a holding cell."

He dropped his briefcase on the oak table. "You're kidding."

"Nope. Your ex put him in this morning."

"Rachel?"

The clerk nodded. "Word is he got smart with her in
chambers. Paid her three hundred dollars then told her to F
off three times."

The courtroom doors swung open and T. Marcus Nettles
waddled in. His beige Neiman Marcus suit was wrinkled,
Gucci tie out of place, the Italian loafers scuffed and dirty.

"About time, Marcus. What happened?"

"That bitch you once called your wife threw me in jail and
left me there since this mornin'." The baritone voice carried
a strain. "Tell me, Paul. Is she really a woman or some hy-
brid with nuts between those long legs?"

He started to say something, then decided to let it go.

"She climbs my ass in front of a jury because I called her
sir—"

"Four times, I heard," the clerk said.

"Yeah. Probably was. After I move for a mistrial, which
she should have granted, she gives my guy twenty years
without a presentence hearin'. Then she wants to give me an
ethics lesson. I don't need that shit. Particularly from some
smart-ass bitch. I can tell you now, I'll be pumpin' money to
both her opponents. Lots of money. I'm going to rid myself
of that problem the second Tuesday in July."

He'd heard enough. "You ready to argue this motion?"

Nettles laid his briefcase on the table. "Why not? I figured
I'd be in that cell all night. Guess the whore has a heart, after
all."

"That's enough, Marcus," he said, his voice a bit firmer than he intended.

Nettles's eyes tightened, a penetrating feral stare that seemed to read his thoughts. "The shit you care? You've been divorced—what?—three years? She must gouge a chunk out of your paycheck every month in child support."

He said nothing.

"I'll be fuckin' damned," Nettles said. "You still got a thing for her, don't you?"

"Can we get on with it?"

"Son of a bitch, you do." Nettles shook his bulbous head.

He headed for the other table to get ready for the hearing. The clerk popped from her chair and walked back to fetch the judge. He was glad she'd left. Courthouse gossip blew from ear to ear like a wildfire.

Nettles settled his portly frame into the armchair. "Paul, my boy, take it from a five-time loser. Once you get rid of 'em, be rid of 'em."

FOUR

5:45 P.M.

KAROL BORYA CRUISED INTO HIS DRIVEWAY AND PARKED THE Oldsmobile. At eighty-one, he was happy to still be driving. His eyesight was amazingly good, and his coordination, though slow, seemed adequate enough for the state to renew his license. He didn't drive much, or far. To the grocery store, occasionally to the mall, and over to Rachel's house at least twice a week. Today he'd ventured only four miles to the MARTA station, where he'd caught a train downtown to the courthouse for the name-change hearing.

He'd lived in northeast Fulton County nearly forty years, long before the explosion of Atlanta northward. The once forested hills of red clay, whose runoff had tracked into the nearby Chattahoochee River, were now covered in commercial development, high-end residential subdivisions, apartments, and roads. Millions lived and worked around him, Atlanta along the way having acquired the designations of *metropolitan* and "Olympic host."

He ambled out to the street and checked the curbside mailbox. The evening was unusually warm for May, good for his arthritic joints, which seemed to sense the approach of fall and downright hated winter. He walked back toward the house and noticed that the wooden eaves needed painting.

He sold his original acreage twenty-four years ago, garnering enough to pay cash for a new house. The subdivision then was one of the newer developments, the street now evolved into a pleasant nook under a canopy of quarter-century timber. His cherished wife, Maya, died two years after the house was completed. Cancer claimed her fast. Too fast. He hardly had time to say good-bye. Rachel was fourteen and brave, he was fifty-seven and scared to death. The prospect of growing old alone had frightened him. But Rachel had always stayed nearby. He was lucky to have such a good daughter. His only child.

He trudged into the house, and was there only a few minutes when the back door burst open and his two grandchildren rushed into the kitchen. They never knocked and he never locked the door. Brent was seven, Marla six. Both hugged him. Rachel followed them inside.

"Grandpa, Grandpa, where's Lucy?" Marla asked.

"Asleep in the den. Where else?" The stray had wandered into the backyard four years ago and never left.

The children bolted to the front of the house.

Rachel yanked open the refrigerator and found a pitcher of tea. "You got a little emotional in court."

"I know I say too much. But I thought of papa. I wish you knew him. He work the fields every day. A Tsarist. Loyal to end. Hated Communists." He paused. "I was thinking, I have no photo of him."

"But you have his name again."

"And for that I thank you, my darling. Did you learn where was Paul?"

"My clerk checked. He was tied up in probate court and couldn't make it."

"How is he doing?"

She sipped her tea. "Okay, I guess."

He studied his daughter. She was so much like her mother. Pearl white skin, frilly auburn hair, perceptive brown eyes that cast the prepossessing look of a woman in charge. And smart. Maybe too smart for her own good.

"How are you doing?" he asked.

"I get by. I always do."

"You sure, daughter?" He'd noticed changes lately. Some drifting, a bit more distance and fragility. A hesitancy toward life that he found disturbing.

"Don't worry about me, Daddy. I'll be fine."

"Still no suitors?" He knew of no men in the three years since the divorce.

"Like I have time. All I do is work and tend those two in there. Not to mention you."

He had to say it. "I worry about you."

"No need."

But she looked away while answering. Perhaps she wasn't quite so certain of herself. "Not good to be old alone."

She seemed to get the message. "You're not."

"I'm not speaking of me, and you know it."

She moved to the sink and rinsed her glass. He decided not to press and reached over and flicked on the counter television. The station was still set to CNN Headline News from the morning. He turned down the volume and felt he had to say, "Divorce is wrong."

She cut him one of her looks. "You going to start with the lecture?"

"Swallow that pride. You should try again."

"Paul doesn't want to."

His gaze held hers. "You both too proud. Think of my grandchildren."

"I did when I divorced. All we did was fight. You know that."

He shook his head. "Stubborn, like your mother." Or was she like him? Hard to tell.

Rachel dried her hands with the dish towel. "Paul will be by about seven to get the kids. He'll bring them home."

"Where you going?"

"Fund-raiser for the campaign. Going to be a tough summer, and I'm not looking forward to it."

He focused on the television and saw mountain ranges, steep inclines, and rocky crags. The sight was instantly familiar. A caption at the bottom left read STOD, GERMANY. He turned up the volume.

"—millionaire contractor Wayland McKoy thinks this area in central Germany may still harbor Nazi treasure. His expedition begins next week into the Harz Mountains of what was once East Germany. These sites have only recently become accessible, thanks to the fall of Communism and the reunification of East and West Germany." The image switched to a tight view of caves in forested inclines. "It's believed that in the final days of World War Two, Nazi loot was hastily stashed inside hundreds of tunnels crisscrossing these ancient mountains. Some were also used as ammunition dumps, which complicates the search, making the venture even more hazardous. In fact, more than two dozen people have lost their lives in this area since World War Two, trying to locate treasure."

Rachel came close and kissed him on the cheek. "I have to go."

He turned from the television. "Paul be here at seven?"

She nodded and headed for the door.

He immediately returned his attention to the television.

FIVE

BORYA WAITED UNTIL THE NEXT HALF HOUR, HOPING HEADLINE News would contain some story repeats. And he was lucky. The same report on Wayland McKoy's search of the Harz Mountains for Nazi treasure appeared at the end of the six-thirty segment.

He was still thinking about the information, twenty minutes later, when Paul arrived. By then he was in the den, a German road map unfolded on the coffee table. He'd bought it at the mall a few years back, replacing the dated *National Geographic* one he'd used for decades.

"Where are the children?" Paul asked.

"Watering my garden."

"You sure that's safe for your garden?"

He smiled. "It's been dry. They can't hurt."

Paul plopped into an armchair, his tie loosened and collar unbuttoned. "That daughter of yours tell you she put a lawyer in jail this morning?"

He didn't look up from the map. "He deserve it?"

"Probably. But she's running for reelection, and he's not one to mess with. That fiery temper is going to get her in trouble one day."

He looked at his former son-in-law. "Just like my Maya. Run off half-crazy in a moment."

"And she won't listen to a thing anybody says."

"Got from her mother, too."

Paul smiled. "I bet." He gestured to the map. "What are you doing?"

"Checking something. Saw on CNN. Fellow claims art is still in Harz Mountains."

"There was a story in *USA Today* on that this morning. Caught my eye. Some guy named McKoy from North Carolina. You'd think people would give up on the Nazi legacy thing. Fifty years is a long time for some three-hundred-year-old canvas to languish in a damp mine. It would be a miracle if it wasn't a mass of mold."

He creased his forehead. "The good stuff already found or lost forever."

"I guess you should know all about that."

He nodded. "A little experience there, yes." He tried to conceal his current interest, though his insides were churning. "Could you buy me copy of that *USA* newspaper?"

"Don't have to. Mine's in the car. I'll go get it."

Paul left through the front door just as the back door opened and the two children trotted into the den.

"Your papa's here," he said to Marla.

Paul returned, handed him the paper, then said to the children, "Did you drown the tomatoes?"

The little girl giggled. "No, Daddy." She tugged at Paul's arm. "Come see Granddaddy's vegetables."

Paul looked at him and smiled. "I'll be right back. That article is on page four or five, I think."

He waited until they left through the kitchen before finding the story and reading every word.

GERMAN TREASURES AWAIT?
By Fran Downing, Staff Writer

Fifty-two years have passed since Nazi convoys rolled through the Harz Mountains into tunnels dug specifically to secret away art and other Reich valuables. Originally, the caverns were used as weapons manufacturing sites and munitions depots. But in the final days of World War II, they became perfect repositories for pillaged loot and national treasures.

Two years ago, Wayland McKoy led an expedition into the Heimkehl Caverns near Uftrugen, Germany, in search of two railroad cars buried under tons of gypsum. McKoy found the cars, along with several old master paintings, toward which the French and Dutch governments paid a handsome finder's fee.

This time McKoy, a North Carolina contractor, real estate developer and amateur treasure hunter, is hoping for bigger loot. He's been a part of four past expeditions and is hoping his latest, which starts next week, will be his most successful.

"Think about it. It's 1945. The Russians are coming from one end, the Americans from another. You're the curator of the Berlin museum full of art stolen from every invaded country. You've got a few hours. What do you put on the train to get out of town? Obviously, the most valuable stuff."

McKoy tells the tale of one such train that left Berlin in the waning days of World War II, heading south for central Germany and the Harz Mountains. No records exist of its destination, and he's hoping the cargo lies within some caverns found only last fall. Interviews with relatives of German soldiers who helped load the train have convinced him of the train's existence. Earlier this year, McKoy used ground-penetrating radar to scan the new caverns.

"Something's in there," McKoy says. "Certainly big enough to be boxcars or storage crates."

McKoy has already secured a permit from German authorities to excavate. He's particularly excited about the prospects of foraging this new site, since, to his knowledge, no one has yet excavated the area. Once a part of East Germany, the region has been off-limits for decades. Current German law provides that McKoy can retain only a small portion of whatever is not claimed by rightful owners. Yet McKoy is undeterred. "It's exciting. Hell, who knows, the Amber Room could be hidden under all that rock."

The excavations will be slow and hard. Backhoes and

bulldozers could damage the treasure, so McKoy will be forced to drill holes in the rocks and then chemically break them apart.

"It's slow going and dangerous, but worth the trouble," he says. "The Nazis had prisoners dig hundreds of caves, where they stored ammunition to keep it safe from the bombers. Even the caves used as art repositories were many times mined. The trick is to find the right cave and get inside safely."

McKoy's equipment, seven employees and a television crew are already waiting in Germany. He plans to head there over the weekend. The nearly $1 million cost is being borne by private investors hoping to cash in on the bonanza.

McKoy says, "There's stuff in the ground over there. I'm sure of it. Somebody's going to find all that treasure. Why not me?"

He looked up from the newspaper. Mother of Almighty God. Was this it? If so, what could be done about it? He was an old man. Realistically, there was little left he could do.

The back door opened and Paul strolled into the den. He tossed the paper on the coffee table.

"You still interested in all that art stuff?" Paul asked.

"Habit of lifetime."

"Would be kind of exciting to dig in those mountains. The Germans used them like vaults. No telling what's still there."

"This McKoy mentions Amber Room." He shook his head. "Another man looking for lost panels."

Paul grinned. "The lure of treasure. Makes for great television specials."

"I saw the amber panels once," he said, giving in to an urge to talk. "Took train from Minsk to Leningrad. Communists had turned Catherine Palace into a museum. I saw the room in its glory." He motioned with his hands. "Ten meters square. Walls of amber. Like a giant puzzle. All the wood carved beautifully and gilded gold. Amazing."

"I've read about it. A lot of folks regarded it as the eighth wonder of the world."

"Like stepping into fairy tale. The amber was hard and shiny like stone, but not cold like marble. More like wood. Lemon, whiskey brown, cherry. Warm colors. Like being in the sun. Amazing what ancient masters could do. Carved figurines, flowers, seashells. The scrollwork so intricate. Tons of amber, all handcrafted. No one ever do that before."

"The Nazis stole the panels in 1941?"

He nodded. "Bastard criminals. Strip room clean. Never seen again since 1945." He was getting angry thinking about it and knew he'd said too much already, so he changed the subject. "You said my Rachel put lawyer in jail?"

Paul sat back in the chair and crossed his ankles on an ottoman. "The Ice Queen strikes again. That's what they call her around the courthouse." He sighed. "Everybody thinks because we're divorced I don't mind."

"It bothers?"

"I'm afraid it does."

"You love my Rachel?"

"And my kids. The apartment gets pretty quiet. I miss all three of 'em, Karl. Or should I say, Karol. That's going to take some getting used to."

"Us both."

"Sorry about not being there today. My hearing got postponed. It was with the lawyer Rachel jailed."

"I appreciate help with petition."

"Any time."

"You know," he said, a twinkle in his eye, "she's seen no man since divorce. Maybe why she's so cranky?" Paul noticeably perked up. He thought he'd read him right. "Claims too busy. But I wonder."

His former son-in-law did not take the bait, and simply sat in silence. He returned his attention to the map. After a few moments, he said, "Braves on TBS."

Paul reached for the remote and punched on the television.

He didn't mention Rachel again, but all through the game he kept glancing at the map. A light green delineated the Harz Mountains, rolling north to south then turning east, the old border between the two Germanies gone. The towns were noted in black. Göttingen. Münden. Osterdode. Warthberg. Stod. The caves and tunnels were unmarked, but he knew they were there. Hundreds of them.

Where was the right cave?

Hard to say anymore.

Was Wayland McKoy on the right track?

SIX

10:25 P.M.

PAUL CRADLED MARLA AND GENTLY CARRIED HER INTO THE house. Brent followed, yawning. A strange feeling always accompanied him when he entered. He and Rachel had bought the two-story brick colonial just after they married, ten years ago. When the divorce came, seven years later, he'd voluntarily moved out. Title remained in both their names and, interestingly, Rachel insisted he retain a key. But he used it sparingly, and always with her prior knowledge, since Paragraph VII of the final decree provided for her exclusive use and possession, and he respected her privacy no matter how much it sometimes hurt.

He climbed the stairs to the second floor and laid Marla in her bed. Both children had bathed at their grandfather's house. He undressed her and slipped her into some *Beauty and the Beast* pajamas. He'd twice taken the children to see the Disney movie. He kissed her good night and stroked her hair until she was sound asleep. After tucking Brent in, he headed downstairs.

The den and kitchen were messy. Nothing unusual. A housekeeper came twice a week since Rachel was not noted for neatness. That was one of their differences. He was a perfectly in place person. Not compulsive, just disciplined. Messes bothered him, he couldn't help it. Rachel didn't seem to mind clothes on the floor, toys strewn about, and a sinkful of dishes.

Rachel Bates had been an enigma from the start. Intelligent, outspoken, assertive, but alluring. That she'd been attracted to him was surprising, since women were never his strong point. There'd been a couple of steady dates in college and one relationship he thought was serious in law school, but Rachel had captivated him. Why, he'd never really understood. Her sharp tongue and brusque manner could hurt, though she didn't mean 90 percent of what she said. At least that's what he told himself over and over to excuse her insensitivity. He was easygoing. Too easygoing. It seemed far less trouble to simply ignore her than rise to the challenge. But sometimes he felt she wanted him to challenge her.

Did he disappoint her by backing down? Letting her have her way?

Hard to say.

He wandered toward the front of the house and tried to clear his head, but each room assaulted him with memories. The mahogany console with the fossil stone top they'd found in Chattanooga one weekend antiquing. The cream-on-sand conversation sofa where they'd sat many nights watching television. The glass credenza displaying Lilliput cottages, something they both collected with zeal, many a Christmas marked by reciprocal gifts. Even the smell evoked fondness. The peculiar fragrance homes seemed to possess. The musk of life, their life, filtered by time's sieve.

He stepped into the foyer and noticed the portrait of him and the kids still on display. He wondered how many divorcées kept a ten by twelve of their ex around for all to see.

And how many insisted that their ex-husband retain a key to the house. They even still possessed a couple of joint investments, which he managed for them both.

The silence was broken by a key scraping the front door lock.

A second later the door opened and Rachel stepped inside. "Kids any trouble?" she asked.

"Never."

He took in the black princess-seamed jacket that cinched her waist and the slim skirt cut above the knee. Long, slender legs led down to low-heeled pumps. Her auburn hair fell in a layered bob, barely brushing the tips of her thin shoulders. Green tiger eyes trimmed in silver dangled from each of her earlobes and matched her eyes, which looked tired.

"Sorry about not making it to the name change," he said. "But your stunt with Marcus Nettles held things up in probate court."

"He's a sexist bastard."

"You're a judge, Rachel, not the savior of the world. Can't you use a little diplomacy?"

She tossed her purse and keys on a side table. Her eyes hardened like marbles. He'd seen the look before. "What do you expect me to do? The fat bastard drops hundred-dollar bills on my desk and tells me to fuck off. He deserved to spend a few hours in jail."

"Do you have to constantly prove yourself?"

"You're not my keeper, Paul."

"Somebody needs to be. You've got an election coming up. Two strong opponents, and you're only a first-termer. Nettles is already talking about bankrolling both of them. Which, by the way, he can afford. You don't need that kind of trouble."

"Screw Nettles."

Last time he'd arranged the fund-raisers, handled advertising, and courted the people needed to secure endorsements, attract the press, and secure votes. He wondered who would run her campaign this time. Organization was not

Rachel's strong suit. So far she hadn't asked for help, and he really didn't expect her to. "You can lose, you know."

"I don't need a political lecture."

"What do you need, Rachel?"

"None of your damn business. We're divorced. Remember?"

He recalled what her father said. "Do you? We've been apart three years now. Have you dated anyone during that time?"

"That's also none of your business."

"Maybe not. But I seem to be the only one who cares."

She stepped close. "What's that supposed to mean?"

"The Ice Queen. That's what they call you around the courthouse."

"I get the job done. Rated highest of any judge in the county last time the *Daily Report* checked stats."

"That all you care about? How fast you clear a docket?"

"Judges can't afford friends. You either get accused of bias or are hated for a lack of it. I'd rather be the Ice Queen."

It was late, and he didn't feel like an argument. He brushed past her toward the front door. "One day you may need a friend. I wouldn't burn all my bridges if I were you." He opened the door.

"You're not me," she said.

"Thank God."

And he left.

SEVEN

HIS UMBER JUMPSUIT, BLACK LEATHER GLOVES, AND CHARCOAL sneakers blended with the night. Even his close-cropped, bottle-dyed chestnut hair, matching eyebrows, and swarthy complexion helped, the past two weeks spent scouring North Africa having left a tan on his Nordic face.

Gaunt peaks rose all around him, a jagged amphitheater barely distinguishable from the pitch sky. A full moon hung in the east. A spring chill lingered in the air that was fresh, alive, and different. The mountains echoed a low peal of distant thunder.

Leaves and straw cushioned his every step, the underbrush thin under gangly trees. Moonlight dappled through the canopy, spotting the trail with iridescence. He chose his steps carefully, resisting the urge to use his penlight, his sharp eyes ready and alert.

The village of Pont-Saint-Martin lay a full ten kilometers to the south. The only way north was a snaking two-lane road that led eventually, after forty more kilometers, to the Austrian border and Innsbruck. The BMW he'd rented yesterday at the Venice airport waited a kilometer back in a stand of trees. After finishing his business he planned to drive north to Innsbruck, where tomorrow an 8:35 A.M. Austrian Airlines shuttle would whisk him to St. Petersburg, where more business awaited.

Silence surrounded him. No church bells clanging or cars screaming past on the autostrada. Just ancient groves of oak, fir, and larch patchworking the mountainous slopes. Ferns, mosses, and wildflowers carpeted the dark hollows. Easy to see why da Vinci included the Dolemites in the background of the *Mona Lisa.*

The forest ended. A grassy meadow of blossoming orange lilies spread before him. The château rose at the far end, a pebbled drive horseshoeing in front. The building was two stories tall, its redbrick walls decorated with gray lozenges. He remembered the stones from his last visit two months ago, surely crafted by masons who'd learned from their fathers and grandfathers.

None of the forty or so dormer windows flickered with light. The oaken front door likewise loomed dark. No fences, dogs, or guards. No alarms. Just a rambling country estate in the Italian Alps owned by a reclusive manufacturer who'd been semiretired for almost a decade.

He knew that Pietro Caproni, the château's owner, slept on the second floor in a series of rooms that encompassed the master suite. Caproni lived alone, except for three servants who commuted daily from Pont-Saint-Martin. Tonight, Caproni was entertaining, the cream-colored Mercedes parked out front probably still warm from a drive made earlier from Venice. His guest was one of many expensive working women. They would sometimes come for the night or the weekend, paid for their trouble in euros by a man who could afford the price of pleasure. Tonight's excursion had been timed to coincide with her visit, and he hoped she would be enough of a distraction to cover a quick in and out.

Pebbles crunched with each step as he crossed the drive and rounded the château's northeast corner. An elegant garden led back to a stone veranda, Italian wrought iron separating tables and chairs from grass. A set of French doors opened into the house, both knobs locked. He straightened his right arm and twisted. A stiletto slipped off its O-ring and slithered down his forearm, the jade handle nestling firmly in his gloved palm. The leather sheath was his own invention, specially designed for a dependable release.

He plunged the blade into the wooden jamb. One twist, and the bolt surrendered. He resecured the stiletto in his sleeve.

Stepping into a barrel-vaulted salon, he gently closed the glass-paneled door. He liked the surrounding decor of neoclassicism. Two Etruscan bronzes adorned the far wall under a painting, *View of Pompeii,* one he knew to be a collector's item. A pair of eighteenth-century *bibliothèques* hugged two Corinthian columns, the shelves brimming with antique volumes. From his last visit he remembered the fine copy of Guicciardini's *Storia d'Italia* and the thirty volumes of Teatro Francese. Both were priceless.

He threaded the darkened furniture, passed between the

columns, then stopped in the foyer and listened up the stairs. Not a sound. He tiptoed across a wheel-patterned marble floor, careful not to scrape his rubber soles. Neapolitan paintings adorned the faux-marble panels. Chestnut beams supported the darkened ceiling two stories above.

He stepped into the parlor.

The object of his quest lay innocently on an ebony table. A match case. Fabergé. Silver and gold with an enameled translucent strawberry red over a guilloche ground. The gold collar was chased with leaf tips, the thumbpiece cabochon sapphire. It was marked in Cyrillic initials, N. R. 1901. Nicholas Romanov. Nicholas II. The last Tsar of Russia.

He yanked a felt bag from his back pocket and reached for the case.

The room was suddenly flooded with light, shafts of incandescent rays from an overhead chandelier burning his eyes. He squinted and turned. Pietro Caproni stood in the archway leading to the foyer, a gun in his right hand.

"*Buona sera,* Signor Knoll. I wondered when you would return."

He struggled to adjust his vision and answered in Italian, "I didn't realize you would be expecting my visit."

Caproni stepped into the parlor. The Italian was a short, heavy-chested man in his fifties with unnaturally black hair. He wore a navy blue terry-cloth robe tied at the waist. His legs and feet were bare. "Your cover story from the last visit didn't check out. Christian Knoll, art historian and academician. Really, now. An easy matter to verify."

His vision settled as his eyes adjusted to the light. He reached for the match case. Caproni's gun jutted forward. He pulled back and raised his arms in mock surrender. "I merely wish to touch the case."

"Go ahead. Slowly."

He lifted the treasure. "The Russian government has been looking for this since the war. It belonged to Nicholas himself. Stolen from Peterhof outside Leningrad sometime in 1944, a soldier pocketing a souvenir from his time in Russia. But what a souvenir. One of a kind. Worth now on the open market about forty thousand U.S. dollars. That's if someone were foolish enough to sell. 'Beautiful loot' is the term, I believe, the Russians use to describe things such as this."

"I'm sure after your liberation this evening it would have quickly found its way back to Russia?"

He smiled. "The Russians are no better than thieves themselves. They want their treasures back only to sell them. Cash poor, I hear. The price of Communism, apparently."

"I am curious. What brought you here?"

"A photograph of this room in which the match case was visible. So I came to pose as a professor of art history."

"You determined authenticity from that brief visit two months ago?"

"I am an expert on such things. Particularly Fabergé." He laid the match case down. "You should have accepted my offer of purchase."

"Far too low, even for 'beautiful loot.' Besides, the piece has sentimental value. My father was the soldier who pocketed the souvenir, as you so aptly describe."

"And you so casually display it?"

"After fifty years, I assumed nobody cared."

"You should be careful of visitors and photos."

Caproni shrugged. "Few come here."

"Just the signorinas? Like the one upstairs now?"

"And none of them are interested in such things."

"Only euros?"

"And pleasure."

He smiled and casually fingered the match case again. "You are a man of means, Signor Caproni. This villa is like a museum. That Aubusson tapestry there on the wall is priceless. Those two Roman capriccios are certainly valued collectibles. Hof, I believe, nineteenth century?"

"Good, Signor Knoll. I'm impressed."

"Surely you can part with this match case."

"I do not like thieves, Signor Knoll. And, as I said during

your last visit, the item is not for sale." Caproni gestured with the gun. "Now you must leave."

He stayed rooted. "What a quandary. You certainly cannot involve the police. After all, you possess a treasured relic the Russian government would very much like returned—pilfered by your father. What else in this villa fits into that category? There would be questions, inquiries, publicity. Your friends in Rome will be of little help, since you will then be regarded as a thief."

"Lucky for you, Signor Knoll, I cannot involve the authorities."

He casually straightened, then twitched his right arm. It was an unnoticed gesture partially obscured by his thigh. He watched as Caproni's gaze stayed on the match case in his left hand. The stiletto released from its sheath and slowly inched down the loose sleeve until settling into his right palm. "No reconsideration, Signor Caproni?"

"None." Caproni backed toward the foyer and gestured again with the gun. "This way, Signor Knoll."

He wrapped his fingers tight on the handle and rolled his wrist forward. One flick, and the blade zoomed across the room, piercing Caproni's bare chest in the hairy V formed by the robe. The older man heaved, stared down at the handle, then fell forward, his gun clattering across the terrazzo.

He quickly deposited the match case into the felt bag, then stepped across to the body. He withdrew the stiletto and checked for a pulse. None. Surprising. The man died fast.

But his aim had been true.

He cleaned the blood off on the robe, slid the blade into his back pocket, then mounted the stairs to the second floor. More faux marble panels lined the upper foyer, periodically interrupted by paneled doors, all closed. He stepped lightly across the floor and headed toward the rear of the house. A closed door waited at the far end of the hall.

He turned the knob and entered.

A pair of marble columns defined an alcove where a king-size poster bed rested. A low-wattage lamp burned on the nightstand, the light absorbed by a symphony of walnut paneling and leather. The room was definitely a rich man's bedroom.

The woman sitting on the edge of the bed was naked. Long, dramatic red hair framed a pair of pyramid-like breasts and exquisite almond-shaped eyes. She was puffing on a thin black-and-gold cigarette and gave him only a disconcerting glance. "And who are you?" she quietly asked in Italian.

"A friend of Signor Caproni's." He stepped into the bedchamber and casually closed the door.

She finished the cigarette, stood, and strutted close, her thin legs taking deliberate strides. "You're dressed strangely for a friend. You look more like a burglar."

"And you seem unconcerned."

She shrugged. "Strange men are my business. Their needs are no different from anyone else's." Her gaze raked him from head to toe. "You have a wicked gleam in your eyes. German, no?"

He said nothing.

She massaged his hands through the leather gloves. "Powerful." She traced his chest and shoulders. "Muscles." She was close now, her erect nipples nearly touching his chest. "Where is the signore?"

"Detained. He suggested I might enjoy your company."

She looked at him, hunger in her eyes. "Do you have the capabilities of the signore?"

"Monetary or otherwise?"

She smiled. "Both."

He took the whore in his arms. "We shall see."

EIGHT

THE CAB JERKED TO A STOP AND KNOLL STEPPED OUT ONTO BUSY Nevsky Prospekt, paying the driver with two twenty-dollar bills. He wondered what happened to the ruble. It wasn't much better than play money anymore. The Russian government openly banned the use of dollars years ago on pain of imprisonment, but the cabdriver didn't seem to care, eagerly demanding and pocketing the bills before whipping the taxi away from the curb.

His flight from Innsbruck had touched down at Pulkovo Airport an hour ago. He'd shipped the match case from Innsbruck overnight to Germany with a note of his success in northern Italy. Before he too returned to Germany, there was one last errand to be performed.

The *prospekt* was packed with people and cars. He studied the green dome of Kazan Cathedral across the street and turned to spy the gilded spire of the distant Admiralty off to the right, partially obscured by a morning fog. He imagined the boulevard's past, when traffic was all horse-drawn and prostitutes arrested during the night swept the cobbles clean. What would Peter the Great think now of his "window to Europe"? Department stores, cinemas, restaurants, museums, shops, art studios, and cafés lined the busy five-kilometer route. Flashing neon and elaborate kiosks sold everything from books to ice cream and heralded the rapid advance of capitalism. What had Somerset Maugham described? *Dingy and sordid and dilapidated.*

Not anymore, he thought.

Change was the reason he was able to even come to St. Petersburg. The privilege of scouring old Soviet records had been extended to outsiders only recently. He'd made two previous trips this year—one six months ago, another two months back—both to the same depository in St. Petersburg, the building he now entered for the third time.

It was five stories with a rough-hewn stone facade, grimy from engine exhaust. The St. Petersburg Commercial Bank operated a busy branch out of one part of the ground floor, and Aeroflot, the Russian national airline, filled the rest. The first through third and fifth floors were all austere government offices: Visa and Foreign Citizen's Registration Department, Export Control, and the regional Agricultural Ministry. The fourth floor was devoted exclusively to a records depository. One of many scattered throughout the country, it was a place where the remnants of seventy-five years of Communism could be stored and safely studied.

Yeltsin had opened the documents to the world through the Russian Archival Committee, a way for the learned to preach his message of anti-Communism. Clever, actually. No need to purge the ranks, fill the gulags, or rewrite history as Khrushchev and Brezhnev managed. Just let historians uncover the multitude of atrocities, thievery, and espionage—secrets hidden for decades under tons of rotting paper and fading ink. Their eventual writings would be more than enough propaganda to serve the needs of the state.

He climbed black iron stairs to the fourth floor. They were narrow in the Soviet style, indicating to the knowledgeable, like himself, that the building was post-revolutionary. A call yesterday from Italy informed him that the depository would be open until 5:00 P.M. He'd visited this one and four others in southern Russia. This facility was unique, since a photocopier was available.

On the fourth floor a battered wooden door opened into a stuffy space, its pale green walls peeling from a lack of ventilation. There was no ceiling, only pipes and ducts caked in asbestos crisscrossing beneath the brittle concrete of the fifth floor. The air was cool and moist. A strange place to house supposedly precious documents.

He stepped across gritty tile and approached a solitary desk. The same clerk with wispy brown hair and a horsy face waited. He'd concluded last time the man to be an involuted, self-depreciating, nouveau Russian bureaucrat. Typical. Hardly a difference from the old Soviet version.

"Dobriy den," he said, adding a smile.

"Good day," the clerk replied.

In Russian, he stated, "I need to study the files."

"Which ones?" An irritating smile accompanied the inquiry, the same look he recalled from two months before.

"I'm sure you remember me."

"I thought your face familiar. The Commission records, correct?"

The clerk's attempt at coyness was a failure. *"Da.* Commission records."

"Would you like me to retrieve them?"

"Nyet. I know where they are. But thank you for your kindness."

He excused himself and disappeared among metal shelves brimming with rotting cardboard boxes, the stale air heavily scented with dust and mildew. He knew a variety of records surrounded him, many an overflow from the nearby Hermitage, most from a fire years ago in the local Academy of Sciences. He remembered the incident well. "The Chernobyl of our culture," the Soviet press labeled the event. But he'd wondered how unintentional the disaster may have been. Things always had a convenient tendency of disappearing at just the right moment in the USSR, and the reformed Russia was hardly any better.

He perused the shelves, trying to recall where he left off last time. It could take years to finish a thorough review of everything. But he remembered two boxes in particular. He'd run out of time on his last visit before getting to them, the depository having closed early for International Women's Day.

He found the boxes and slid both off the shelf, placing them on one of the bare wooden tables. About a meter square, each box was heavy, maybe twenty-five or thirty kilograms. The clerk still sat toward the front of the depository. He realized it wouldn't be long before the impertinent fool sauntered back and made a note of his latest interest.

The label on top of both boxes read in Cyrillic, EXTRAORDINARY STATE COMMISSION ON THE REGISTRATION AND INVESTIGATION OF THE CRIMES OF THE GERMAN-FASCIST OCCUPIERS AND THEIR ACCOMPLICES AND THE DAMAGE DONE BY THEM TO THE CITIZENS, COLLECTIVE FARMS, PUBLIC ORGANIZATIONS, STATE ENTERPRISES, AND INSTITUTIONS OF THE UNION OF SOVIET SOCIALIST REPUBLIC.

He knew the Commission well. Created in 1942 to resolve problems associated with the Nazi occupation, it eventually did everything from investigating concentration camps liberated by the Red Army to valuing art treasures looted from Soviet museums. By 1945 the Commission evolved into the primary sender of thousands of prisoners and supposed traitors to the gulags. It was one of Stalin's concoctions, a way to maintain control, and eventually employed thousands, including field investigators who searched western Europe, northern Africa, and South America for art pillaged by the Germans.

He settled down into a metal chair and started sifting page by page through the first box. The going was slow, thanks to the volume and the heavy Russian and Cyrillic diatribes. Overall, the box was a disappointment, mostly summary reports of various Commission investigations. Two long hours passed and he found nothing of interest. He started on the second box, which contained more summary reports. Toward the middle, he came to a stack of field reports from investigators. Acquisitors, like himself. But paid by Stalin, working exclusively for the Soviet government.

He scanned the reports one by one.

Many were unimportant narratives of failed searches and disappointing trips. There were some successes, though, the recoveries noted in glowing language. Degas's *Place de la Concorde*. Gauguin's *Two Sisters*. Van Gogh's last painting, *The White House at Night*. He even recognized the investigators' names. Sergei Telegin. Boris Zernov. Pyotr Sabsal. Maxim Voloshin. He'd read other field reports filed by them in other depositories. The box contained a hundred or so reports, all surely forgotten, of little use today except to the few who still searched.

Another hour passed, during which the clerk wandered back three times on the pretense of helping. He'd declined each offer, anxious for the irritating little man to mind his own business. Near five o'clock he found a note to Nikolai Shvernik, the merciless Stalin loyalist who had headed the Extraordinary Commission. But this memo was unlike the others. It was not sealed on official Commission stationery. Instead, it was handwritten and personal, dated November 26, 1946, the black ink on onionskin nearly gone:

Comrade Shvernik,

I hope this message finds you in good health. I visited Donnersberg but could not locate any of the Goethe manuscripts thought there. Inquiries, discreet of course, revealed previous Soviet investigators may have removed the items in November 1945. Suggest a recheck of Zagorsk inventories. I met with Ÿxo yesterday. He reports activity by Loring. Your suspicions seem correct. The Harz mines were visited repeatedly by various work crews, but no local workers were employed. All persons were transported in and out by Loring. Yantarnaya komnata may have been found and removed. It is impossible to say at this time. Ÿxo is following additional leads in Bohemia and will report directly to you within the week.

Danya Chapaev

Clipped to the tissue sheet were two newer sheets of paper, both photocopies. They were KGB information memos dated March, seven years ago. Strange they were

there, he thought, tucked indiscriminately among fifty-plus-
year-old originals. He read the first note typed in Cyrillic:

```
Ýxo is confirmed to be Karol Borya, once em-
ployed by Commission, 1946—1958. Immigrated to
United States, 1958, with permission of then-
government. Named changed to Karl Bates. Cur-
rent address: 959 Stokeswood Avenue. Atlanta,
Georgia (Fulton County), USA. Contact made.
Denies any information on yantarnaya komnata
subsequent to 1958. Have been unable to lo-
cate Danya Chapaev. Borya claimed no knowledge
of Chapaev's whereabouts. Request additional
instructions on how to proceed.
```

Danya Chapaev was a name he recognized. He'd looked
for the old Russian five years ago but had been unable to find
him, the only one of the surviving searchers he hadn't interviewed. Now there may be another. Karol Borya, aka Karl
Bates. Strange, the nickname. The Russians seemed to delight in code words. Was it affection or security? Hard to tell.
References like Wolf, Black Bear, Eagle, and Sharp Eyes
he'd seen. But Ýxo? "Ears." That was unique.

He flipped to the second sheet, another KGB memo typed
in Cyrillic that contained more information on Karol Borya.
The man would now be eighty-three years old. A jeweler by
trade, retired. His wife died a quarter century back. He had a
daughter, married, who lived in Atlanta, Georgia, and a grandchild. Seven-year-old information, granted. But still more
than *he* possessed on Karol Borya.

He glanced again at the 1946 document. Particularly the
reference to Loring. It was the second time he'd seen that
name among reports. Couldn't be Ernst Loring. Too young.
More likely the father, Josef. The conclusion was becoming
more and more inescapable that the Loring family had long
been on the trail, as well. Maybe the trip to St. Petersburg
had been worth the trouble. Two direct references to *yantar-*

naya komnata, rare for Soviet documents, and some new information.

A new lead.

Ears.

"Will you be through soon?"

He looked up. The clerk stared down at him. He wondered
how long the bastard had been standing there.

"It's after five," the man said.

"I didn't realize. I will be finished shortly."

The clerk's gaze roamed across the page in his hand, trying to steal a look. He nonchalantly tabled the sheet. The
man seemed to get the message and headed back to his desk.

He lifted the papers.

Interesting the KGB had been searching for two former-
Extraordinary Commission members as late as a few years
ago. He'd thought the search for *yantarnaya komnata* ended
in the mid-1970s. That was the official account, anyway.
He'd encountered only a few isolated references dated to the
eighties. Nothing of recent vintage, until today. The Russians don't give up, he'd give them that. But considering the
prize, he could understand. He didn't give up either. He'd
tracked leads the past eight years. Interviewed old men with
failing memories and tight tongues. Boris Zernov. Pyotr
Sabsal. Maxim Voloshin. Searchers, like himself, all looking
for the same thing. But none knew anything. Maybe Karol
Borya would be different. Maybe he knew where Danya
Chapaev was. He hoped both men were still alive. It was certainly worth a flight to the United States to find out. He'd
been to Atlanta once. During the Olympics. Hot and humid,
but impressive.

He glanced around for the clerk. The impish man stood on
the other side of the cluttered shelves, busily replacing files.
Quickly, he folded the three sheets and pocketed them. He
had no intention of leaving anything for another inquisitive
mind to find. He replaced the two boxes on the shelf and
headed for the exit. The clerk was waiting with the door
open.

"Dobriy den," he told the clerk.

"Good day to you."

He left and the lock immediately clicked behind him. He imagined it would not take long for the fool to report the visit, surely receiving a gratuity in the post a few days from now for his attentiveness. No matter. He was pleased. Ecstatic. He had a new lead. Maybe something definitive. The start of a trail. Maybe even an acquisition.

The acquisition.

He bounded down the stairs, the words from the memo ringing in his ears.

Yantarnaya komnata.

The Amber Room.

NINE

BURG HERZ, GERMANY
7:54 P.M.

KNOLL STARED OUT THE WINDOW. HIS BEDCHAMBER OCCUPIED the upper reaches of the castle's west turret. The citadel belonged to his employer, Franz Fellner. It was a nineteenth-century reproduction, the original burned and sacked to the foundation by the French when they stormed through Germany in 1689.

Burg Herz, "Castle Heart," was an apt name, since the fortress rested nearly in the center of a unified Germany. Franz's father, Martin, acquired the building and surrounding forest after World War I, when the previous owner guessed wrong and backed the Kaiser. Knoll's bedroom, his home for the past eleven years, once served as the head steward's chambers. It was spacious, private, and equipped with a bath. The view below extended for kilometers and encompassed grassy meadows, the wooded heights of the Rothaar, and the muddy Eder flowing east to Kassel. The head steward had attended the senior Fellner every day for the last twenty years of Martin Fellner's life, the steward himself dying only a week after his master. Knoll had heard the gossip, all attesting they'd been more than employer and employee, but he'd never placed much merit in rumor.

He was tired. The last two months, without question, had been exhausting. A long trip to Africa, then a run through Italy, and finally Russia. He'd come a long way from a three-bedroom apartment in a government high-rise thirty kilometers north of Munich, his home until he was nineteen. His father was a factory worker, his mother a music teacher. Memories of his mother always evoked fondness. She was a Greek his father met during the war. He'd always called her by her first name, Amara, which meant "unfading," a perfect description. From her he inherited his sharp brow, pinched nose, and insatiable curiosity. She also hammered into him a passion for learning and named him Christian, as she was a devout believer.

His father molded him into a man, but that bitter fool also instilled a sense of anger. Jakob Knoll fought in Hitler's army as a fervent Nazi. To the end he supported the Reich. He was a hard man to love, but equally hard to ignore.

He turned from the window and glanced over at the nightstand beside the four-poster bed.

A copy of *Hitler's Willing Executioners* lay on top. The volume had caught his eye two months ago. One of a rash of books published lately on the psyche of the German people during the war. How did so many let such barbarism exist from so few? Were they willing participants, as the writer suggested? Hard to say about everyone. But his father was definitely one. Hate came easy to him. Like a narcotic. What was it he many times quoted from Hitler? *I go the way Providence dictates with the assurance of a sleepwalker.*

And that was exactly what Hitler had done—straight to

his downfall. Jakob Knoll likewise died bitter, twelve years after Amara succumbed to diabetes.

Knoll was eighteen and alone when his genius IQ led to a scholarship at the University of Munich. Humanities had always interested him, and during his senior year he earned a fellowship to Cambridge University in art history. He recalled with amusement the summer he fell in briefly with neo-Nazi sympathizers. At the time those groups were not nearly so vocal as today, outlawed as they were by the German government. But their unique look at the world hadn't interested him. Then or now. Nor had hate. Both were unprofitable and counterproductive.

Particularly when he found women of color so alluring.

He spent only a year at Cambridge before dropping out and hiring on to work for Nordstern Fine Art Insurance Limited in London as a claims adjuster. He recalled how quickly he made a name for himself after retrieving a Dutch master thought lost forever. The thieves called, demanding a ransom of twenty million pounds or the canvas would be burned. He could still see the shock on his superiors' faces when he flatly told the thieves to burn it. But they hadn't. He knew they wouldn't. And a month later he recovered the painting after the culprits, in desperation, tried to sell it back to the owner.

More successes came equally as easy.

Three hundred million dollars' worth of old Masters taken from a Boston museum found. A $12 million Jean-Baptiste Oudry, stolen in northern England from a private collector recovered. Two magnificent Turners filched from the Tate Gallery in London located in a ramshackle Parisian apartment.

Franz Fellner met him eleven years ago, when Nordstern dispatched him to do an inventory on Fellner's collection. Like any careful collector Fellner insured his known art assets, the ones that sometimes appeared in European art or American specialty magazines, the publicity a way to make a name for himself, spurring black marketeers to seek him

out with truly valuable treasures. Fellner lured him away
from Nordstern with a generous salary, a room at Burg Herz,
and the excitement that came from stealing back some of hu-
manity's greatest creations. He possessed a talent for searching, enjoying immensely the challenge of finding what
people went to enormous lengths to hide. The women he
came across were equally enticing. But killing particularly
excited him. Was that his father's legacy? Hard to say. Was
he sick? Depraved? Did he really care? No. Life was good.

Damn good.

He stepped away from the window and entered the bathroom. The oriel above the toilet was hinged open and cool
evening air rid the tiles of moisture from his earlier shower.
He studied himself in the mirror. The brown dye used the
past couple of weeks was gone, his hair once again blond.
Disguises were not his usual forte, but he'd deemed a change
of look wise under the circumstances. He'd shaved while
bathing, his tanned face smooth and clean. His face still carried a confident air, the image of a forthright man with strong
tastes and convictions. He splashed a bit of cologne onto his
neck and dried his skin with a towel, then slipped on his dinner jacket.

The telephone on the nightstand rang in the outer room.
He crossed the bedchamber and answered before the third
ring.

"I'm waiting," the female voice said.

"And patience is not one of your virtues?"

"Hardly."

"I'm on my way."

Knoll descended the spiral staircase. The narrow stone
path wound clockwise, copied from a medieval design that
forced invading right-handed swordsmen to battle the central turret as well as castle defenders. The castle complex
was huge. Eight massive towers adorned with half timbers
accommodated more than a hundred rooms. Mullion and
dormer windows enlivened the outside and provided exqui-

site views of the rich forested valleys beyond. The towers were grouped in an octagon around a spacious inner court-yard. Four halls connected them, all the buildings topped by a steeply pitched slate roof that bore witness to harsh German winters.

He turned at the base of the stairs and followed a series of slate tiled corridors toward the chapel. Barrel vaults loomed overhead. Battle-axes, spears, pikes, visored helmets, suits of mail—all collectors' pieces—lined the way. He'd person-ally acquired the largest piece of armor, a knight standing nearly eight feet tall, from a woman in Luxembourg. Flem-ish tapestries adorned the walls, all originals. The lighting was soft and indirect, the rooms warm and dry.

An arched door at the far end opened out to a cloister. He exited and followed a breezeway to a pillared doorway. Three stone faces carved into the castle facade watched his steps. They were a remnant of the original seventeenth-century structure, their identities unknown, though one legend pro-claimed them to be of the castle's master builder and two as-sistants, the men killed and walled into the stone so that they could never build another similar structure.

He approached the Chapel of Saint Thomas. An interest-ing label, since it was not only the name of an Augustinian monk who founded a nearby monastery seven centuries ago, but also the first name of old Martin Fellner's head steward.

He shoved the heavy oak door inward.

She was standing in the center aisle, just beyond a gilded grille that separated the foyer from six oak pews. Incandes-cent fixtures illuminated a black-and-gold rococo altar be-yond and cast her in shadows. The bottle-glass and bull's-eye windows left and right were dark. The stained-glass heraldic signs of castle knights loomed unimpressive, awaiting re-vivement by the morning sun. Little worship occurred here. The chapel was now a display room for gilded reliquaries— Fellner's collection, one of the most extensive in the world, rivaled most European cathedrals.

He smiled at his host.

Monika Fellner was thirty-four and the eldest daughter of his employer. The skin that covered her tall, svelte frame carried the swarthy tint of her mother's, who'd been a Lebanese her father passionately loved forty years before. But old Martin had not been impressed with his son's choice of wife and eventually forced a divorce, sending her back to Lebanon, leaving two children behind. He often thought Monika's cool, tailored, almost untouchable air the result of her mother's rejection. But that wasn't something she would ever voice or he would ever ask. She stood proud, like always, her tangled dark curls falling in carefree wisps. A flick of a smile creased her lips. She wore a taupe brocade jacket over a tight chiffon skirt, the slit rising all the way up to thin supple thighs. She was the sole heir to the Fellner fortune, thanks to the untimely death of her older brother two years ago. Her name meant "devout to God." Yet she was anything but.

"Lock it," she said.

He snapped the lever down.

She strutted toward him, her heels clicking off the ancient marble floor. He met her at the open gate in the grille. Immediately below her was the grave of her grandfather, MARTIN FELLNER 1868–1941 etched into the smooth gray marble. The old man's last wish was that he be buried in the castle he so loved. No wife accompanied him in death. The elder Fellner's head steward lay beside him, more letters carved in stone marking that grave.

She noticed his gaze down to the floor.

"Poor grandfather. To be so strong in business, yet so weak in spirit. Must have been a bitch to be queer back then."

"Maybe it's genetic?"

"Hardly. Though I have to say, a woman can sometimes provide an interesting diversion."

"Your father wouldn't want to hear that."

"I don't think he'd care right now. It's you he's rather upset with. He has a copy of the Rome newspaper. There's a front-page story on the death of Pietro Caproni."

"But he also has the match case."

She smiled. "You think success smooths anything?"

"I've found it to be the best insurance for job security."

"You didn't mention killing Caproni in your note yesterday."

"It seemed an unimportant detail."

"Only you would consider a knife in the chest unimportant. Father wants to talk with you. He's waiting."

"I expected that."

"You don't seem concerned."

"Should I be?"

She stared hard. "You're a hard bastard, Christian."

He realized that she possessed none of her father's sophisticated air, but in two ways they were much alike—both were cold and driven. Newspapers linked her with man after man, wondering who might eventually snag her and the resulting fortune, but he knew that no one would ever control her. Fellner had been meticulously grooming her the past few years, readying her for the day when she'd take over his communications empire along with his passion for collecting, a day that would surely soon arrive. She'd been educated outside Germany in England and the United States, adopting an even sharper tongue and brassy attitude along the way. But being rich and spoiled hadn't helped her personality either.

She reached out and patted his right sleeve. "No stiletto tonight?"

"Do I need it?"

She pressed close. "I can be quite dangerous."

Her arms went around him. Their mouths fused, her tongue searching with excitement. He enjoyed her taste and savored the passion she freely offered. When she withdrew, she bit his lower lip hard on the way. He tasted blood.

"Yes, you can." He dabbed the wound with a handkerchief.

She reached out and unzipped his trousers.

"I thought you said Herr Fellner was waiting."

"There's plenty of time." She pushed him down on the floor, directly atop her grandfather's grave. "And I didn't wear any underwear."

TEN

KNOLL FOLLOWED MONIKA ACROSS THE CASTLE'S GROUND floor to the collection hall. The space consumed the better part of the northwest tower and was divided into a public room, where Fellner displayed his notable and legal items, and the secret room, where only he, Fellner, and Monika ventured.

They entered the public hall and Monika locked the heavy wooden doors behind them. Lighted cases stood in rows like soldiers at attention and displayed a variety of precious objects. Paintings and tapestries lined the walls. Frescoes adorned the ceiling with images depicting Moses giving laws to the people, the building of Babel, and the translation of the Septuagint.

Fellner's private study was off the north wall. They entered, and Monika strolled across the parquet to a row of bookcases, all inlaid oak and gilded in heavy baroque style. He knew the volumes were all collectibles. Fellner loved books. His ninth-century Beda Venerabilis was the oldest and most valuable he possessed, Knoll had been lucky enough to find a stash in a French parish rectory a few years back, the priest more than willing to part with them in return for a modest contribution to both the church and himself.

Monika withdrew a black controller from her jacket pocket and clicked the button. The center bookcase slowly revolved on its axis. White light spilled from a room beyond. Franz Fellner was standing amidst a long windowless space, the gallery cleverly hidden between the junction of two grand halls. High-pitched ceilings and the castle's oblong shape provided more architectural camouflage. Its thick stone walls were all soundproofed and a special handler filtered the air.

More collection cases stood in staggered rows, each illuminated by carefully placed halogen lights. Knoll wove a path through the cases, noticing some of the acquisitions. A jade sculpture he'd stolen from a private collection in Mexico, not a problem since the supposed owner had likewise stolen it from the Jalapa City Museum. A number of ancient African, Eskimo, and Japanese figurines retrieved from an apartment in Belgium, war loot thought long destroyed. He was especially proud of the Gauguin sculpture off to the left, an exquisite piece he'd liberated from a thief in Paris.

Paintings adorned the walls. A Picasso self-portrait. Correggio's *Holy Family.* Botticelli's *Portrait of a Lady.* Dürer's *Portrait of Maximillian I.* All originals, thought lost forever.

The remaining stone wall was draped in two enormous Gobelin tapestries, looted by Hermann Göring during the war, recovered from another supposed owner two decades ago, and still hotly sought by the Austrian government.

Fellner stood beside a glass case containing a thirteenth-century mosaic depicting Pope Alexander IV. He knew it to be one of the old man's favorites. Beside him was the enclosure with the Fabergé match case. A tiny halogen light illuminated the strawberry-red enamel. Fellner had obviously polished the piece. He knew how his employer liked to personally prepare each treasure, more insurance to prevent strange eyes from seeing his acquisitions.

Fellner was a lean hawk of a man with a craggy face the color of concrete and emotions to match. He wore a pair of wire-rimmed spectacles that framed suspicious eyes. Surely, Knoll had often thought, they once bore the bright-eyed look of an idealist. Now they carried the pallor of a man approaching eighty, who'd built an empire from magazines, newspapers, television, and radio, but lost interest in making money after crossing the multibillion-dollar mark. His competitive nature was currently channeled into other, more private ventures. Activities where men with lots of money and limitless nerve could superachieve.

Fellner yanked a copy of the *International Daily News* off the collection case and thrust it forward. "You want to tell me why this was necessary?" The voice bore the rasp of a million cigarettes.

He knew the newspaper was one of Fellner's corporate possessions, and that a computer in the outer study was fed daily with articles from around the world. The death of a wealthy Italian industrialist was certainly something that would catch the old man's eye. At the bottom of the front page was the article:

> Pietro Caproni, 58, founder of Due Mori Industries was found in his northern Italian estate yesterday with a fatal knife wound in the chest. Also found stabbed to death was Carmela Terza, 27, identification at the scene listing her residence as Venice. Police found evidence of a forced entry from a ground-floor door but have so far discovered nothing missing from the villa. Caproni was retired from Due Mori, the conglomerate he built into one of Italy's premier producers of wool and ceramics. He remained active as a major shareholder and consultant, and his death leaves a void in the company.

Fellner interrupted his reading. "We've had this discussion before. You've been warned to indulge your peculiarities on your own time."

"It was necessary, Herr Fellner."

"Killing is never necessary, if you do your job correctly."

He glanced over at Monika, who was watching with apparent amusement. "Signor Caproni intruded on my visit. He was waiting for me. He'd become suspicious from my previous trip. Which I made, if you recall, at your insistence."

Fellner seemed to immediately get the message. The older man's face softened. He knew his employer well.

"Signor Caproni did not want to share the match case without a fight. I simply obliged, concluding you desired the piece regardless. The only alternative was to leave without it and risk exposure."

"The signore did not offer the opportunity to leave? After all, he couldn't very well telephone the police."

He thought a lie better than the truth. "The signore actually wanted to shoot me. He was armed."

Fellner said, "The newspaper makes no mention of that."

"Evidence of the press's unreliability," he said with a smile.

"And what of the whore?" Monika said. "She armed, too?"

He turned toward her. "I was unaware you harbored such sympathy for working women. She understood the risks, I'm sure, when she agreed to become involved with a man like Caproni."

Monika stepped closer. "You fuck her?"

"Of course."

Fire lit her eyes. But she said nothing. Her jealousy was almost as amusing as it was surprising. Fellner broke the moment, conciliatory as always.

"Christian, you retrieved the match case. I appreciate that. But killing does nothing but draw attention. That's the last thing we desire. What if your semen is traced by DNA?"

"There was no semen other than the signore's. Mine was in her stomach."

"What about fingerprints?"

"I wore gloves."

"I realize you are careful. For that I'm grateful. But I am an old man who merely wants to pass what I have accumulated to my daughter. I do not desire to see any of us in jail. Am I clear?"

Fellner sounded exasperated. They'd had this discussion before, and he genuinely hated disappointing him. His employer had been good to him, generously sharing the wealth they'd meticulously accumulated. In many ways he was more like a father than Jakob Knoll had ever been. Monika, though, was nothing like a sister.

He noticed the look in her eyes. The talk of sex and death was surely arousing. Most likely she'd visit his room later.

"What did you find in St. Petersburg?" Fellner finally asked.

He reported the references to *yantarnaya komnata,* then showed both of them the sheets he'd stolen from the archives. "Interesting the Russians were still inquiring about the Amber Room, even recently. This Karol Borya, though, *Ỳxo,* is somebody new."

"Ears?" Fellner spoke perfect Russian. "A strange designation."

Knoll nodded. "I think a trip to Atlanta may be worth the effort. Perhaps *Ỳxo* is still alive. He might know where Chapaev is. He was the only one I did not find five years ago."

"I would think the reference to Loring is also further corroboration, " Fellner said. "That's twice you have found his name. The Soviets were apparently quite interested in what Loring was doing."

Knoll knew the history. The Loring family dominated the Eastern European steel and arms market. Ernst Loring was Fellner's main rival in collecting. He was a Czech, the son of Josef Loring, possessed of an air of superiority bred since youth. Like Pietro Caproni, a man definitely accustomed to having his way.

"Josef was a determined man. Ernst, unfortunately, did not inherit his father's character. I wonder about him," his employer said. "Something has always troubled me about him—that irritating cordiality he thinks I accept." Fellner turned to his daughter. "What about it, *liebling*? Should Christian head for America?"

Monika's face stiffened. At these moments she was most

like her father. Inscrutable. Guarded. Furtive. Certainly, in the years ahead, she'd do him proud. "I want the Amber Room."

"And I want it for you, *liebling*. I've searched forty years. But nothing. Absolutely nothing. I've never understood how tons of amber could simply vanish." Fellner turned toward him. "Go to Atlanta, Christian. Find Karol Borya, this *Ýxo*. See what he knows."

"You realize that if Borya is dead we are out of leads. I have checked the depositories in Russia. Only the one in St. Petersburg has any information of note."

Fellner nodded.

"The clerk in St. Petersburg is certainly on someone's payroll. He was once again attentive. That's why I kept the sheets."

"Which was wise. I'm sure Loring and I are not the only ones interested in *yantarnaya komnata*. What a find that would be, Christian. You'd almost want to tell the world."

"Almost. But the Russian government would want it returned, and if found here, the Germans would surely confiscate. It would make an excellent bargaining chip for the return of treasure the Soviets carted away."

"That's why *we* need to find it," Fellner said.

He leveled his gaze. "Not to mention the bonus you promised."

The old man chuckled. "Quite right, Christian. I have not forgotten."

"Bonus, Father?"

"Ten million euros. I promised years ago."

"And I'll honor it," Monika made clear.

Damn right she would, Knoll thought.

Fellner stepped from the display case. "Ernst Loring is surely looking for the Amber Room. He could well be the benefactor of that technocrat in St. Petersburg. If so, he knows about Borya. Let's not delay on this, Christian. You need to stay a step ahead."

"I intend to."

"Can you handle Suzanne?" the old man quizzed, a mischievous smile on his gaunt face. "She will be aggressive."

He noticed Monika openly bristle at the mention. Suzanne Danzer worked for Ernst Loring. Highly educated and possessed of a determined intent that could be lethal if necessary, only two months back she'd raced him across southwestern France looking for a pair of nineteenth-century jeweled Russian wedding crowns. More "beautiful loot" hidden away for decades by poachers. Danzer had won that race, finding the crowns with an old woman in the Pyrenees near the Spanish border. The woman's husband had liberated them from a Nazi collaborator after the war. Danzer had been unrelenting in securing the prize, a trait he greatly admired.

"I would expect no less of her," he said.

Fellner extended his hand. "Good hunting, Christian."

He accepted the gesture, then turned to leave, heading for the far wall. A rectangle parted in the stone as the bookcase on the other side swung open again.

"And keep *me* informed," Monika called out.

ELEVEN

WOODSTOCK, ENGLAND
10:45 P.M.

SUZANNE DANZER SAT UP FROM THE PILLOW. THE TWENTY-YEAR-old slept soundly beside her. She took a moment and studied his lean nakedness. The young man projected the assurance of a show horse. What a pleasure it had been screwing him.

She stood from the bed and crept across hardwood planks. The darkened bedroom was on the third floor of a sixteenth-century manor house, the estate owned by Audrey Whiddon. The old woman had served three terms in the House of Com-

mons and eventually acquired the title of lady, purchasing
the manor house at foreclosure after the previous owner de-
faulted on a minor mortgage. The elder Whiddon still sometimes visited, but Jeremy, her only grandson, was now its
main resident.

How easy it had been to latch on to Jeremy. He was flighty
and spirited, more interested in ale and sex than finance and
profit. Two years at Oxford and already dropped twice for
academic deficiencies. The old lady loved him dearly and
used what influences she still retained to get the boy back in,
hoping for no more disappointments, but Jeremy seemed un-
accommodating.

Suzanne had been searching nearly two years for the last
snuffbox. Four constituted the original collection. There was
a gold box with a mosaic on the cover. An oval one trimmed
with translucent green and red berries. Another fashioned of
hard stone with silver mounts. And an enameled Turkish
market box adorned with a scene of the Golden Horn. All
were created in the nineteenth century by the same master
craftsman—his mark distinctively etched into the bottom—
and looted from a private collection in Belgium during
World War II.

They were thought lost, melted for their gold, stripped of
their jewels, the fate of many precious objects. But one sur-
faced five years ago at a London auction house. She'd been
there and bought it. Her employer, Ernst Loring, was fascinated by the intricate workmanship of antique snuffboxes
and possessed an extensive collection. Some legitimate,
bought on the open market, but most covertly acquired from
possessors like Audrey Whiddon. The box bought at auction
had generated an ensuing court battle with the heirs of the
original owner. Loring's legal representatives finally won,
but the fight was costly and public, her employer harboring
no desire of a repeat. So the acquisition of the remaining
three was delegated to her surreptitious acquiring.

Suzanne had found the second in Holland, the third in Fin-
land, the fourth quite unexpectedly when Jeremy tried to

peddle it at another auction house, unknown to his grandmother. The alert auctioneer had recognized the piece and,
knowing that he couldn't sell it, profited when she paid him
ten thousand pounds to learn its whereabouts. She possessed
many such sources at auction houses all over the world, people who kept their eyes open for stolen treasure, things they
couldn't legally handle but could sell all too easily.

She finished dressing and combed her hair.

Fooling Jeremy had been easy. Like always, her fashion-
model features, saucer-round azure eyes, and trim body
played well. All masked a mien of controlled calm and made
her appear as something other than what she was, something
not to be feared, something easy to master and contain. Men
quickly felt comfortable with her, and she'd learned that
beauty could be a far better weapon than bullets or blades.

She tiptoed from the bedroom and down a wooden staircase, careful to minimize the squeaks. Dainty Elizabethan
stencils decorated the towering walls. She'd once imagined
living in a similar house with a husband and children. But
that was before her father taught her the value of independence and the price of dedication. He'd also worked for
Ernst Loring, dreaming one day of buying his own estate.
But he never realized that ambition, dying in a plane crash
eleven years ago. She'd been twenty-five years old, just out
of college, yet Loring never hesitated, immediately allowing
her to succeed her father. She'd learned her craft on the job
and quickly discovered that she, like her father, instinctively
possessed the ability to search, and she greatly enjoyed the
chase.

She turned at the bottom of the stairs, slipped through
the dining hall, and entered an oak-paneled piano room. The
windows highlighting the adjacent grounds loomed dark,
the white Jacobean ceiling muted. She approached the table
and reached for the snuffbox.

Number four.

It was eighteen-carat gold, the hinged cover enameled *en
plein* with an impregnation of Danaë by Jupiter in a shower

of even more gold. She drew the tiny box close and gazed at the image of the plump Danaë. How had men once believed such obesity attractive? But apparently they had, since they found the need to fantasize that their gods desired such a butterball. She flipped the box over and traced her fingernail over the initials.

B. N.

Its craftsman.

She yanked a cloth from the pocket of her jeans. The case, less than four inches long, easily dissolved into its crimson folds. She stuffed the bundle into her pocket and then crossed the ground floor to the library.

Growing up on the Loring estate came with obvious advantages. A fine home, the best tutors, access to art and culture. Loring made sure the Danzer family was well cared for. But the isolation of Castle Loukov deprived her of childhood friends. Her mother died when she was three, and her father traveled constantly. It was Loring who took the time with her, and books became her trusted companions. She read once that the Chinese symbolized books with the power to ward off evil spirits. And for her they did. Stories became her escape. Particularly English literature. Marlowe's tragedies on kings and potentates, the poetry of Dryden, Locke's essays, Chaucer's tales, Malory's *Morte d'Arthur*.

Earlier, when Jeremy had shown her around the ground floor, she'd noticed one particular book in the library. Casually, she'd slipped the leather volume from the shelf and found the expected garish swastika bookplate inside, the inscription reading: EX LIBRIS ADOLF HITLER. Two thousand of Hitler's books, all from his personal library, had been hastily evacuated from Berchtesgaden and stashed in a nearby salt mine just days before the end of the war. American soldiers later found them, and they were eventually cataloged into the Library of Congress. But some were stolen before that happened. Several had turned up through the years. Loring owned none, desiring no reminders of the horror of Nazism, but he knew other collectors who did.

She slipped the book off the shelf. Loring would be pleased with this added treasure.

She turned to leave.

Jeremy stood naked in the darkened doorway.

"Is it the same one you looked at before?" he asked. "Grandmother has so many books. She'll not miss one."

She approached close and quickly decided to use her best weapon. "I enjoyed tonight."

"So did I. You didn't answer my question."

She gestured with the book. "Yes. It's the same one."

"You require it?"

"I do."

"Will you come back?"

A strange question considering the situation, but she realized what he truly wanted. So she reached down and grasped him where she knew he could not resist. He instantly responded to her gentle strokes. "Perhaps," she said.

"I saw you in the piano room. You're not some woman who just got out of a bad marriage, are you?"

"Does it matter, Jeremy? You enjoyed yourself." She continued to stroke him. "You're enjoying yourself now, aren't you?"

He sighed.

"And everything here is your grandmother's anyway. What do you care?"

"I don't."

She released her hold. His organ stood at attention. She kissed him gently on the lips. "I'm sure we'll be seeing one another again." She brushed past him and headed for the front door.

"If I hadn't given in, would you have harmed me to get the book and the box?"

She turned back. Interesting that someone so immature about life could be perceptive enough to understand the depths of her desires. "What do you think?"

He seemed to genuinely consider the inquiry. Perhaps the hardest he'd considered anything in a while.

"I think I'm glad I fucked you."

TWELVE

SUZANNE ANGLED THE PORSCHE HARD TO THE RIGHT, AND THE
911 Speedster's coil-spring suspension and torque steering
grabbed the tight curve. She'd earlier hinged the glass-fiber
hood back, allowing the afternoon air to whip her layered
bob. She kept the car parked at the Ruzyně airport, the 120
kilometers from Prague to southwestern Bohemia an easy
hour's drive. The car was a gift from Loring, a bonus two
years ago after a particularly productive year of acquisitions.
Metallic slate gray, black leather interior, plush velvet carpet. Only 150 of the model were produced. Hers bore a gold
insigne on the dash. *Drahá.* "Little darling," the nickname
Loring bestowed upon her in childhood.

She'd heard the tales and read the press on Ernst Loring.
Most portrayed him as baleful, stern, and dismissive, with
the energy of a zealot and the morals of a despot. Not far off
the mark. But there was another side of him. The one she
knew, loved, and respected.

Loring's estate occupied a three-hundred-acre tract in
southwestern Czech, only kilometers from the German border. The family had flourished under Communist rule, their
factories and mines in Chomutov, Most, and Teplice vital to
the old Czechoslovakia's once supposed self-sufficiency.
She'd always thought it amusing that the family uranium
mines north in Jáchymov, manned with political prisoners—
the worker death toll nearly 100 percent—were officially
considered irrelevant by the new government. It was likewise unimportant that, after years of acid rain, the Sad
Mountains had been transformed into eerie graveyards of

rotting forests. A mere footnote that Teplice, once a thriving spa town near the Polish border, was renowned more for the short life expectancy of its inhabitants than for its refreshing warm water. She'd long ago noticed that no photos of the region were contained in the fancy picture books vendors hawked outside Prague Castle to the millions who visited each year. Northern Czech was a blight. A reminder. Once a necessity, now something to be forgotten. But it was a place where Ernst Loring profited, and the reason why he lived in the south.

The Velvet Revolution of 1989 assured the demise of the Communists. Three years later Czech and Slovakia divorced, hastily dividing the country's spoils. Loring benefited from both events, quickly allying himself with Havel and the new government of the Czech Republic, a name he thought dignified but lacking in punch. She'd heard his views about the changes. How his factories and foundries were in demand more than ever. Though spawned in Communism, Loring was a tried and true capitalist. His father, Josef, and his grandfather before that had been capitalists.

What did he say all the time? *All political movements need steel and coal.* Loring supplied both, in return for protection, freedom, and a more than modest return on investment.

The manor suddenly loomed on the horizon. Castle Loukov. A former knight's *hrad,* the site a formidable headland overshadowing the swift Orlík Stream. Built in the Burgundian-Cistercian style, its earliest construction began in the fifteenth century, but it wasn't finished until the mid-seventeenth century. Triple sedilia and leaf capitals lined the towering walls. Oriels dotted vine-covered ramparts. A clay roof flashed orange in the midday sun.

A fire ravaged the entire complex during World War II, the Nazis confiscating it as a local headquarters, and the Allies finally bombing it. But Josef Loring wrestled back title, allying himself with the Russians who liberated the area on their way to Berlin. After the war the elder Loring resurrected his industrial empire and expanded, ultimately bequeathing everything to Ernst, his only surviving child, a move the government wholly supported.

Clever, industrious men were also always in demand, her employer had said many times.

She downshifted the Porsche to third. The engine groaned, then forced the tires to grab dry pavement. She twisted up the narrow road, the black asphalt surrounded by thick forest, and slowed at the castle's main gate. What once accommodated horse-drawn carriages and deterred aggressors had been widened and paved to easily accept cars.

Loring stood outside in the courtyard, dressed casually, wearing work gloves, apparently tending his spring flowers. He was tall and angular, with a surprisingly flat chest and strong physique for a man in his late seventies. Over the past decade she'd watched the silkened ash blond hair fade to the point of a lackluster gray, a matching goatee carpeting his creased jaw and wrinkled neck. Gardening had always been one of his obsessions. The greenhouses outside the walls were packed with exotic plants from around the world.

"*Dobriy den,* my dear," Loring called out in Czech.

She parked and exited the Porsche, grabbing her travel bag out of the passenger's seat.

Loring clapped dirt from his gloves and walked over. "Good hunting, I hope?"

She withdrew a small cardboard box from the passenger's seat. Neither Customs in London nor Prague questioned the trinket after she explained that it had been bought at a Westminister Abbey gift shop for less than thirty pounds. She was even able to produce a receipt, since she'd stopped by that very shop on the way to the airport and bought a cheap reproduction, one she trashed at the airport.

Loring yanked off his gloves and lifted the lid, studying the snuffbox in the graying afternoon. "Beautiful," he whispered. "Perfect."

She reached back into her bag and extracted the book.

"What is this?" he asked.

"A surprise."

He returned the gold treasure to the cardboard box, then gingerly cradled the volume, unfolding the front cover, marveling at the bookplate.

"*Drahá,* you amaze me. What a wonderful bonus."

"I recognized it instantly and thought you'd like it."

"We can certainly sell or trade this. Herr Greimel loves these, and I would very much like a painting he possesses."

"I knew you'd be happy."

"This should make Christian take notice, huh? Quite an unveiling at our next gathering."

"And Franz Fellner."

He shook his head. "Not anymore. I believe now it's Monika. She seems to be taking over everything. Slowly but surely."

"Arrogant bitch."

"True. But she's also no fool. I spoke to her at length recently. A bit impatient and eager. Seems to have inherited her father's spirit, if not his brains. But, who knows? She's young—maybe she'll learn. I'm sure Franz will teach her."

"And what of my benefactor. Any similar thoughts of retirement?"

Loring grinned. "What would I do?"

She gestured to the blossoms. "Garden?"

"Hardly. What we do is so invigorating. Collecting carries such thrills. I am as a child at Christmas opening packages."

He cradled his two treasures and led her inside his woodworking shop, which consumed the ground floor of a building adjacent to the courtyard. "I received a call from St. Petersburg," he told her. "Christian was in the depository again. In the Commission records. Fellner obviously is not giving up."

"Find anything?"

"Hard to say. The idiot clerk should have gone through the boxes by now, but I doubt he has. Says it will take years. He seems far more interested in getting paid than working. But he was able to see that Knoll discovered a reference to Karol Borya."

She realized the significance.

"I don't understand this obsession of Franz's," Loring said. "So many things waiting to be found. Bellini's *Madonna and Child,* gone since the war. What a find that would be. Van Eyck's altarpiece of the Mystical Lamb. The twelve old masters stolen from the Treves Museum in '68. And those impressionist works stolen in Florence. There are not even any photos of those for identification purposes. Anyone would love to acquire just one of them."

"But the Amber Room is at the top of everyone's collection list," she said.

"Quite right, and that seems to be the problem."

"You think Christian will try to find Borya?"

"Without a doubt. Borya and Chapaev are the only two searchers left alive. Knoll never found Chapaev five years ago. He's probably hoping Borya knows Chapaev's whereabouts. Fellner would love the Amber Room to be Monika's first unveiling. There is no doubt in my mind that Franz will send Knoll to America, at least to try to find Borya."

"But shouldn't that be a dead end?"

"Exactly. Literally. But only if necessary. Let's hope Borya still has a tight lip. Maybe the old man finally died. He has to be approaching ninety. Go to Georgia, but stay out of the way unless forced to act."

A thrill ran through her. How wonderful to battle Knoll again. Their last encounter in France had been invigorating, the sex afterwards memorable. He was a worthy opponent. But dangerous. Which made the adventure that much more exciting.

"Careful with Christian, my dear. Not too close. You may have to do some unpleasant things. Leave him to Monika. They deserve one another."

She pecked the old man on the cheek with a soft kiss. "Not to worry. Your *drahá* will not let you down."

Thirteen

KAROL BORYA SETTLED INTO THE CHAISE LONGUE AND READ again the one article he always consulted when he needed to remember details. It was from the *International Art Review,* October 1972. He'd found it on one of his regular forays downtown to the library at Georgia State University. Outside of Germany and Russia, the media had shown little interest in the Amber Room. Fewer than two dozen English accounts had been printed since the war, most rehashes of historical facts or a pondering on the latest theory on what might have happened. He loved how the article began, a quote from Robert Browning, still underlined in blue ink from his first reading: *Suddenly, as rare things will, it vanished.*

That observation was particularly relevant to the Amber Room. Unseen since 1945, its history was littered with political turmoil and marked by death and intrigue.

The idea came from Frederick I of Prussia, a complicated man who traded his precious vote as an elector of the Holy Roman Emperor to secure a hereditary kingship of his own. In 1701, he commissioned panels of amber for a study in his Charlottenburg palace. Frederick amused himself daily with amber chessmen, candlesticks, and chandeliers. He quaffed beer from amber tankards and smoked from pipes fitted with amber mouthpieces. Why not a study faced ceiling to floor with carved amber paneling? So he charged his court architect, Andreas Schülter, with the task of creating such a marvel.

The original commission was granted to Gottfried Wolf-

fram, but in 1707, Ernst Schact and Gottfried Turau replaced
the Dane. Over four years Schact and Turau labored, meticulously searching the Baltic coast for jewel-grade amber.
The area had for centuries yielded tons of the substance, so
much that Frederick trained whole details of soldiers in its
gathering. Eventually, each rough chunk was sliced to no
more than five millimeters thick, polished, and heated to
change its color. The pieces were then fitted jigsaw style into
mosaic panels of floral scrollwork, busts, and heraldic symbols. Each panel included a relief of the Prussian coat of
arms, a crowned eagle in profile, and was backed in silver to
enhance its brilliance.

The room was partially completed in 1712, when Peter the
Great of Russia visited and admired the workmanship. A
year later Frederick I died and was succeeded by his son,
Frederick William I. As sons sometimes do, Frederick William hated everything his father loved. Harboring no desire
to spend any more crown money on his father's caprice, he
ordered the amber panels dismantled and packed away.

In 1716, Frederick William signed a Russian-Prussian
alliance with Peter the Great against Sweden. To commemo-
rate the treaty, the amber panels were ceremonially presented
to Peter and transported to St. Petersburg the following January. Peter, more concerned with building the Russian Navy
than with collecting art, simply stored them away. But, in
gratitude, he reciprocated the gift with 248 soldiers, a lathe,
and a wine cup he crafted himself. Included among the soldiers were fifty-five of his tallest guardsmen, this in recogni-
tion of the Prussian king's passion for tall warriors.

Thirty years passed until Empress Elizabeth, Peter's
daughter, asked Rastrelli, her court architect, to display the
panels in a study at the Winter Place in St. Petersburg. In
1755 Elizabeth ordered them carried to the summer palace
in Tsarskoe Selo, thirty miles south of St. Petersburg, and
installed in what came to be known as the Catherine Palace.

It was there that the Amber Room was perfected.

Over the next twenty years, forty-eight square meters of additional amber panels, most emblazoned with the Romanov crest and elaborate decorations, were added to the original thirty-six square meters, the additions necessary since the thirty-foot walls in the Catherine Palace towered over the original room the amber had graced. The Prussian king even contributed to the creation, sending another panel, this one with a bas-relief of the two-headed eagle of the Russian tsars. Eighty-six square meters of amber were eventually crafted, the finished walls dotted with fanciful figurines, floral garlands, tulips, roses, seashells, monograms, and rocaille, all in glittering shades of brown, red, yellow, and orange. Rastrelli framed each panel in a cartouche of boiserie, Louis Quinze style, separating them vertically by pairs of narrow mirrored pilasters adorned with bronze candelabra, everything gilded to blend with the amber.

The centers of four panels were dotted with exquisite Florentine mosaics fashioned from polished jasper and agate and framed in gilded bronze. A ceiling mural was added, along with an intricate parquet floor of inlaid oak, maple, sandalwood, rosewood, walnut, and mahogany, itself as magnificent as the surrounding walls.

Five Königsberg masters labored until 1770, when the room was declared finished. Empress Elizabeth was so delighted that she routinely used the space to impress foreign ambassadors. It also served as a *kunstkammer,* a cabinet of curiosities for her and later tsars, the place where royal treasures could be displayed. By 1765, seventy amber objects—chests, candlesticks, snuffboxes, saucers, knives, forks, crucifixes, and tabernacles—graced the room. In 1780, a corner table of encrusted amber was added. The last decoration came in 1913, an amber crown on a pillow, the piece purchased by Tsar Nicholas II.

Incredibly, the panels survived 170 years and the Bolshevik Revolution intact. Restorations were done in 1760, 1810, 1830, 1870, 1918, 1935, and 1938. An extensive restoration was planned in the 1940s, but on June 22, 1941, German troops invaded the Soviet Union. By July 14, Hitler's army had taken Belarus, most of Latvia, Lithuania, and the Ukraine, reaching the Liga River less than a hundred miles from Leningrad. On September 17, Nazi troops took Tsarskoe Selo and the palaces in and around it, including the Catherine Palace, which had become a state museum under the Communists.

In the days before its capture, museum officials hastily shipped all the small objects in the Amber Room to eastern Russia. But the panels themselves had proved impossible to remove. In an effort to conceal them, a layer of wallpaper was slapped over, but the disguise fooled no one. Hitler ordered Erich Koch, gauleiter of East Prussia, to return the Amber Room to Königsberg, which, in Hitler's mind, was where it rightly belonged. Six men took thirty-six hours to dismantle the panels, and twenty tons of amber was meticulously packed in crates and shipped west by truck convoy and rail, eventually reinstalled in the Königsberg castle, along with a vast collection of Prussian art. A 1942 German news article proclaimed the event a "return to its true home, the real place of origination and sole place of origination of the amber." Picture postcards were issued of the restored treasure. The exhibit became the most popular of all Nazi museum spectacles.

The first Allied bombardment of Königsberg occurred in August 1944. Some of the mirrored pilasters and a few of the smaller amber panels were damaged. What happened after that was unclear. Sometime between January and April 1945, as the Soviet Army approached Königsberg, Koch ordered the panels crated and hidden in the cellar of the Blutgericht restaurant. The last German document that mentioned the Amber Room was dated January 12, 1945, and noted that the panels were being packed for transport to Saxony. At some point Alfred Rohde, the room's custodian, supervised the loading of crates onto a truck convoy. Those crates were last seen on April 6, 1945, when trucks left Königsberg.

Borya set the article aside.

Each time he read the words his mind always returned to the opening line. *Suddenly, as rare things will, it vanished.*

How true.

He took a moment and thumbed through the file spread across his lap. It contained copies of other articles he'd collected through the years. He casually glanced over a few, his memory triggered by more details. It was good to remember.

To a point.

He rose from the chaise longue and stepped from the patio to twist off the faucet. His summer garden glistened from a good soaking. He'd waited all day to water, hoping it might rain, but the spring so far had been dry. Lucy watched from the patio, perched upright, her feline eyes studying his every move. He knew she didn't like the grass, particularly wet grass, finicky about her fur ever since achieving indoor status.

He grabbed the file folder. "Come, little kitty, inside."

The cat followed him through the back door and into the kitchen. He tossed the folder on the counter next to his dinner, a bacon-wrapped fillet marinating in teriyaki. He was about to start boiling some corn when the doorbell rang.

He shuffled out of the kitchen and headed toward the front of the house. Lucy followed. He peered through the peephole at a man dressed in a dark business suit, white shirt, and striped tie. Probably another Jehovah's Witness or Mormon. They often came by about this time, and he liked talking to them.

He opened the door.

"Karl Bates? Once known as Karol Borya?"

The question caught him off guard, and his eyes betrayed him with an affirmative response.

"I'm Christian Knoll," the man said.

A faint German accent, which he instantly disliked, laced the words. A business card reiterating the name in raised black letters along with the label PROCURER OF LOST ANTIQUITIES was thrust forward but not offered. The address and phone number was Munich, Germany. He studied his visitor. Mid-forties, broad shouldered, wavy blond hair, sun-leathered skin tanned the color of cinnamon, and gray eyes that dominated an icy face—one that demanded attention.

"Why you want me, Mr. Knoll?"

"May I?" His visitor indicated a desire to come in, as he repocketed the card.

"Depends."

"I want to talk about the Amber Room."

He considered a protest but decided against it. He'd actually been expecting a visit for years.

Knoll followed him into the den. They both sat. Lucy skirted in to investigate, then took up a perch in an adjacent chair.

"You work for Russians?" he asked.

Knoll shook his head. "I could lie and say yes, but no. I'm employed by a private collector searching for the Amber Room. I recently learned of your name and address from Soviet records. It seems you once were on a similar quest."

He nodded. "Long time ago."

Knoll slipped a hand into his jacket and extracted three folded sheets. "I found these references in the Soviet records. They refer to you as *Ỹxo*."

He scanned the papers. Decades had passed since he'd last read Cyrillic. "It was my name in Mauthausen."

"You were a prisoner?"

"For many months." He rolled over his right arm and pointed to the tattoo. "10901. I try to remove, but can't. German craftsmanship."

Knoll motioned to the sheets. "What do you know of Danya Chapaev?"

He noted with interest Knoll's ignoring of the ethnic jab. "Danya was my partner. We teamed till I leave."

"How did you come to work for the Commission?"

He eyed his visitor, debating whether to answer. He hadn't talked about that time in decades. Only Maya knew it all, the information dying with her years ago. Rachel knew enough to understand and never forget. Should he talk about it? Why not? He was an old man on borrowed time. What did it matter anymore?

"After death camp I return to Belarus, but my homeland was gone. Germans like locust. My family was dead. Commission seemed good place to help rebuild."

"I've studied the Commission closely. An interesting organization. The Nazis did their share of looting, but the Soviets far outmatched them. Soldiers seemed satisfied with mundane luxuries like bicycles and watches. Officers, though, sent boxcars and planeloads of artwork, porcelain, and jewelry back home. The Commission apparently was the largest looter of all. Millions of items, I believe."

He shook his head in defiance. "Not looting. Germans destroy land, homes, factories, cities. Kill millions. Back then, Soviets think reparation."

"And now?" Knoll seemed to have sensed his hesitancy.

"I agree. Looting. Communists worse than Nazis. Amazing how time opens eyes."

Knoll was apparently pleased with the concession. "The Commission turned into a travesty, wouldn't you say? It eventually helped Stalin send millions to gulags."

"Which is why I leave."

"Is Chapaev still alive?"

The question came quick. Unexpected. Surely designed to elicit an equally quick response. He almost smiled. Knoll was good. "Have no idea. Not seen Danya since I leave. KGB came years back. Big smelly Chechen. I tell him same thing."

"That was very bold, Mr. Bates. The KGB should not be taken so lightly."

"Many years make me bold. What was he to do? Kill an old man? Those days are gone, Herr Knoll."

His shift from *Mr.* to *Herr* was intentional but, again, Knoll did not react. Instead, the German changed the subject.

"I've interviewed a lot of the former searchers. Telegin.

Zernov. Voloshin. I never could find Chapaev. I didn't even know about you until a few days ago."

"Others not mention me?"

"If they had, I would have come sooner."

Which was not surprising. Like him, they'd all been taught the value of a tight lip.

"I know the Commission's history," Knoll said. "It hired searchers to scour Germany and eastern Europe for art. A race against the army for the right to pillage. But it was quite successful and managed to get the Trojan gold, the Pergamum Altar, Raphael's *Sistine Madonna,* and the entire Dresden Museum collection, I believe."

He nodded. "Many, many things."

"As I understand, only now are some of those objects seeing the light of day. Most have been secreted away in castles or locked in rooms for decades."

"I read stories. Glasnost." He decided to get to the point. "You think I know where Amber Room is?"

"No. Otherwise you would have already found it."

"Maybe better stay lost."

Knoll shook his head. "Someone with your background, a lover of fine art, surely would not want such a masterpiece destroyed by time and elements."

"Amber last forever."

"But the form into which it is crafted does not. Eighteenth-century mastics could not be that effective."

"You are right. Those panels found today would be like jigsaw puzzle from box."

"My employer is willing to fund the reassembling of that puzzle."

"Who is employer?"

His visitor grinned. "I cannot say. That person prefers anonymity. As you well know, the world of collecting can be a treacherous place for the known."

"They seek a grand prize. Amber Room not seen in over fifty years."

"But imagine, Herr Bates, excuse me, Mr. Bates—"

"It's Borya."

"Very well. Mr. Borya. Imagine the room restored to its former glory. What a sight that would be. As of now, only a few color photographs exist, along with some black and whites that certainly do no justice to its beauty."

"I saw those pictures when searching. I also saw room before war. Truly magnificent. No photo could ever capture. Sad, but it seems lost forever."

"My employer refuses to believe that."

"Evidence good that panels were destroyed when Königsberg was carpet bombed in 1944. Some think they rest at bottom of Baltic. I investigate *Wilhelm Gustloff* myself. Ninety-five hundred dead when Soviets send ship to bottom. Some say Amber Room in cargo hold. Moved from Königsberg by truck to Danzig, then loaded for trip to Hamburg."

Knoll shifted in the chair. "I, too, looked into the *Gustloff.* The evidence is contradictory, at best. Frankly, the most credible story I researched was that the panels were shipped out of Königsberg by the Nazis to a mine near Göttingen along with ammunition. When the British occupied the area in 1945, they exploded the mine. But, as with all other versions, ambiguities exist."

"Some even swore Americans find and ship across Atlantic."

"I heard that, too. Along with a version proposing the Soviets actually found and stored the panels somewhere unbeknownst to anyone now in power. Given the sheer volume of what was looted, that is entirely possible. But given the value and desire for the return of this treasure, not probable."

His visitor seemed to know the subject well. He'd reread all those theories earlier. He stared hard at the granite face, but blank eyes betrayed nothing of what the German was thinking. He recalled the practice it took to so inconspicuously post such a barrier. "Have you no concern for the curse?"

Knoll grinned. "I've heard of it. But such things are for the uninformed or the sensationalist."

"How rude I have been," he suddenly said. "You want a drink?"

"That would be nice," Knoll said.

"I be right back." He motioned to the cat sacked out on the chair. "Lucy will keep you company."

He stepped toward the kitchen and gave his visitor one last glance before pushing through the swinging door. He filled two glasses with ice and poured some tea. He also deposited the still marinating fillet in the refrigerator. He actually wasn't hungry anymore, his mind racing, like in the old days. He glanced down at the file folder with articles still lying on the counter.

"Mr. Borya?" Knoll called out.

The voice was accompanied by footsteps. Perhaps it was better the articles not be seen. He quickly yanked open the freezer and slid the folder onto the top rack next to the ice maker. He slammed the door shut just as Knoll pushed through the swinging door and into the kitchen. "Yes, Herr Knoll?"

"Might I use your rest room?"

"Down hall. Off the den."

"Thank you."

He didn't believe for a moment that Knoll needed to use the bathroom. More likely he needed to change a tape in a pocket recorder without the worry of interruption, or use the pretense as an opportunity to look around. It was a trick he'd utilized many times in the old days. The German was becoming annoying. He decided to have a little fun. From the cabinet beside the sink he retrieved the laxative his aging intestines forced him to take at least a couple of times a week. He trickled the tasteless granules into one of the tea glasses and stirred them in. Now the bastard really would need a bathroom.

He brought the chilled glasses into the den. Knoll returned and accepted the tea, downing several long swallows.

"Excellent," Knoll said. "Truly an American beverage. Iced tea."

"We proud of it."

"We? You consider yourself American?"

"Here many years. My home now."

"Is not Belarus independent again?"

"Leaders there no better than Soviets. Suspend constitution. Mere dictators."

"Did not the people give the Belarussian president that latitude?"

"Belarus is more like province of Russia, not true independence. Slavery takes centuries to shed."

"You do not seem to care for Germans or Communists."

He was tiring of the conversation, remembering how much he hated Germans. "Sixteen months in death camp can change your heart."

Knoll finished the tea. The ice cubes jangled as the glass banged the coffee table.

He went on, "The Germans and Communists rape Belarus and Russia. Nazis used Catherine Palace as barracks, then for target practice. I visit after war. Little left of regal beauty. Did not the Germans try and destroy Russian culture? Bombed palaces to rubble to teach us a lesson."

"I am not a Nazi, Mr. Borya, so I cannot answer your question."

A moment of strained silence passed. Then Knoll asked, "Why don't we quit sparring. Did you find the Amber Room?"

"As I said, room lost forever."

"Why don't I believe you?"

He shrugged. "I'm old man. Soon I die. No reason to lie."

"Somehow I doubt that last observation, Mr. Borya."

He grabbed Knoll's gaze with his own. "I tell you story— maybe it help with your search. Months before Mauthausen fell, Göring came to camp. He forced me to help torture four Germans. Göring had them tied naked to stakes in freezing cold. We poured water over them till dead."

"And the purpose?"

"Göring wanted *das Bernstein-zimmer*. The four men

were some who evacuate amber panels from Königsberg before Russians invade. Göring wanted Amber Room, but
Hitler got it first."

"Any of the soldiers reveal information?"

"Nothing. Just yell *'Mein Führer'* until freeze to death. I
still see their frozen faces in my dreams sometimes. Strange,
Herr Knoll, in a sense I owe my life to a German."

"How so?"

"If one of four talk, Göring would have tied me to stake
and kill same way." He was tired of remembering. He
wanted the bastard out of his house before the laxative took
effect. "I hate Germans, Herr Knoll. I hate Communists. I
told KGB nothing. I tell you nothing. Now, go."

Knoll seemed to sense that further inquiry would be fruit-
less, and he stood. "Very well, Mr. Borya. Let it not be said I
pressed. I will bid you a good night."

They walked to the foyer, and he opened the front door.
Knoll stepped outside, turned, and extended his hand to
shake. A casual gesture, seemingly more out of politeness
than duty.

"A pleasure, Mr. Borya."

He thought again about the German soldier, Mathias, as
he'd stood naked in the freezing cold, and how he'd responded to Göring.

He spat on the outstretched palm.

Knoll said nothing, nor did he move for a few seconds.
Then, calmly, the German slipped a handkerchief from his
trouser pocket and wiped the spittle away as the door
slammed in his face.

FOURTEEN

BORYA ONCE AGAIN SCANNED THE ARTICLE FROM *INTERNATIONAL Art Review* magazine and found the part he remembered:

> . . . Alfred Rohde, the man who supervised the evacuation of the Amber Room from Königsberg, was quickly apprehended after the war and summoned before Soviet authorities. The so-called Extraordinary State Commission on Damage Done by the Fascist-German Invaders was looking for the Amber Room and wanted answers. But Rohde and his wife were found dead on the morning they were to appear for questioning. Dysentery was the official cause, plausible since epidemics were raging at the time from polluted water, but speculation abounded they had been killed in order to protect the location of the Amber Room.
>
> On the same day, Dr. Paul Erdmann, the physician who signed the Rohdes' death certificates, disappeared.
>
> Erich Koch, Hitler's personal representative in Prussia, was ultimately arrested and tried by the Poles for war crimes. Koch was sentenced to death in 1946, but his execution was continuously postponed at the request of Soviet authorities. It was widely believed that Koch was the only man left alive who knew the actual whereabouts of the crates that left Königsberg in 1945. Paradoxically, Koch's continued survival was dependent on his not revealing their location, since there was no reason to believe the Soviets would intervene in his behalf once they again possessed the Amber Room.

In 1965, Koch's lawyers finally obtained Soviet assurance that his life would be spared once the information was revealed. Koch then announced that the crates were walled into a bunker outside Königsberg but claimed he was unable to remember the exact location as a result of Soviet rebuilding after the war. He went to his grave without revealing where the panels lay.

In the decades following, three West German journalists died mysteriously while searching for the Amber Room. One fell down the shaft of a disused salt mine in Austria, a place rumored to be a Nazi loot depository. Two others were killed by hit-and-run drivers. George Stein, a German researcher who long investigated the Amber Room, supposedly committed suicide. All these events fueled speculation of a curse associated with the Amber Room, making the search for the treasure even more intriguing.

He was upstairs in what was once Rachel's room. Now it was a study where he kept his books and papers. There was an antique writing desk, an oak filing cabinet, and a club chair where he liked to sit and read. Four walnut bookcases held novels, historical treatises, and classical literature.

He'd come upstairs after eating dinner, still thinking about Christian Knoll, and found more articles in one of the cabinets. They were all short, mainly fluff, containing no real information. The rest were still in the freezer. He needed to retrieve them, but didn't feel like climbing back up the stairs again afterward.

By and large the newspaper and magazine accounts on the Amber Room were contradictory. One would say the panels disappeared in January 1945, another April. Did they leave in trucks, by rail, or on the sea? Different writers offered different perspectives. One account noted that the Soviets torpedoed the *Wilhelm Gustloff* to the bottom of the Baltic with the panels, another mentioned bombing the ship from the air. One was sure that seventy-two crates left Königsberg, the next noted twenty-six, another eighteen. Several accounts were sure the panels burned in Königsberg during the bombing. Another tracked leads implying they made it surreptitiously across the Atlantic to America. It was difficult to extract anything useful, and no article ever mentioned the source of information. It could be double to triple hearsay. Or even worse, pure speculation.

Only one, an obscure publication, *The Military Historian,* noted the story of a train leaving occupied Russia sometime around May 1, 1945, with the crated Amber Room supposedly on board. Witness accounts vouched that the crates were offloaded in the tiny Czechoslovakian town of Týnec-nad-Sázavou. There, they were supposedly trucked south and stored in an underground bunker that housed the headquarters of Field Marshal von Schörner, commander of the million-strong German army, still holding out in Czechoslovakia. But the article noted that an excavation of the bunker by the Soviets in 1989 found nothing.

Close to the truth, he thought. Real close.

Seven years ago, when he first read the article, he'd wondered about its source, even tried to contact the author, but was unsuccessful. Now a man named Wayland McKoy was burrowing into the Harz Mountains near Stod, Germany. Was he on the right track? The only thing clear was that people had died searching for the Amber Room. What happened to Alfred Rohde and Erich Koch was documented history. So were the other deaths and disappearances. Coincidence? Perhaps. But he wasn't so sure. Particularly given what happened nine years ago. How could he forget. The memory haunted him every time he looked at Paul Cutler. And he wondered many times if two more names should not be added to the list of casualties.

A squeak came from the hall.

Not a sound the house usually made when empty.

He looked up, expecting to see Lucy bound into the room, but the cat was nowhere to be seen. He laid the articles aside and pushed himself up from the chair. He shuffled out into the second-floor foyer and peered down, past an oak banister, to the foyer below. Narrow sidelights framing the front door were dark, the ground floor illuminated by a single den lamp. Upstairs was dark, too, except for the floor lamp in the study. Just ahead, his bedroom door was open, the room black and quiet.

"Lucy? Lucy?"

The cat did not respond. He listened hard. No more sounds. Everything appeared quiet. He turned and started back into the study. Suddenly, someone lunged at him from behind, out of the bedroom. Before he could turn, a powerful arm locked around his neck, yanking him off the ground. The scent of latex bloomed from sheathed hands.

"Können wir reden mehr, Ỳxo."

The voice was that of his visitor, Christian Knoll. He easily translated.

Now we talk further, Ears.

Knoll squeezed his throat hard, and his breath faltered.

"Miserable damn Russian. Spit on my hand. Who the fuck you think you are? I've killed for less."

He said nothing, the experience of a lifetime cautioning silence.

"You will tell me what I want to know, old man, or I will kill you."

He remembered similar words said fifty-two years ago. Göring informing the naked soldiers of their fate right before water was poured. What had the German soldier, Mathias, said?

It is an honor to defy your captor.

Yes, it still was.

"You know where Chapaev is, don't you?"

He tried to shake his head.

Knoll's grip tightened. "You know where *das Bernstein-zimmer* rests, don't you?"

He was about to pass out. Knoll loosened his grip. Air rushed into his lungs.

"I'm not someone to take lightly. I traveled a long way for information."

"I tell nothing."

"You sure? You said earlier that your time is short. Now it is shorter than you imagined. What of your daughter? Your grandchildren. Would you not like a few more years with them?"

He would, but not enough to be cowed by a German. "Go fuck, Herr Knoll."

His frail body was launched out over the stairs. He tried to cry out, but before he could muster the breath he pounded headfirst onto oak runners and rolled. His limbs splayed. Arms and legs raked the spindles as gravity sent him tumbling end over end. Something cracked. Consciousness flickered in and out. Pain seared his back. He finally settled spine first on the hard tile, agony radiating through his upper body. His legs were numb. The ceiling spun. He heard Knoll bound down the stairs, then watched him reach down and jerk him up by his hair. Ironic. He owed his life to a German, and now a German would take it.

"Ten million euros is one thing. But no Russian pissant will spit on me."

He tried to amass enough saliva to spit again, but his mouth was dry, his jaw frozen.

Knoll's arm encircled his neck.

FIFTEEN

SUZANNE DANZER WATCHED THROUGH THE WINDOW AND HEARD the crack as Knoll snapped the old man's neck. She saw the body go limp, the head left at an unnatural angle.

Knoll then shoved Borya aside and kicked the man's chest.

She'd picked up Knoll's trail this morning, after arriving in Atlanta on a flight from Prague. His actions so far had been predictable, and she initially located him as he cruised the neighborhood on a scouting mission. Any competent Acquisitor always studied the landscape first, making sure a lead was not a trap.

And if Knoll was anything, he was good.

He'd stayed downtown in his hotel most of the day, and she'd followed him earlier when he first visited Borya. But instead of returning to his hotel, Knoll waited in a car three blocks over and then backtracked to the house after dark. She'd watched as he entered through a rear door, the entrance apparently unlocked as the knob turned on the first try.

Obviously, the old man had been uncooperative. Knoll's temper was legendary. He'd tossed Borya down the stairs as casually as one tossed paper into the trash, then snapped the neck with apparent pleasure. She respected her adversary's talents, knew of the stiletto he sported on his forearm and his unhesitating ability to use it.

But she was not without talents of her own.

Knoll stood and looked around.

Her vantage point provided a clear view. The black jumpsuit and black cap she wore over her blond hair helped blend her into the night. The room the window opened into, a front parlor, was unlit.

Did he sense her?

She shrank below the sill into the tall hollies surrounding the house, careful with the prickly leaves. The night was warm. Sweat beaded on her forehead at the edge of the cap's elastic. She cautiously edged back up and saw Knoll disappear up the stairs. Six minutes later he returned, his hands empty, his jacket was once again smooth, his tie perfect. She watched as he bent down and checked Borya's pulse and then moved toward the back of the house. A few seconds later she heard a door open and close.

She waited ten minutes before creeping around to the rear

of the house. With gloved hands, she twisted the knob and
stepped inside. The scent of antiseptic and old age lingered
in the air. She crossed the kitchen and headed toward the
foyer.

In the dining room a cat suddenly bisected her path. She
stopped, her heart pounding, and cursed the creature.

She sucked in a breath and entered the den.

The decor hadn't changed since her last visit, three years
ago. The same hand-tufted camelback sofa, chiming wall
clock, and iron Cambridge lamps. The lithographs on the
wall had initially intrigued her. She'd wondered if any might
be originals, but a close inspection last time revealed all to
be copies. She'd broken in one evening after Borya left, her
search revealing nothing on the Amber Room other than
some magazine and newspaper reports. Nothing of any
value. If Karol Borya knew anything of substance on the
Amber Room, he certainly hadn't written it down or did not
keep the information in his house.

She bypassed the body in the foyer and mounted the
stairs. Another quick check in the study revealed nothing
except that Borya had apparently been reading some of
the Amber Room material recently. Several articles were
strewn across the same tan chair she remembered from before.

She crept back downstairs.

The old man lay facedown. She tried for a pulse. None.

Good.

Knoll saved her the trouble.

Sixteen

RACHEL STEERED THE CAR INTO HER FATHER'S DRIVEWAY. THE mid-May morning sky was an inviting blue. The garage door was up, the Oldsmobile resting outside, dew sparkling on its maroon exterior. The sight was strange, since her father usually parked the car inside.

The house had changed little since her childhood. Red brick, white trim, charcoal shingled roof. The magnolia and dogwoods in front, planted twenty years ago when the family first moved in, now loomed tall and bushy along with hollies and junipers encircling the front and sides. The shutters were showing their age, and mildew was slowly advancing up the brick. The outside needed attention and she made a mental note to talk to her father about it.

She parked and the kids bolted out, running around to the back door.

She checked her father's car. Unlocked. She shook her head. He simply refused to lock anything. The morning *Constitution* lay in the driveway, and she walked down and retrieved it, then followed the concrete path around back. Marla and Brent were calling for Lucy in the backyard.

The kitchen door was also unlocked. The light over the sink was on. As careless as her father was about locks, he was downright neurotic about lights, burning one only when absolutely necessary. He would surely have switched it off last night before going to bed.

She called out, "Dad? You here? How many times do I have to tell you about leaving the door unlocked?"

The kids called for Lucy, then pushed through the swinging door toward the dining room and den.

"Daddy?" Her voice was louder.

Marla ran back into the kitchen. "Granddaddy's asleep on the floor."

"What do you mean?"

"He's asleep on the floor by the stairs."

She rushed from the kitchen to the foyer. The odd angle of her father's neck instantly told her he wasn't sleeping.

"WELCOME TO THE HIGH MUSEUM OF ART," THE GREETER SAID TO each person passing through the wide glass doors. "Welcome. Welcome." People continued to file through the turnstile one at a time. Paul waited his turn in line.

"Morning, Mr. Cutler," the greeter said. "You didn't have to wait. Why didn't you come on up?"

"That wouldn't be fair, Mr. Braun."

"Membership on the board should have some privilege, shouldn't it?"

Paul smiled. "You would think. Is there a reporter here waiting for me? I was to meet him at ten."

"Yep. Fellow's been in the front gallery since I opened."

He headed off, his leather heels clicking against the shiny terrazzo. The four-story atrium was open all the way to the ceiling, semicircular pedestrian ramps girdled the towering walls on each floor, people milled up and down, and the rumble of muted conversations floated across the conditioned air.

He could think of no better way to spend a Sunday morning than at the museum. He'd never been much of a churchgoer. It wasn't that he didn't believe. It was just that admiring real human endeavor seemed more satisfying than pondering some omnipotent being. Rachel was the same way. He often wondered if their lackadaisical attitude toward religion affected Marla and Brent. Maybe the children needed exposure, he once argued. But Rachel had disagreed.

Let them make up their own minds in their own time. She was staunchly antireligion.

Just one more of their debates.

He sauntered into the front gallery, its canvases a tantalizing sample of what awaited throughout the rest of the building. The reporter, a skinny, brisk-looking man with a scraggly beard and a camera bag slung over his right shoulder, stood in front of a large oil.

"Are you Gale Blazek?"

The young man turned and nodded.

"Paul Cutler." They shook hands, and he motioned to the painting. "Lovely, isn't it?"

"Del Sarto's last, I believe," the reporter said.

He nodded. "We were fortunate to talk a private collector into lending it to us for a while, along with several other nice canvases. They're on the second floor with the rest of the fourteenth- and eighteenth-century Italians."

"I'll make a point to see them before I leave."

He noticed the huge wall clock. 10:15 A.M. "Sorry I'm late. Why don't we wander around and you can ask your questions."

The man smiled and withdrew a microrecorder from the shoulder bag. They strolled across the expansive gallery.

"I'll just get right into it. How long have you been on the museum's board?" the reporter asked.

"Nine years now."

"You a collector?"

He grinned. "Hardly. Only some small oils and a few watercolors. Nothing substantial."

"I've been told your talents lie in organization. The administration speaks highly of you."

"I love my volunteer work. This place is special to me."

A noisy group of teenagers poured in from the mezzanine.

"Were you educated in the arts?"

He shook his head. "Not really. I earned a BA from Emory in political science and took a few graduate courses in art history. Then I found out what art historians make and went to law school." He left out the part about not getting accepted on the first try. Not from vanity—it was just that after thirteen years it really didn't matter any longer.

They skirted the edge of two women admiring a canvas of St. Mary Magdalene.

"How old are you?" the reporter asked.

"Forty-one."

"Married?"

"Divorced."

"Me, too. How you handling it?"

He shrugged. No need to make any comment on the record about that. "I get by."

Actually, divorce meant a sparse two-bedroom apartment and dinners eaten either alone or with business associates, except the two nights a week he ate with the kids. Socializing was confined to State Bar functions, which was the only reason he served on so many committees, something to occupy his spare time and the alternate weekends he didn't have the kids. Rachel was good about visitation. Any time, really. But he didn't want to interfere with her relationship with the children, and he understood the value of a schedule and the need for consistency.

"How about you describe yourself for me."

"Excuse me?"

"It's something I ask all the people I profile. They can do it far better than I could. Who better to know you than you?"

"When the administrator asked me to do this interview and show you around, I thought the piece was on the museum, not me."

"It is. For next Sunday's *Constitution* magazine section. But my editor wants some side boxes on key people. The personalities behind the exhibits."

"What about the curators?"

"The administrator says you're one of the real central figures around here. Somebody he can really count on."

He stopped. How could he describe himself? Five foot ten, brown hair, hazel eyes? The physique of somebody who runs three miles a day? No. "How about plain face on a plain body with a plain personality. Dependable. The kind of guy you'd want to be in a foxhole with."

"The kind of guy who makes sure your estate gets handled right after you're gone?"

He'd not said anything about being a probate lawyer. Obviously, the reporter had done some homework. "Something like that."

"You mentioned foxholes. Ever been in the military?"

"I came along after the draft. Post-Vietnam and all that."

"How long have you practiced law?"

"Since you know I'm a probate lawyer, I assume you also know how long I've practiced."

"Actually, I forgot to ask."

An honest answer. Fair enough. "I've been at Pridgen and Woodworth thirteen years now."

"Your partners speak highly of you. I talked to them Friday."

He raised an eyebrow in puzzlement. "Nobody mentioned anything about that."

"I asked them not to. At least until after today. I wanted our talk to be spontaneous."

More patrons filed in. The chamber was getting crowded and noisy. "Why don't we walk into the Edwards Gallery. Less folks. We have some excellent sculptures on display." He led the way across the mezzanine. Sunlight poured past the walkways through tall sheets of thick glass laced into a white porcelain edifice. A towering jewel-toned ink drawing graced the far north wall. The aroma of coffee and almonds drifted from an open café.

"Magnificent," the reporter said, looking around. "What did the *New York Times* call it? The best museum a city's built in a generation?"

"We were pleased with their enthusiasm. It helped stock the galleries. Donors immediately felt comfortable with us."

Ahead stood a polished red-granite monolith in the center of the atrium. He instinctively moved toward it, never passing without stopping for a moment. The reporter followed. A list of twenty-nine names was etched into stone. His eyes always gravitated to the center:

YANCY CUTLER
JUNE 4, 1936–OCTOBER 23, 1998
DEDICATED LAWYER
PATRON OF THE ARTS
FRIEND OF THE MUSEUM

MARLENE CUTLER
MAY 14, 1938–OCTOBER 23, 1998
DEVOTED WIFE
PATRON OF THE ARTS
FRIEND OF THE MUSEUM

"Your father was on the board, wasn't he?" the reporter asked.

"He served thirty years. Helped raise the money for this building. My mother was active, too."

He stood silent. Reverent, as always. It was the only memorial of his parents that existed. The airbus exploded far out to sea. Twenty-nine people dead. The entire museum board of directors, spouses, and several employees. No bodies found. No explanation for the cause other than a curt conclusion by Italian authorities that separatist terrorists had been responsible. The Italian Minister of Antiquities, on board, had been presumed the target. Yancy and Marlene Cutler were simply in the wrong place at the wrong time.

"They were good people," he said. "We all miss them."

He turned, leading the reporter into the Edwards Gallery. An assistant curator raced across the atrium.

"Mr. Cutler, please wait." The woman hurried over, a look of concern on her face. "A call just came for you. I'm sorry. Your ex-father-in-law has died."

SEVENTEEN

KAROL BORYA WAS BURIED AT 11 A.M., THE MIDSPRING MORNING cloudy and overcast with a lingering chill, unusual for May. The funeral was well attended. Paul officiated, introducing three of Borya's longtime friends who delivered moving eulogies. He then said a few words of his own.

Rachel stood in front, with Marla and Brent at her side. The mitered priest at St. Methodius Orthodox Church presided, Karol having been a regular parishioner. The ceremony was unhurried, tearful, and enhanced by a choir performance of Tchaikovsky and Rachmaninov. Interment was in the Orthodox cemetery adjacent to the church, a rolling patch of red clay and Bermuda grass shaded by mushrooming sycamore trees. As the coffin was lowered into the ground, the priest's final words rang true, "From dust you come, to dust you go."

Though Borya fully adopted American culture, he'd always retained a religious connection with his homeland, strictly adhering to Orthodox doctrine. Paul didn't remember his ex-father-in-law as an overly devout man, just one who solemnly believed and transferred that belief into a good life. The old man had mentioned many times that he'd liked to be buried in Belarus, among the birch groves, marshlands, and sloping fields of blue flax. His parents, brothers, and sisters lay in mass graves, the exact locations dying with the SS officers and German soldiers who slaughtered them. Paul thought about talking with somebody at the State Department on the possibility of a foreign burial, but

Rachel vetoed the idea, saying she wanted her father and mother nearby. Rachel also insisted the postfuneral gathering occur at her house, and about seventy-some people wandered in and out over two hours. Neighbors supplied food and drinks. She politely talked to everyone, accepted condolences, and expressed thanks.

Paul watched her carefully. She seemed to be holding up well. Around two o'clock, she disappeared upstairs. He found her in their former bedroom, alone. It'd been a while since he was last inside.

"You okay?" he asked.

She was perched on the edge of the four-poster bed, staring at the carpet, her eyes swollen from crying. He stepped closer.

"I knew this day would come," she said. "Now they're both gone." She paused. "I remember when Mama died. I thought it was the end of the world. I couldn't understand why she'd been taken away."

He'd often wondered if that was the source of her antireligious beliefs. Resentment for a supposed merciful God who would so callously deprive a young girl of her mother. He wanted to hold her, comfort her, tell her he loved her and always would. But he stood still, fighting back tears.

"She used to read to me all the time. Strange, but what I remember most was her voice. So gentle. And the stories she'd tell. Apollo and Daphne. Perseus' battles. Jason and Medea. Everybody else got fairy tales." She smiled weakly. "I got mythology."

The comment was one of the rare times she'd ever mentioned anything specific about her childhood. The subject was not one she dwelled upon, and she'd made it clear in the past that she considered any inquiry an intrusion.

"That why you read the same kind of stuff to the kids?"

She wiped the tears from her cheek and nodded.

"Your father was a good man. I loved him."

"Even though you and I didn't make it, he always thought of you as his son. Told me he always would." She looked at him. "It was his fondest wish that we get back together."

His too, but he said nothing.

"Seems all you and I ever did was fight," she said. "Two stubborn people."

He had to say, "That's not all we did."

She shrugged. "You always were the optimist in the house."

He noticed the family picture angled atop the chest of drawers. They'd had it taken a year before the divorce. He, Rachel, and the kids. Their wedding picture was also still there, like the one downstairs.

"I'm sorry about last Tuesday night," she said. "What I said when you left. You know how my mouth can be sometimes."

"I shouldn't have meddled. What happened with Nettles was none of my business."

"No, you're right. I overreacted with him. My temper gets me into more trouble." She brushed away more tears. "I've got so much to do. This summer is going to be difficult. I wasn't planning on a contested race this time. Now this."

He didn't voice the obvious. Maybe if she exercised a little diplomacy the lawyers appearing before her wouldn't feel so threatened.

"Look, Paul, could you handle Dad's estate? I just can't deal with that right now."

He reached out and lightly squeezed her shoulder. She did not resist the gesture. "Sure."

Her hand went up to his. It was the first time they'd touched in months. "I trust you. I know it'll get done right. He would have wanted you to handle things. He respected you."

She withdrew her hand.

He did, too. He started thinking like a lawyer. Anything to take his mind away from the moment. "You know where the will is?"

"Look around the house. It's probably in the study. It might be in his safe deposit box at the bank. I don't know. He gave me the key."

She walked over to the dresser. Ice Queen? Not to him. He recalled their first encounter twelve years ago at an Atlanta Bar Association meeting. He was a quiet first-year associate at Pridgen & Woodworth. She was an aggressive assistant district attorney. Two years they dated until she finally suggested they marry. They'd been happy in the beginning and the years passed quickly. What went wrong? Why couldn't things be good again? Maybe she was right. Perhaps they were better friends than lovers.

He hoped not.

He accepted the safe deposit key she offered and said, "Don't worry, Rach. I'll take care of things."

He left Rachel's house and drove straight to Karol Borya's. It was less than a half-hour journey through a combination of busy commercial boulevards and hectic neighborhood streets.

He parked in the driveway and saw Borya's Oldsmobile nestled in the garage. Rachel had given him the house key, and he unlocked the front door, his eyes immediately drawn to the foyer tiles, then up the staircase spindles, some splintered in half, others jutting at odd angles. The oak steps bore no evidence of an impact, but the police said the old man slammed into one and then tumbled to his death, his eighty-one-year-old neck breaking in the process. An autopsy confirmed the injuries and their apparent cause.

A tragic accident.

Standing in the stillness, an odd combination of regret and sadness shuddered through him. Always before he'd enjoyed coming over, talking art and the Braves. Now the old man was gone. Another link to Rachel severed. But a friend was gone, too. Borya was like a father to him. They'd become especially close after his parents were killed. Borya and his father had been good friends, linked by art. He now remembered both men with a pang in his heart.

Good men gone forever.

He decided to take Rachel's advice and first look upstairs

in the study. He knew there was a will. He'd drafted it a few years back and doubted that Borya would have gone to anyone else to modify the language. A copy was certainly back at the firm in the retired files and, if necessary, he could use that. But the original could be worked through probate faster.

He climbed the stairs and searched the study. Magazine articles lay strewn on the club chair, a few scattered on the carpet. He shuffled through the pages. All concerned the Amber Room. Borya had spoken of the object many times through the years, his conviction the words of a White Russian who longed to see the treasure restored to the Catherine Palace. Beyond that, though, he hadn't realized the man's rather intense interest, apparently enough to collect articles and clippings dating back thirty years.

He rifled through the desk drawers and filing cabinets and found no will.

He scanned the bookshelves. Borya loved to read. Homer, Hugo, Poe, and Tolstoy lined the shelves, along with a volume of Russian fairy tales, a set of Churchill's *Histories,* and a leather-bound copy of Ovid's *Metamorphoses.* He seemed to also like southern writers, works by Flannery O'Connor and Katherine Anne Porter formed part of the collection.

His eyes were drawn to the banner on the wall. The old man had bought it at a kiosk in Centennial Park during the Olympics. A silver knight on a rearing horse, sword drawn, a six-ended golden cross adorning the shield. The background was blood red, the symbol of valor and courage, Borya had said, trimmed in white to embody freedom and purity. It was the national emblem of Belarus, a defiant symbol of self-determination.

A lot like Borya himself.

Borya had loved the Olympics. They'd gone to several events, and were there when Belarus won the gold in women's rowing. Fourteen other medals came to the nation—six silver and eight bronze, in discus, heptathlon, gymnastics, and wrestling—Borya proud of every one. Though American by osmosis, his former father-in-law was without a doubt a White Russian at heart.

He retreated downstairs and carefully searched the drawers and cabinets, but found no will. The map of Germany was still unfolded on the coffee table. The *USA Today* he'd given Borya was there, too.

He wandered into the kitchen and searched on the off chance that important papers were stashed there. He once handled a case where a woman stored her will in the freezer, so on a lark, he yanked open the refrigerator's double doors. The sight of a file angled beside the ice maker surprised him.

He removed and opened the cold manila folder.

More articles on the Amber Room, dating back to the 1940s and 1950s, but some as recent as two years ago. He wondered what they were doing in the freezer. Deciding that finding the will was, at the moment, more important, he decided to keep the folder and head for the bank.

The street sign for the Georgia Citizens Bank on Carr Boulevard read 3:23 P.M. when Paul rolled into the busy parking lot. He'd banked at Georgia Citizens for years, ever since working for them prior to law school.

The manager, a mousy man with fading hair, initially refused access to Borya's safe deposit box. After a quick phone call to the office, Paul's secretary faxed a letter of representation, which he signed, attesting he was attorney for the estate of Karol Borya, deceased. The letter seemed to satisfy the manager. At least there was something now in the file to show an heir who complained that the safe deposit box was empty.

Georgia law contained a specific provision that allowed estate representatives access to safe deposit boxes to search for wills. He'd utilized the law many times and most bank managers were familiar with the provisions. Occasionally, though, a difficult one came along.

The man led him into the vault and the array of stainless

steel boxes. Possession of the key for number 45 seemed to further confirm his authenticity. He knew the law required the manager to stay, view the contents, and inventory exactly what was removed and by whom. He unlocked the box and slid the narrow rectangle out, metal screeching against metal.

Inside was a single bunch of paper, rubber-banded together. One document was blue-backed, and he immediately recognized the will he'd drawn years ago. About a dozen white envelopes were bound to it. He shuffled through them. All came from a Danya Chapaev and were addressed to Borya. Neatly trifolded in the stack were copies of letters from Borya to Chapaev. All the script was in English. The last document was a plain white envelope, sealed, with Rachel's name scrawled on the front in blue ink.

"The letters and this envelope are attached to the will. Mr. Borya obviously intended them a unit. There's nothing else in the box. I'll take it all."

"We've been instructed in situations like this to release only the will."

"It was bound together. These envelopes may relate to the will. The law states that I can have them."

The manager hesitated. "I'll have to call downtown to our general counsel's office for an okay."

"What's the problem? There's nobody to complain about anything. I wrote this will. I know what it says. Mr. Borya's only heir was his daughter. I'm here on her behalf."

"I still need to check with our lawyer."

He'd had enough. "You do that. Tell Cathy Holden that Paul Cutler is in your bank being jacked around by somebody who obviously doesn't know the law. Tell her if I have to go to court and get an order allowing me to have what I should have anyway, the bank's going to compensate me the two hundred and twenty dollars an hour I'm going to charge for the trouble."

The manager seemed to consider the words. "You know our general counsel?"

"I used to work for her."

The manager pondered his predicament quietly, then finally said, "Take 'em. But sign here."

EIGHTEEN

Danya,

How my heart aches every day for what happened to Yancy Cutler. What a fine man, his wife such a good woman. All the rest of the people on that plane were good people, too. Good people shouldn't die so violent or so sudden. My son-in-law grieves deeply and it pains me to think I may be responsible. Yancy telephoned the night before the crash. He was able to locate the old man you mentioned whose brother worked at Loring's estate. You were right. I should never have asked Yancy to inquire again while in Italy. It wasn't right to involve others. The burden rests with you and me. But why have we survived? Do they not know where we are? What we know? Maybe we're no longer a threat? Only those who ask questions and get too close draw their attention. Indifference is perhaps far better than curiosity. So many years have passed, the Amber Room seems more a memory than a wonder of the world. Does anybody really care anymore? Stay safe and well, Danya. Keep in touch.
Karol

Danya,

The KGB came today. A fat Chechen who smelled like a sewer. He said he found my name in the Commission records. I thought the trail was too old and too cold to follow.

But I was wrong. Be careful. He asked whether you are still alive. I told him the usual. I think we are the only two of the old ones left. All those friends gone. So sad. Maybe you're right. No more letters, just in case. Particularly now, since they know where I am. My daughter is about to have a child. My second grandchild. A girl this time, they tell me. Modern science. I liked the old ways when you wondered. But a little girl would be nice. My grandson is such a joy. I hope your grandchildren are well. Be safe, old friend.
Karol

Dear Karol,

The clipping enclosed is from the Bonn newspaper. Yeltsin arrived in Germany proclaiming he knew where the Amber Room was located. The newspapers and magazines buzzed with the announcement. Did it reach across the ocean to you? He claimed scholars uncovered the information from Soviet records. The Extraordinary Commission for Crimes against Russia, Yeltsin called us. Ha! All the fool did was extract a half billion marks in aid from Bonn, then apologized, saying the records weren't for the Amber Room but other treasures pilfered from Leningrad. More Russian bullshit. The Russians, Soviets, Nazis. All the same. The current talk about restoring Russian heritage is more propaganda. What they do is sell our heritage. The papers every day are full of stories about paintings, sculptures, and jewels being sold. A rummage sale of our history. We must keep the panels safe. No more letters, at least for awhile. The photo of your granddaughter is appreciated. The joy she must bring you. Good health, my friend.
Danya

Danya,

I hope this letter finds you well. It's been too long since we last wrote. I thought perhaps after three years, it may be safe. There have been no more visits, and I have read few reports on anything concerning the panels. Since we last com-

municated, my daughter and her husband divorced. They
love each other, yet simply cannot live together. My grandchildren are well. I hope yours are, too. We are both old. It
would be nice to venture and see if the panels are really
there. But neither of us can make the journey. Besides, it
might still be too dangerous. Somebody was watching when
Yancy Cutler asked questions about Loring. I know in my
heart that bomb was not meant for an Italian minister. I still
grieve for the Cutlers. So many have died looking for the
Amber Room. Perhaps it should stay lost. No matter. Neither
of us can protect it much longer. Good health, old friend.
Karol

Rachel,

My precious darling. My only child. Your father now rests
in peace with your mother. We are surely together, for a merciful God would not deny two people who loved each other
the opportunity of eternal happiness. I have penned this note
to say what perhaps should have been said in life. You have
always been aware of my past, what I did for the Soviets before emigrating. I pilfered art. Nothing more than a thief, but
one sanctioned and encouraged by Stalin. I rationalized it at
the time with my hatred for the Nazis, but I was wrong. We
stole so much from so many, all in the name of reparations.
What we sought most was the Amber Room. Ours by heritage, stolen by invaders. The letters bound to this note tell
some of the story of our search. My old friend Danya and I
looked hard. Did we ever find it? Perhaps. Neither of us
really went and looked. Too many were watching in those
days and, by the time we narrowed the trail, both of us realized the Soviets were far worse than the Germans. So we left
it alone. Danya and I vowed never to reveal what we knew,
or perhaps simply what we thought we knew. Only when
Yancy volunteered to make discreet inquiries, checking information that I once thought credible, did I inquire again.
He was making an inquiry on his last trip to Italy. Whether
that blast on the plane was attributable to his questions or

something else will never be known. All I know is that the search for the Amber Room has proved dangerous. Maybe the danger comes from what Danya and I suspect. Maybe not. I haven't heard from my old comrade in many years. My last letter to him went unanswered. Perhaps he is with me now, too. My precious Maya. My friend Danya. Good companions for eternity. Hopefully it will be many years before you join us, my darling. Have a good life. Be successful. Take care of Marla and Brent. I love them so. I'm very proud of you. Be good. Maybe give Paul another chance. But never, absolutely never concern yourself with the Amber Room. Remember the story of Phaëthon and the tears of the Heliades. Heed his ambition and their grief. Maybe the panels will be found one day. I hope not. Politicians should not be entrusted with such a treasure. Leave it in its grave. Tell Paul I'm so sorry. I love you.

NINETEEN

6:34 P.M.

PAUL'S HEART POUNDED AS RACHEL LOOKED UP FROM HER FAther's final note, tears falling from her sad eyes. He could feel the pain. Hard to tell where his stopped and hers started.

"He wrote so elegantly," she said.

He agreed.

"He learned English well, read incessantly. He knew more about participial phrases and dangling modifiers than I ever did. I think his broken speech was just a way to hold on to his heritage. Poor Daddy."

Her auburn hair was tied in a ponytail. She wore no makeup, was dressed only in a white terry-cloth robe over a flannel nightgown. The house was finally clear of all the mourners. The children were in their rooms, still upset from the emotional day. Lucy was scampering through the dining room.

"Have you read all these letters?" Rachel asked.

He nodded. "After I left the bank. I went back to your father's house and got the rest of this stuff."

They were sitting in Rachel's dining room. Their old dining room. The two folders with news articles on the Amber Room, a German map, the *USA Today,* the will, all the letters, and the note to Rachel were fanned out on the table. He'd told her what he found and where. He also told her about the *USA* article her father specifically asked for Tuesday and his questions on Wayland McKoy.

"Daddy was watching something on CNN about that when I left the kids with him. I remember the name." Her body sagged in the chair. "What was that file doing in the freezer? That's not like him. What's going on, Paul?"

"I don't know. But Karol was obviously interested in the Amber Room." He pointed to Borya's last note. "What did he mean about Phaëthon and the tears of the Heliades?"

"Another story Mama used to tell me when I was little. Phaëthon, the mortal son of Helios, God of the Sun. I was fascinated by it. Daddy loved mythology. He said thinking about fantasy was one of the things that got him through Mauthausen." She shuffled through the clippings and photocopies, glancing closely at a few. "He thought he was responsible for what happened to your parents and the rest of the people on that plane. I don't understand."

Neither did he. And he'd thought of little else during the past two hours. "Weren't your parents in Italy on museum business?" asked Rachel.

"The whole board went. The trip was to secure loans of works from Italian museums."

"Daddy seemed to think there was a connection."

He also recalled something else Borya wrote. *I should never have asked Yancy to inquire again while in Italy.*

What did he mean, *again*?

"Don't you want to know what happened?" Rachel suddenly asked, her voice rising.

He'd not liked that tone years ago and didn't appreciate it now. "I never said that. It's just that six years have passed, and it would be nearly impossible to find out. My God, Rachel, they never even found bodies."

"Paul, your parents may have been murdered, and you don't want to do anything about it?"

Impetuous and stubborn. What had Karol said? *Got both traits from her mother.* Right.

"I didn't say that either. There's just nothing practical that can be done."

"We can find Danya Chapaev."

"What do you mean?"

"Chapaev. He may still be alive." She looked down at the envelopes, the return addresses. "Kehlheim couldn't be that hard to find."

"It's in southern Germany. Bavaria. I found it on the map."

"You looked?"

"Not hard to spot. Karol circled it."

She unfolded the map and saw for herself. "Daddy said they knew something on the Amber Room but never went to check. Maybe Chapaev could tell us what that was?"

He couldn't believe what she was saying. "Did you read what your father said? He told you to leave the Amber Room alone. Finding Chapaev is the one thing he *didn't* want you doing."

"Chapaev might know more about what happened to your parents."

"I'm a lawyer, Rachel, not an international investigator."

"Okay. Let's take this to the police. They could look into it."

"That's far more practical than your first suggestion. But the trail's still years old."

Her face hardened. "I hope to hell Marla and Brent don't

inherit your complacency. I'd like to think they'd want to know what happened if a plane blew out of the sky with you and me on it."

She knew exactly how to push his buttons. It was one of the things he most resented about her. "Did you read those articles?" he asked. "People have died searching for the Amber Room. Maybe my parents. Maybe not. One thing's for certain. Your father didn't want you involved. And you're way out of your league. What you know about art could fit inside a thimble."

"Along with your nerve."

He stared hard into her angry eyes, bit his tongue, and tried to be understanding. She'd buried her father this morning. Still, one word kept reverberating through his brain.

Bitch.

He took a deep breath before quietly saying, "Your second suggestion is the most practical. Why don't we let the police handle this." He paused. "I realize how upset you are. But, Rachel, Karol's death was an accident."

"Trouble is, Paul, if it wasn't, then add my father to the list of casualties along with your parents." She cut him one of her looks. The kind he'd seen too many times before. "Still want to be practical?"

TWENTY

WEDNESDAY, MAY 14, 10:25 A.M.

RACHEL FORCED HERSELF TO CLIMB OUT OF BED AND GET THE children dressed. She then dropped the kids off at school and reluctantly headed for the courthouse. She'd not been in her chambers since last Friday, having taken Monday and Tuesday off.

Throughout the morning her secretary made things easy, running interference, rerouting calls, deflecting lawyers and the other judges. Originally the week had been scheduled for civil jury trials, but they were all hastily postponed. An hour ago she'd called the Atlanta police department and requested somebody from Homicide be sent to her chambers. She wasn't the most popular judge with the police. Everyone seemed to assume that since she was once a hard-nosed prosecutor, she'd be a pro-police judge. But her rulings, if they could be labeled, tended to be defense-oriented. *Liberal* was the term the Fraternal Order of Police and the press liked to use. *Traitor,* was the description she'd been told a lot of the narcotics detectives whispered. But she didn't care. The Constitution was there to protect people. The police were supposed to work within its bounds, not outside them. Her job was to make sure they didn't take any shortcuts. How many times had her father preached, *when government comes before law, tyranny is not far behind.*

And if anyone should know, he should.

"Judge Cutler," her secretary said through the speakerphone. Most times they were simply Rachel and Sami; only when someone came around was she labeled *judge.* "A Lieutenant Barlow is here from the Atlanta police. In response to your call."

She quickly dabbed her eyes with a tissue. The picture of her father on the credenza had triggered more tears. She stood and smoothed her cotton skirt and blouse.

The paneled door opened and a thin man with wavy black hair strutted in. He closed the door behind him and introduced himself as Mike Barlow, assigned to the homicide division.

She regained her judicial composure and offered a seat. "I appreciate your coming over, Lieutenant."

"No problem. The department always tries to accommodate the bench."

But she wondered. The tone was irritatingly cordial, bordering on condescending.

"After you called, I pulled the incident report on your father's death. I'm sorry about your loss. It appears to be one of those accidents that sometimes happen."

"My father was fairly independent. Still drove a car. He had no real health problems, and he'd climbed those stairs for years without a problem."

"Your point?"

She was liking his tone even less. "You tell me."

"Judge, I get the message. But there's nothing here to suggest foul play."

"He survived a Nazi concentration camp, Lieutenant. I think he could climb stairs."

Barlow seemed unpersuaded. "The report says nothing appears missing. His wallet was on the dresser. The televisions, stereo, VCR were all there. Both doors were unlocked. No evidence of forced entry anywhere. Where's the burglary?"

"My father left the doors unlocked all the time."

"That's not smart, but it doesn't appear to have contributed to his death. Look, I agree, no evidence of robbery could lead to an implication of murder, but there's nothing to suggest anyone was even around when he died."

She was curious. "Did your people search the house?"

"I've been told they looked around. Nothing elaborate. There seemed no need. I'm curious, what do you think was the motive for murder? Your father have enemies?"

She did not answer him. Instead she asked, "What did the medical examiner say?"

"Broken neck. Caused by the fall. No evidence of other trauma except bruising on the arms and legs from the fall. Again, Judge, what makes you think your father's death was something other than accidental?"

She considered telling him about the file in the freezer, Danya Chapaev, the Amber Room, and Paul's parents. But the arrogant ass didn't even want to be here, and she'd sound like a conspiratorial nut. He was right. There was no proof her father had been shoved down the stairs. Nothing that connected his death to any "curse of the Amber Room," as some of the articles suggested. So what if her father was interested in the subject? He loved art. Once worked with it every day. So what if he was reading articles in his study, stashed more in his freezer, unfolded a German map in the den, and possessed a keen interest in a man heading for Germany to dig in forgotten caves? A huge leap from that to murder. Maybe Paul was right. She decided to let it lie with this guy.

"Nothing, Lieutenant. You're quite right. Just a tragic fall. Thanks for coming by."

Rachel sat sullen in her office and thought back to when she was sixteen, her father explaining for the first time about Mauthausen, and how the Russians and Dutch worked the stone quarry, hauling tons of boulders up a long series of narrow steps to the camp where more prisoners chiseled them into bricks.

The Jews, though, weren't so lucky. Each day they were tossed down the cliff into the quarry simply for sport, their screams echoing as bodies flew through the air, bets taken by the guards on how many times flesh and bones would bounce before being silenced by death. Eventually, her father explained, the SS had to stop the hurling because it so disrupted the work.

Not because they were killing people, she remembered him saying, *only because it affected the work.*

Her father cried that day, one of the few times ever, and so had she. Her mother had told her about his war experiences and what he'd done afterward, but her father hardly mentioned the time. She'd always noticed the smeared tattoo on his right forearm, wondering when he'd explain.

They forced us to run into electric fence. Some did willingly, tired of torture. Others were shot, hanged, or injected in the heart. The gas came later.

She'd asked how many died in Mauthausen. And he told her without hesitation that 60 percent of the two hundred thousand never made it out. He arrived in April 1944. The Hungarian Jews came shortly thereafter, every one of them slaughtered like sheep. He'd helped heave the bodies from the gas chamber to the oven, a daily ritual, commonplace, like taking out the garbage, the guards used to say. She remembered him telling her about one night in particular, toward the end, when Hermann Göring marched into the camp wearing a pearl gray uniform.

Evil on two legs, he called him.

Göring had ordered four Germans murdered, her father part of the detail that poured water over their naked bodies until they froze to death. Göring stood impassive the whole time, rubbing a piece of amber, wanting to know something about the Amber Room. Of all the horror that happened in Mauthausen, her father said, that night with Göring was what stayed with him.

And set his course in life.

After the war, he was sent to interview Göring in prison during the Nürnberg trials.

Did he remember you? she'd asked.

My face in Mauthausen meant nothing to him.

But Göring recalled the torture, saying he greatly admired the soldiers for holding out. German superiority, breeding, he'd said. Her love for her father multiplied tenfold after finally hearing about Mauthausen. What he endured was unimaginable and just to survive was an accomplishment. But to survive with his sanity intact seemed nothing short of a miracle.

Sitting in the quiet of her chambers, Rachel cried. That precious man was gone. His voice forever silent, his love only a memory. For the first time in her life she was alone. Her parents' entire family had either perished in the war or were inaccessible, somewhere in Belarus, strangers really, linked merely by genes. Only her two children were left. She remembered how they'd ended that conversation about Mauthausen twenty-four years ago.

Daddy, did you ever find the Amber Room?

He stared back at her with woeful eyes. She wondered then and now if there was something he wanted to tell her. Something she needed to know. Or was it better she not know? Hard to tell. And his words didn't help.

Never did, my darling.

But his tone was reminiscent of when he once explained there really was a Santa Claus, an Easter Bunny, a Tooth Fairy. Hollow words that simply needed to be said. Now, after reading the letters between her father and Danya Chapaev and the note penned in his own hand, she was convinced that there was more to the story. Her father harbored a secret, and apparently had done so for years.

But he was gone.

Only one lead left.

Danya Chapaev.

And she knew what had to be done.

Rachel stepped off the elevator on the twenty-third floor and marched toward the paneled doors labeled PRIDGEN & WOODWORTH. The law firm consumed the entire twenty-third and twenty-fourth floors of the downtown high-rise, its probate division on the twenty-third.

Paul started with the firm right out of law school. She'd worked first with the DA's office, then with another Atlanta firm. They met eleven months later and married two years after that. Their courtship typical of Paul, never in a hurry to do anything. So careful. Deliberate. Afraid to take a chance, play the odds, or risk failure. She'd been the one to suggest marriage, and he readily agreed.

He was a handsome man, always had been. Not rugged, or dashing, just attractive in an ordinary way. And he was honest. Along with possessing a fanatical dependability. But his unbending dedication to tradition had slowly turned irksome. Why not vary Sunday dinner every once in a while? Roast, potatoes, corn, snap peas, rolls, and iced tea. Every Sunday for years. Not that Paul required it, only that the same thing always satisfied him. In the beginning, she'd liked that predictability. It was comforting. A known commodity that stabilized her world. Toward the end it became a tremendous pain in the ass.

But why?

Was a routine so bad?

Paul was a good, decent, successful man. She was proud of him, though she rarely voiced it. He was next in line to head the probate division. Not bad for a forty-one-year-old who needed two tries to get into law school. But Paul knew probate law. He studied nothing else, concentrating on all its nuances, even serving on legislative committees. He was a recognized expert on the subject, and Pridgen & Woodworth paid him enough money to prevent another firm from luring him away. The firm handled thousands of estates, many quite substantial, and most she knew were attributable to the statewide reputation of Paul Cutler.

She pushed through the doors and followed the maze of corridors to Paul's office. She'd called before leaving her chambers, so he was expecting her. She went straight in, closed the door, and announced, "I'm going to Germany."

Paul looked up. "You're what?"

"I didn't stutter. I'm going to Germany."

"To find Chapaev? He's probably dead. He didn't even return your father's last letter."

"I need to do something."

Paul stood from the desk. "Why do you always have to do something?"

"Daddy knew about the Amber Room. I owe it to him to check it out."

"Owe it to him?" His voice was rising. "You owe it to him to respect his last wish, which was to stay out of whatever it was. *If anything,* by the way. Damn, Rachel, you're forty years old. When are you going to grow up?"

She stayed surprisingly calm, considering how she felt about his lectures. "I don't want to fight, Paul. I need you to look after the children. Will you do that?"

"Typical, Rachel. Fly off the handle. Do the first thing that comes to mind. No thought. Just do it."

"Will you watch the kids?"

"If I said no, would you stay?"

"I'd call your brother."

Paul sat back down. His expression signaled surrender.

"You can stay at the house," she said. "It'll be easier on the kids. They're still pretty upset over Daddy."

"They'd be even more upset if they knew what their mother was doing. And have you forgotten about the election? It's less than eight weeks away, and you have two opponents working their asses off to beat you, now with Marcus Nettles's money."

"Screw the election. Nettles can have the damn judgeship. This is more important."

"What's more important? We don't even know what *this* is. What about your docket? How can you just up and leave?"

She notched two points for a nice try, but that wasn't going to discourage her. "The chief judge understood. I told him I needed some time to grieve. I haven't taken a vacation in two years. I have the leave accrued."

Paul shook his head. "You're going on a wild goose chase to Bavaria for an old man who's probably dead, looking for something that's probably lost forever. You're not the first one to search for the Amber Room. People have devoted their whole lives to looking, and found nothing."

She wasn't going to budge. "Daddy knew something important. I can feel it. This Chapaev may know also."

"You're dreaming."

"And you're pathetic." She instantly regretted the words and tone. There was no need to hurt him.

"I'm going to ignore that because I know you're upset," he slowly said.

"I'm leaving tomorrow evening on a flight to Munich. I need a copy of Daddy's letters and the articles from his files."

"I'll drop them off on the way home." His voice was filled with total resignation.

"I'll call from Germany and let you know where I'm staying." She headed for the door. "Pick up the kids at day care tomorrow."

"Rachel."

She stopped but did not turn back.

"Be careful."

She opened the door and left.

PART TWO

Twenty-one

KNOLL LEFT HIS HOTEL AND CAUGHT A MARTA TRAIN TO THE Fulton County Courthouse. The KGB information sheet he'd pilfered from the St. Petersburg records depository indicated that Rachel Cutler was a lawyer and an office address was provided. But a visit to the law firm yesterday revealed that she'd left the firm four years earlier after being elected a superior court judge. The receptionist was more than courteous, providing the new phone number and office location at the courthouse. He decided that a call might bring a quick rebuke. A face-to-face unannounced visit seemed the best approach.

Five days had elapsed since he'd killed Karol Borya. He needed to ascertain what, if anything, the daughter knew about the Amber Room. Perhaps her father had mentioned something over the years. Perhaps she knew about Chapaev. A long shot, but he was rapidly running out of leads, and he needed to exhaust all the possibilities. A trail that once seemed promising was growing cold.

He boarded a crowded elevator and rose to the courthouse's sixth floor. The corridors were lined with crowded courtrooms and busy offices. He wore the light gray business suit, striped shirt, and pale yellow silk tie bought yesterday at a suburban men's store. He'd intentionally kept the colors soft and conservative.

He pushed through glass doors marked CHAMBERS OF THE HONORABLE RACHEL CUTLER and stepped into a quiet anteroom. A thirtyish black female waited behind a desk. The nameplate read, SAMI LUFFMAN. In his best English, he said, "Good morning."

The woman smiled and returned the greeting.

"My name is Christian Knoll." He handed her a card, similar to the one used with Pietro Caproni, except this one proclaimed only ART COLLECTOR, not academician, and bore no address. "I was wondering if I could speak to Her Honor?"

The woman accepted the card. "I'm sorry, Judge Cutler is not in today."

"It's quite important I speak to her."

"May I ask if this concerns a pending case in our court?"

He shook his head, cordial and innocent. "Not at all. It is a personal matter."

"The judge's father died last weekend and—"

"Oh, I'm so sorry," he said, feigning emotion. "How terrible."

"Yes, it was awful. She's very upset and decided to take a little time off."

"That's so unfortunate, for both her and me. I am in town only until tomorrow and was hoping to talk to Judge Cutler before I leave. Perhaps you could forward a message and she could call my hotel?"

The secretary seemed to be considering the request, and he took the moment to study a framed photograph hanging behind her on the papered wall. A woman was standing before another man, right arm raised as if taking an oath. She had shoulder-length auburn hair, an upturned nose, and intense eyes. She wore a black robe, so it was hard to tell about her figure. Her smooth cheeks were flushed with a tinge of rouge and her slight smile appeared appropriate for the solemn circumstance. He motioned to the photo. "Judge Cutler?"

"When she was sworn in, four years ago."

It was the same face he'd seen at Karol Borya's funeral Tuesday, standing in front of the assembled mourners, hugging two small children, a boy and a girl.

"I could give Judge Cutler your message, but I don't know if you would hear from her."

"Why is that?"

"She's leaving town later today."

"A long journey?"

"She's going to Germany."

"Such a wonderful place." He needed to know where, so he tried the three major points of entry. "Berlin is exquisite this time of year. As are Frankfurt and Munich."

"She's going to Munich."

"Ah! A magical city. Perhaps it will help with her grief?"

"I hope so."

He'd learned enough. "I thank you, Ms. Luffman. You have been most helpful. Here is the information on my hotel." He fabricated a place and room number, no need now for contact. "Please let Judge Cutler know I came by."

"I'll try," she said.

He turned to leave but gave the framed photograph on the wall one last look, freezing the image of Rachel Cutler in his mind.

He left the sixth floor and descended to street level. A bank of pay phones spread across one wall. He stepped over and dialed overseas to the private line in Franz Fellner's study. It was almost 5 P.M. in Germany. He wasn't sure who would answer or even who he was reporting to now. Power was clearly in transition—Fellner was phasing himself out while Monika assumed control. But the old man was not the type to let go easily, especially with something like the Amber Room at stake.

"Guten tag," Monika answered after two rings.

"You on secretary duty today?" he asked in German.

"About time you called in. It's been a week. Any luck?"

"We should get something straight. I don't check in like a schoolboy. Give me a job and leave me alone. I'll call when necessary."

"Touchy, aren't we?"

"I require no supervision."

"I'll remind you of that the next time you're between my legs."

He smiled. Hard to back her down. "I found Borya. He said he knew nothing."

"And you believed him?"

"Did I say that?"

"He's dead, right?"

"A tragic fall down the stairs."

"Father will not like this."

"I thought you were in charge?"

"I am. And frankly it matters not. But Father's right—you take too many risks."

"I took no unnecessary risks."

In fact, he'd been quite cautious. Careful on his first visit to touch nothing other than the tea glass, which he removed on the later visit. And when he returned the second time his hands were gloved.

"Let's say I decided the course necessary under the circumstances."

"What did he do, insult your pride?"

Amazing how she could read him even from four thousand miles away. He never realized himself to be so transparent. "That's unimportant."

"One day your luck will run out, Christian."

"You sound like you look forward to the day."

"Not really. You'll be hard to replace."

"In which way?"

"Every way, you bastard."

He smiled. Good to know he got under her skin, too. "I've learned Borya's daughter is on her way to Munich. She might be going to see Chapaev."

"What makes you think that?"

"The way Borya dodged me, and something he said about the panels."

Maybe better stay lost.

"The daughter could simply be vacationing."

"I doubt that. Too much of a coincidence."

"You going to follow her?"

"Later today. There's something I need to handle first."

TWENTY-TWO

SUZANNE WATCHED CHRISTIAN KNOLL FROM ACROSS THE MEZ-zanine. She was seated inside a crowded waiting room, CLERK OF COURT, TRAFFIC FINES stenciled on the outer glass wall. About seventy-five people waited their turn to approach a Formica counter and dispose of citations, the whole scene chaotic, stale cigarette smoke lingering in the air despite several NO SMOKING signs.

She'd been following Knoll since Saturday. Monday, he'd made two trips to the High Museum of Art and one to a downtown Atlanta office building. Tuesday, he attended Karol Borya's funeral. She'd watched the graveside service from across the street. He'd done little yesterday, a trip to the public library and a shopping mall, but today he was up early and on the move.

Her short blond hair was stuffed beneath a tendriled, brownish-red wig. Extra makeup splotched her face, and her eyes were shielded by a pair of cheap sunglasses. She wore tight jeans, a collarless 1996 Atlanta Olympics jersey, and tennis shoes. A cheap black bag was slung over one shoulder. She fit right in with the crowd, a *People* magazine open in her lap, her eyes constantly shifting from the page to the phone bank across the hectic mezzanine.

Five minutes ago she'd followed Knoll to the sixth floor

and watched while he entered Rachel Cutler's chambers. She recognized the name and knew the connection. Knoll was obviously not giving up, most likely now reporting to Monika Fellner what he learned. That bitch would definitely be a problem. Young. Aggressive. Hungry. A worthy successor to Franz Fellner, and a nuisance in more ways than one.

Knoll hadn't stayed long in Rachel Cutler's office, certainly not long enough to meet with her. So she'd backed off, fearful he might notice her presence, unsure if the disguise would be effective camouflage. She'd worn a different ensemble each day, careful not to repeat anything he might recognize. Knoll was good. Damn good. Fortunately, she was better.

Knoll hung up the phone and headed for the street.

She tossed the magazine aside and followed.

KNOLL FLAGGED A CAB AND RODE BACK TO HIS HOTEL. HE'D sensed somebody Saturday night at Borya's house after he twisted the old man's neck. But he definitely detected Suzanne Danzer on Monday, and every day since. She'd disguised herself well. But too many years in the field had honed his abilities. Little escaped him now. He'd almost been expecting her. Ernst Loring, Danzer's employer, wanted the Amber Room as much as Fellner did. Loring's father, Josef, had been obsessed with amber, amassing one of the largest private collections in the world. Ernst had inherited both the objects and his father's desire. Many times he'd heard Loring preach on the subject, and watched while he traded or bought amber pieces from other collectors, Fellner included. Surely Danzer had been dispatched to Atlanta to see what he was doing.

But how did she know where to find him?

Of course. The nosy clerk in St. Petersburg. Who else? The idiot must have stolen a look at the KGB sheet before he tabled it. He was certainly on the take, with Loring one of several likely benefactors—now the primary benefactor, since Danzer was here.

The cab pulled up to the Marriott and Knoll jumped out. Somewhere behind, Danzer was certainly following. She was probably registered here, as well. She would most likely duck into one of the ground-floor rest rooms and modify her disguise, switching wigs and accessories, maybe making a quick run to change clothes, probably paying one of the bell-boys or concierges to alert her if he left the building.

He headed straight for his eighteenth-floor room. Inside, he dialed Delta reservations.

"I need a flight from Atlanta to Munich. Is there one leaving today?"

Computer keys were punched.

"Yes, sir, we have an outbound at 2:35 P.M. A direct flight to Munich."

He had to be sure there were no other flights. "Anything sooner or later?"

More keys were punched. "Not with us."

"How about another airline?"

More punching. "That's the only direct flight from Atlanta to Munich today. You could connect, though, on two others."

He gambled she was on the direct flight and not another to New York, Paris, Amsterdam, or Frankfurt with a connection into Munich. He confirmed the reservation, then hung up and quickly packed his travel bag. He needed to time his arrival at the airport precisely. If Rachel Cutler wasn't on the flight he'd chosen, he'd have to pick up her trail another way, perhaps when she called her office to let her secretary know where she could be reached. He could call back, give a correct phone number, and tickle her curiosity until she returned his call.

He headed down to check out. The lobby was busy. People rushing everywhere. But he quickly noticed a pixie brunette, fifty yards away, perched at an outside table in one of the lounges dotting the center atrium. As he suspected, Danzer had changed clothes. A peach-colored jumpsuit and

sunglasses, more stylish and darker than before, replaced the
grunge look.

He paid the clerk for the room, then headed outside for a
cab to the airport.

✹━ ┰

SUZANNE EYED THE TRAVEL BAG. KNOLL WAS LEAVING? THERE
was no time to return to her room. She'd have to follow and
see where he went. That was exactly why she always packed
light and included nothing she couldn't do without or replace.

She stood, threw five dollars on the table for a drink she'd
sipped only twice, then headed toward the revolving doors
and the street.

✹━ ┰

KNOLL EXITED THE CAB AT HARTSFIELD INTERNATIONAL AIRPORT
and checked his watch—1:25 P.M. He tossed the driver three
tens, folded the leather travel bag across his right arm, and
marched inside the south terminal.

He was curious to see how far Danzer would go, so he ignored the electronic kiosk and headed for one of the Delta
check-in lines and watched as Danzer slipped across the terminal to another line, this one not as long. She was surely
wondering where he was headed. But her dilemma was complicated. She'd need a ticket to follow him deeper into the
terminal. So she'd probably buy whatever seat she could,
anything that would give her access to the concourses beyond.

She'd clearly been caught off guard by his sudden exit
since she still wore the same brunette wig, peach jumpsuit,
and dark sunglasses from the Marriott. A bit sloppy. She
should carry a backup. Something to vary the look, if disguise was her only means of camouflage. He preferred electronic surveillance. It allowed the luxury of distance between
hunter and hunted.

He stood patiently and, at his turn, obtained a boarding

pass and checked his bag. The stiletto was stashed inside, the only safe place since the blade would have never survived the metal detectors. Danzer was already out of her line, now positioned at the far end of the busy security checkpoint, ticket in hand.

He almost smiled.

She was so predictable.

After passing through the detectors, he cruised down a long escalator to the transportation mall. Danzer lingered twenty yards back. At the bottom of the escalator, he scampered with the rest of the afternoon travelers to the automatic trains. He boarded the front car and noticed Danzer climb into the second car, positioning herself near the forward windows.

He knew the airport well. The trains moved between six concourses, the International Concourse being farthest away. At the first stop, Concourse A, he and fifty other people stepped off. Danzer surely was wondering what he was doing, certainly familiar enough with Hartsfield to know that no international flights used concourses A through D. Perhaps he's taking a domestic flight to another American city, she might be thinking.

He loitered as if waiting for somebody. Instead he silently ticked off the seconds. Timing was critical. Danzer waited too, fifty feet away, trying to seem disinterested, apparently confident he noticed nothing. He waited exactly one minute then paraded toward the escalator.

The steps slowly rose.

It was thirty yards up to the busy concourse. Broad skylights four stories above admitted the bright sun. An aluminum median separated the up escalator from the down, a silk plant sprouting from it every twenty feet. The other escalator heading back toward the transportation mall was sparsely populated. No surveillance cameras or security guards were in sight.

He waited for the precise moment, then gripped the rubber handrail and slid across the median, landing on the down escalator. He was now headed in the opposite direction and, as he passed Danzer, he tipped his head in mock salute.

The look on her face said it all.

He needed to move fast. It wouldn't be long before she copied his action. He sidestepped the few travelers ahead of him and kept repeating, "Airport security, please step aside."

His timing was perfect. A train roared into the station, heading outbound. The doors parted. A robotic voice announced, "Please move away from the doors to the center of the aisle." People streamed on. He glanced back and saw Danzer slide across the median, her move not quite as graceful as his. She stumbled for a moment, then regained her balance.

He stepped onto the train.

"The doors are now closing," the robotic voice announced.

Danzer raced off the escalator straight for the train, but was too late. The doors closed and the train roared from the station.

He exited at the International Concourse. Danzer would eventually head that way, but the flight to Munich was surely boarding and by the time she either ran through the transportation mall or waited for the next train he'd be gone. The concourse was huge, the largest international flight terminal in America. Five stories. Twenty-four gates. It would take an hour just to walk through and check every one.

He stepped onto the escalator and started up. The same bright airy feel permeated the space except, periodically, recessed showcases displayed a variety of Mexican, Egyptian, and Phoenician art. Nothing extravagant or precious, just ordinary pieces, placards at the bottom noting the particular Atlanta museum or collector that made the loan.

At the top of the escalator he followed more travelers to the right. The aroma of coffee wafted from a Starbuck's. A crowd was poised at W.H. Smith's buying periodicals and newspapers. He studied the departure screens. Over the next thirty minutes a dozen or so flights were leaving the gates. Danzer would have no way to know which one, if any, he was taking.

He scanned the screen for the flight to Munich, found the gate, and marched down the concourse. When he arrived the flight was already boarding. He stepped into line and said at his turn, "Full flight today?"

The attendant concentrated on the video monitor. "Yes, sir. All full."

Now, even if Danzer found him, there was no way she could follow. He headed for the gate, thirty or so people ahead of him. He glanced toward the front of the line and noticed a woman sporting shoulder-length auburn hair dressed in a striking, dark-blue pants suit. She was handing her boarding pass to the attendant and entering the Jetway.

The face was instantly recognizable.

Rachel Cutler.

Perfect.

TWENTY-THREE

ATLANTA, GEORGIA
FRIDAY, MAY 16, 9:15 A.M.

SUZANNE STROLLED INTO THE OFFICE. PAUL CUTLER ROSE FROM behind an oversize walnut desk and stepped toward her.

"I appreciate your taking the time to see me," she said.

"Not a problem, Ms. Myers."

Cutler used the surname she'd provided the receptionist. She knew Knoll liked to use his own name. More of his arrogance. She preferred anonymity. Less chance of leaving a lasting impression.

"Why don't you call me Jo?" she said.

She took the seat offered her and studied the middle-aged lawyer. He was tall and lean with light brown hair, not bald, just thinning. He was dressed in the expected white shirt, dark pants, and silk tie, but the suspenders added a touch of maturity. He flashed a disarming smile and she liked his glinting hazel eyes. He appeared diffident and unassuming, someone she quickly decided could be charmed.

Luckily, she'd dressed for the part. A chestnut wig was pinned to the top of her head. Blue contact lenses tinted her eyes. A pair of octagonal clear lenses in gold frames added to the illusion. The crepe skirt with a double-breasted jacket and peak lapels had been bought yesterday at Ann Taylor and carried a distinctive feminine touch, the idea being to draw attention away from her face. When she sat, she crossed her legs, slowly exposing black stockings, and she tried to smile a bit more than usual.

"You're an art investigator?" Cutler asked. "Must be interesting work."

"It can be. But I'm sure your job is equally challenging."

She quickly took in the room's decor. A framed Winslow print hung over a leather settee, a Kupka watercolor on either side. Diplomas dotted another wall, along with numerous professional memberships and awards from the American Bar Association, Society of Probate Lawyers, and the Georgia Trial Lawyers Association. Two color photographs were apparently taken in what looked to be a legislative chamber—Cutler shaking hands with the same older man.

She motioned to the art. "A connoisseur?"

"Hardly. I do a little collecting. I'm active, though, with our High Museum."

"You must derive a lot of pleasure from that."

"Art is important to me."

"Is that why you agreed to see me?"

"That, and simple curiosity."

She decided to get down to business. "I went by the Fulton County Courthouse a little while ago. The secretary at your ex-wife's office indicated Judge Cutler was out of town. She wouldn't tell me where she'd gone and suggested I come talk to you."

"Sami called a little while ago and said this concerns my former father-in-law?"

"Yes, it does. Judge Cutler's secretary confirmed to me that a man visited yesterday, looking for your ex-wife. A tall, blond European. He used the name Christian Knoll. I've been tailing Knoll all week, but lost him yesterday afternoon at the airport. I fear he might be following Judge Cutler."

Concern waved across her host's face. Excellent. She'd guessed right.

"Why would this Mr. Knoll follow Rachel?"

She was gambling by being frank. Maybe fear would lower his barriers and she could learn exactly where Rachel Cutler had gone. "Knoll came to Atlanta to talk with Karol Borya." She decided to omit any reference that Knoll actually talked to Borya Saturday night. No need to make too much of a connection. "He must have learned that Borya died and sought out the daughter. It's the only logical explanation why he went to her office."

"How did he, or you, know anything about Karol?"

"You must know what Mr. Borya did when he was a Soviet citizen."

"He told us. But how do you know?"

"The records for the Commission Mr. Borya once worked for are now public in Russia. It's an easy matter to study the history. Knoll is looking for the Amber Room, and was probably hoping Borya knew something about it."

"But how did he know where to find Karol?"

"Last week Knoll perused records in a depository in St. Petersburg. These have become available for inspection only recently. He learned the information there."

"That doesn't explain why you're here."

"As I indicated, I followed Knoll."

"How did you know Karol died?"

"I didn't until I arrived in town Monday."

"Ms. Myers, what's all the interest in the Amber Room? We're talking about something that's been lost for over fifty years. Don't you think if it could have been found, it would have by now?"

"I agree, Mr. Cutler. But Christian Knoll thinks otherwise."

"You said you lost him in the airport yesterday. What makes you think he's following Rachel?"

"Just a hunch. I searched the concourses but never could find him. I noted several international flights that left within a few minutes after Knoll dodged me. One was to Munich. Two to Paris. Three to Frankfurt."

"She was on the one to Munich," he said.

Paul Cutler appeared to be warming to her. Starting to trust. To believe. She decided to take advantage of the moment. "Why is Judge Cutler going to Munich so soon after her father died?"

"Her father left a note about the Amber Room."

Now was time to press. "Mr. Cutler, Christian Knoll is a dangerous man. When he's after something, nothing gets in the way. I'd wager he was on that flight to Munich, too. It's important I speak with your ex-wife. Do you know where she's staying?"

"She said she'd call from there, but I haven't heard from her."

Concern laced the words. She glanced at her watch. "It's nearly three-thirty in Munich."

"I was thinking the same thing before you arrived."

"Do you know exactly where she was headed?" He didn't answer. She pressed harder. "I understand I'm a stranger to you. But I assure you I'm a friend. I need to find Christian Knoll. I can't go into the details because of confidentiality, but I strongly believe he is looking for your ex-wife."

"Then I think I ought to contact the police."

"Knoll would mean nothing to local law enforcement. This is a matter for the international authorities."

He hesitated, as if considering her words, weighing the

options. Calling the police would take time. Involving European agencies even more time. She was here now, ready to act. The choice should be an easy one, and she wasn't surprised when he made it.

"She went to Bavaria to find a man named Danya Chapaev. He lives in Kehlheim."

"Who is Chapaev?" she asked, innocently.

"A friend of Karol's. They worked together at the Commission years ago. Rachel thought Chapaev might know about the Amber Room."

"What would lead her to believe that?"

He reached into a desk drawer and removed a bundle of letters. He handed them to her. "See for yourself. It's all there."

She took a few minutes and scanned each letter. Nothing definite or precise, just hints to what the two might have known or suspected. Enough, though, to cause her concern. There was no question now that she had to stop Knoll from teaming up with Rachel Cutler. That was exactly what the bastard planned to do. He learned nothing from the father, so he tossed him down the stairs and decided to charm the daughter to see what he could learn. She stood. "I appreciate the information, Mr. Cutler. I'm going to see if your ex-wife can be located in Munich. I have contacts there." She extended her hand to shake. "I want to thank you for your time."

Cutler stood and accepted the gesture. "I appreciate your visit and the warning, Ms. Myers. But you never did say what *your* interest is."

"I'm not at liberty to divulge that, but suffice it to say that Mr. Knoll is wanted for some serious charges."

"Are you with the police?"

"Private investigator hired to find Knoll. I work out of London."

"Strange. Your accent is more East European than British."

She smiled. "Quite right. Originally, I'm from Prague."

"Can you leave a phone number? Perhaps if I hear from Rachel, I can put the two of you in touch."

"No need. I'll check back with you later today or tomorrow, if that's all right."

She turned to leave and noticed the framed picture of an older man and woman. She motioned. "A handsome couple."

"My parents. Taken about three months before they died."

"I'm so sorry."

He accepted her condolences with a slight nod of the head, and she left the office without saying anything more. The last time she'd seen that same older couple they, and twenty or so others, were climbing out of the rain into an Alitalia airbus, preparing to leave Florence for a short hop across the Ligurian Sea to France. The explosives she'd paid to store on board were safe in the luggage compartment, the timer ticking away, set for zero thirty minutes later over open water.

Twenty-four

MUNICH, GERMANY
4:35 P.M.

RACHEL WAS AMAZED. SHE'D NEVER BEEN IN A BEER HALL. AN oompah band, complete with trumpets, drums, an accordion, and cowbells blasted an earsplitting din. Long wooden tables were knotted with revelers, the aroma of tobacco, sausage, and beer thick and strong. Perspiring waiters in lederhosen and women in flaring dirndl dresses eagerly served one-liter tankards of dark beer. *Maibock,* she heard it called, a seasonal brew served only this time of year to herald the arrival of warm weather.

Most of the two hundred or so people surrounding her appeared to be enjoying themselves. She'd never cared for beer, always thought it an acquired taste, so she ordered a Coke along with a roasted chicken for dinner. The desk clerk at her hotel suggested the hall, discouraging her from the nearby Hofbrauhaus where tourists flocked.

Her flight from Atlanta arrived earlier that morning and, disregarding advice she'd always heard, she rented a car, checked into a hotel, and enjoyed a long nap. She would drive tomorrow to Kehlheim, about seventy kilometers to the south, within shouting distance of Austria and the Alps. Danya Chapaev had waited this long, he could wait another day, assuming he was even there to find.

The change of scenery was doing her good, though it was strange to look around at barrel-vaulted ceilings and the colorful costumes of the beer garden employees. She'd traveled overseas only once before, three years ago to London and a judicial conference sponsored by the State Bar of Georgia. Television programs about Germany had always interested her, and she'd dreamed about one day visiting. Now she was here.

She munched her chicken and enjoyed the spectacle. It took her mind off her father, the Amber Room, and Danya Chapaev. Off Marcus Nettles and the coming election. Maybe Paul was right and this was a total waste of time. But she felt better just being here, and that counted for something.

She paid her bill with euros obtained at the airport and left the hall. The late afternoon was cool and comfortable, sweater weather back home, a midspring sun casting the cobblestones in alternating light and shadows. The streets were crowded with thousands of tourists and shoppers, the buildings of the old town an intriguing mix of stone, half-timber, and brick, a villagelike atmosphere of the quaint and medieval. The entire area was pedestrian only, vehicles limited to an occasional delivery truck.

She turned west and strolled back toward the *Marienplatz*.

Her hotel sat on the far side of the open square. A food market lay between, the stalls brimming with produce, meat, and cooked specialties. An outdoor beer garden spread out to the left. She remembered a little about Munich. Once the capital of Bavaria, home of the Duke and Elector, seat of the Wittelsbachs who ruled the area for 750 years. What had Thomas Wolfe called it? *A touch of German heaven.*

She passed several tourist groups with guides spouting French, Spanish, and Japanese. In front of the town hall she encountered an English group, the accent twinged with the cockney twang she remembered from her previous trip to England. She lingered at the back of the group, listening to the guide, staring up at the blaze of Gothic ornamentation rising before her. The tour group inched across the square, stopping on the far side, opposite the town hall. She followed and noticed the guide studying her watch. The clock face high above read 4:58 P.M.

Suddenly, the windows in the clock tower swung open and two rows of brightly colored enameled copper figurines danced out on a turntable. Music flooded the square. Bells clanged for five o'clock, echoed by more bells in the distance.

"This is the *glockenspiel*," the guide said over the noise. "It comes to life three times a day. Eleven, noon, and now at five. The figures on top are reenacting a tournament that used to accompany sixteenth-century German royal weddings. The figures below are performing the Dance of the Coppers."

The colorful figures twirled to the tune of lively Bavarian music. Everyone in the street stopped, their necks craned upward. The vignette lasted two minutes, then stopped, and the square sprang back to life. The tour group moved off and crossed one of the side streets. She lingered for a few seconds and watched the clock windows fully close, then followed across the intersection.

The blare of a horn shattered the afternoon.

She jerked her head to the left.

The front end of a car approached her. Fifty feet. Forty. Twenty. Her eyes focused on the hood and the Mercedes emblem, then on the lights and words that signified taxi.

Ten feet.

The horn still blared. She needed to move, but her feet wouldn't respond. She braced herself for the pain, wondering if the impact or the slam to the cobblestones would hurt worse.

Poor Marla and Brent.

And Paul. Sweet Paul.

An arm wrapped around her neck, and she was jerked back.

Brakes squealed. The taxi slid to a stop. The smell of burning rubber steamed from the pavement.

She turned to see who now held her. The man was tall and lean, with a shock of corn-colored hair brushed across a tanned brow. Thin lips like slits cut with a razor creased a handsome face, the complexion a dusky hue. He was dressed in a wheat-colored twill shirt and checkered trousers.

"You okay?" he asked in English.

The peak of the moment had spent her emotions. She instantly realized how close she'd come to dying. "I think so."

A crowd gathered. The cabdriver was out of the car, looking on.

"She's okay, folks," her savior said. Then he said something in German and people started to leave. He spoke to the taxi driver in German, who responded and then sped off.

"The driver is sorry. But he said you appeared out of nowhere."

"I thought this was pedestrian only," she said. "I wasn't concerned about a car."

"The taxis are not supposed to be here, but they find a way. I reminded the driver of that, and he decided that leaving was the best course."

"There should be a sign or something."

"America, right? Everything has a sign in America. Not here."

She calmed down. "Thanks for what you did."

Two rows of even white teeth flashed a perfect smile. "My pleasure." He extended a hand. "I am Christian Knoll."

She accepted the offer. "Rachel Cutler. And I'm glad you were there, Mr. Knoll. I never saw that taxi."

"It would have been unfortunate otherwise."

She grinned. "Quite." She started to shake uncontrollably, the aftershock of what had almost just happened.

"Please, let me buy you a drink to calm you down."

"That's not necessary."

"You are shaking. Some wine would be good."

"I appreciate it, but—"

"As a reward for my effort."

That would be hard to refuse, so she surrendered. "Okay, maybe a little wine might be the thing."

She followed Knoll to a café about four blocks away, the twin copper towers of the main cathedral looming directly across the street. Clothed tables sprouted across the cobblestones, each filled with people cradling steins of dark beer. Knoll ordered a beer for himself and her a glass of Rhineland wine, the clear liquid dry, bitter, and good.

Knoll had been right. Her nerves were flustered. That was the closest she'd ever come to death. Strange her thoughts at the time. Brent and Marla were understandable. But Paul? She'd clearly thought of him, her heart aching for an instant.

She sipped the wine and let the alcohol and ambience soothe her nerves.

"I have a confession to make, Ms. Cutler," Knoll said.

"How about Rachel?"

"Very well. Rachel."

She sipped more wine. "What kind of confession?"

"I was following you."

The words got her attention. She set the wineglass down. "What do you mean?"

"I was following you. I have been since you left Atlanta."

She rose from the table. "I think perhaps the police should be involved in this."

Knoll sat impassive and sipped his beer. "I have no problem with that, if you so desire. I only ask that you hear me out first."

She considered the request. They were seated in the open. Beyond a wrought-iron railing, the street was full of evening shoppers. What would it hurt to hear him out? She sat back down. "Okay, Mr. Knoll, you've got five minutes."

Knoll set the mug on the table. "I traveled to Atlanta earlier in the week to meet your father. On arrival I learned of his death. Yesterday, I appeared at your office and learned of your trip here. I even left my name and number. Your secretary did not pass my message on?"

"I haven't talked with my office. What business did you have with my father?"

"I am looking for the Amber Room and thought he could be of assistance."

"Why are you looking for the Amber Room?"

"My employer seeks it."

"As do the Russians, I'm sure."

Knoll smiled. "True. But, after fifty years, we regard it as 'finders keepers,' I believe is the American saying."

"How could my father help?"

"He searched many years. Finding the Amber Room was given a high priority by the Soviets."

"That was fifty-plus years ago."

"With this particular prize, the passage of time is meaningless. If anything, it makes the search all the more intriguing."

"How did you locate my father?"

Knoll stuffed a hand into a pocket and handed her some folded sheets. "I discovered those last week in St. Petersburg. They led me to Atlanta. As you'll see, the KGB visited him a few years ago."

She unfolded and read. The typed words were in Cyrillic. An English translation appeared to the side in blue ink. She instantly noticed who'd signed the top sheet. Danya Chapaev. She also noted what was written on the KGB sheet about her father:

```
Contact made. Denies any information on yan-
tarnaya komnata subsequent to 1958. Have been
unable to locate Danya Chapaev. Borya claimed
no knowledge of Chapaev's whereabouts.
```

But her father had known exactly where Chapaev lived. He'd corresponded with him for years. Why had he lied? And her father never mentioned anything about the KGB visiting him. Nor much about the Amber Room. It was a little unnerving to think the KGB had known about her, Marla, and Brent. She wondered what else her father held back.

"Unfortunately, I was not able to speak with your father," Knoll said. "I arrived too late. I am truly sorry about your loss."

"When did you arrive?"

"Monday."

"And you waited till yesterday to go by my office?"

"I learned of your father's death and did not want to intrude on your grief. My business could be postponed."

The connection to Chapaev started to ease her tension. This man may be credible, but she cautioned herself against complacency. After all, though handsome and charming, Christian Knoll was still a stranger. Worse yet, a stranger in a foreign country. "Were you on my flight over?"

He nodded. "I barely made it onto the plane."

"Why did you wait till now to speak up?"

"I was unsure of your visit. If it was personal, I did not want to interfere. If it concerned the Amber Room, I intended on approaching you."

"I don't appreciate being followed, Mr. Knoll. Not one damn bit."

His gaze soldered onto hers. "Perhaps it is fortunate I did."

The taxi flashed through her mind. Maybe he was right?

"And Christian will do fine," he said.

She told herself to back off. No need to be so hostile. He's right. He saved her life. "Okay. Christian it is."

"Does your trip involve the Amber Room?"

"I'm not sure I should answer that."

"If I were a danger, I would simply have let the taxi hit you."

A good point, but not necessarily good enough.

"Frau Cutler, I am a trained investigator. Art is my speciality. I speak the language here and am familiar with this country. You may be an excellent judge, but I would assume you are a novice investigator."

She said nothing.

"I am interested in information on the Amber Room, nothing more. I have shared with you what I am privy to. I only ask the same in return."

"And if I decline and go to the police?"

"I will simply disappear from sight, but will keep you under surveillance to learn what you do. It is nothing personal. You are a lead I intend to explore to the end. I simply thought we could work together and save time."

There was something rugged and dangerous about Knoll that she liked. His words came clear and direct, the voice sure. She searched his face hard for portents, but found none. So she made the kind of quick decision she was accustomed to making in court.

"Okay, Mr. Knoll. I've come to find Danya Chapaev. Apparently the same name on this sheet. He lives in Kehlheim."

Knoll lifted the mug and took a pull of beer. "That's south of here, toward the Alps near Austria. I know the village."

"He and my father were apparently interested in the Amber Room. Obviously, more so than I ever realized."

"Any idea what Herr Chapaev would know?"

She decided not to mention anything about the letters just yet. "Nothing other than they once worked together, as you seem to already know."

"How did you come by the name?"

She decided to lie. "My father talked of him for many years. They were close once."

"I can be of valuable assistance, Frau Cutler."

"In all honesty, Mr. Knoll, I was hoping for some time alone."

"I understand completely. I recall when my father died. It was very hard."

The sentiment sounded genuine, and she appreciated the concern. But he was still a stranger.

"You need assistance. If this Chapaev is privy to information, I can help develop it. I have a vast knowledge of the Amber Room. Knowledge that can help."

She said nothing.

"When do you plan to head south?" Knoll asked.

"Tomorrow morning." She answered too quickly.

"Let me drive you."

"I wouldn't want my children accepting rides from strangers. Why should I do the same?"

He smiled. She liked it.

"I was open and frank with your secretary about my identity and intentions. Quite a trail for somebody who intended to harm you." He downed the rest of his beer. "In any event, I would simply follow you to Kehlheim anyway."

She made another quick decision. One that surprised her. "All right. Why not. We'll go together. I'm staying at the Hotel Waldeck. A couple of blocks that way."

"I'm across the street from the Waldeck at the Elisabeth."

She shook her head and smiled. "Why doesn't that surprise me?"

Knoll watched Rachel Cutler disappear into the crowd.

That went quite well.

He tossed a few euros on the table and left the café. He rounded several corners and recrossed the *Marienplatz*. Past the food market, busy with early diners and revelers, he headed for Maximilianstrasse, an elegant boulevard lined with museums, government offices, and shops. The pillared portico of the National Theater rose ahead. In front, a line of taxis wrapped the statue of Max Joseph, Bavaria's first king, patiently waiting for fares from the evening's early performance. He crossed the street and walked to the fourth taxi in line. The driver was standing outside, arms folded, propped against the Mercedes' exterior.

"Good enough?" the driver asked in German.

"More than enough."

"My performance afterwards convincing?"

"Outstanding." He handed the man a wad of euros.

"Always a pleasure doing business with you, Christian."

"You, too, Erich."

He knew the driver well, having used him before when in Munich. The man was both reliable and corruptible, two qualities he sought in all his operatives.

"You getting soft, Christian?"

"How so?"

"You only wanted her frightened, not killed. So unlike you."

He smiled. "Nothing like a brush with death to breed trust."

"You want to fuck her or something?"

He didn't want to say much more, but he also wanted the man available in the future. He nodded and said, "A good way to get into the pants."

The driver counted off the bills. "Five hundred euros is a lot for a piece of ass."

But he considered the Amber Room and the ten million euros it would bring him. Then reconsidered Rachel Cutler and her attractiveness, which had lingered after she'd left.

"Not really."

TWENTY-FIVE

PAUL WAS CONCERNED. HE'D SKIPPED LUNCH AND STAYED IN THE office, hoping Rachel would call. It was after 6:30 P.M. in Germany. She'd mentioned the possibility of staying in Munich one night before heading to Kehlheim. So he wasn't sure if she'd call today, or tomorrow after she made it south to the Alps, or if she'd call at all.

Rachel was outspoken, aggressive, and tough. Always had been. That independent spirit was what made her a good judge. But it also made her hard to know, and even harder to like. Friends didn't come easy. But down deep, she was warm and caring. He knew that. Unfortunately, the two of them were like grease and fire. But were they, really? They both thought a quiet dinner at home better than a crowded restaurant. A video rental preferable to the theater. An afternoon with the kids at the zoo heaven, compared with a night out on the town. He realized she missed her father. They'd been close, particularly after the divorce. Karol had tried hard to get them back together.

What had the old man's note said?

Maybe give Paul another chance.

But it was no use. Rachel was determined that they were to live apart. She'd rebuffed every attempt he made at a reconciliation. Maybe it was time he obliged her and gave up. But there was something there. Her lack of a social life. Her reliance and trust in him. And how many men possessed a key to their ex-wife's house? How many still shared the title to property? Or continued to maintain a joint account for stocks? She'd never once insisted that their Merrill Lynch account be closed, and he'd managed it the last three years without her ever questioning his judgment.

He stared at the phone. Why hadn't she called? What was going on? Some man, Christian Knoll, was supposedly looking for her. Perhaps he was dangerous. Perhaps not. All the information he possessed was the word of a rather attractive brunette with bright blue eyes and shapely legs. Jo Myers. She'd been calm and collected, handling his questions well, her answers quick and to the point. It was almost as if she could sense his apprehension toward Rachel, the doubts he harbored about her traveling to Germany. He'd volunteered a little too much, and that fact bothered him. Rachel had no business in Germany. Of that he was sure. The Amber Room was not her concern, and it was doubtful Danya Chapaev was even still alive.

He reached across his desk and retrieved his former father-in-law's letters. He found the note penned to Rachel and scanned down the page about halfway:

> *Did we ever find it? Perhaps. Neither of us really went and looked. Too many were watching in those days and, by the time we narrowed the trail, both of us realized the Soviets were far worse than the Germans. So we left it alone. Danya and I vowed never to reveal what we knew, or perhaps simply what we thought we knew. Only when Yancy volunteered to make discreet inquiries, checking information that I once thought credible, did I inquire again. He was making an inquiry on his last trip to Italy. Whether that blast on the plane was attributable to his questions or something else will never be known. All I know is that the search for the Amber Room has proved dangerous.*

He read a little farther and again found the warning:

But never, absolutely never, concern yourself with the Amber Room. Remember the story of Phaëthon and the tears of the Heliades. Heed his ambition and their grief.

He'd read a lot of the classics, but couldn't recall the specifics. Rachel had been evasive three days ago when he asked her about the story at the dining room table.

He turned to his computer terminal and accessed the Internet. He selected a search engine and typed "Phaëthon and the Heliades." The screen noted over a hundred sites. He randomly checked a couple. The third was the best, a Web page titled "The Mythical World of Edith Hamilton." He scanned through until he found the story of Phaëthon, a bibliography noting the account was from Ovid's *Metamorphoses*.

He read the story. It was colorful and prophetic.

Phaëthon, the illegitimate son of Helios, the Sun God, finally found his father. Feeling guilty, the Sun God granted his son one wish, and the boy immediately chose to take his father's place for a day, piloting the sun chariot across the sky from dawn to dusk. The father realized his son's folly and tried in vain to dissuade the boy, but he would not be deterred. So Helios granted the wish, but warned the boy how difficult the chariot was to command. None of the Sun God's cautions seemed to mean anything. All the boy saw was himself standing in the wondrous chariot, guiding the steeds that Zeus himself could not master.

Once airborne, though, Phaëthon quickly discovered that his father's warnings were correct, and he lost control of the chariot. The horses darted to the top of the sky, then plunged close enough to the earth to set the world ablaze. Zeus, having no choice, unleashed a thunderbolt that destroyed the chariot and killed Phaëthon. The mysterious river Eridanus received him and cooled the flames that engulfed his body. The Naiads, in pity for one so bold and so young, buried him. Phaëthon's sisters, the Heliades, came to his grave and mourned. Zeus, taking pity on their sorrow, turned them into poplar trees that sprouted sadly murmuring leaves on the bank of the Eridanus.

He read the last lines of the story on the screen:

WHERE SORROWING THEY WEEP INTO THE STREAM FOREVER
EACH TEAR AS IT FALLS SHINES IN THE WATER
A GLISTENING DROP OF AMBER.

He instantly recalled the copy of Ovid's *Metamorphoses* he'd seen on Borya's bookshelves. Karol was trying to warn Rachel, but she wouldn't listen. Like Phaëthon, she'd raced off on a foolish quest, not understanding the dangers or appreciating the risks. Would Christian Knoll be her Zeus? The one to hurl a thunderbolt.

He stared at the phone. Ring, dammit.

What should he do?

He could do nothing. Stay with the kids, look after them, and wait for Rachel to return from her wild goose chase. He could call the police and perhaps alert the German authorities. But if Christian Knoll was nothing more than a curious investigator, Rachel would soundly chastise him. Alarmist Paul, she'd say.

And he didn't need to hear that.

But there was a third option. The one most appealing. He glanced at his watch. 1:50 P.M. 7:50 in Germany. He reached for the phone book, found the number, and dialed Delta Airlines. The reservation clerk came on the line.

"I need a flight to Munich from Atlanta, leaving tonight."

TWENTY-SIX

SUZANNE MADE GOOD TIME. SHE'D LEFT PAUL CUTLER'S OFFICE yesterday and immediately flew to New York, where she caught the Concorde leaving at 6:30 for Paris. Arriving a little after 10 P.M. local time, an Air France shuttle to Munich placed her on the ground by 1 A.M. She'd managed a little sleep at an airport hotel and then sped south in a rented Audi, following autobahn E533 straight to Oberammergau, then west on a snaking highway to the alpine lake called Förggensee, east of Füssen.

The village of Kehlheim was a tumbled collection of frescoed houses capped by ornate, gabled roofs that nestled close to the lake's east shore. A steepled church dominated the town center, a rambling *marktplatz* surrounding. Forested slopes cradled the far shores. A few white-winged sailboats flitted across the blue-gray water like butterflies in a breeze.

She parked south of the church. Vendors filled the cobbled square, set up for what appeared to be a Saturday morning market. The air reeked of raw meat, damp produce, and spent tobacco. She strolled through the mélange swarming with spring sojourners. Children played in noisy groups. Hammer blows echoed in the distance. An older man at one of the booths, with silver hair and an angled nose, caught her attention. He wasn't far from the age Danya Chapaev should be. She approached and admired his apples and cherries.

"Beautiful fruit," she said in German.

"My own," the older man said.

She bought three apples, smiled broadly, and warmed to him. Her image was perfect. Reddish-blond wig, fair skin, hazel eyes. Her breasts were enhanced two sizes by a pair of external silicone inserts. She'd padded her hips and thighs, as well, the fitted jeans two sizes larger to accommodate the manufactured bulk. A plaid flannel shirt and tan prairie boots rounded out the disguise. Sunglasses shielded her eyes, dark, but not enough to draw attention. Later, eyewitnesses would surely describe a busty, heavyset blonde.

"Do you know where Danya Chapaev lives?" she finally asked. "He's an old man. Lived here awhile. A friend of my grandfather. I came to deliver a present but lost directions to where he lives. I only found the village by luck."

The older man shook his head. "How careless, Fräulein."

She smiled, soaking in the rebuke. "I know. But I'm like that. My mind stays a thousand miles away."

"I don't know where a Chapaev lives. I'm from Nessel-wang, to the west. But let me get someone from here."

Before she could stop him, he yelled to another man across the square. She didn't want to draw too much attention to her inquiry. The two men spoke in French, a language she wasn't overly proficient in, but she caught an occasional word here and there. Chapaev. North. Three kilometers. Near the lake.

"Eduard knows Chapaev. Says he lives north of town. Three kilometers. Right beside the lakeshore. That road there. Small stone chalet with a chimney."

She smiled and nodded at the information, then heard the man from across the square call out, "Julius! Julius!"

A boy of about twelve scampered toward the stall. He had light brown hair and a cute face. The vendor spoke to the lad, then the boy ran toward her. Behind, a flock of ducks sprang from the lake, up into the milky morning sky.

"You looking for Chapaev?" the boy asked. "That's my grandpapa. I can show you."

His young eyes scanned her breasts. Her smile broadened. "Then lead the way."

Men of all ages were so easy to manipulate.

TWENTY-SEVEN

RACHEL GLANCED ACROSS THE FRONT SEAT AT CHRISTIAN KNOLL. They were speeding south on autobahn E533, thirty minutes south of Munich. The terrain framed by the Volvo's tinted windows featured ghostly peaks emerging from a curtain of haze, snow whitening the folds of the highest altitudes, the slopes below clothed in verdant fir and larch.

"It's beautiful out there," she said.

"Spring is the best time to visit the Alps. This your first time in Germany?"

She nodded.

"You will very much like the area."

"You travel a lot?"

"All the time."

"Where's home?"

"I have an apartment in Vienna, but rarely do I stay there. My work takes me all over the world."

She studied her enigmatic chauffeur. His shoulders were broad and muscular, his neck thick, his arms long and powerful. He was again dressed casually. Plaid chamois cloth shirt, jeans, boots, and smelled faintly of sweet cologne. He was the first European man she'd ever really talked with at length. Maybe that was the fascination. He'd definitely piqued her interest.

"The KGB sheet said you have one child. Is there a husband?" Knoll asked.

"Used to be. We're divorced. And there are two children."

"Divorce is rather prevalent in America."

"I hear a hundred or more a week in my court."

Knoll shook his head. "Such a shame."

"People can't seem to live together."

"Is your ex-husband a lawyer?"

"One of the best." A Volvo whizzed by in the left-hand lane. "Amazing. That car's got to be going over a hundred miles an hour."

"Closer to one hundred and twenty," Knoll said. "We're doing nearly a hundred."

"That's a definite difference from home."

"Is he a good father?" Knoll asked.

"My ex? Oh, yes. Very good."

"Better father than husband?"

Strange, the questions. But she didn't mind answering, the anonymity of a stranger lessening the intrusion. "I wouldn't say that. Paul's a good man. Any woman would be thrilled to have him."

"Why weren't you?"

"I didn't say I wasn't. I simply said we couldn't live together."

Knoll seemed to sense her hesitancy. "I did not mean to pry. It's just that people interest me. With no permanent home or roots, I enjoy probing others. Simple curiosity. Nothing more."

"It's okay. No offense taken." She sat silent for a few moments, then said, "I should have called and told Paul where I'm staying. He's watching the children."

"You can let him know this evening."

"He's not happy I'm even here. He and my father said I should stay out of it."

"You discussed this with your father before his death?"

"Not at all. He left me a note with his will."

"Then why are you here?"

"Just something I have to do."

"I can understand. The Amber Room is quite a prize. People have searched for it since the war."

"So I've been told. What makes it so special?"

"Hard to say. Art has such a varying effect on people. The interesting thing about the Amber Room was that it moved everyone in the same way. I've read accounts from the nineteenth and the early part of the twentieth century. All agree it was magnificent. Imagine, an entire room paneled in amber."

"It sounds amazing."

"Amber is so precious. You know much about it?" Knoll asked.

"Very little."

"Just fossilized tree resin, forty to fifty millions of years old. Sap hardened by the millennia into a gem. The Greeks called it *elektron,* 'substance of the sun,' for the color and because, if you rub a piece with your hands, it produces an electric charge. Chopin used to finger chains of it before he played the piano. It warms to the touch and carries away perspiration."

"I didn't know that."

"The Romans believed if you were a Leo, wearing amber would bring you luck. If you were a Taurus, trouble was ahead."

"Maybe I should get some. I'm a Leo."

He smiled. "If you believe in that sort of thing. Medieval doctors prescribed amber vapor to treat sore throats. The boiling fumes are very fragrant and supposedly possessed medicinal qualities. The Russians call it 'incense from the sea.' They also—I'm sorry, I may be boring you."

"Not at all. This is fascinating."

"The vapors can ripen fruit. There's an Arab legend about a certain Shah who ordered his gardener to bring him fresh pears. Problem was, pears were out of season and the fruit would not be ready for another month. The Shah threatened to behead the gardener if he didn't produce ripe pears. So the gardener picked a few unripe pears and spent the night praying to Allah and burning amber incense. The next day, in response to his prayers, the pears were rosy and sweet, ready to eat." Knoll shrugged. "Whether that's true or not, who knows? But amber vapor does contain ethylene, and that stimulates early ripening. It can also soften leather. The Egyptians used the vapor in the mummifying process."

"My only knowledge is from jewelry, or the pictures I've seen with insects and leaves inside."

"Francis Bacon called it 'a more than royal tomb.' Scientists look at amber as a time capsule. Artists think of it like paint. There are over two hundred and fifty colors. Blue and green the rarest. Red, yellow, brown, black, and gold most common. Whole guilds emerged in the Middle Ages that controlled distribution. The Amber Room was crafted in the eighteenth century, the very epitome of what man could do with the substance."

"You know the subject well."

"My job."

The car slowed.

"Our exit," Knoll said as they sped off the autobahn, down a short ramp, and braked at the bottom. "From here we go west by highway. It's not far to Kehlheim." He turned the wheel right and quickly worked the gears, regaining speed.

"Who do you work for?" she asked.

"I cannot say. My employer is a private person."

"But obviously wealthy."

"How so?"

"To send you across the globe looking for art. That's not a hobby for a poor man."

"Did I say my employer was a man?"

She grinned. "No, you didn't."

"Nice try, Your Honor."

Green meadows sprinkled with copses of tall fir lined the highway. She brought down the window and soaked in the crystalline air. "We're rising, aren't we?"

"The Alps start here and spread south to Italy. It will get cool before we make it to Kehlheim."

She'd wondered earlier why he'd worn a long-sleeved shirt and long pants. She'd dressed in a pair of khaki walking shorts and short-sleeved button-down. Suddenly she realized this was the first time she'd driven anywhere with a man other than Paul since the divorce. It was always the children, her father, or a girlfriend.

"I meant what I said yesterday. I am sorry about your father," Knoll said.

"He was very old."

"The terrible thing about parents. One day we lose them."

He sounded like he meant it. Expected words. Surely said out of courtesy. But she appreciated the sentiment.

And found him even more intriguing.

TWENTY-EIGHT

11:45 A.M.

RACHEL STUDIED THE OLD MAN WHO OPENED THE DOOR. HE was short with a narrow face topped by shaggy silver hair. Graying peach fuzz dusted his withered chin and neck. His frame was spare, his skin the shade of talcum, the face wizened like a walnut. He was at least eighty, and her first thought was of her father and how much the man reminded her of him.

"Danya Chapaev? I'm Rachel Cutler. Karol Borya's daughter."

The old man stared deep. "I see him in your face and eyes."

She smiled. "He'd be proud of that fact. May we come in?"

"Of course," Chapaev said.

She and Knoll entered the tiny house. The one-story building was formed from old timber and aging plaster, Chapaev's the last of several chalets that straggled from Kehlheim on a wooded lane.

"How did you find my place?" Chapaev asked. His English was much better than her father's.

"We asked in town where you lived," she said.

The den was homey and warm from a small fire that crackled in a stone hearth. Two lamps burned beside a quilt sofa, where she and Knoll sat. Chapaev slipped down into a wooden rocking chair facing them. The scent of cinnamon and coffee drifted in the air. Chapaev offered a drink, but they declined. She introduced Knoll, then told Chapaev about her father's death. The old man was surprised by the news. He sat in silence for a while, tears welling up in his tired eyes.

"He was a good man. The best," Chapaev finally said.

"I'm here, Mr. Chapaev—"

"Danya, please. Call me Danya."

"All right. Danya. I'm here because of the letters you and my father sent to each other about the Amber Room. I read them. Daddy said something about the secret you two share and being too old now to go and check. I came to find out what I could."

"Why, child?"

"It seemed important to Daddy."

"Did he ever speak with you about it?"

"He talked little about the war and what he did afterwards."

"Perhaps he had a reason for his silence."

"I'm sure he did. But Daddy's gone now."

Chapaev sat silent, seeming to contemplate the fire. Shadows flickered across his ancient face. She glanced at Knoll, who was watching their host closely. She'd been forced to say something about the letters, and Knoll had reacted. Not surprising, since she'd intentionally withheld the information. She figured there'd be questions later.

"Perhaps it's time," Chapaev softly said. "I wondered when. Maybe now is the moment."

Beside her, Knoll sucked a long breath. A chill tingled down her spine. Was it possible this old man knew where the Amber Room was located?

"Such a monster, Erich Koch," Chapaev whispered.

She did not understand. "Koch?"

"A gauleiter," Knoll said. "One of Hitler's provincial governors. Koch ruled Prussia and Ukraine. His job was to squeeze every ton of grain, every ounce of steel, and every slave laborer he could from the region."

The old man sighed. "Koch used to say that if he found a Ukrainian fit to sit at his table, he'd shoot him. I guess we should be grateful for his brutality. He managed to convert forty million Ukrainians, who greeted the invaders as liberators from Stalin, into seething partisans who hated Germans. Quite an accomplishment."

Knoll said nothing.

Chapaev went on. "Koch toyed with the Russians and the Germans after the war, using the Amber Room to stay alive. Karol and I watched the manipulation, yet could say nothing."

"I don't understand," she said.

Knoll said, "Koch was tried in Poland after the war and sentenced to die as a war criminal. The Soviets, though, repeatedly postponed his execution. He claimed to know where the Amber Room was buried. It was Koch who ordered it removed from Leningrad and moved to Königsberg in 1941. He also ordered its evacuation west in 1945. Koch used his supposed knowledge to stay alive, reasoning that the Soviets would kill him as soon as he revealed the location."

She now began to remember some of what she'd read in the articles her father saved. "He eventually got an assurance, though, didn't he?"

"In the mid-1960s," Chapaev said. "But the fool claimed he was unable to remember the exact location. Königsberg by then was renamed Kaliningrad and was part of the Soviet Union. The town was bombed to rubble during the war, and the Soviets bulldozed everything, then rebuilt. Nothing re-

mained of the former city. He blamed everything on the Soviets. Said they destroyed his landmarks. Their fault he
couldn't find the location now."

"Koch never knew anything, did he?" Knoll asked.

"Nothing. A mere opportunist trying to stay alive."

"Then tell us, old man, did you find the Amber Room?"

Chapaev nodded.

"You saw it?" Knoll asked.

"No. But it was there."

"Why did you keep it secret?"

"Stalin was evil. The devil incarnate. He pilfered and stole
Russia's heritage to build the Palace of the Soviets."

"The what?" she asked.

"An immense skyscraper in Moscow," Chapaev said.
"And he wanted to top the thing with a huge statue of Lenin.
Can you imagine such a monstrosity? Karol, me, and all the
others were collecting for the Museum of World Art that was
to be a part of that palace. It was going to be Stalin's gift to
the world. Nothing different from what Hitler planned in
Austria. A huge museum of pilfered art. Thank God Stalin
never built his monument either. It was all madness. Nothing
sane. And nobody could stop the bastard. Only death did him
in." The old man shook his head. "Utter, total madness.
Karol and I were determined to do our part and never say
anything about what we thought we found in the mountains.
Better to leave it buried than to be a showpiece for Satan."

"How did you find the Amber Room?" she asked.

"Quite by accident. Karol stumbled onto a railroad worker
who pointed us to the caves. They were in the Russian sec-
tor, what became East Germany. The Soviets even stole that,
too, though that was one theft I agreed with. Such awful
things happen whenever Germany unites. Wouldn't you say,
Herr Knoll?"

"I do not opine on politics, Comrade Chapaev. Besides,
I'm Austrian, not German."

"Odd. I thought I detected a Bavarian twang to your accent."

"Good ears for a man your age."

Chapaev turned toward her. "That was your father's nick-name. *Ýxo*. Ears. They called him that in Mauthausen. He was the only one in the barracks who spoke German."

"I didn't know that. Daddy spoke little of the camp."

Chapaev nodded. "Understandable. I spent the last months of the war in one myself." The old man stared hard at Knoll. "To your accent, Herr Knoll, I used to be good at such things. German was my specialty."

"Your English is quite good, too."

"I have a talent for language."

"Your former job certainly demanded powers of observation and communication."

She was curious at the friction that seemed to exist. Two strangers, yet they acted as though they knew one another. Or, more accurately, hated one another. But the sparring was delaying their mission. She said, "Danya, can you tell us where the Amber Room is?"

"In the caves to the north. The Harz Mountains. Near Warthberg."

"You sound like Koch," Knoll said. "Those caves have been scoured clean."

"Not these. They were in the eastern portion. The Soviets chained them off. Refused to let anyone inside. There are so many. It would take decades to explore them all, and they are like rat mazes. The Nazis wired most with explosives and stored ammunition in the rest. That's one reason Karol and I never went to look. Better to let the amber rest quietly than risk exploding it."

Knoll slipped a small notebook and pen from his back pocket. "Draw a map."

Chapaev worked a few minutes on a sketch. She and Knoll sat silent. Only the crackle of the fire and the pen moving across the paper broke the stillness. Chapaev handed the pad back to Knoll.

"The right one can be found by the sun," Chapaev said. "The opening points due east. A friend who visited the area recently said the entrance is now chained shut with iron bars, the designation BCR-65 on the outside. The German authorities have yet to sweep the inside for explosives, so no one has ventured in as yet. Or so I am told. I drew a tunnel map as best I could remember. You will have to dig at the end. But you will hit the iron door that leads into the chamber after a few feet."

Knoll said, "You've kept this secret for decades. Yet now you freely tell two strangers?"

"Rachel is not a stranger."

"How do you know she's not lying about who she is?"

"I see her father in her, clearly."

"Yet you know nothing about me. You haven't even inquired as to why I'm here."

"If Rachel brought you, that is good enough for me. I am an old man, Herr Knoll. My time is short. Someone needs to know what I know. Maybe Karol and I were right. Maybe not. Nothing may be there at all. Why don't you go see to be sure." Chapaev turned to her. "Now if that's all you wanted, my child, I'm tired and would like to rest."

"All right, Danya. And thank you. We'll see if the Amber Room's there."

Chapaev sighed. "Do that, my child. Do that."

"VERY GOOD, COMRADE," SUZANNE SAID IN RUSSIAN AS CHA-paev opened the bedroom door. The old man's guests had just left, and she heard the car drive away. "Have you ever considered an acting career? Christian Knoll is hard to fool. But you did wonderfully. I almost believed you myself."

"How do you know Knoll will go to the cave?"

"He's eager to please his new employer. He wants the Amber Room so bad, he'll take the chance and look, even if he thinks it's a dead end."

"What if he thinks it's a trap?"

"No reason to suspect anything, thanks to your remarkable performance."

Chapaev's eyes locked on his grandson, the boy gagged and bound to an oak chair beside the bed.

"Your precious grandson greatly appreciates your performance." She stroked the child's hair. "Don't you, Julius?"

The boy tried to jerk back, humming behind the tape across his mouth. She raised the sound-suppressed pistol close to his head. His young eyes widened as the barrel nestled to his skull.

"There is no need for that," Chapaev quickly said. "I did as you asked. I drew the map exactly. No tricks. Though my heart aches for what may happen to poor Rachel. She doesn't deserve this."

"Poor Rachel should have thought of that before she decided to involve herself. This is not her fight, nor is it her concern. She should have left well enough alone."

"Could we go out into the other room?" he asked.

"As you wish. I don't think dear Julius will be traveling anywhere. Do you?"

They walked into the den. He closed the bedroom door. "The boy does not deserve to die," he quietly said.

"You are perceptive, Comrade Chapaev."

"Do not call me that."

"You're not proud of your Soviet heritage?"

"I have no Soviet heritage. I was White Russian. Only against Hitler did I join with them."

"You harbored no reservations about stealing treasure for Stalin."

"A mistake of the times. Dear god. Fifty years I've kept the secret. Never once have I said a word. Can't you accept that and let my grandson live?"

She said nothing.

"You work for Loring, don't you?" he asked. "Josef is surely dead. It must be Ernst, the son."

"Again, very perceptive, Comrade."

"I knew one day you would come. It was the chance I took. But the boy is not a part of this. Let him go."

"He's a loose end. As you have been. I read the correspondence between yourself and Karol Borya. Why couldn't you leave it alone? Let the matter die. How many more have you corresponded with? My employer does not desire to take any more chances. Borya's gone. The other searchers are gone. You are all that's left."

"You killed Karol, didn't you?"

"Actually, no. Herr Knoll beat me to it."

"Rachel does not know?"

"Apparently not."

"That poor child, the danger she is in."

"Her problem, Comrade, as I have said."

"I expect you to kill me. In some ways I welcome it. But please let the boy go. He cannot identify you. He does not speak Russian. He understood nothing we have said. Certainly that's not your actual appearance. The boy could never help the police."

"You know I cannot do that."

He lunged toward her, but muscles that perhaps once scaled cliffs and shimmied out of buildings had atrophied with age and disease. She easily sidestepped his meaningless attempt.

"There is no need for this, Comrade."

He fell to his knees. "Please. I beg you in the name of the Virgin Mary, let the boy go. He deserves a life." Chapaev hinged his body forward and pressed his face tight to the floor. "Poor Julius," he muttered through tears. "Poor, poor Julius."

She aimed the gun at the back of Chapeav's skull and considered his request.

"*Dasvidániya*, Comrade."

TWENTY-NINE

"WEREN'T YOU A LITTLE ROUGH ON HIM?" RACHEL SAID.

They were speeding north on the autobahn, Kehlheim and Danya Chapaev an hour south. She was driving. Knoll had said he'd take over in a little while and navigate the twisting roads through the Harz Mountains.

He glanced up from the sketch Chapaev had drawn. "You must understand, Rachel, I have been doing this many years. People lie far more than they tell the truth. Chapaev says the Amber Room rests in one of the Harz caves. That theory has been explored a thousand times. I pushed to be sure if he was being truthful."

"He appeared sincere."

"I am suspicious that, after all these years, the treasure is simply waiting at the end of a dark tunnel."

"Didn't you say there are hundreds of tunnels and most haven't been explored? Too dangerous, right?"

"That's correct. But I am familiar with the general area Chapaev describes. I have searched caves there myself."

She told him about Wayland McKoy and the ongoing expedition.

"Stod is only forty kilometers from where we will be," Knoll said. "Lots of caves there, as well, supposedly full of loot. If you believe what the treasure hunters say."

"You don't?"

"I have learned that anything worth having is usually already owned. The real hunt is for those who possess it. You would be surprised how many missing treasures are simply lying on a table in somebody's bedroom or hanging on the wall, as free as a trinket bought in a department store. People think time protects them. It doesn't. Back in the 1960s, a Monet was found in a farmhouse by a tourist. The owner had taken it in exchange for a pound of butter. Stories like that are endless, Rachel."

"That what you do? Search for those opportunities?"

"Along with other quests."

They drove on, the terrain flattening and then rising as the highway crossed central Germany and veered northwest into mountains. After a stop on the side of the road, Rachel moved to the passenger seat. Knoll pulled the car back on the highway. "These are the Harz. The northernmost mountains in central Germany."

The peaks were not the towering snowy precipices of the Alps. Instead the slopes rose at gentle angles, rounded at the top, covered in fir, beech, and walnut trees. Towns and villages were nestled throughout in tiny valleys and wide ravines. Off in the distance the silhouette of even higher peaks were visible.

"Reminds me of the Appalachians," she said.

"This is the land of Grimm," Knoll said. "The kingdom of magic. In the Dark Ages, it was one of the final venues for paganism. Fairies, witches, and goblins were supposed to roam out there. It is said the last bear and lynx in Germany were killed somewhere nearby."

"It's gorgeous," she said.

"Silver used to be mined here, but that stopped in the tenth century. Then came gold, lead, zinc, and barium oxide. The last mine closed before the war in the 1930s. That's where most of the caves and tunnels came from. Old mines the Nazis made good use of. Perfect hiding places from bombers, and tough for ground troops to invade."

She watched the winding road ahead and thought about Knoll's mention of the Brothers Grimm. She half expected to see the goose that laid the golden egg, or the two black stones that were once cruel brothers, or the Pied Piper luring rats and children with a tune.

An hour later they entered Warthberg. The dark outline of a bulwark wall encased the compact village, softened only by arching tresses and conical-roofed bastions. The architectural difference from the south was obvious. The red roofs and timeworn ramparts of Kehlheim were replaced with half-timbered facades sheathed in dull slate. Fewer flowers adorned the windows and the houses. There was a definite glow of medieval color, but it seemed tempered by a shellac of self-consciousness. Not a whole lot different, she concluded, from the contrast between New England and the Deep South.

Knoll parked in front of an inn with the interesting name of Goldene Krone. "Golden Crown," he told her before disappearing inside. She waited outside and studied the busy street. An air of commercialism sprang from the shop windows lining the cobbled lane. Knoll returned a few minutes later.

"I obtained two rooms for the night. It is nearly five o'clock, and daylight will last another five or six hours. But we'll head up into the hills in the morning. No rush. It has waited fifty years."

"It stays daylight that long around here?"

"We're halfway to the Arctic Circle, and it is almost summer."

Knoll lifted both their bags out of the rental. "I'll get you settled, then there are a few things I need to buy. After, we can have dinner. I noticed a place driving in."

"That'd be nice," she said.

❧━

KNOLL LEFT RACHEL IN HER ROOM. HE'D NOTICED THE YELLOW phone booth driving in and quickly retraced a path back toward the town wall. He didn't like using hotel room phones. Too much record keeping. The same was true for mobile phones. An obscure pay booth was always safer for a quick long-distance call. Inside, he dialed Burg Herz.

"About time. What's going on?" Monika asked as she answered the phone.

"I am trying to find the Amber Room."

"Where are you?"

"Not far away."

"I'm in no mood, Christian."

"The Harz Mountains. Warthberg." He told her about Rachel Cutler, Danya Chapaev, and the cave.

"We've heard this before," Monika said. "Those mountains are like ant mounds, and nobody has ever found a damn thing."

"I have a map. What could it hurt?"

"You want to screw her, don't you?"

"The thought crossed my mind."

"She's learning a bit too much, wouldn't you say?"

"Nothing of any consequence. I had no choice but to take her along. I assumed Chapaev would be more at ease with Borya's daughter than with me."

"And?"

"He was forthcoming. Too open, if you ask me."

"Careful with this Cutler woman," Monika said.

"She thinks I'm searching for the Amber Room. Nothing more. There is no connection between me and her father."

"Sounds like you're developing a heart, Christian."

"Hardly." He told her about Suzanne Danzer and the episode in Atlanta.

"Loring is concerned about what we're doing," Monika said. "He and Father talked yesterday for a long time on the phone. He was definitely picking for information. A bit obvious for him."

"Welcome to the game."

"I don't need amusement, Christian. What I want is the Amber Room. And, according to Father, this appears to be the best lead ever."

"I'm not so sure about that."

"Always so pessimistic. Why do you say that?"

"Something about Chapaev bothers me. Hard to say. Just something."

"Go to the mine, Christian, and look. Satisfy yourself. Then fuck your judge and get on with the job."

RACHEL DIALED THE PHONE BESIDE THE BED AND GAVE AN AT&T overseas operator her credit card number. After eight rings, the answering machine clicked on at her house and her voice instructed a caller to leave a message.

"Paul, I'm in a town called Warthberg in central Germany. Here's the hotel and number." She told him about the Goldene Krone. "I'll call tomorrow. Kiss the kids for me. Bye."

She glanced at her watch. 5:00 P.M. Eleven o'clock in the morning in Atlanta. Maybe he took the kids to the zoo or a movie. She was glad they were with Paul. It was a shame they couldn't be with him every day. Children need a father, and he needed them. That was the hardest thing about divorce, knowing a family was no more. She'd sat on the bench a year, divorcing others, before her own marriage fell apart. Many times, while listening to evidence she really did not need to hear, she'd wondered why couples who once loved one another suddenly had nothing good to say. Was hate a prerequisite to divorce? A necessary element? She and Paul didn't hate one another. They'd sat down, calmly divided their possessions, and decided what was best for the children. But what choice did Paul have? She'd made it clear the marriage was over. The subject was not open to debate. He'd tried hard to talk her out of it, but she was determined.

How many times had she asked herself the same question? Had she done the right thing? How many times had she come to the same conclusion?

Who knows?

Knoll arrived at her room, and she followed him to a quaint stone building that he explained had once been a staging inn, now transformed into a restaurant.

"How do you know that?" she asked.

"I inquired earlier when I stopped by to see how late it stayed open."

The inside was a Gothic stone crypt with vaulted ceilings, stained-glass windows, and wrought-iron lanterns. Knoll commandeered one of the trestle tables on the far side. Two hours had passed since they arrived in Warthberg. She'd taken the time for a quick bath and a change of clothes. Her escort had changed, too. Jeans and boots replaced by wool slacks, a colorful sweater, and tan leather shoes.

"What did you do after you left earlier?" she asked as they sat down.

"Purchased what we will need tomorrow. Flashlights, a shovel, bolt cutter, two jackets. It will be chilly inside the mountain. I noticed that you wore a pair of ankle boots today. Wear them tomorrow—you will need good footing."

"You act like you've done this before."

"Several times. But we have to be careful. No one is supposed to venture into the mines without a permit. The government controls access to keep people from blowing themselves up."

"I assume we're not worrying with permits?"

"Hardly. That's why it took so long. I bought from several merchants. Not enough in one place to draw attention."

A waiter sauntered over and took their orders. Knoll ordered a bottle of wine, a vigorous red the waiter insisted was local.

"How do you like your adventure so far?" he asked.

"Beats the courtroom."

She glanced around the intimate eatery. About twenty others were scattered at the tables. Mainly twosomes. One foursome. "You think we'll find what we're looking for?"

"Very good," he said.

She was perplexed. "What do you mean?"

"No mention of our goal."

"I assumed you wouldn't want to advertise our intentions."

"You assume right. And I doubt it."

"Still don't trust what you heard this morning?"

"It's not that I don't trust. I have just heard it all before."

"But not from my father."

"Your father isn't the one leading us."

"You still think Chapaev lied?"

The waiter brought their wine and food orders. Knoll's was a steaming slab of pork, hers a roasted chicken, both with potatoes and salad. She was impressed with the fast service.

"How about I reserve judgment until in the morning," Knoll said. "Give the old man the benefit of the doubt, as you Americans say."

She smiled. "I think that'd be a good idea."

Knoll gestured to dinner. "Shall we eat and talk about more pleasant matters?"

After dinner Knoll led her back to the Goldene Krone. It was nearly 10 P.M., yet the sky was still backlit, the evening air like fall in north Georgia.

"I do have a question," she said. "If we find the Amber Room, how will you keep the Russian government from reclaiming the panels?"

"There are legal avenues available. The panels have been abandoned for more than fifty years. Possession surely will count for something. Besides, the Russians may not even want them back. They have re-created the room with new amber and new technology."

"I didn't know that."

"The room in the Catherine Palace has been recrafted. It has taken over two decades. The loss of the Baltic states, when the Soviet Union collapsed, meant they were forced to buy the amber on the open market. That proved expensive. But benefactors donated money. Ironically, a German manufacturing concern made the largest contribution."

"All the more reason why they'd want the panels back. The originals would be far more precious than copies."

"I don't think so. The amber would be of different color and quality. It would not work to mix those pieces."

"So the panels would not be intact, if found?"

He shook his head. "The amber was originally glued to slabs of solid oak with a mastic of beeswax and tree sap. The Catherine Palace was hardly temperature controlled, so as the wood expanded and contracted for over two hundred years, the amber progressively fell off. When the Nazis stole them, almost thirty percent had already dropped off. It is estimated that another fifteen percent was lost during transport to Königsberg. So all there would be now is a pile of pieces."

"Then what good are they?"

He grinned. "Photographs exist. If you have the pieces, it would not be difficult to reassemble the whole room. My hope is that the Nazis packed them well, since my employer is not interested in re-creations. The original is what matters."

"Sounds like an interesting man."

He smiled. "Nice try . . . again. But I never said *he*."

They arrived at the hotel. Upstairs, at her room, Knoll stopped outside her door.

"How early in the morning?" she asked.

"We'll leave at seven-thirty. The clerk downstairs says breakfast is available after seven. The area we seek is not far, about ten kilometers."

"I appreciate everything you've done. Not to mention saving my life."

Knoll tipped his head. "My pleasure."

She smiled at the gesture.

"You've mentioned your husband, but no one else. Is there a man in your life?"

The question came suddenly. A bit too fast. "No." She instantly regretted her honesty.

"Your heart still longs for your ex-husband, doesn't it?"

Not any of this man's business, but for some reason she wanted to answer. "Sometimes."

"Does he know?"

"Sometimes."

"How long has it been?"

"Since what?"

"Since you made love to a man."

His gaze lingered longer than she expected. This man was intuitive, and it bothered her. "Not long enough that I'd hop in bed with a total stranger."

Knoll smiled. "Perhaps that stranger could help your heart forget?"

"I don't think that's what I need. But thanks for the offer." She inserted her key and opened the lock, then glanced back. "I think this is the first time I've ever actually been propositioned."

"And surely not the last." He bowed his head and smiled. "Good night, Rachel." And he walked off, toward the staircase and his own room.

But something grabbed her attention.

Interesting how rebukes seemed to challenge him.

THIRTY

SUNDAY, MAY 18, 7:30 A.M.

KNOLL EXITED THE HOTEL AND STUDIED THE MORNING. A COTton fog wrapped the quiet village and surrounding valley. The sky was gloomy, a late-spring sun straining hard to warm the day. Rachel leaned against the car, apparently ready. He walked over. "The fog will help conceal our visit. Being Sunday is good, too. Most people are in church."

They climbed into the car.

"I thought you said this was a bastion of paganism," she said.

"That's for the tourist brochures and travel guides. Lots of

Catholics live in these mountains, and have for centuries. They are a religious people."

The Volvo snarled to life, and he quickly navigated out of Warthberg, the cobbled streets nearly deserted and damp from a morning chill. The road east from town wound up and then down into another fog-draped valley.

"This area reminds me even more of the Great Smoky Mountains in North Carolina," Rachel said. "They're veiled like this, too."

He followed the map Chapaev provided and wondered if this was a wild goose chase. How could tons of amber stay hidden for more than half a century? Many had looked. Some had even died. He was well aware of the so-called curse of the Amber Room. But what harm could there be in a quick look into one more mountain? At least the journey would be interesting, thanks to Rachel Cutler.

Over a crest in the road they dropped back into another valley, thick stands of misty beech towering on either side. He came to where Chapaev's road map ended and parked in a pocket of woods. He said, "The rest of the way is on foot."

They climbed out and he retrieved a caver's pack from the trunk.

"What's in there?" Rachel asked.

"What we require." He slid the shoulder straps on. "Now we are merely a couple of hikers, out for the day."

He handed her a jacket. "Hang on to it. You're going to need it once we're underground."

He'd donned his jacket in the hotel room, the stiletto sheathed on his right arm beneath the nylon sleeve. He led the way into the forest, and the grassy terrain rose as they moved north from the highway. They followed a defined trail that wound the base of a tall range, while offshoots traced paths higher along wooded slopes toward the summits. Dark entrances to three shafts loomed in the distance. One was chained shut with an iron gate, a sign—GEFAHR-ZUTRITT VERBOTEN-EXPLOSIV—posted on the rough granite.

"What does that say?" Rachel asked.

"Danger. No Admittance. Explosives."

"You weren't kidding about that."

"These mountains were like bank vaults. The Allies found the German national treasury in one. Four hundred tons of art from Berlin's Kaiser Friedrich Museum was stashed here, too. The explosives were better than troops and watch dogs."

"Is some of that art what Wayland McKoy's after?" she asked.

"From what you told me, yes."

"You think he'll have any luck?"

"Hard to say. But I seriously doubt millions of dollars in old canvases are still waiting around here to be found."

The smell of damp leaves was thick in the heavy air.

"What was the point?" Rachel asked as they walked. "The war was lost. Why hide all that stuff?"

"You have to think like a German in 1945. Hitler ordered the army to fight to the last man or be executed. He believed if Germany held out long enough the Allies would eventually join him against the Bolsheviks. Hitler knew how much Churchill hated Stalin. He also read Stalin correctly and accurately predicted what the Soviets had in mind for Europe. Hitler thought Germany could remain intact by playing off the Soviets. He reasoned the Americans and the British would eventually join him against the Communists. Then, all those treasures could be saved."

"Foolishness," Rachel said.

"Madness is a better description."

Sweat beaded on his brow. His leather boots were stained from dew. He stopped and surveyed the various shaft entrances in the distance, along with the sky. "None point east. Chapaev said the opening faced east. And according to him it should be marked BCR-65."

He moved deeper into the trees. Ten minutes later, Rachel pointed and yelled, "There."

He stared ahead. Through the trees, another shaft entrance was visible, the opening barred by iron. A rusty sign affixed to the bars read BCR-65. He checked the sun. East.

Son of a bitch.

They approached close and he slid off the cave pack. He glanced around. No one was in sight, and no sounds disturbed the silence beyond the birds and an occasional rustle from fox squirrels. He examined the bars and gate. All the iron was purpled from heavy oxidation. A steel chain and hasp lock held the gate firmly shut. The chain and lock were definitely newer. Nothing unusual, though. German federal inspectors routinely resecured the shafts. He slipped bolt cutters from the cave pack.

"Nice to see you're prepared," Rachel said.

He snapped the chain and it slinked to the ground. He slid the cutters back into the pack and pulled open the gate.

The hinges screamed.

He stopped. No use attracting unnecessary attention.

He worked the gate open slowly, the tear of metal on metal quieter. Ahead was an arched opening about five meters high and four meters wide. Lichens clung to the blackened stone beyond the entrance and the stale air reeked of mold. Like a grave, he thought. "This opening is wide enough to accept a truck."

"Truck?"

"If the Amber Room is inside, so are trucks. There is no other way the crates could have been transported. Twenty tons of amber is heavy. The Germans would have driven trucks into the cave."

"They didn't have forklifts?"

"Hardly. We're talking about the end of the war. The Nazis were desperate to hide their treasure. No time for finesse."

"How did the trucks get up here?"

"Fifty years have passed. There were many roads and fewer trees then. This whole area was a vital manufacturing site."

He pulled two flashlights and a thick coil of twine from his pack, then reshouldered it. He closed the gate behind them and draped the chain and lock back across the bars, providing the appearance that the opening was still bolted shut.

"We might have company," he said. "That should keep people moving to another cavern. Many are unobstructed, much easier to enter."

He handed her a flashlight. Their two narrow beams pierced only meters ahead in the forbidding blackness. A piece of rusted iron protruded from the rock. He tied the end of the twine securely and handed the coil to Rachel.

"Unravel it on the way in. This is how we'll find our way out if we get disoriented."

He cautiously led the way forward, their flashlights revealing a rugged passage deep into the bowels of the mountain. Rachel followed him after slipping on her jacket.

"Be careful," he said. "This tunnel could be mined. That would explain the chaining."

"Comforting to know."

"Nothing worth having is ever easy to obtain."

He stopped and glanced back toward the entrance forty meters behind them. The air had turned fetid and cold. He fished Chapaev's drawing from his pocket and studied the route with the flashlight. "There should be a fork ahead. Let's see if Chapaev is right."

A suffocating pall permeated the air. Rotten. Nauseating.

"Bat guano," he said.

"I think I'm going to vomit."

"Breathe shallow and try to ignore it."

"That's like trying to ignore cow manure on your upper lip."

"These shafts are full of bats."

"Lovely."

He grinned. "In China, bats are revered as the symbol of happiness and long life."

"Happiness stinks."

A fork in the tunnel appeared. He stopped. "The map says to go right." He did. Rachel followed, the twine unraveling behind her.

"Let me know if you get to the end of the coil. I have more," he said.

The odor lessened. The new tunnel was tighter than the main shaft, yet still large enough for a transport truck. Dark capillaries branched off periodically. The echo of chirping bats, waiting for night, loomed clear.

The mountain was most certainly a labyrinth. They all were. Miners in search of ore and salt had burrowed for centuries. How wonderful it would be if this shaft turned out to be the one that led to the Amber Room. Ten million euros. All his. Not to mention Monika's gratitude. Perhaps then Rachel Cutler would be sufficiently excited to let him into her pants. Her rebuke last night had been more arousing than insulting. He wouldn't be surprised if her ex-husband was the only man she'd ever been with. And that thought was intoxicating. Nearly a virgin. Certainly one since her divorce. What a pleasure having her was going to be.

The shaft started to narrow and rise.

His mind snapped back to the tunnel.

They were at least a hundred meters into the granite and limestone. Chapaev's diagram showed another fork ahead.

"I'm out of string," Rachel said.

He stopped and handed her a new coil.

"Tie the ends tight."

He studied the diagram. Supposedly their destination was just ahead. But something wasn't right. The tunnel was not wide enough now for a vehicle. If the Amber Room had been hidden here, it would have been necessary to carry the crates. Eighteen, if he remembered correctly. All cataloged and indexed, the panels wrapped in cigarette paper. Was there another chamber ahead? Nothing unusual for rooms to be carved out of the rock. Nature did some. Others were man-made. According to Chapaev, slabs of rock and silt blocked a doorway to one such chamber twenty meters ahead.

He walked on, careful with each step. The deeper into the mountain, the higher the risk of explosives. His flashlight beam broke the darkness ahead, and his eyes focused on something.

He stared hard.

What the hell?

⚜━━

SUZANNE RAISED THE BINOCULARS AND STUDIED THE ENTRANCE to the mine. The sign she'd attached to the iron gate three years ago, BCR-65, was still there. The ploy seemed to have worked. Knoll was getting careless. He'd raced straight to the mine, Rachel Cutler in tow. It was a shame things had come to this, but little choice remained. Knoll was certainly interesting. Exciting even. But he was a problem. A big problem. Her loyalty to Ernst Loring was absolute. Beyond reproach. She owed Loring everything. He was the family she'd never been allowed. All her life the old man had treated her as a daughter, their relationship perhaps closer than the one he possessed with his two natural sons, their love of precious art the glue bonding them to one another. He'd been so excited when she gave him the snuffbox and the book. Pleasing him gave her a sense of satisfaction. So a choice between Christian Knoll and her benefactor was simply no choice at all.

Still, it was too bad. Knoll had his good points.

She stood on the forested ridge undisguised, her blond hair looped to her shoulders, a turtleneck sweater wrapping her chest. She lowered the binoculars and reached for the radio controller, extending the retractable antenna.

Knoll obviously hadn't sensed her presence, thinking he'd rid himself of her in the Atlanta airport.

Not hardly, Christian.

A flick of a switch and the detonator activated.

She checked her watch.

Knoll and his damsel should be deep inside by now. More than enough distance to never get out. The authorities repeatedly warned the public about exploring the caverns. Explosives were common. Many had died through the years, which was why the government started licensing exploration. Three years ago there'd been an explosion in this same shaft, arranged by her when a Polish reporter crept too close. She'd lured him with visions of the Amber Room, the accident ultimately attributed to another unauthorized exploration, the body never found, buried under the rubble that Christian Knoll should be studying right about now.

KNOLL EXAMINED THE WALL OF ROCK AND SAND. HE'D SEEN A tunnel end before. This wasn't a natural cessation. An explosion had caused what lay before him, and there was no way to shovel through the ceiling-to-floor debris.

And there was no iron door on the other side, either.

That much he knew.

"What is it?" Rachel asked.

"There was an explosion here."

"Maybe we made a wrong turn?"

"Not possible. I followed Chapaev's directions precisely."

Something was definitely wrong. His mind reeled off the facts. Chapaev's information offered with no resistance. The chain and lock newer than the gate. The iron hinges still working. The trail easy to follow. Too damn easy.

And Suzanne Danzer? In Atlanta? Maybe not.

The best thing to do was head back to the entrance, enjoy Rachel Cutler, then get out of Warthberg. He'd planned to kill her all along. No need to have a live source of information available for another Acquisitor to tap. Danzer was already on the trail. So it was only a matter of time before she tracked down Rachel and talked to her, perhaps learning about Chapaev. Monika wouldn't like that. Maybe Chapaev really did know where the Amber Room lay but had intentionally led them on this chase. So he decided to get rid of Rachel Cutler here and now, then head back to Kehlheim and squeeze information from Chapaev, one way or the other.

"Let's go," he said. "Roll up the string back to the entrance. I'll follow."

They started back through the maze, Rachel leading the way. His light revealed her firm ass and shapely thighs through tan jeans. He studied her slender legs and narrow shoulders. His groin started to respond.

The first fork appeared, then the second.

"Wait," he said. "I want to see what's down here."

"This way is out," she said, pointing left toward the string.

"I know. But while we're here. Let's see. Leave the string. We know the way from here."

She tossed the twine ball down and turned right, still leading the way.

He flicked his right arm. The stiletto released and slid down. He palmed the handle.

Rachel stopped and turned back, her light momentarily on him.

His light caught her shocked face as she saw the glistening blade.

⚷━ ▪

SUZANNE POINTED THE RADIO CONTROLLER AND PRESSED THE button. The signal sped through the morning air to the explosive charges she'd set in the rock last night. Not enough of an explosion to draw attention from Warthberg, six kilometers away, but more than enough to bring the mountain down inside.

Ending another problem.

⚷━ ▪

THE GROUND SHOOK. THE CEILING CRUMBLED. KNOLL TRIED TO steady himself.

Now he knew. It *was* a trap.

He turned and raced toward the entrance. Rock cascaded in a shower of stone and blinding dust. The air fouled. He held the flashlight in one hand, stiletto in the other. He quickly pocketed the knife and yanked his shirt out, using the clean hem to shield his nose and mouth.

More rock rained down.

The light toward the entrance ahead grew dusty and thick, veiled in a cloud, then obliterated behind boulders. It was now impossible to go that way.

He turned again and darted in the opposite direction, hoping there was another way out of the maze. Thankfully, his flashlight still worked. Rachel Cutler was nowhere to be seen. But it didn't matter. The rocks had saved him the trouble.

He raced deeper into the mountain, down the main shaft, past the point where he last saw her standing. The explosions seemed to have centered behind him, the walls and ceiling ahead stable, though the entire mountain now vibrated.

More rock pounded onto itself behind him. Definitely only one way to go now. A fork appeared in the shaft. He stopped and oriented himself. The original entrance behind him had faced east. So west lay ahead. The left fork appeared to go south, the right north. But, who knows? He had to be careful. Not too many turns. It would be easy to get lost, and he didn't want to die wandering underground until he either starved or dehydrated.

He lowered his shirttail and sucked in a lungful of air. He tried to recall what he could about the mines. Never was there only one way in or out. The sheer depth and extent of the tunnels demanded multiple entrances. During the war, though, the Nazis sealed off most of the portals, trying to secure their hiding places. He now hoped this mine wasn't one of those. What encouraged him was the air. Not as stale as when they were deeper inside.

He raised his hand. A slight breeze drifted from the left fork. Should he take the chance? Too many more turns and he'd never find his way back. Total darkness possessed no reference points, his present position known only because of the main shaft's orientation. But he could easily lose that frame of reference with a couple of indiscriminate moves.

What should he do?

He stepped left.

Fifty meters and the tunnel forked again. He held up his hand. No breeze. He recalled reading once that the miners designed their safety routes all in the same direction. One left turn meant all left turns until you were out. What choice did he have? Go left.

Two more forks. Two more lefts.

A shaft of light appeared ahead. Faint. But there. He scurried forward and turned the corner.

Daylight loomed a hundred meters away.

THIRTY-ONE

KEHLHEIM, GERMANY
11:30 A.M.

PAUL GLANCED IN THE REARVIEW MIRROR. A CAR RAPIDLY APproached, its lights flashing and siren hee-hawing. The green-and-white compact, POLIZEI on the doors in blue letters, zoomed past in the opposite lane and disappeared around a bend.

He drove on, entering Kehlheim ten kilometers later.

The quiet village was littered with brightly painted buildings that ringed a cobbled square. He wasn't much of a traveler. Only one trip overseas to Paris two years ago for the museum—a chance to tour the Louvre had been too enticing to pass up. He'd asked Rachel to go with him. She'd refused. Not a good idea for an ex-wife, he remembered her saying. He was never quite sure what she meant, though he sincerely thought she would have liked to go.

He'd been unable to get a flight out of Atlanta until yesterday afternoon, taking the children to his brother's house early in the morning. The lack of a call from Rachel worried him. But he'd not checked the answering machine since

9 A.M. yesterday. His flight was protracted by stops in Amsterdam and Frankfurt, which didn't get him into Munich until two hours ago. He'd cleaned up the best he could in an airport bathroom, but could definitely use a shower, shave, and change of clothes.

He cruised into the town square and parked in front of what appeared to be a grocery market. Bavaria obviously wasn't a Sunday place. All the buildings were closed down. The only activity was centered near the church, whose steeple was the highest point in the village. Parked cars hunched in tight rows across uneven cobbles. A group of older men stood on the church steps talking. Beards, dark coats, and hats predominated. He should have brought a jacket himself, but he'd packed in a hurry with only the essentials.

He walked over. "Excuse me. Any of you speak English?"

One man, seemingly the oldest of the four said, "*Ja.* A little."

"I'm looking for a man named Danya Chapaev. I understand he lives here."

"Not anymore. Dead now."

He was afraid of that. Chapaev had to have been old. "When did he die?"

"Last night. Killed."

Had he heard right? Killed? Last night? His greatest fear welled up inside him. The question immediately formed in his mind. "Was anyone else hurt?"

"*Nein.* Just Danya."

He remembered the police car. "Where did this happen?"

He motored out of Kehlheim and followed the proffered directions. The house appeared ten minutes later, easy to spot with four police cars angled in front. A uniformed, stone-faced man stood guard at the open front door. Paul approached, but was stopped immediately.

"*Nicht eintreten. Kriminelle szene,*" the policeman said.

"English, please."

"No entrance. Crime scene."

"Then I need to speak to the person in charge."

"I'm in charge," a voice said from inside, the English laced with a guttural German accent.

The man who approached the front doorway was middle-aged. Tufts of unruly black hair crowned a craggy face. A dark blue overcoat draped his thin frame down to the knees, an olive suit and knit tie showing underneath.

"I am Fritz Pannik. Inspector with the federal police. And you?"

"Paul Cutler. A lawyer from the United States."

Pannik brushed past the door guard. "What is a lawyer from America doing here on a Sunday morning?"

"Looking for my ex-wife. She came to see Danya Chapaev."

Pannik cut a look at the policeman.

He noticed the curious expression. "What is it?"

"A woman was asking directions to this house yesterday in Kehlheim. She is a suspect in this murder."

"You have a description?"

Pannik reached into his coat pocket and withdrew a notepad. He flipped open the leather flap. "Medium height. Reddish-blond hair. Big breasts. Jeans. Flannel shirt. Boots. Sunglasses. Hefty."

"That's not Rachel. But it could be somebody else."

He quickly told Pannik about Jo Myers, Karol Borya, and the Amber Room, describing his female visitor as she appeared. Thin, moderately chested, chestnut hair, blue eyes, a pair of octagonal gold frames. "I got the impression the hair wasn't hers. Call it lawyer intuition."

"But she read the letters Chapaev and this Karol Borya sent to one another?"

"Thoroughly."

"Did the envelopes note this location on them?"

"Only the town name."

"Is there more to the story?"

He told the inspector about Christian Knoll, Jo Myers's concerns, and his own.

"And you came to warn your ex-wife?" Pannik asked.

"More to see if she was okay. I should have come with her in the first place."

"But you considered her trip a waste of time?"

"Absolutely. Her father expressly asked her not to get involved." Beyond Pannik's shoulders, two policemen moved about inside. "What happened in there?"

"If you have the stomach, I'll show you."

"I'm a lawyer," he said, as if that meant anything. He didn't mention that he'd never handled a criminal case in his life and had never visited a crime scene before. But curiosity drove him. First Borya dead, now Chapaev murdered. But Karol had fallen down the stairs.

Or had he?

He followed Pannik inside. The warm room carried a peculiar, sickeningly sweet odor. Mystery novels always talked about the smell of death. Was that it?

The house was small. Four rooms. A den, kitchen, bedroom, and bath. From what he could see the furniture was old and tattered, yet the place was clean and cozy, the tranquillity shattered by the sight of an old man sprawled across a threadbare carpet, a large splotch of crimson leading from two holes in the skull.

"Shot point-blank," Pannik said.

His eyes were riveted on the corpse. Bile started to rise in his throat. He fought the urge, but to no avail.

He rushed from the room.

He was bent over, retching. The little bit he'd eaten on the plane was now puddled on the damp grass. He took a few deep breaths and got hold of himself.

"Finished?" Pannik asked.

He nodded. "You think the woman did that?"

"I don't know. All I know is that a female asked where Chapaev lived, and the grandson offered to show her the way. They left the marketplace together yesterday morning. The old man's daughter got concerned last night when the

boy did not come home. She came over and found the boy
tied up in the bedroom. Apparently the woman had a problem killing children, but didn't mind shooting an old man."

"The boy okay?"

"Shook up, but all right. He confirmed the description, but
could offer little more. He was in the other room. He re-
members hearing voices talking. But he couldn't determine
any of the conversation. Then his papa and the woman came
in for a moment. They spoke in another language. I tried a
few sample words, and it appears they were speaking Russian. Then the old man and the woman left the room. He
heard a shot. Silence after that till his mother arrived a few
hours later."

"She shot the man square in the head?"

"At close range, too. The stakes must be high."

A policeman walked from inside. *"Nichts im haus hin-
sichtlich des Bernstein-zimmer."*

Pannik looked at him. "I had them search the house for
anything on the Amber Room. There's nothing there."

A radio crackled from the hip of the German standing
guard at the front door. The man slipped the transmitter from
his waist, then approached Pannik. In English the policeman
said, "I have to go. A call has come for search and rescue.
I'm on duty this weekend."

"What's happened?" Pannik asked.

"Explosion in one of the mines near Warthberg. An
American woman has been pulled out, but they're still
searching for a man. Local authorities have requested our
help."

Pannik shook his head. "A busy Sunday."

"Where's Warthberg?" Paul immediately asked.

"In the Harz Mountains. Four hundred kilometers to the
north. They sometimes use our Alpine rescue teams when
there are mishaps."

Wayland McKoy and Karol's interest in the Harz Mountains flashed through his mind. "An American woman was
found? What's her name?"

Pannik seemed to sense the point of the inquiry and turned

to the officer. Words passed between them, and the officer talked back into the radio.

Two minutes later, the words came through the speaker: *"Die frau ist Rachel Cutler. Amerikanerin."*

THIRTY-TWO

3:10 P.M.

THE POLICE CHOPPER KNIFED NORTH THROUGH THE MAY AFTERnoon. Past Würzburg it started to rain. Paul sat next to Pannik, a team of search-and-rescue personnel strapped in behind them.

"A group of hikers heard the explosions and alerted authorities," Pannik said over the roar of the turbine. "Your ex-wife was pulled out near an entrance to one of the shafts. She's been taken to a local hospital, but managed to tell her rescuers about the man. His name is Christian Knoll, Herr Cutler."

He listened with great concern. But all he could see was Rachel lying in a hospital, bleeding. What was going on? What had Rachel gotten into? How had Knoll found her? What happened in that mine? Were Marla and Brent in any danger? He needed to call his brother and alert him.

"Seems Jo Myers was right," Pannik said.

"Did the reports mention Rachel's condition?"

Pannik shook his head.

The helicopter flew first to the scene of the explosion— the mine entrance was deep in the forest at the base of one of the higher mounds. The nearest clearing opened a half kilometer to the west, and the rescue personnel were deposited there to hike back. He and Pannik remained in the chopper and flew east of Warthberg to a regional hospital, where Rachel had been taken.

Inside, he headed straight for her fourth-floor room. Rachel was dressed in a blue gown. A large bandage lay across her scalp. She smiled from the bed when she saw him. "Why did I know you'd be here?"

He stepped closer. Her cheeks, nose, and arms were scraped and bruised. "I didn't have much else to do this weekend, so why not a trip to Germany."

"The children okay?"

"They're fine."

"How did you get here so fast?"

"I left yesterday."

"Yesterday?"

Before he could explain, Pannik, standing quiet at the door, stepped closer. "Frau Cutler, I'm Inspector Fritz Pannik, federal police."

Paul told Rachel about Jo Myers, Christian Knoll, and what happened to Danya Chapaev.

Shock invaded Rachel's face. "Chapaev's dead?"

"I need to call my brother," Paul said to Pannik, "and have him watch the kids closely. Maybe even alert the Atlanta police."

"You think they're in danger?" she asked.

"I don't know what to think, Rachel. You've got yourself into something really bad. Your father warned you to stay out of this."

"What do you mean?"

"Don't play coy. I can read Ovid. He wanted you to stay the hell out of this. Now Chapaev is dead."

Her face tightened. "That's not fair, Paul. I didn't do that. I didn't know."

"But perhaps you pointed the way," Pannik made clear.

Rachel stared at the inspector, the realization clear on her face. Suddenly, Paul regretted chastising her. He wanted to help shoulder the blame, like always. "That's not entirely true," he said. "I showed the woman the letters. She learned about Kehlheim from me."

"And would you have done that if you did not think Frau Cutler to be in danger?"

No, he wouldn't have. He looked at Rachel. Tears welled in her eyes.

"Paul's right, Inspector. It's my fault. I wouldn't leave well enough alone. He and my father warned me."

"What of this Christian Knoll?" Pannik asked. "Tell me about him."

Rachel reported what she knew, which wasn't much. Then she said, "The man saved me from getting run down by a car. He was charming and courteous. I sincerely thought he wanted to help."

"What happened in the mine?" Pannik asked.

"We were following Chapaev's map. The tunnel was fairly wide, and all of a sudden it felt like an earthquake and an avalanche bisected the shaft. I turned back toward the entrance and started running. I only made it about halfway when the rocks knocked me down. Luckily, I wasn't buried. I lay there till some hikers came in and got me."

"And Knoll?" Pannik asked.

She shook her head. "I called out to him after the cave-in stopped, but nothing."

"He's probably still in there," Pannik said.

"Was it an earthquake?" Paul asked.

"We have no earthquakes here. Probably explosives from the war. The shafts are full of them."

"Knoll said the same thing," Rachel said.

The hospital room door opened, and a stocky policeman motioned to Pannik. The inspector excused himself and stepped outside.

"You're right," Rachel said. "I should have listened."

He wasn't interested in her concessions. "We need to get out of here and back home."

Rachel said nothing, and he was about to press the point when Pannik returned.

"The shaft has been cleared. No one else was found inside. There was another entrance, unblocked, out a far tunnel. How did you and Herr Knoll get to the mine?"

"We drove a rental car, then hiked."

"What kind of car?"

"A maroon Volvo."

"No car was found at the highway," Pannik said. "This Knoll is gone."

The inspector seemed to know something more. Paul asked, "What else did that policeman tell you?"

"That shaft was never used by the Nazis. No explosives were inside. Yet this is the second explosion there in three years."

"Meaning what?"

"Meaning something quite strange is going on."

Paul left the hospital and hitched a ride in a police car to Warthberg. Pannik tagged along. Being a federal inspector gave him certain rank and privileges.

"Similar to your FBI," Pannik said. "I work for the nationwide police force. The locals cooperate with us all the time."

Rachel told them Knoll rented two rooms in the Goldene Krone. Pannik's badge gained immediate access to Rachel's room, which was tidy, bed made, suitcase gone. Knoll's room was empty, too. No maroon Volvo anywhere in sight.

"Herr Knoll left this morning," the hotel proprietor said. "Paid for both rooms and left."

"What time?"

"Around ten-thirty."

"You didn't hear about the explosion?"

"There are many explosions in the mines, Inspector. I don't pay much attention to who is involved."

"Did you see Knoll return this morning?" Pannik asked.

The man shook his balding head. They thanked the proprietor and stepped outside.

Paul said to Pannik, "Knoll's got a five-hour head start, but maybe the car could be spotted by a bulletin."

"Herr Knoll doesn't interest me. The most he's done right now is trespass."

"He left Rachel to die in that mine."

"That's no crime either. The woman is the one I seek. A murderess."

Pannik was right. But he realized the inspector's quandary. No accurate description. No real name. No physical evidence. No background. No nothing.

"Any idea where to look?" he asked.

Pannik stared out at the quiet village square. *"Nein,* Herr Cutler. Not a one."

THIRTY-THREE

CASTLE LOUKOV, CZECH REPUBLIC
5:10 P.M.

SUZANNE ACCEPTED THE PEWTER GOBLET FROM ERNST LORING and wedged herself comfortably into an Empire chair. Her employer seemed pleased with the report.

She said, "I waited a half hour at the scene and left when the authorities started to arrive. No one emerged from the mine shaft."

"I will check with Fellner tomorrow on the pretense of something else. Perhaps he will say if something happened to Christian."

She sipped her wine, pleased with the day's activity. She'd driven straight from central Germany to Czech, crossing the border and speeding south to Loring's castle estate. The three hundred kilometers had been an easy two-and-a-half-hour trek in the Porsche.

"Very clever, maneuvering Christian like that," Loring said. "He is a difficult one to lead."

"He was too eager. But I have to say, Chapaev was quite convincing." She sipped more wine. The fruity vintage was

Loring's own. "A shame. The old man was dedicated. He'd kept quiet a long time. Unfortunately, I had no choice but to silence him."

"It was good to leave the child unharmed."

"I don't kill children. He knew nothing more than what the other witnesses at the market would report. He was my leverage to get the old man to do what I wanted."

Loring's face bore a heavy, tired look. "I wonder when it will end. Every few years we seem forced to tend to this matter."

"I read the letters. Leaving Chapaev around would have been an unnecessary risk. More loose ends that would eventually have led to problems."

"Regretfully, *drahá,* you are right."

"Were you able to learn anything more from St. Petersburg?"

"Only that Christian was definitely in the Commission records again. He noticed Father's name on a document Knoll was reading, but it was gone when he checked after Knoll left."

"Good thing Knoll is no longer a problem. With Borya and Chapaev gone, things should now be secure."

"I am afraid not," Loring said. "There is another problem."

She set her wine aside. "What?"

"An excavation has started near Stod. An American entrepreneur looking for treasure."

"People don't give up, do they?"

"The lure is too intoxicating. Hard to say for sure if this latest venture is in the right cavern. Unfortunately, there is no way to know until the cavern is explored. All I know is that he is in the generally correct area."

"We have a source?"

"Directly on the inside. He has kept me informed, but even he doesn't know for sure. Unfortunately, Father kept that precise information close to himself . . . not even trusting his son."

"You want me to travel there?"

"Please. Keep an eye on things. My source is reliable, but greedy. He demands too much and, as you know, greed is something I cannot tolerate. He's expecting contact from a woman. My personal secretary has been the only one to talk with him so far, and only by telephone. The source knows nothing of me. He will know you by Margarethe. If anything is found, make sure the situation stays contained. No trail leading out. If the location is unrelated, forget it, and, if need be, eliminate the source. But, please, let's try to minimize the killing."

She knew what he meant. "I had no choice with Chapaev."

"I understand, *drahá,* and I appreciate the efforts. Hopefully, that death will be the end of the so-called curse of the Amber Room."

"Along with two more."

The old man grinned. "Christian and Rachel Cutler?"

She nodded.

"I believe you are pleased with your efforts. Strange, I thought I sensed a hesitancy the other day regarding Christian. Maybe a small attraction?"

She lifted the goblet and toasted her employer. "Nothing I can't live without."

⚜

KNOLL SPED SOUTH TOWARD FÜSSEN. THERE WERE TOO MANY police in and around Kehlheim to stay the night there. He'd fled Warthberg and returned south to the Alps to talk with Danya Chapaev, only to learn the old man had been murdered during the night. The police were searching for a woman who'd asked directions to the house yesterday and left the marketplace with Chapaev's grandson. Her identity was unknown. But not to him.

Suzanne Danzer.

Who else? Somehow she'd picked up the trail and beat him to Chapaev. All that information Chapaev had freely provided came from her. No question about it. He'd been sucked into a trap and nearly killed.

He recalled what Juvenal said in his *Satires. Revenge is the delight of a mean spirit and petty mind. Proof of this is no one rejoices more in revenge than a woman.*

Right. But he preferred Byron. *Men love in haste but detest at leisure.*

There'd be hell to pay when their paths crossed again. Bloody damn painful hell. Next time he'd have the advantage. He'd be ready.

The narrow streets of Füssen overflowed with spring tourists drawn by Ludwig's castle south of town. It was an easy matter to blend into the evening rush of revelers searching for dinner and spirits in the busy cafés. He paused for a half hour and ate in one of the least crowded, listening to delightful chamber music echoing from a spring concert across the street. After, he found a phone booth near his hotel and called Burg Herz. Franz Fellner answered.

"I heard about an explosion in the mountains today. A woman was pulled out, and they are still looking for the man."

"I won't be found," he said. "It was a trap." He told Fellner what happened from the time he left Atlanta to the moment he learned of Chapaev's murder a little while ago. "Interesting that Rachel Cutler may have survived. But it does not matter. She'll surely head back to Atlanta."

"You are sure Suzanne is involved?"

"Somehow she got ahead of me."

Fellner chuckled. "Perhaps you are getting old, Christian?"

"I was not careful enough."

"Cocksure is a better explanation," Monika suddenly said. She was obviously on an extension.

"I wondered where you were."

"Your mind was probably on how you were going to fuck her."

"How fortunate I am to have you to remind me of all my shortcomings."

Monika laughed. "Half the fun of all this, Christian, is watching you work."

He said, "It appears this trail is now frozen. Perhaps I should move on to other acquisitions?"

"Tell him, child," Fellner said.

"An American, Wayland McKoy, is excavating near Stod. Claims he's going to find the Berlin museum art, maybe the Amber Room. He's done this before with some success. Check it out just to be sure. At the very least you might pick up some good information, maybe a new acquisition."

"Is this excavation well known?"

"It's in the local papers, and CNN International ran several pieces on it," Monika said.

"We were aware of it before you traveled to Atlanta," Fellner said, "but thought Borya worth an immediate inquiry."

"Is Loring interested in this new dig?" he asked.

"He seems interested in everything else we do," Monika said.

"You're hoping Suzanne will be dispatched?" Fellner asked.

"More than hoping."

"Good hunting, Christian."

"Thank you, sir, and when Loring calls to learn if I'm dead, don't disappoint him."

"Need a little anonymity?"

"It would help."

THIRTY-FOUR

WARTHBERG, GERMANY
8:45 P.M.

RACHEL STROLLED INTO THE RESTAURANT AND FOLLOWED PAUL to a table, savoring the warm air laced with a scent of cloves and garlic. She was starving and feeling better. The full bandage from the hospital had been replaced with gauze and tape to the side of her head. She wore a pair of chinos and a long-sleeved shirt Paul bought at a local store, her tattered clothes from this morning no longer wearable.

Paul had checked her out of the hospital two hours ago. She was fine except for the bump on her head and a few cuts and scrapes. She'd promised the doctor to take it easy the next couple of days, Paul telling him they were headed back to Atlanta anyway.

A waiter stepped over, and Paul asked what type of wine she'd like.

"A good red would be nice. Something local," she said, remembering last night's dinner with Knoll.

The waiter departed.

"I called the airline," Paul said. "There's a flight out of Frankfurt tomorrow. Pannik said he could arrange to get us to the airport."

"Where is the inspector?"

"Went back to Kehlheim to see about the investigation on Chapaev. He left a phone number."

"I can't believe all my stuff's gone."

"Knoll obviously wanted nothing left to trace you."

"He appeared so sincere. Charming, in fact."

Paul seemed to sense the attraction in her voice. "You liked him?"

"He was interesting. Said he was an investigator looking for the Amber Room. "

"That appeals to you?"

"Come on, Paul. Wouldn't you say that we live a mundane life? Work and home. Think about it. Traveling the world, looking for lost art—that would excite anyone."

"The man left you to die."

Her face tightened. That tone of his did it every time. "But he also saved my life in Munich."

"I should have come with you to start with."

"I don't recall inviting you." Her irritation was building. Why did it swell so easily? Paul was only trying to help.

"No, you didn't invite me. But I still should have come."

She was surprised by his reaction to Knoll. Hard to tell if he was jealous or concerned.

"We need to go home," he said. "There's nothing left here. I'm worried about the children. I can still see Chapaev's body."

"You believe the woman who came to see you killed Chapaev?"

"Who knows? But she certainly. knew where to look, thanks to me."

Now seemed the right time. "Let's stay, Paul."

"What?"

"Let's stay."

"Rachel, haven't you learned your lesson? People are dying. We need to get out of here, before it's us. You were lucky today. Don't push it. This isn't some adventure novel. This is real. And foolishness. Nazis. Russians. We're out of our league."

"Paul, Daddy must have known something. Chapaev, too. We owe it to them to try."

"Try what?"

"There's one trail left to follow. Remember Wayland McKoy. Knoll told me Stod is not far from here. He might be on to something. Daddy was interested in what he was doing."

"Leave it alone, Rachel."

"What would it hurt?"

"That's exactly what you said about finding Chapaev."

She shoved her chair back and stood. "That's not fair, and you know it." Her voice rose. "If you want to go home, go. I'm going to talk to Wayland McKoy."

A few other diners started to notice. She hoped none of them spoke English. Paul's face carried the usual look of resignation. He'd never really known what to do with her. It was another of their problems. Impetuousness was foreign to his personality. He was a meticulous planner. No detail too small. Not obsessive. Just consistent. Had he ever done a spontaneous thing in his life? Yes. He'd flown here virtually on the spur of the moment. And she was hoping that counted for something.

"Sit down, Rachel," he quietly said. "For once could we discuss something rationally?"

She sat. She wanted him to stay, but would never admit it.

"You've got an election campaign to run. Why don't you channel all this energy into that?"

"I have to do this, Paul. Something is telling me to go on."

"Rachel, in the last forty-eight hours two people have turned up out of nowhere, both looking for the same thing, one possibly a killer, the other callous enough to leave you for dead. Karol is gone. So is Chapaev. Maybe your father was murdered. You were awfully suspicious about that before coming over here."

"I still am, and that's part of this. Not to mention your parents. They may have been victims also."

She could almost hear his analytical mind working. Weighing the options. Trying to think of the next argument to convince her to come home with him.

"All right," he said. "We'll go to see McKoy."

"You serious?"

"What I am is crazy. But I don't plan to leave you alone over here."

She reached over and squeezed his hand. "You watch my back and I'll watch yours. Okay?"

He grinned. "Yeah, right."

"Daddy would be proud."

"Your father is probably turning in his grave. We're ignoring everything he wanted."

The waiter arrived with the wine and poured two glasses. She raised her glass. "To success."

He returned the toast. "Success."

She sipped the wine, pleased Paul was staying. But the vision flashed through her mind once again. What she saw as her flashlight revealed Christian Knoll the second before the explosion. A knife blade gleaming in his hand.

Yet she'd said nothing to Paul or Inspector Pannik. Easy to guess at both their reactions, especially Paul's.

She looked at her ex-husband, remembered her father and Chapaev, and thought of the children.

Was she doing the right thing?

PART THREE

THIRTY-FIVE

WAYLAND MCKOY MARCHED INTO THE CAVERN. COLD DAMP AIR enveloped him, and darkness overtook the morning light. He marveled at the ancient shaft. *Ein Silberbergwerk.* A silver mine. Once the "treasury of the Holy Roman Emperors," the earth now lay spent and abandoned, a sordid reminder of the cheap Mexican silver that drove most of the Harz's mines out of business by 1900.

The whole area was spectacular. Knots of pine-clad hills, stunted scrub, and alpine meadows, all beautiful and rugged, yet an eeriness permeated. As Goethe had said in *Faust: Where witches held their Sabbath.*

It had once been the southwestern corner of East Germany, in the dreaded forbidden zone, and stilted border posts continued to dot the forest. The minefields, shrapnel-scattering trap guns, guard dogs, and barbed-wire fences were now gone. *Wende,* unification, had put an end to the need for containing an entire population and opened opportunities. Ones he was now exploiting.

He made his way down the wide shaft. The trail was marked every thirty meters by a hundred-watt bulb, and an electrical cord snaked a path back to the generator outside. The rock face was sharp, the floor rubble strewn, the work of an initial team he'd sent in last weekend to clear the passage.

That had been the easy part. Jackhammers and air guns. No need to worry about long-lost Nazi explosives, the tunnel had been sniffed by dogs and surveyed by demolitionists. The lack of anything even remotely concerned with explosives was worrisome. If this was indeed the right mine, the one Germans used to stash the art from Berlin's Kaiser Friedrich museum, then it would almost certainly have been mined. Yet nothing had been found. Just rock, silt, sand, and thousands of bats. The nasty little bastards populated off-shoots of the main shaft during winter, and of all the species in the world, this one had to be endangered. Which ex-plained why the German government had been so hesitant about granting him an exploration permit. Luckily, the bats left the mine every May, not to return until mid-July. A pre-cious forty-five days to explore. That had been all the Ger-man government would grant. His permit required the mine be empty when the beasts returned.

The deeper he strolled into the mountain, the larger the shaft became—which also was troublesome. The normal routine was for the tunnels to narrow, eventually becoming impassable, the miners excavating until it proved impossible to burrow any farther. All the shafts were a testament to cen-turies of mining, each generation trying to better the one be-fore and uncover a vein of previously undetected ore. But for all its width, the size of this shaft still concerned him. It was simply far too narrow to stash anything as large as the loot he was searching for.

He approached his three-man work crew. Two men stood on ladders, another below, each boring holes at sixty-degree angles into the rock. Cables fed air and electricity. The genera-tors and compressors stood fifty meters behind him, outside in the morning air. Harsh, hot, blue-white lights illuminated the scene and drenched the crew in sweat.

The drills stopped and the men slipped off their ear pro-tection. He, too, slipped off his sound muffs. "Any idea how we're doin'?" he asked.

One of the men shoved fogged goggles from his eyes and mopped the perspiration on his brow. "We've moved about a foot forward today. No way to tell how much farther, and I'm afraid to jackhammer."

Another of the men reached for a jug. Slowly, he filled the drilled holes with solvent. McKoy stepped close to the wall of rock. The porous granite and limestone instantly drank in the brown syrup from each hole, the caustic chemical expanding, creating fissions in the stone. Another goggled man approached with a sledgehammer. One blow and the rock shattered in sheets, crumbling to the ground. Another few inches forward now excavated.

"Slow goin'," he said.

"But the only way to do it," came a voice from behind.

McKoy turned to see *Herr Doktor* Alfred Grumer standing in the cavern. He was tall, with spindly arms and legs, gaunt to the point of caricature, a graying Vandyke beard bracketing pencil-thin lips. Grumer was the resident expert on the dig, possessed of a degree from the University of Heidelberg in art history. McKoy had latched on to Grumer three years ago during his last venture into the Harz mines. The man boasted both expertise and greed, two attributes he not only admired but also needed in his business associates.

"We're runnin' out of time," McKoy said.

Grumer stepped close. "There's another four weeks left on your permit. We'll get through."

"Assumin' there's something to get through to."

"The chamber is there. The radar soundings confirm it."

"But how goddamned far into that rock?"

"That's hard to say. But something is in there."

"And how the hell did it get there? You said the radar soundin's confirmed multiple sizable metallic objects." He motioned back beyond the lights. "That shaft is hardly big enough for three people to walk through."

A thin grin lined Grumer's face. "You assume this is the only way in."

"And you assume I'm a bottomless money pit."

The other men reset their drills and started a new bore. McKoy drifted back into the shaft, beyond the lights, where it was cooler and quieter. Grumer followed. He said, "If we don't make some progress by tomorrow, the hell with this drillin'. We're going to dynamite."

"Your permit requires otherwise."

He ran a hand through his wet black hair. "Fuck the permit. We need progress, and fast. I've got a television crew waitin' in town that's costing me two thousand a day. And those fat-ass bureaucrats in Bonn don't have a bunch of investors flying here tomorrow, expectin' to see art."

"This cannot be rushed," Grumer said. "There is no telling what awaits behind the rock."

"There's supposed to be a huge chamber."

"There is. And it contains something."

He softened his tone. It wasn't Grumer's fault the dig was going slow. "Somethin' gave the ground radar multiple orgasms, huh?"

Grumer smiled. "A poetic way of putting it."

"You better damn well hope so or we're both screwed."

"The German word for 'cave' is *höhle*," Grumer said. "The word for 'hell' is *hölle*. I have always thought the similarity was not without significance."

"Fuckin' damn interesting, Grumer. But not the right sentiment at the moment, if you get my drift."

Grumer seemed unconcerned. As always. Another thing about this man that irritated the hell out of him.

"I came down to tell you we have visitors," Grumer said.

"Not another reporter?"

"An American lawyer and a judge."

"The lawsuits have started already?"

Grumer flashed one of his condescending grins. He wasn't in the mood. He should fire the irritating fool. But Grumer's contacts within the Ministry of Culture were too valuable to dispense with. "No lawsuits, Herr McKoy. These two speak of the Amber Room."

His face lit up.

"I thought you might be interested. They claim to have information."

"Crackpots?"

"Don't appear to be."

"What do they want?"

"To talk."

He glanced back at the wall of rock and the whining drills. "Why not? Nothing the hell goin' on here."

PAUL TURNED AS THE DOOR TO THE TINY SHED SWUNG OPEN. HE watched a grizzly bear of a man with a bull neck, thick waist, and bushy black hair enter the whitewashed room. A bulging chest and arms swelled a cotton shirt that was embroidered with MCKOY EXCAVATIONS, and an intense gaze through dark eyes immediately assessed the situation. Alfred Grumer, whom he and Rachel had met a few minutes ago, followed the man inside.

"Herr Cutler, Frau Cutler, this is Wayland McKoy," Grumer said.

"I don't want to be rude," McKoy said, "but this is a critical time around here, and I don't have a lot of time to chitchat. So what can I do for you?"

Paul decided to get to the point. "We've had an interesting last few days—"

"Which one of you is the judge?" McKoy asked.

"Me," Rachel said.

"What's a lawyer and judge from Georgia doin' in the middle of Germany bothering me?"

"Looking for the Amber Room," Rachel said.

McKoy chuckled. "Who the hell isn't?"

"You must think it's nearby, maybe even where you're digging," Rachel said.

"I'm sure you two legal eagles know that I'm not about to discuss any of the particulars of this dig with you. I have investors that demand confidentiality."

"We're not asking you to divulge anything," Paul said. "But you may find what's happened to us the past few days interesting." He told McKoy and Grumer everything that'd occurred since Karol Borya died and Rachel had been pulled from the mine.

Grumer settled down on one of the stools. "We heard about that explosion. Never found the man?"

"Nothing to find. Knoll was long gone." Paul explained what he and Pannik learned in Warthberg.

"You still haven't said what you want," McKoy said.

"You can start with some information. Who's Josef Loring?"

"A Czech industrialist," McKoy said. "He's been dead about thirty years. There was talk he found the Amber Room right after the war, but nothin' was ever verified. Another rumor for the books."

Grumer said, "Loring was noted for lavish obsessions. He owned a very extensive art collection. One of the largest private amber collections in the world. I understand his son still has it. How would your father know of him?"

Rachel explained about the Extraordinary Commission and her father's involvement. She also told them about Yancy and Marlene Cutler and her father's reservations about their deaths.

"What's Loring's son's name?" she asked.

"Ernst," Grumer said. "He must be eighty now. Still lives on the family estate in southern Czech. Not all that far from here."

There was something about Alfred Grumer that Paul simply did not like. The furrowed brow? The eyes that seemed to consider something else as the ears listened? For some reason, the German reminded him of the housepainter who two weeks ago tried to take the estate he represented for $12,300, easily settling for $1,250. No compunction about lying. More deception than truth in everything he said. Somebody not to be trusted.

"You have your father's correspondence?" Grumer asked Rachel.

Paul didn't want to show him, but thought the gesture would be a demonstration of their good faith. He reached into his back pocket and withdrew the sheets. Grumer and McKoy studied each letter in silence. McKoy particularly seemed riveted. When they finished, Grumer asked, "This Chapaev is dead?"

Paul nodded.

"Your father, Mrs. Cutler—by the way, are you two married?" McKoy asked.

"Divorced," Rachel said.

"And travelin' all over Germany together?"

Rachel's face screwed tight. "Is that relevant to anything?"

McKoy gave her a curious look. "Maybe not, Your Honor. But you two are the ones disruptin' my morning with questions. Like I was sayin', your father worked with the Soviets, looking for the Amber Room?"

"He was interested in what you're doing here."

"He say anythin' in particular?"

"No," Paul said. "But he watched the CNN report and wanted the *USA Today* account. The next thing we knew, he was studying a German map and reading old articles on the Amber Room."

McKoy ambled over and plopped down in an oak swivel chair. The springs groaned from the weight. "You think we might have the right tunnel?"

"Karol knew something about the Amber Room," Paul said. "So did Chapaev. My parents may have even known something. And somebody may have wanted them all kept quiet."

"But do you have anything that shows they were the target of that bomb?" McKoy asked.

"No," Paul said. "But after Chapaev's death, I have to wonder. Karol was very remorseful about what happened to my parents. I'm beginning to believe there's more to it than I thought."

"Too many coincidences, huh?"

"You could say that."

"What about the tunnel Chapaev directed you to?" Grumer asked.

"Nothing there," Rachel said. "And Knoll thought the collapsed end was from an explosion. At least that's what he said."

McKoy grinned. "Wild goose chase?"

"Most likely," Paul said.

"Any explanation as to why Chapaev would send you on a dead end?"

Rachel had to concede that she had no explanation. "But

what about this Loring? Why would my father be concerned enough to have the Cutlers make inquiries about him?"

"The rumors concerning the Amber Room are wide-spread. So many, it is hard to keep them straight anymore. Your father may have been checking another lead," Grumer said.

"You know anything about this Christian Knoll?" Paul asked Grumer.

"*Nein.* Never heard the name."

"You here for a piece of the action?" McKoy suddenly asked.

Paul smiled. He'd half expected a sales pitch. "Hardly. We're not treasure hunters. Just a couple of folks deep into something we probably have no business in. Since we were in the neighborhood, we thought a look might be worth the trip."

"I've been diggin' in these mountains for years—"

The shed door burst open. A grinning man in filthy over-alls said, "We're through!"

McKoy sprang from the chair. "Hot damn, Almighty. Call the TV crew. Tell 'em to get over here. And nobody goes inside till I get there."

The worker sprinted off.

"Let's go, Grumer."

Rachel thrust forward, blocking McKoy's path to the door. "Let us come."

"The shit for?"

"My father."

McKoy hesitated a few seconds, then said, "Why not? But stay the hell out of the way."

THIRTY-SIX

AN UNCOMFORTABLE FEELING SWEPT OVER RACHEL. THE SHAFT was wide but tighter than the one yesterday, and the entrance had faded behind them. Twenty-four hours earlier she'd almost been buried alive. Now she was back underground, following a trail of exposed bulbs deep inside another German mountain. The path ended in an open gallery with walls of gray-white rock surrounding her, the farthest wall broken by a black slit. A worker was swinging a sledgehammer, widening the slit into an aperture large enough for a person to pass through.

McKoy unclamped one of the flood lamps and stepped to the opening. "Anyone look inside?"

"No," a worker said.

"Good." McKoy lifted an aluminum pole from the sand and clicked the lamp to the end. He then extended the telescopic sections until the light was about ten feet away. He approached the opening and shoved the glow into the darkness.

"Son of a bitch," McKoy said. "The chamber's huge. I see three trucks. Oh, shit." He withdrew the light. "Bodies. Two I can see."

Footsteps approached from behind. Rachel turned to see three people racing toward them, video cameras, lights, and battery packs in hand.

"Get that stuff ready," McKoy said. "I want the initial look documented for the show." McKoy turned toward Rachel and Paul. "I sold the video rights. Going to be a TV special on this. But they wanted everything as it happened."

Grumer came close. "Trucks, you say?"

"Looks like Büssing NAGs. Four and half ton. German. "

"That's not good."

"What do you mean?"

"There would have been no transports available to move the Berlin museum material. It would have been hand carried."

"The fuck you talkin' about?"

"Like I said, Herr McKoy, the Berlin material was transported by rail then by truck to the mine. The Germans would not have discarded the vehicles. They were far too valuable, needed for other tasks."

"We don't know what the hell happened, Grumer. Could be the fuckin' krauts decided to leave the trucks, who knows?"

"How did they get inside the mountain?"

McKoy got close in the German's face. "Like you said earlier, there could be another way in."

Grumer shrank back. "As you say, Herr McKoy."

McKoy rammed a finger forward. "No. As *you* say." The big man turned his attention to the video crew. Lights blazed. Two cameras were shouldered. An audio man arched a boom mike and stood back out of the way. "I go in first. Film it from my perspective."

The men nodded.

And McKoy stepped into the blackness.

PAUL WAS THE LAST TO ENTER. HE FOLLOWED TWO WORKERS who dragged light bars into the chamber, blue-white rays evaporating the darkness.

"This chamber is natural," Grumer said, his voice echoing.

Paul studied the rock, which rose to an arch at least sixty feet high. The sight reminded him of the ceiling in some grand cathedral, except that the ceiling and walls were draped in helicities and speleothems that sparkled in the bright light. The floor was soft and sandy, like the shaft leading in. He sucked in a breath and did not particularly care for the stale smell in the air. The video lights were aimed at the far wall. Another opening, or at least what was left of one, came into view. It was larger than the shaft they'd used, more than enough room to admit the transports, rock and rubble packed tight in the archway.

"The other way in, huh?" McKoy said.

"*Ja.*" Grumer said. "But strange. The whole idea of hiding was to be able to retrieve. Why shut it off like that?"

Paul turned his attention to the three trucks. They were parked at odd angles, all eighteen tires deflated, the rims crushed from the weight. The dark canvas awnings draped over the long beds were still there but moldy, the steel cabs and frames heavily rusted.

McKoy moved deeper into the room, a cameraman following. "Don't worry about the audio. We'll dub that over later, get video right now."

Rachel walked ahead.

Paul stepped close behind her. "Strange, isn't it? Like walking through a grave."

She nodded. "Exactly what I was thinking."

"Look at this," McKoy said.

The lights revealed two bodies sprawled in the sand, rock and rubble on either side. Nothing was left but bones, tattered clothes, and leather boots.

"They were shot in the head," McKoy said.

A worker brought a light bar close.

"Try not to touch anything until we have a full photographic record. The Ministry will require that." Grumer's voice was firm.

"Two more bodies are over here," one of the other workers said.

McKoy and the camera crew moved in that direction. Grumer and the others followed, as did Rachel. Paul lingered with the two bodies. The clothing had rotted, but even in the dim light the remnants appeared to be some type of uniform. The bones had grayed and blackened, flesh and muscle long since yielding to dust. There definitely was a hole in each skull. Both appeared to have been lying on their backs, their spine and ribs still neatly arranged. A knife bayonet lay to one side, attached to what was left of a stitched belt. A leather pistol holder was empty.

His eyes drifted farther to the right.

Partially covered by the sand, in the shadows, he noticed something black and rectangular. Ignoring what Grumer said, he reached down and grabbed it.

A wallet.

He carefully parted the cracked leather fold. Tattered remnants of what appeared to have once been money lined the bill compartment. He slipped a finger into one of the side flaps. Nothing. Then the other. Bits of a card slid out. The edges were frayed and fragile, most of the ink faded, but some of the writing remained. He strained to read the letters.

AUSGEGEBEN 15-3-51. VERFÄLLT 15-3-55. GUSTAV MÜLLER.

There were more words, but only scattered letters had survived, nothing legible. He cradled the wallet in his palm and started back toward the main group. He rounded the rear of a transport and suddenly spotted Grumer off to one side. He was about to approach and ask about the wallet when he saw that Grumer was bent over another skeleton. Rachel, McKoy, and the others were gathered ten meters off to the left, their backs to them, cameras still whining, McKoy talking to the lens. Workers had erected a telescopic stand and hoisted a halogen light bar at the center, generating more than enough light to see Grumer searching the sand around the bones.

Paul retreated into the shadows behind one of the trucks and continued to watch. Grumer's flashlight traced the bones embedded in the sand. He wondered what carnage had raged through here. Grumer's light finished its survey at the end of an outstretched arm, the remains of finger bones clear. He focused hard. There were letters etched in the sand. Some gone from time, but three remained, spread across with irregular spaces in between.

O   I   C.

Grumer stood and snapped three pictures, his flash strobing the scene.

Then the German bent down and lightly brushed all three letters from the sand.

MCKOY WAS IMPRESSED. THE VIDEO SHOULD BE SPECTACULAR. Three rusted World War II German transports found relatively intact deep inside an abandoned silver mine. Five bodies, all with holes in their heads. What a show it would make. His percentage of the residuals would be impressive.

"Got enough exterior shots?" he asked one of the cameramen.

"More than."

"Then let's see what the fuck's in these things." He grabbed a flashlight and moved toward the nearest transport. "Grumer, where are you?"

The *Doktor* stepped up from behind.

"Ready?" McKoy asked.

Grumer nodded.

So was he.

The sight inside each bed should be of wooden crates hastily assembled and haphazardly packed, many using centuries-old draperies, costumes, and carpets as padding. He'd heard stories of how curators in the Hermitage used Nicholas II and Alexandra's royal garb to pack painting after painting shipped east, away from the Nazis. Priceless articles of clothing indiscriminately stuffed in cheap wooden crates. Anything to protect the canvases and fragile ceramics. He hoped the Germans had been equally frivolous. If this was the right chamber, the one that contained the Berlin museum inventory, the find should be the cream of the collection. Perhaps Vermeer's *Street of Delft,* or da Vinci's *Christ's Head,* or Monet's *The Park.* Each one would bring millions on the open market. Even if the German government insisted on retaining ownership—which was likely— the finder's fee would be millions of dollars.

He carefully parted the stiff canvas and shined the light inside.

The bed was empty. Nothing but rust and sand.

He darted to the next truck.

Empty.

To the third.

Empty, as well.

"Mother of fuckin' god," he said. "Shut those damn cameras off."

Grumer shined his light inside each bed. "I was afraid of this."

He was not in the mood.

"All the signs said this may not be the chamber," Grumer said.

The smug German seemed to almost enjoy his predicament. "Then why the hell didn't you tell me back in January?"

"I did not know then. The radar soundings indicated something large and metallic was here. Only in the past few days, as we got close, did I begin to suspect this may be a dry site."

Paul approached. "What's the problem?"

"The problem, Mr. Lawyer, is the goddamn beds are empty. Not one son-of-a-bitchin' thing in any of 'em. I just spent a million dollars to retrieve three rusted trucks. How the fuck do I explain that to the people flyin' here tomorrow expectin' to get rich from their investment?"

"They knew the risks when they invested," Paul said.

"Not a one of the bastards is goin' to admit that."

Rachel asked, "Were you honest with them about the risk?"

"About as honest as you can be when you're pannin' for money." He shook his head in disgust. "Jesus Christ Almighty damn."

THIRTY-SEVEN

KNOLL TOSSED HIS TRAVEL BAG ON THE BED AND SURVEYED THE cramped hotel room. The Christinenhof rose five stories, its exterior half timbered, its interior breathing history and hospitality. He'd intentionally chosen a room on the third floor, street side, passing on the more luxurious and expensive garden side. He wasn't interested in ambience, only location, since the Christinenhof sat directly across from the Hotel Garni, where Wayland McKoy and his party occupied the entire fourth floor.

He'd learned from an eager attendant in the town's tourist office of McKoy's excavation. He'd also been told that tomorrow a group of investors was due in town—rooms in the Garni had been blocked off, two other hotels assisting with the overflow. "Good for business," the attendant had said. Good for him, too. Nothing better than a crowd for a distraction.

He unzipped the leather bag and removed an electric razor.

Yesterday had been a tough day. Danzer had bested him. Probably gloating right now to Ernst Loring how she lured him into the mine. But why kill him? Never before had their jousts escalated to such finality. What had raised the stakes? What was so important that Danya Chapaev, himself, and Rachel Cutler needed to die? The Amber Room? Perhaps. Certainly more investigation was needed, and he intended doing just that once this side mission was accomplished.

He'd taken his time on the drive north from Füssen to Stod. No real hurry. The Munich newspapers reported yesterday's explosion in the Harz mine, mentioning Rachel Cutler's name and the fact that she survived. There was no reference to him, only that they were still searching for an unidentified white male, but rescue crews were not hopeful of finding anything. Surely Rachel had told the authorities about him, and the police would have learned that he'd checked out of the Goldene Krone with both his and Rachel's things. Yet not a mention. Interesting. A police ploy? Possibly. But he didn't care. He'd committed no crime. Why would the police want him? For all they knew, he was scared to death and decided to get out of town, a near brush with death enough to frighten anyone. Rachel Cutler was alive and surely on the way back to America, her German adventure nothing more than an unpleasant memory. Back to the life of a big-city judge. Her father's quest for the Amber Room would die with him.

He'd showered this morning but hadn't shaved, so his neck and chin now felt like sandpaper and itched. He took a moment and retrieved the pistol at the bottom of his travel bag. He softly massaged the smooth, nonreflective polymer, then palmed the weapon, finger on the trigger. It was no more than thirty-five ounces, a gift from Ernst Loring, one of his new CZ-75Bs.

"I had them expand the clip to fifteen shots," Loring had said when he presented him with the weapon. "No ten-round bureaucrat's magazine. So it's identical to our original model. I recalled your comment on not liking the subsequent factory modification down to ten shots. I also had the safety framemounted and adjusted so the gun can be carried in the cocked and locked position, as you noted. That change is now on all the models."

Loring's Czech foundries were the largest small-arms producers in Eastern Europe, their craftsmanship legendary. Only in the past few years had western markets opened fully to his products, high tariffs and import restrictions going the way of the Iron Curtain. Thankfully, Fellner had allowed him to retain the gun, and he appreciated the gesture.

"I also had the barrel tip threaded for a sound suppressor," Loring had said. "Suzanne has one identical. I thought you two would enjoy the irony. The playing field leveled, so to speak."

He screwed the sound suppressor to the end of the short barrel and popped in a fresh clip of bullets.

Yes. He greatly enjoyed the irony.

He tossed the gun on the bed and grabbed his razor. On the way into the bathroom he stopped for a moment at the room's only window. The front entrance of the Garni stood across the street, stone pilasters rose on either side of a heavy brass door, the street side rooms rising six stories. He'd learned the Garni was the most expensive hotel in town. Obviously Wayland McKoy liked the best. He'd also learned, while checking in, that the Garni possessed a large restaurant and meeting room, two amenities the expedition seemed to require. The Christinenhof's staff had been glad that they didn't have to cater to the constant needs of such a large group. He'd smiled at that observation. Capitalism was so different from European socialism. In America, hotels would have fought one another for that kind of business.

He stared through a black wrought-iron grille protecting the window. The afternoon sky loomed gray and dingy, as a thick bank of clouds rolled in from the north. From what he'd been told, the expedition personnel usually arrived back around six o'clock each day. He'd start his field work then, dining in the Garni, learning what he could from the dinner talk.

He glanced down at the street. First one way, then the next. Suddenly, his eyes locked on a woman. She was weaving a path through the crowded pedestrian-only lane. Blond hair. Pretty face. Dressed casually. A leather bag slung over her right shoulder.

Suzanne Danzer.

Undisguised. Out in the open.

Fascinating.

He tossed the razor on the bed, stuffed the gun beneath his jacket and into a shoulder harness, then bolted for the door.

A STRANGE FEELING FILLED SUZANNE. SHE STOPPED AND glanced back. The street was crowded, a midday lunch crowd milling about in full force. Stod was a busy town. Fifty thousand or so inhabitants, she'd learned. The oldest part of town spread in all directions, the blocks full of half-timbered multistory stone and brick buildings. Some were clearly ancient, but most were reproductions built in the 1950s and 1960s, after bombers left their mark in 1945. The builders did a good job, decorating everything with rich moldings, life-size statues, and bas-reliefs, everything had been specifically created to be photographed.

High above her, the Abbey of the Seven Sorrows of the Virgin dominated the sky. The monstrous structure had been erected in the fifteenth century in honor of the Virgin Mary's help in turning the tide of a local battle. The baroque building crowned a rocky bluff overlooking both Stod and the muddy Eder River, a clear personification of ancient defiance and lordly power.

She stared upward.

The abbey's towering edifice seemed to lean forward, curving slightly inward, its twin yellow towers connected by a balcony that faced due west. She imagined a time when monks and prelates surveyed their domain from that lofty perch. "The Fortress of God," she recalled one medieval chronicler proclaiming of the site. Alternating amber and white-colored stone walls lined the exterior, capped by a rust-colored tile roof. How fitting. Amber. Maybe it was an omen. And if she believed in anything other than herself, she might have taken notice. But, at the moment, the only thing she noticed was the feeling of being watched.

Certainly Wayland McKoy would arouse interest. Maybe that was it. Somebody else was here. Searching. Watching. But where? Hundreds of windows lined the narrow street, most up several stories. The cobblestones were crowded with too many faces to digest. Someone could be in disguise. Or maybe somebody was a hundred meters up on the balcony of the abbey gazing down. She could just make out tiny silhouettes in the midday sun, tourists apparently enjoying a grand view.

No matter.

She turned and entered the Hotel Garni.

She approached the front desk and told the male clerk in German, "I need to leave a message for Alfred Grumer."

"Certainly." The man pushed her a pad.

She wrote, *I will be at the Church of St. Gerhard, 10:00 P.M. Be there. Margarethe.* She folded the note.

"I'll see *Herr Doktor* Grumer receives it," the clerk said.

She smiled and handed him five euros for his trouble.

KNOLL STOOD INSIDE THE CHRISTINENHOF'S LOBBY AND CARE-fully parted the sheers for a ground-floor view of the street. He watched while less than a hundred feet away Suzanne Danzer stopped and looked around.

Did she sense him?

She was good. Her instincts sharp. He'd always liked Jung's comparisons of how the ancients viewed women as either Eve, Helen, Sophia, or Mary—corresponding to im-pulsive, emotional, intellectual, and moral. Danzer certainly possessed the first three, but nothing about her was moral. She was also one other thing—dangerous. But her guard was probably down, thinking he was buried under tons of rock in a mine forty kilometers away. Hopefully, Franz Fellner passed the word to Loring that his whereabouts were un-known, the ploy buying the time he'd need to figure out what was going on. Even more important, it would buy time to de-cide how to settle the score with his attractive colleague.

What was she doing here, out in the open, headed into the Hotel Garni? It was too much of a coincidence that Stod hap-pened to be the headquarters for Wayland McKoy, that par-ticular hotel where McKoy and his people were staying. Did she have a source on the excavation? If so, nothing unusual there. He'd many times cultivated sources on other digs so Fellner could have first crack at whatever might be uncov-ered. Adventurers were usually more than eager to sell at least some of their bounty on the black market, no one the wiser since everything they found was thought lost anyway. The practice avoided unnecessary government hassles and annoying seizures. The Germans were notorious for confiscating the best of what was pulled from the ground. Strict reporting requirements and heavy penalties governed violators. But greed could always be counted on to prevail, and he'd made several excellent purchases for Fellner's private collection from unscrupulous treasure hunters.

A light rain began to fall. Umbrellas sprouted. Thunder rolled in the distance. Danzer appeared back out of the Garni. He retreated to the window's edge. Hopefully, she wouldn't cross the street and enter the Christinenhof. There was nowhere to hide in the cramped lobby.

He was relieved when she casually rolled up her jacket collar and strolled back down the street. He headed for the front door and cautiously peered out. Danzer entered another hotel just down the street, the Gebler, as the sign out front announced, its cross-beamed facade sagging from the weight of centuries. He'd passed it on his way to the Christinenhof. It made sense she'd stay there. Nearby, convenient. He retreated back into the lobby and watched through the window, trying not to appear conspicuous to the few people loitering around. Fifteen minutes passed, and still she did not reappear.

He smiled.

Confirmation.

She was there.

THIRTY-EIGHT

1:15 P.M.

PAUL STUDIED ALFRED GRUMER WITH HIS LAWYER EYES, EXAM-
ining every facet of the man's face, gauging a reaction, cal-
culating a likely response. He, McKoy, Grumer, and Rachel
were back in the shed outside the mine. Rain peppered the
tin roof. Nearly three hours had passed since the initial find,
and McKoy's mood, like the weather, had only dampened.

"What the fuck's going on, Grumer?" McKoy said.

The German was perched on a stool. "Two possible ex-
planations. One, the trucks were empty when they were
driven in the cavern. Two, somebody beat us inside."

"How could somebody beat us to it? It took four days to
bore into that chamber, and the other way out is sealed shut
with tons of crap."

"The violation could have happened long ago."

McKoy took a deep breath. "Grumer, I have twenty-eight
people flyin' in here tomorrow. They've invested a shitload
of money into this rat hole. What am I supposed to say to
'em? Somebody beat us to it?"

"The facts are the facts."

McKoy shot from the chair, rage in his eyes. Rachel cut
him off. "What good is that going to do?"

"It'd make me feel a whole lot better."

"Sit down," Rachel said.

Paul recognized her court voice. Strong. Firm. A tone that
allowed no hint of doubt. A tone she'd used too many times
in their own home.

The big man backed off. "Jesus Christ. This is some shit."

He sat back down. "Looks like I might need a lawyer. The judge here certainly can't do it. You available, Cutler?"

He shook his head. "I do probates. But my firm has a lot of good litigators and contract-law specialists."

"They're all across the pond and you're here. Guess who's elected."

"I assume all the investors signed waivers and acknowledgments of the risk?" Rachel asked.

"Lot of damn good that'll do. These people have money and lawyers of their own. By next week, I'll be waist deep in legal bullshit. Nobody'll believe I didn't know this was a dry hole."

"I don't agree with you," Rachel said. "Why would anyone assume you'd dig knowing there was nothing to find? Sounds like financial suicide."

"Maybe that little hundred-thousand-dollar fee I'm guaranteed whether we find anythin' or not?"

Rachel turned toward Paul. "Maybe you should call the firm. This guy does need a lawyer."

"Look, let me make somethin' clear," McKoy said. "I have a business to run back home. I don't do this for a livin'. It costs to do this kind of shit. On the last dig, I charged the same fee and made it back with more. Those investors got a good return. Nobody complained."

"Not this time," Paul said. "Unless those trucks are worth something, which I doubt. And that's assuming you can even get them out of there."

"Which you can't," Grumer said. "That other cavern is impassable. It would cost millions to clear it."

"Fuck off, Grumer."

Paul stared at McKoy. The big man's expression was familiar, a combination of resignation and worry. Lots of clients looked that way at one time or another. Actually, though, he wanted to stay around. In his mind he saw Grumer in the cavern again, brushing letters from the sand. "Okay, McKoy. If you want my help, I'll do what I can."

Rachel gave him a strange gaze, her thoughts easy to read. Yesterday he'd wanted to go home and leave all this intrigue to the authorities. Yet here he was, volunteering to represent Wayland McKoy, piloting his own chariot of fire across the sky at the whim of forces he did not understand and could not control.

"Good," McKoy said. "I can use the help. Grumer, make yourself useful and arrange rooms for these folks at the Garni. Put them on my tab."

Grumer did not appear pleased at being ordered around, but the German did not argue, and he headed for the phone.

"What's the Garni?" Paul asked.

"Where we're staying in town."

Paul motioned to Grumer. "He there, too?"

"Where else?"

Paul was impressed with Stod. It was a considerable city interlaced with venerable thoroughfares that seemed to have been taken straight from the Middle Ages. Row after row of black-and-white half-timbered buildings lined the cobbled lanes, pressed tight like books on a shelf. Above everything, a monstrous abbey capped a steep mountain spur high—the slopes leading up thick with larch and beech trees bursting in a spring flourish.

He and Rachel drove into town behind Grumer and McKoy, their path winding deep into the old town, ending just before the Hotel Garni. A small parking lot reserved for guests waited farther down the street, toward the river, just outside the pedestrian-only zone.

Inside the hotel he learned that McKoy's party dominated the fourth floor. The entire third floor had already been reserved for investors arriving tomorrow. After some haggling by McKoy and palm pressing of a few euros, the clerk made a room available on the second floor. McKoy asked if they wanted one or two rooms, and Rachel had immediately said one.

Upstairs, his suitcase had barely hit the bed before Rachel said, "Okay, what are you up to, Paul Cutler?"

"What are *you* up to? One room. I thought we were divorced. You like to remind me about it enough."

"Paul, you're up to something, and I'm not letting you out of my sight. Yesterday you were busting a gut to go home. Now you volunteer to represent this guy? What if he's a crook?"

"All the more reason he needs a lawyer."

"Paul—"

He motioned to the double bed. "Night and day?"

"What?"

"You going to keep me in your sight night and day?"

"It's not anything we both haven't seen before. We were married seven years."

He smiled. "I might get to like this intrigue."

"Are you going to tell me?"

He sat on the edge of the bed and told her what happened in the underground chamber, then showed her the wallet, which he'd kept all afternoon in his back pocket. "Grumer dusted the letters away on purpose. No doubt about it. That guy is up to something."

"Why didn't you tell McKoy?"

He shrugged. "I don't know. I thought about it. But, like you say, he may be a crook."

"You're sure the letters were *O-I-C*?"

"As best I could make out."

"You think this has anything to do with Daddy and the Amber Room?"

"There's no connection at this point, except Karol was real interested in what McKoy was doing. But that doesn't necessarily mean anything."

Rachel sat down beside him. He noticed the cuts and scrapes on her arms and face that had scabbed over. "This guy McKoy latched on to us kind of quick," she said.

"We may be all he's got. He doesn't seem to like Grumer much. We're just two strangers who came out of the woodwork. No interest in anything. No ax to grind. I guess we're deemed safe."

Rachel cradled the wallet and studied closely the scraps of decaying paper. "*Ausgegeben* 15-3-51. *Verfällt* 15-3-55. *Gustav Müller.* Should we get somebody to translate?"

"Not a good idea. Right now, I don't trust anyone, present company excepted of course. I suggest we find a German-English dictionary and see for ourselves."

Two blocks west of the Garni they found a translation dictionary in a cluttered gift shop, a thin volume apparently printed for tourists with common words and phrases.

"*Ausgegeben* means 'issued,' " he said. "*Verfällt,* 'expires,' 'ends.' " He looked at Rachel. "The numbers have to be dates. The European way. Backwards. Issued March 15, 1951. Expires March 15, 1955. Gustav Müller."

"That's postwar. Grumer was right. Somebody beat McKoy to whatever was there. Sometime after March 1951."

"But what?"

"Good question."

"It had to be serious. Five bodies with holes in their heads?"

"And important. All three trucks were clean. Not a scrap of anything left to find."

He tossed the dictionary back on the shelf. "Grumer knows something. Why go to all the trouble of taking pictures then dusting the letters away? What's he documenting? And who for?"

"Maybe we should tell McKoy?"

He thought about the suggestion, then said, "I don't think so. Not yet, at least."

THIRTY-NINE

10:00 P.M.

SUZANNE PUSHED THROUGH A VELVET CURTAIN SEPARATING THE outer gallery and portal from the inner nave. The Church of St. Gerhard was empty. A message board outside proclaimed the sanctuary open until 11 P.M., which was the central reason she'd chosen the place for the meeting. The other was locale—blocks from Stod's hotel district, on the edge of old town, far away from the crowds.

The building's architecture was clearly Romanesque with lots of brick and a lofty front adorned by twin towers. Lucid, spatial proportions dominated. Blind arcades loomed in playful patterns. A beautifully adorned chancel stretched from the far end. The high altar, sacristy, and choir stalls were empty. A few candles flickered from a side altar, their glint like stars on the gilded ornamentation high overhead.

She walked forward and stopped at the base of a gilded pulpit. Chiseled figures of the Four Evangelists encircled her. She glanced at the steps leading up. More figures lined both sides. Allegories of Christian values. Faith, Hope, Charity, Prudence, Fortitude, Temperance, and Justice. She recognized the carver instantly. Riemenschneider. Sixteenth century. The pulpit above was empty. But she could imagine the bishop addressing the congregation, extolling the virtues of God and the advantages in believing.

She crept to the nave's far end, her eyes and ears alert. The quiet was unnerving. Her right hand was stuffed in her jacket pocket, ungloved fingers wrapped around a Sauer .32 automatic, a present from Loring three years back out of his private collection. She'd almost brought the new CZ-75B Loring gave her. It had been her suggestion that Christian be given one identical. Loring had smiled at the irony. Too bad Knoll would never get a chance to use his.

The corner of her eye caught a sudden movement. Her fingers tightened around the gun stock, and she spun. A tall, gaunt man pushed through a curtain and walked toward her.

"Margarethe?" he softly said.

"Herr Grumer?"

The man nodded and came close. He smelled of bitter beer and sausage.

"This is dangerous," he said.

"No one knows of our relationship, *Herr Doktor.* You have simply come to church to speak with your God."

"We need to keep it that way."

His paranoia did not concern her. "What have you learned?"

Grumer reached under his jacket and pulled out five photographs. She studied them in the bare light. Three trucks. Five bodies. Letters in the sand.

"The transports are empty. There is another entrance into the chamber blocked with rubble. The bodies are definitely postwar. The clothing and equipment give that away."

She gestured to the photo that showed letters in the sand. "How was this handled?"

"With a brush of my hand."

"Then why photograph them?"

"So you would believe me."

"And so you could up the price?"

Grumer smiled. She hated the pallor of greed.

"Anything more?"

"Two Americans have appeared at the site."

She listened while Grumer told her about Rachel and Paul Cutler.

"The woman is the one involved with the mine explosion near Warthberg. They have McKoy thinking about the Amber Room."

The fact that Rachel Cutler survived was interesting. "She say anything about another survivor in that explosion?"

"Only that there was one. A Christian Knoll. He left Warthberg after the explosion and took Frau Cutler's belongings."

Her guard suddenly stiffened. Knoll was alive. The situation, which a moment ago was entirely under control, now seemed frightening. But she needed to complete her mission. "Does McKoy still listen to you?"

"As much as he wants to. He's upset about the trucks being empty. Afraid investors on the dig will sue him. He's enlisted Herr Cutler's legal assistance."

"They are strangers."

"But I believe he trusts them more than me. The Cutlers also have letters that passed between Frau Cutler's father and a man named Danya Chapaev. They concern the Amber Room."

Old news. The same letters she'd read in Paul Cutler's office. But she needed to act interested. "You've seen these letters?"

"I have."

"Who has them now?"

"Frau and Herr Cutler."

A loose end that needed attention. "Obtaining the letters could up your worth considerably."

"I thought as much."

"And what is your price, Herr Grumer?"

"Five million euros."

"What makes you worth that?"

Grumer gestured to the photos. "I believe these show my good faith. That is clear evidence of postwar looting. Is that not what your employer seeks?"

She did not answer his inquiry, merely saying, "I'll pass the price along."

"To Ernst Loring?"

"I never said who I work for, nor should that matter. As I understand the situation, no one has related the identity of my benefactor."

"But Herr Loring's name has been mentioned by both the Cutlers and Frau Cutler's father."

This man was quickly becoming another loose end that would require tending. As were the Cutlers. How many more would there be? "Needless to say," she said, "the letters are important, as is what McKoy is doing. Along with time. I want this resolved quickly and am willing to pay for speed."

Grumer tipped his head. "Would tomorrow be soon enough for the letters? The Cutlers have rooms at the Garni."

"I'd like to be there."

"Tell me where you're staying, and I'll call when the way is clear."

"I'm at the Gebler."

"I know the place. You'll hear from me by eight A.M."

The curtain at the far end parted. A robed prior strolled

silently down the center aisle. She glanced at her watch. Nearly 11 P.M. "Let's head outside. He's probably here to close the building."

⚓━━━▪

KNOLL RETREATED INTO THE SHADOWS. DANZER AND A MAN emerged from the Church of St. Gerhard through sculptured bronze doors and stood on the front portico, not twenty meters away, the cobbled street beyond dark and empty.

"I'll have an answer tomorrow," Danzer said. "We will meet here."

"I don't think that's possible." The man gestured to a sign affixed to the stone next to the bronze portal. "Services are held here on Tuesdays at nine."

Danzer glanced at the announcement. "Quite right, Herr Grumer."

The man motioned off to the sky, the abbey sparkling gold and white in floodlight against the clear night. "The church there stays open to midnight. Few visit late. How about ten-thirty?"

"Fine."

"And a down payment would be nice to show your benefactor's good faith. Shall we say a million euros?"

Knoll did not know this man, but the idiot was being foolish trying to squeeze Danzer. He respected her abilities more than that, and this Grumer should, too. He was obviously an amateur she was using to learn what Wayland McKoy was doing.

Or was it more?

A million euros? Only the down payment?

The man named Grumer descended the stone steps to the street and turned east. Danzer followed, but went west. He knew where she was staying, that's how he'd found the church, following her from the Gebler. Certainly her presence complicated matters, but right now it was this Grumer who really interested him.

He waited for Danzer to disappear around a corner, then

headed after his quarry. He stayed back—an easy matter to follow the man to the Garni.

Now he knew.

And he also knew exactly where Suzanne Danzer would be at ten-thirty tomorrow night.

RACHEL SWITCHED OFF THE BATHROOM LIGHT AND STEPPED toward the bed. Paul was propped upright reading the *International Herald Tribune* he'd bought at the souvenir shop earlier when they'd found the German/English dictionary.

She thought about her ex-husband. In divorce after divorce, she watched people revel in destroying one other. Every little detail of their lives, unimportant years ago, suddenly became vital to their assertions of mental cruelty, or abuse, or simply to prove the marriage irretrievably broken as the law required. Was there really pleasure in that? How could there be? Thankfully, they'd not done that. She and Paul had settled their differences on a dismal Thursday afternoon, sitting calmly around the dining room table. The same one where, last Tuesday, Paul had told her about her father and the Amber Room. She'd been rough on him last week. There was no need to say that he was spineless. Why was she like that? It was so unlike her courtroom demeanor, where her every word and action was calculated.

"Your head still hurt?" Paul asked.

She sat on the bed, the mattress firm, a down comforter soft and warm. "A little."

The image of a glistening knife strobed through her mind. Had Knoll actually meant the blade for her? Was she doing the right thing by not telling Paul? "We need to call Pannik. Let him know what's happening and where we are. He's got to be wondering."

Paul looked up from the newspaper. "I agree. We'll do it tomorrow. Let's be sure if there's anything here first."

She thought again of Christian Knoll. His self-assurance had intrigued her and stirred feelings long suppressed. She

was forty years old and had loved only her father, a short ro-
mance in college she thought was the real thing, and Paul.
She hadn't been a virgin when she and Paul married, but neither was she experienced. Paul had been a shy, retiring sort
who easily found comfort within himself. He was certainly
no Christian Knoll, but he was loyal, faithful, and honest.
Why had that once seemed boring to her? Was it her own
immaturity? Probably. Marla and Brent adored their father.
And they were his number one priority. Hard to fault a man
for loving his children and being faithful to his wife. So what
happened? They grew apart? That was the easiest explanation. But had they really? Maybe stress took its toll. God
knows they both stayed under pressure. Laziness, though,
seemed the best explanation. Not wanting to simply work at
what she knew to be right. She'd read a phrase once—*the
contempt of familiarity*—that supposedly described what,
sadly, many marriages produced. An apt observation.

"Paul, I appreciate your doing all this. More than you
know."

"I'd be lying if I said this wasn't fascinating. Besides, I
might get a new client for the firm. Sounds like Wayland
McKoy is going to need a lawyer."

"I have a feeling all hell's going to break loose around
here tomorrow, when those investors get here."

Paul tossed the newspaper to the carpet. "I think you're
right. It could get interesting." He then switched off the bedside light. The wallet from the underground chamber lay
next to the lamp, her father's letters beside it.

She switched off the lamp on her side.

"This is really strange," he said. "Sleeping together for the
first time in three years."

She curled under the comforter on her side. She wore one
of his long-sleeved twill shirts, full of the comforting scent
she remembered from seven years of marriage. Paul turned
on his side, his back facing her, seemingly making sure her
space was hers. She decided to make a move and spooned
closer. "You're a good man, Paul Cutler."

Her arm wrapped around him. She felt him tense and wondered if it was nerves or shock.

"You're not so bad yourself," he said.

FORTY

TUESDAY, MAY 20, 9:10 A.M.

PAUL FOLLOWED RACHEL DOWN THE DANK SHAFT TO THE CHAMber harboring the three trucks. He'd learned in the shed that McKoy had been underground since 7 A.M. Grumer had yet to appear at the site, which was nothing unusual according to the man on duty, since Grumer rarely appeared before midmorning.

They entered the lit chamber.

He took a moment and studied the three vehicles more closely. In yesterday's excitement there'd been no time for a detailed look. All the headlights, rearview mirrors, and windshields were whole. The barrel-shaped canvas beds were likewise relatively intact. Except for an icing of rust, the flattened tires, and moldy canvas, it was as though the vehicles could have been driven right out of their rocky garage.

Two of the cab doors were open. He glanced inside one. The leather seat was ripped and brittle from decay. The dials and gauges on the instrument panel were silent and still. Not a scrap of paper or anything tangible lay in sight. He found himself wondering where the trucks came from. Had they once transported German troops? Or Jews headed for the camps? Did they bear witness to the Russian advance on Berlin, or the Americans' simultaneous rush from the west? Strange, this surreal sight so deep inside a German mountain.

A shadow flared across the rock wall, revealing movement from the other side of the farthest vehicle.

"McKoy?" he called out.

"Over here."

He and Rachel rounded the trucks. The big man turned to face them.

"These are without a doubt Büssing NAGs. Four-and-a-half-ton diesels. Twenty feet long. Seven and a half feet wide. Ten feet high." McKoy moved close to a rusted side panel and banged it with his fist. Brownish-red snow fluttered to the sand below, but the metal held. "Solid steel and iron. These things can carry almost seven tons. Slow as hell, though. No more than twenty, twenty-one miles per hour, tops."

"What's the point?" Rachel asked.

"The point, Your Honor, is these damn things weren't used to haul a bunch of paintin's and vases. These were precious. Big haulers. For heavy loads. And the Germans sure didn't just dump 'em in a mine."

"Meaning?" Rachel said.

"This whole thing doesn't make a damn bit of sense." McKoy reached into his pocket and brought out a folded piece of paper, handing it to Paul. "I need you to look at this."

He unfolded the sheet and walked close to one of the light bars. It was a memorandum. He and Rachel read it in silence:

GERMAN EXCAVATIONS CORPORATION
6798 Moffat Boulevard
Raleigh, North Carolina 27615

To: Potential Partners
From: Wayland McKoy, CEO
Re: **Own a Piece of History and Get a Free Vacation to Germany**

German Excavations Corporation is pleased to be a sponsor and partner of the following program along with these contributing companies: Chrysler Motor Company (Jeep Division), Coleman, Eveready, Hewlett-Packard, IBM, Saturn Marine, Boston Electric Tool Company, and Olympus America, Inc.

In the waning days of World War II, a train left Berlin loaded with 1,200 art treasures. It reached the outskirts of the city of Magdeburg and was then diverted southward toward the Harz Mountains and was never seen again. We have an expedition now ready to locate and excavate that train.

Under German law, the rightful owners have ninety days to claim their artworks. Unclaimed works are then put up for auction with 50 percent of the proceeds going to the German government and 50 percent to the expedition and its sponsoring partners. An inventory list of the train can be provided on request. Minimum estimated value of the artwork, $360 million—with 50 percent going to the government. The partners' remaining sum of $180 million will be divided according to units purchased, less art claimed by original owners, less auction fees, taxes, etc.

All the partners' monies will be returned by funds of the presold media rights. All partners and spouses will be our guests in Germany for the expedition. Bottom line: We have found the proper place. We have the contract. We have the research. We have the media sold. We have the experience and the equipment to effect excavation. German Excavations Corporation has a 45-day permit to dig. So far, the rights to 45 units at $25,000 per unit for the final stage of the expedition (Phase III) have been sold. We have about 10 units left at $15,000 per unit. Please feel free to call me if you're interested in this exciting investment.

Sincerely,
Wayland McKoy
President,
German Excavations Corporation

"That's what I sent to potential investors," McKoy said.

"What do you mean by 'All the partners' monies will be returned by funds of the presold media rights'?" Paul asked McKoy.

"Just what it says. A bunch of companies paid for the rights to film and broadcast what we find."

"But that presupposes you find something. They didn't pay you up front, did they?"

McKoy shook his head. "Shit, no."

"Trouble is," Rachel said, "you didn't say that in the letter. The partners could think, and rightfully so, that you already have the money."

Paul pointed to the second paragraph. " 'We have an expedition now ready to locate and excavate that train.' That sounds like you actually found it."

McKoy sighed. "I thought we did. The ground radar said there was somethin' big in here." McKoy motioned to the trucks. "And there damn well is."

"This true about the forty-five units at twenty five thousand dollars each?" Paul asked. "That's $1.25 million."

"That's what I raised. Then I sold the units for the other one hundred fifty thousand. Sixty investors in all."

Paul motioned to the letter. "*Partners* is what you call them. That's different from investor."

McKoy grinned. "Sounds better."

"Are these other listed companies also investors?"

"They supplied equipment either by donation or at reduced rates. So, in a sense, yes. They don't expect anythin' in return, though."

"You dangled sums like three hundred sixty million dollars, half maybe going to the partners, that can't be true."

"Damn well is. That's what researchers value the Berlin museum stuff."

"Assuming the art can be found," Rachel said. "Your problem, McKoy, is the letter misleads. It could even be construed as fraudulent."

"Since we're going to be so close, why don't you two call me Wayland. And, little lady, I did what was necessary to get the money. I didn't lie to anybody, and I wasn't interested in bilkin' these people. I wanted to dig and that's what I did. I didn't keep a dime, except what they were told I'd get up front."

Paul waited for a rebuke on "little lady," but none came. Instead, Rachel said, "Then you've got another problem. There's not a word in that letter about any hundred-thousand-dollar fee to you."

"They were all told. And, by the way, you're a real ray of sunshine through this storm."

Rachel did not back down. "You need to hear the truth."

"Look, half that hundred thousand went to Grumer for his time and trouble. He was the one who got the permit from the government. Without that, there'd have been no dig. The rest I kept for my time. This trip is costin' me plenty. And I didn't take my cut till the end. Those last units paid me and Grumer, along with our expenses. If I hadn't raised that, I was prepared to borrow it, that's how strong I felt about this venture."

Paul wanted to know, "When are the partners getting here?"

"Twenty-eight with their spouses are due after lunch. That's all that accepted the trips we offered."

He started thinking like a lawyer, studying each word in the letter, analyzing the diction and syntax. Was the proposal fraudulent? Maybe. Ambiguous? Definitely. Should he tell McKoy about Grumer and show him the wallet? Explain about the letters in the sand? McKoy was still an unknown commodity. A stranger. But weren't most clients? Perfect strangers one minute, trusted confidants the next. No. He decided to keep quiet and wait a little longer and see what developed.

SUZANNE ENTERED THE GARNI AND CLIMBED A MARBLE STAIR-case to the second floor. Grumer had called ten minutes ago and informed her that McKoy and the Cutlers had left for the excavation site. Grumer waited at the end of the second floor hall.

"There," he said. "Room Twenty-one."

She stopped at the door, a slab of paneled oak stained dark, its jamb tattered from time and abuse. The lock was part of the doorknob, a tarnished piece of brass that accepted a regular key. No dead bolt. Lock picking had never been her specialty, so she slipped the letter opener commandeered from the concierge's desk into the jamb and worked the point, easily sliding the latch bolt out of the strike plate.

She opened the door. "Careful with our search. Let's not announce our visit."

Grumer started with the furniture. She moved to the luggage and discovered only one travel bag. She rifled through the clothes—mainly men's—and found no letters. She checked the bathroom. The toiletries were also mainly men's. Then she searched the more obvious places. Under the mattress and bed, on top of the armoire, beneath the drawers in the nightstands.

"The letters are not here," Grumer said.

"Search again."

They did. This time not caring about neatness. When they finished the room was a wreck. But still, no letters. Her patience was running thin. "Get to the site, *Herr Doktor,* and find those letters or there'll be not one euro paid to you. Understand?"

Grumer seemed to sense she was in no mood and only nodded before leaving.

FORTY-ONE

KNOLL THRUST HIS ERECT MEMBER DEEPER. MONIKA WAS hunched on all fours, back to him, her firm ass arched high, her head buried deep into a goose-down pillow.

"Come on, Christian. Show me what that bitch from Georgia missed."

He pumped harder, sweat beading on his brow. She reached back and gently massaged his balls. She knew exactly how to work him. And that fact alone bothered him. Monika knew him far too well.

He grasped her thin waist with both hands and torqued her body forward. She accepted the gesture and sighed like a cat after a satisfying kill. He felt her come a moment later, a deep moan confirming her delight. He pounded a few more seconds, then came, too. She continued her testicle massage, milking every drop of his pleasure.

Not bad, he thought. Not bad at all.

She released her hold. He withdrew and relaxed onto the bed. She lay beside him, belly down. He caught his breath and allowed the last spasms of orgasm to shudder through him. He kept his body still, not giving the bitch the satisfaction of knowing he enjoyed it.

"Hell of a lot better than some mousy lawyer, huh?"

He shrugged. "Never got to sample the wares."

"What about that Italian whore you sliced up. Good?"

He kissed his index finger and thumb. "*Buono.* Well worth whatever she charged."

"And Suzanne Danzer?"

The resentment was clear. "Your jealousy is so unbecoming."

"Don't flatter yourself."

Monika raised up on one elbow. She'd been waiting in his room when he arrived a half hour ago. Burg Herz was only an hour west of Stod. He'd returned to his home base for further instructions, deciding a face-to-face talk with his employer was better than the telephone.

"I don't get it, Christian. What is it you see in Danzer? You prefer the finer things of life, not some charity case raised by Loring."

"That charity case, as you say, graduated with honors from the University of Paris. She speaks a dozen languages, that I know of. She is well versed in the arts and can fire a sidearm with expert accuracy. She is also attractive, and an excellent lay. I'd say Suzanne has some admirable credentials."

"Like one-upping you?"

He grinned. "To the devil her due, yes. But payback is truly hell."

"Don't make this personal, Christian. Violence draws too much attention. The world is not your personal playground."

"I am well aware of my duties and my limits."

Monika shot him a wiry grin, one he'd never liked. She seemed determined to make this as difficult as possible. It was so much easier when Fellner ran the show. Now business mixed with pleasure. Maybe that wasn't such a good idea.

"Father should be through with his meeting. He said for us to come to the study."

He pushed up from the mattress. "Then let us not keep him waiting."

He followed Monika into her father's study. The old man sat behind an eighteenth-century walnut desk Fellner had purchased in Berlin two decades ago. He sucked on an ivory pipe with an amber mouthpiece, another rare collectible that once belonged to Alexander II of Russia, liberated from another thief in Romania.

Fellner looked tired, and Knoll hoped their remaining time together would not be short. That'd be a shame. He'd miss their banter on classical literature and art, along with their political debates. He'd learned a lot from his years at Burg Herz—a working education obtained while scouring the world for lost treasure. He appreciated the opportunity that had been extended, grateful for the life, determined to do what the old man wanted till the end.

"Christian. Welcome back. Sit. Tell me everything that happened." Fellner's tone was upbeat, his face alight with a warm smile.

He and Monika sat. He reported what he'd learned about Danzer and her meeting the night before with a man named Grumer.

"I know him," Fellner said. "*Herr Doktor* Alfred Grumer. An academic whore. Moves from university to university. But is connected in the German government and sells that influence. Not surprising a man like McKoy would attach himself to him."

"Obviously Grumer is Danzer's source at the site," Monika said.

"I agree," Fellner said. "And Grumer wouldn't be around unless there was a profit to be made. This may be more interesting than first thought. Ernst is intent on this. He called again this morning inquiring. Apparently he's concerned for your good health, Christian. I told him we had not heard from you in days."

"All of this certainly fits the pattern," Knoll said.

"What pattern?" Monika asked.

Fellner grinned at his daughter. "Perhaps it is time, *liebling,* you know it all. What do you say, Christian?"

Monika looked perturbed. He loved her obvious confusion. The bitch needed to realize she didn't know everything.

Fellner slid open one of the drawers and extracted a thick file. "Christian and I have followed this for years." Across the desk he spread an assortment of newspaper clippings and magazine articles.

"The first death we know of was in 1957. A German reporter from one of my Hamburg newspapers. He came here, looking for an interview. I indulged him, he was remarkably well informed, and a week later he was hit by a bus in Berlin. Witnesses swore he was pushed.

"The next death came two years later. Another reporter. Italian. A car forced him off an alpine road. Two more deaths in 1960, a drug overdose and a robbery gone wrong. From 1960 to 1970 there were a dozen more all over Europe. Reporters. Insurance adjusters. Police investigators. Their demises ranged from supposed suicides to three outright murders.

"My dear, all these people were looking for the Amber Room. Christian's predecessors, my first two Acquisitors, kept a close watch on the press. Anything that might seem related was thoroughly investigated. In the 1970s and '80s the incidents waned. Only six we know of during those twenty years. The last was a Polish reporter killed in a mine explosion three years ago." He looked at Monika. "I'm not sure of the exact location, but it was near where Christian's mishap occurred."

"I'd wager in the same mine," Knoll said.

"Very strange, wouldn't you say? Christian finds a name in St. Petersburg, Karol Borya, the next thing we know the man's dead along with his former colleague. *Liebling,* Christian and I have long thought Loring knows far more of the Amber Room than he wants to admit."

"His father loved amber," Monika said. "So does he."

"Josef was a secretive man. More so than Ernst. It was hard to ever know what he was thinking. Many times we talked on the subject of the Amber Room. I even offered a joint venture once—an all-out search for the panels—but he refused. Called it a waste of time and money. But something about his denials bothered me. So I started keeping this file, checking everything I could. I learned there were too many deaths, too many coincidences for it all to be random. Now

Suzanne is trying to kill Christian. And paying a million euros for mere information on a treasure dig." Fellner shook his head. "I would say the trail we thought ice cold has warmed considerably."

Monika gestured to the clippings fanned on the desk. "You think all those people were murdered?"

"Is there any other logical conclusion?" Fellner said.

Monika stepped close to the desk and thumbed through the articles. "We were on target with Borya, weren't we?"

"I would say so," Knoll said. "How, I'm not sure. But it was enough for Suzanne to kill Chapaev and try to eliminate me."

"That dig site could be important," Fellner said. "I think the time for sparring is over. You have my permission, Christian, to handle the situation at will."

Monika stared at her father. "I thought I was to be in charge."

Fellner smiled. "You must indulge an old man one last quest. Christian and I have worked this for years. I feel we may be on to something. I ask your permission, *liebling,* to intrude on your domain."

Monika managed a weak smile, clearly not pleased. But, Knoll thought, what could she say? Never had she openly defied her father, though privately she'd many times vented her anger over his perpetual patience. Fellner was raised in the old school, where men ruled and women gave birth. He commanded a financial empire that dominated the European communications market. Politicians and industrialists courted his favor. But his wife and son were dead, and Monika was the only remaining Fellner. So he'd been forced to mold a woman into *his* image of a man. Luckily, she was tough. And smart.

"Of course, Father. Do as you wish."

Fellner reached over and cupped his daughter's hand. "I know you don't understand. But I love you for your deference."

Knoll couldn't resist. "Something new."

Monika shot him a hard glance.

Fellner chuckled. "Quite right, Christian. You know her well. You two will make quite a team."

Monika retreated to a chair.

Fellner said, "Christian, return to Stod and find out what is going on. Handle Suzanne however you desire. Before I die I want to know about the Amber Room, one way or the other. If you have any doubts, remember that mine shaft and your ten million euros."

He stood. "I assure you, I will not forget either."

FORTY-TWO

STOD
1:45 P.M.

THE GARNI'S GRAND SALON WAS FULL. PAUL STOOD OFF TO THE side next to Rachel, watching the drama unfold. Certainly, if ambience counted, the room's decor should definitely help Wayland McKoy. Colorful, thickly framed maps of old Germany hung from oak-paneled walls. A shimmering brass chandelier, burnished antique chairs, and a richly designed Oriental carpet rounded out the atmosphere.

Fifty-six people filled the chairs, their faces a mixture of wonder and exhaustion. They'd been bussed straight from Frankfurt, after arriving by air four hours ago. Their ages varied from early thirties to mid-sixties. Race varied, too. Most were white, two black couples, both older, and one Japanese pair. They all seemed eager and anticipatory.

McKoy and Grumer stood at the front of the long room along with five of the excavation's employees. A television with VCR rested on a metal stand. Two somber men sat in the rear, notebooks in hand, and appeared to be reporters. McKoy wanted to exclude them, but both flashed identification from ZDF, a German news organization that had optioned the story, and insisted on staying. "Just watch what you say," Paul had warned.

"Welcome, partners," McKoy said, smiling like a television evangelist. A murmur of conversation receded.

"There's coffee, juice, and danish outside. I know you've had a long journey and are tired. Jet lag's hell, right? But I'm sure you're also anxious to hear how things are goin'."

The direct approach had been Paul's idea. McKoy had favored stalling, but Paul had argued that would do nothing but arouse suspicions. "Keep the tone pleasant and mild," he'd warned. "No 'fuck you' every other word like I heard yesterday, okay?" McKoy repeatedly assured him he was housebroken, fully schooled on how to handle a crowd.

"I know the question on all your minds. Have we found anythin'? No, not yet. But we did make progress yesterday." He motioned to Grumer. "This is *Herr Doktor* Alfred Grumer, professor of art antiquities at the University of Mainz. *Herr Doktor* is our resident expert on the dig. I'll let him explain what happened."

Grumer stepped forward, looking the part of an elderly professor in a tweed wool jacket, corduroy pants, and knit tie. He stood with his right hand stuffed in his trouser pocket, his left arm free. With a disarming smile he said, "I thought I would tell you a little something about how this venture came about.

"Looting art treasure is a time-honored tradition. The Greeks and Romans always stripped a defeated nation of their valuables. Crusaders during the fourteenth and fifteenth centuries pilfered all across Eastern Europe and the Middle East. Western European churches and cathedrals continue to be adorned with their plunder.

"In the seventeenth century, a more refined method of stealing began. After a military defeat the great royal collections— there were no museums in those days—were purchased rather than stolen. An example. When Tsarist armies occupied Berlin in 1757, Frederick II's collections were not touched. To have tampered with them would have been regarded as bar-

baric, even by the Russians, who were themselves deemed barbarians by Europeans.

"Napoleon was perhaps the greatest looter of all. Germany's, Spain's, and Italy's museums were stripped clean so the Louvre could be stocked full. After Waterloo, at the Congress of Vienna in 1815, France was ordered to return the stolen art. Some was, but a lot remained the property of France and can still be seen in Paris."

Paul was impressed with how Grumer handled himself. Like a teacher in class. The group seemed fascinated by the information.

"Your President Lincoln issued an order during the American Civil War that called for the protection of Southern classical works of art, libraries, scientific collections, and precious instruments. A conference in Brussels in 1874 endorsed a similar proposal. Nicholas II, the Russian Tsar, proposed even more ambitious protections, which were approved at the Hague in 1907, but these codes proved of limited value during the two world wars following.

"Hitler completely ignored the Hague Convention and mimicked Napoleon. The Nazis created an entire administrative department that did nothing but steal. Hitler wanted to build a supershowcase—the Führermuseum—to be the largest collection of art in the world. He intended to locate this museum in Linz, Austria, his birthplace. The *Sonderauftrag Linz,* Hitler called it. Special Mission Linz. It was to become the heart of the Third Reich, designed by Hitler himself."

Grumer paused a moment, seemingly allowing the information to be absorbed.

"Plunder for Hitler, though, served another purpose. It demoralized the enemy, and this was especially true in Russia, where the Imperial palaces around Leningrad were decimated in full view of local townspeople. Not since the Goths and Vandals had Europe witnessed so spiteful an assault on human culture. Museums all over Germany were stocked full with stolen art, particularly the Berlin museums. It was in the waning days of the war, with the Russians and Ameri-

cans close, that a trainload of this art was evacuated from
Berlin south to the Harz Mountains. Here, in this region
where we are right now."

The television sprang to life with a panning image of a
mountain range. Grumer pointed a controller and paused the
video on a forested scene.

"The Nazis loved hiding things underground. The Harz
Mountains now surrounding us were used extensively, since
they were the closest underground depositories to Berlin.
Examples of what was found after the war proves this point.
The German national treasury was hidden here along with
over a million books, paintings of all descriptions, and tons
of sculptures. But perhaps the strangest cache was found not
far from here. An American team of soldiers reported finding
a fresh brick wall, nearly two meters thick, five hundred meters into the mountain. It was removed, and a locked steel
door waited on the other side."

Paul watched the partners' faces. They were riveted. He
was, too.

"Inside, the Americans found four enormous caskets. One
was decorated with a wreath and Nazi symbols, the name
Adolf Hitler on the side. German regimental banners draped
the other three coffins. A jeweled scepter and orb, two
crowns, and swords were also found. The whole thing had a
theatrical arrangement, like a shrine. Imagine what these
soldiers thought. Here was the tomb of Hitler. But, alas, it
wasn't. Instead the coffins contained the remains of Field
Marshal von Hindenburg, Hindenburg's wife, Frederick the
Great, and Frederick William I."

Grumer pointed the remote control and released the video.
The color image shifted to the inside of the underground
chamber. McKoy had traveled to the site earlier and remade
the video from yesterday, an edited version to buy a little time
with the partners. Grumer now used that video to explain the
digging, the three transports, and the bodies. Fifty-six pairs
of eyes were glued to the screen.

"Finding these trucks is most exciting. Obviously, something of great value was moved here. Trucks were a precious

commodity, and to forfeit three in a mountain meant a lot was at stake. The five bodies only add to the mystery."

"What did you find inside the trucks?" came the first question from the audience.

McKoy stepped to the front. "They're empty."

"Empty?" several asked at once.

"That's right. All three beds were bare." McKoy motioned to Grumer, who popped in another videotape.

"This is not unusual," Grumer said.

An image rematerialized, an area of the chamber intentionally not filmed on the first tape.

"This shows the other entrance to the chamber." Grumer pointed at the screen. "We hypothesize there may be another chamber past this point. That's where we will now dig."

"You're telling us the trucks are empty," an older man asked.

Paul realized that this was the hard part. The questions. Reality. But they'd gone over everything, he and Rachel prepping McKoy like a witness about to be cross-examined. Paul had approved the strategy of saying there may be another chamber. Hell, there might be. Who knows? At least it would keep the partners happy a few days until McKoy's crew could burrow into the other entrance and learn for sure.

McKoy fended off the challenges well, each inquiry answered completely and with a smile. The big man was right. He did know how to work a crowd. Paul's eyes constantly scanned the spacious salon, trying to gauge the individual reaction.

So far, so good.

Most seemed satisfied with the explanation.

Toward the back of the room, at the double doorway leading out to the lobby, he noticed a woman slip in. She was short, with medium-length blond hair, and stayed in the shadows, making it hard to distinguish her face. Yet there was something familiar about her.

"Paul Cutler here is my legal counsel," McKoy said.

He turned at the mention of his name.

"Mr. Cutler is available to assist *Herr Doktor* Grumer and

myself in the event we have any legal difficulties at the site. We don't expect any, but Mr. Cutler, a lawyer from Atlanta, has graciously volunteered his time."

He smiled at the group, uncomfortable with the loose representations but powerless to say anything. He acknowledged the crowd, then turned back to the doorway.

The woman was gone.

FORTY-THREE

SUZANNE SCAMPERED OUT OF THE HOTEL. SHE'D SEEN AND heard enough. McKoy, Grumer, and both Cutlers were there and apparently busy. By her count, five workers were there, as well. According to Grumer's information, that left two other people on the payroll, probably at the site standing guard.

She'd caught Paul Cutler's momentary glance, but his notice shouldn't be a problem. Her physical appearance was far different from last week in his Atlanta office. To be safe, she'd stayed in the shadows and lingered only a few moments, long enough to see what was going on and take inventory. She'd taken a chance going to the Garni, but she didn't trust Alfred Grumer. He was too German, too greedy. A million euros? The fool must be dreaming. Did he think her benefactor that gullible?

Outside, she hustled back to her Porsche, then sped east to the excavation and parked in thick woods about a half kilometer away. After a quick hike, she found a work shed and shaft entrance. The generators outside hummed. No trucks, cars, or people were visible.

She slipped into the open shaft and followed a trail of

bulbs to a semidarkened gallery. Three halogen light bars were dark, the only available illumination was what spilled from a cavernous chamber beyond. She crept over and tested the air above one of the lights. Warm. She looked down and discovered that the trio of lamps had been unplugged.

In the shadows across the gallery she caught the glimpse of a form lying prone. She stepped close. A man in coveralls lay in the sand. She tried a pulse. Weak, but there.

She glanced into the chamber through an opening in the rock. A shadow danced across the far wall. She crouched low and slipped inside. No shadows betrayed her entrance, the powderlike sand cushioning each step. She decided not to ready her gun until she saw who was there.

She made it to the nearest truck and bent down, looking out from beneath the chassis. A pair of legs and boots stood on the side of the farthest truck. The feet moved right. Casual, unhurried. Her presence was obviously unknown. She stood still and decided to stay anonymous.

The legs stopped toward the rear of the farthest transport.

Canvas cracked. Whoever it was must be looking in a truck bed. She used the moment to slip around to the front end of the closest transport and dash to the hood of the next truck. Whoever it was now stood catty-corner to her on the opposite side. She carefully peered around at the figure twenty feet away.

Christian Knoll.

A chill swept through her.

———⚹——

KNOLL CHECKED INSIDE THE LAST TRUCK BED. EMPTY. THESE trucks had been picked clean. There was nothing in any of the cabs or beds. But who'd done that? McKoy? No way. He'd heard nothing in town about a significant find. Besides, there'd be remnants. Packing crates. Filler material. Yet nothing was here. And would McKoy leave a rich site guarded by only one easily overpowered man if he'd found a fortune in stolen art? The more logical explanation was these trucks were empty when McKoy breached the chamber.

But how?

And the bodies. Were they robbers from decades ago? Perhaps. Nothing unusual about that. Many of the Harz chambers had been pillaged, most by U.S. and Soviet armies that raped the region after the war, some later by scavengers and treasure hunters before the government took control of the area. He stepped to one of the bodies and stared down at the blackened bones. This whole scenario was strange. Why was Danzer so interested in what was obviously nothing? Interested enough to cultivate a covert source that wanted a million euros merely as a downpayment for information.

What kind of information?

A feeling surged through him. One he'd learned to trust. One that told him in Atlanta that Danzer was on his trail. One that told him now that somebody else was in the chamber.

He told himself to keep his moves casual. A sudden turn would spook his visitor. Instead, he slowly strolled down the length of the truck and led whoever it was farther from the entrance, placing himself in between. The intruder, though, intentionally avoided the light bars, allowing no shadow to betray any movement. He stopped and crouched, staring beneath the three transports for legs and feet.

There were none.

SUZANNE STOOD RIGID BEFORE ONE OF THE CRUSHED WHEEL ASsemblies. She'd followed Knoll deeper into the chamber and heard when his footsteps stopped. He was making no effort to mask sound, and that worried her. Did he sense her? Like in Atlanta? Maybe he was looking underneath the trucks as she'd done. If so, there'd be nothing to see. But he wouldn't hesitate long. She was not used to such an adversary. Most of her opponents did not possess the cunning of Christian Knoll. And once he ascertained it was her, there'd be hell to pay. Surely by now he'd learned about Chapaev, realized the mine had been a trap, and narrowed the list of likely suspects who would have set that trap to one.

Knoll's path across the chamber was also cause for concern.

He was leading her in. The bastard knew.

She withdrew the Sauer, her finger instantly wrapped around the trigger.

KNOLL TWISTED HIS RIGHT ARM AND RELEASED THE STILETTO. He palmed the lavender-jade handle and prepared himself. He stole another look beneath the trucks. No feet. Whoever it was obviously had used the wheel mounts as protection. He decided to act and pivoted off the rusted hood of the nearest transport and landed on the other side.

Suzanne Danzer stood twenty feet away, hugging a rear wheel mount. Shock filled her face at the sight of him. Her gun came up and leveled. He leaped in front of the adjacent transport. Two muffled shots exited the barrel, the bullets ricocheting off the rock wall.

He rose up and hurled the stiletto.

SUZANNE DIVED TO THE GROUND, ANTICIPATING THE KNIFE. IT was Knoll's trademark, and the tip had glistened in the light as he landed for the first assault. She realized that her shots would only be enough to momentarily distract him, so when Knoll rebounded, cocked his wrist, and propelled the blade her way, she was ready.

The stiletto swooshed past, slicing into the petrified canvas of the nearest transport's bed, its blade piercing the thin layer of rigid cloth down to the handle. There'd be only a second before he charged. She fired another shot in Knoll's direction. Again, the bullet damaged only rock.

"Not this time, Suzanne," Knoll slowly said. "You're mine."

"You're unarmed."

"Are you sure?"

She stared down at her gun, wondering how many shots were left in the clip. Four? Her eyes scanned the chamber, her mind reeling. Knoll was between her and the only way out. She needed something to stop the bastard long enough to allow her to escape this rat cage. Her eyes surveyed the rock walls, trucks, and lights.

The lights.

Darkness would be her ally.

She quickly popped the magazine from the pistol and replaced it with the spare from her pocket. Now she had seven shots. She aimed at the nearest light bar and fired. Lamps exploded in an electrical shower of sparks and smoke. She rose and darted for the opening, firing at the other light bar. Another blinding explosion flared, then extinguished and the chamber was plunged into total darkness. She set her course just as the last bits of light faded and hoped she ran straight.

If not, a wall of rock would be waiting for her.

⚷━━ ▪

KNOLL DASHED FOR THE STILETTO AS THE FIRST LIGHT BAR EXploded. He realized there'd be only a few more seconds of vision, and Danzer was right, without the knife he was unarmed. A gun would be nice. He'd foolishly left the CZ-75B in his hotel room, thinking it not necessary for this short foray. He actually preferred the stealth of a blade to a gun, but fifteen rounds would have come in handy right now.

He yanked the stiletto free of the canvas and turned. Danzer was racing for the opening to the shaft. He readied himself for another throw.

A light bar exploded in a blinding flash.

Then the room congealed into darkness.

⚷━━ ▪

SUZANNE RAN STRAIGHT AHEAD AND BISECTED THE OPENING leading out to the gallery. Ahead, the main shaft was strung with bulbs. She focused on the glow closest to her and raced straight for it, then charged down the narrow shaft, using her gun to rake the bulbs clean and extinguish the trail.

⚷━━ ▪

KNOLL WAS BLINDED BY THE LAST FLASH. HE CLOSED HIS EYES and told himself to stand still, stay calm. What had Monika said about Danzer earlier?

Charity case.

Hardly. Dangerous as hell was a better description.

The acrid odor of an electrical burn filled his nostrils. The chamber started to cool from the darkness. He opened his eyes. Black slowly dissolved and even darker forms appeared. Beyond the opening, past the gallery to the main shaft, lights flashed as bulbs exploded.

He ran toward them.

SUZANNE RACED FOR DAYLIGHT. FOOTSTEPS ECHOED FROM BEhind. Knoll was coming. She had to move fast. She emerged into a dim afternoon and sprinted through thick forest toward her car. The half kilometer would take a minute or so to traverse. Hopefully she had enough of a lead on Knoll to give her time. Maybe he wouldn't know which direction she went after exiting.

She zigzagged past tall pines, through dense ferns, breathing hard, commanding her legs to keep moving.

KNOLL EXITED THE TUNNEL AND QUICKLY TOOK STOCK OF THE surroundings. Off to his right, clothing flashed through the trees fifty meters away. He took in the shape of the runner.

A woman.

Danzer.

He sprinted in her direction, stiletto in hand.

SUZANNE REACHED THE PORSCHE AND LEAPED IN. SHE REVVED the engine, slammed the gear shift into first, and plunged the accelerator to the floor. Tires spun, then grabbed, and the car lurched forward. In the rearview mirror, she saw Knoll emerge from the trees, knife in hand.

She sped to the highway and stopped, then cocked her head out the window and saluted before speeding away.

KNOLL ALMOST SMILED AT THE GESTURE. PAYBACK FOR HIS mocking of her in the Atlanta airport. Danzer was probably proud of herself, pleased with her escape, another one-up on him.

He checked his watch. 4:30 P.M.

No matter.

He knew exactly where she'd be in six hours.

FORTY-FOUR

4:45 P.M.

PAUL WATCHED THE LAST PARTNER FILE OUT OF THE SALON. Wayland McKoy had smiled at each one, shook their hands, and assured them that things were going to be great. The big man seemed pleased. The meeting had gone well. For nearly two hours they'd fended questions, lacing their answers with romantic notions of greedy Nazis and forgotten treasure, using history as a narcotic to dull the investors' curiosity.

McKoy walked over. "Friggin' Grumer was pretty good, huh?" Paul, McKoy, and Rachel were now alone, all the partners upstairs, settling into their rooms. Grumer had left a few minutes ago.

"Grumer did handle himself well," Paul said. "But I'm not comfortable with this stalling."

"Who's stallin'? I intend to excavate that other entrance, and it could lead to another chamber."

Rachel frowned. "Your ground radar soundings indicate that?"

"Shit if I know, Your Honor."

Rachel took the rebuke with a smile. She seemed to be warming to McKoy, his abrupt attitude and sharp tongue not all that different from her own.

"We'll bus the group out to the site tomorrow and let 'em get an eyeful," McKoy said. "That should buy us a few more days. Maybe we'll get lucky with the other entrance."

"And pigs will fly," Paul said. "You've got a problem, McKoy. We need to be thinking through your legal position. How about I contact my firm and fax them that solicitation letter. The litigation department can look at it."

McKoy sighed. "What's that goin' to cost me?"

"Ten thousand retainer. We'll work off that at two-fifty an hour. After, it's by the hour, paid by the month, expenses on you."

McKoy sucked in a deep breath. "There goes my fifty thousand. Damn good thing I haven't spent it."

Paul wondered if it was time McKoy knew about Grumer. Should he show him the wallet? Tell him about the letters in the sand? Perhaps he knew all along about the chamber being barren and simply withheld the information. What had Grumer said yesterday? Something about suspecting the site was dry. Maybe they could blame everything on him, a foreign citizen, and claim justifiable reliance. *If not for Grumer, McKoy wouldn't have dug.* That way the partners would be forced to go after Grumer in the German courts. Costs would skyrocket, perhaps making litigation an economic impracticability. Maybe enough of a problem to send the wolves in retreat. He said, "There's something else I need—"

"Herr McKoy," Grumer said as he rushed into the salon. "There's been an incident at the site."

———※———

RACHEL STUDIED THE WORKER'S SKULL. A KNOT THE SIZE OF A hen's egg sprouted beneath the man's thick brown hair. She, Paul, and McKoy were in the underground chamber.

"I was standing out there," the man motioned to the outer gallery, "and the next thing I knew, everything went black."

"You didn't see or hear anyone?" McKoy asked.

"Nothing."

Workers were busy replacing the blown-out bulbs in the light bars. One lamp was already glowing again. She studied the scene. Smashed lights, bulbs obliterated in the main shaft, one of the canvas awnings ripped down the side.

"The guy must have got me from behind," the man said, rubbing the back of his head.

"How do you know it was a guy?" McKoy asked.

"I saw him," another worker said. "I was in the shed outside going over the tunnel routes for the area. I saw a woman race out of the shaft with a gun in her hand. A man came out right after. He had a knife. They both disappeared into the woods."

"You go after 'em?" McKoy asked.

"Shit, no."

"Why the hell not?"

"You pay me to dig, not be a hero. I headed in here. Place was black as soot. I went back out and got a flashlight. That's when I found Danny lying in the gallery."

"What did the woman look like?" Paul asked.

"Blonde, I think. Short. Fast as a jackrabbit."

Paul nodded. "She was at the hotel earlier."

McKoy said, "When?"

"While you and Grumer were talking. Came in for a minute then left."

McKoy understood. "Just the fuck long enough to see if we were all there."

"Looks that way," Paul said. "I think it was the same woman from my office. Different look, but there was something familiar about her."

"Lawyer intuition shit?" McKoy said.

"Something like that."

"Did you get a look at the man?" Rachel asked the worker.

"Tall guy. Light hair. With a knife."

"Knoll," she said.

Visions of the knife blade from the mine flashed through her mind. "They're here, Paul. Both of them are here."

Rachel was uneasy when she and Paul climbed the Garni's stairs to their second-floor room. Her watch read 8:10 P.M. Earlier, Paul had telephoned Fritz Pannik but got only an answering service. He left a message about Knoll and the woman, his suspicions, and asked the inspector to call. But there was no return message waiting at the front desk.

McKoy had insisted they eat dinner with the partners. Fine by her—the more crowds, the better. She, Paul, McKoy, and Grumer had divided the group between them, the talk all of the dig and what might be found. Her thoughts, though, stayed on Knoll and the woman.

"That was tough," she said. "I had to watch every word I said so no one could say later I misled them. Maybe this wasn't such a bright idea?"

Paul turned down the hall toward their room. "Look who's not adventurous now."

"You're a respected lawyer. I'm a judge. McKoy has latched on to us like Velcro. If he did bilk these people, we could become accomplices. Your daddy used to say all the time, 'If you can't run with the big dogs, get back under the porch.' I'm ready to climb back under."

He fished the room key from his pocket. "I don't think McKoy ripped anybody off. The more I study that letter, the more I read it as ambiguous, not false. I also think McKoy is genuinely shocked by the find. Now, Grumer—him, I'm not so sure about."

He unlocked the door and switched on the overhead light.

The room was wrecked. Drawers were yanked out. The armoire door swung open. The mattress was askew with the sheets half off. All their clothes lay strewn on the floor.

"The maid service in this place sucks," Paul said.

She wasn't amused. "This doesn't bother you? Somebody's searched this place. Oh, shit. Daddy's letters. And that wallet you found."

Paul closed the door. He slipped off his coat and yanked out his shirttail. A body wallet wrapped his abdomen. "Going to be a little difficult for anybody to find."

"Mother of God. I'll never berate your obsessiveness again. That was damn smart, Paul Cutler."

He lowered his shirt. "Copies of your daddy's letters are back at the office in the safe just in case."

"You expected this?"

He shrugged. "I didn't know what to expect. I just wanted to be prepared. With Knoll and the woman now around, anything can happen."

"Maybe we should get out of here. That judges' campaign waiting back home doesn't seem so bad right now. Marcus Nettles is a piece of cake compared to this."

Paul was calm. "I think it's time we do something else."

Instantly, she understood. "I agree. Let's go find McKoy."

❧————

PAUL WATCHED MCKOY ATTACK THE DOOR. RACHEL STOOD BE-hind him. The effects of three huge steins of beer showed in the intensity of McKoy's pounding.

"Grumer, unlock this goddamned door," McKoy screamed.

The door opened.

Grumer was still dressed in the long-sleeved shirt and trousers worn at dinner. "What is it, Herr McKoy? Has there been another incident?"

McKoy pushed into the room, shoving Grumer aside. Paul and Rachel followed. Two bedside lamps burned soft. Grumer had obviously been reading. An English copy of Polk's *Dutch Influence on German Renaissance Painting* lay parted on the bed. McKoy grabbed Grumer by the shirt and slammed him hard against the wall, rattling the picture frames.

"I'm a North Carolina redneck. Right now, a half-drunk North Carolina redneck. You may not know what that means, but I'll tell you it ain't good. I'm in no damn mood, Grumer. No damn fuckin' mood at all. Cutler tells me you dusted away letters in the sand. Where are the pictures?"

"I know nothing of what he says."

McKoy released his grip and rammed a fist into Grumer's stomach. The man doubled over, choking for air.

McKoy yanked him up. "Let's try it one more time. Where are the pictures?"

Grumer struggled for breath, coughing up bile, but managed to point to the bed. Rachel grabbed the book. Inside were a clutch of color photographs showing the skeleton and letters.

McKoy dropped Grumer to the carpet and studied the pictures. "I want to know why, Grumer. What the hell for?"

Paul wondered if he should issue a caution on the violence, but decided that Grumer had it coming. Besides, McKoy probably wouldn't listen anyway.

Grumer finally answered. "Money, Herr McKoy."

"Fifty thousand dollars I paid you wasn't enough?"

Grumer said nothing.

"Unless you want to start coughin' up blood, you'd better tell me everything."

Grumer seemed to get the message. "About a month ago, I was approached by a man—"

"Name."

Grumer caught a breath. "He gave no name."

McKoy reared back his fist.

"Please . . . it is true. No name at all, and he talked only by telephone. He'd read about my employment on this dig and offered twenty thousand euros for information. I saw no harm. He told me a woman named Margarethe would contact me."

"And?"

"I met her last evening."

"Did she or you search our room?" Rachel asked.

"Both of us. She was interested in the letters from your father."

"She say why?" McKoy asked.

"*Nein.* But I think I may know." Grumer was starting to breathe normally again, but his right arm hugged his stomach. He propped himself up against the wall. "Have you ever heard of *Retter der Verlorenen Antiquitäten*?"

"No," McKoy said. "Enlighten me."

"It is a group of nine people. Their identities unknown, but all are wealthy art lovers. They employ locators, their own personal collectors, called Acquisitors. The ingenious part of their association is as the name implies. 'Retrievers of *Lost* Antiquities.' They steal only what is already stolen. Each member's Acquisitor jousts for a prize. It's a sophisticated and expensive game, but a game nonetheless."

"Get to the point," McKoy said.

"This Margarethe, I suspect, is an Acquisitor. She never said, nor implied, but I believe my guess correct."

"What about Christian Knoll?" Rachel asked.

"The same. These two are competing for something."

"I'm gettin' the urge to beat the fuck out of you again," McKoy said. "Who does Margarethe work for?"

"Only a guess, but I would say Ernst Loring."

The name got Paul's attention, and he saw that Rachel was listening, too.

"From what I have been told, the club members are very competitive. There are thousands of lost objects to retrieve. Most from the last war, but many have been stolen from museums and private collections throughout the world. Quite clever, actually. To steal the stolen. Who's going to complain?"

McKoy moved toward Grumer. "You're tryin' my patience. Get to the damn point."

"The Amber Room," Grumer said between breaths.

Rachel forced a hand into McKoy's chest. "Let him explain."

"Again, this is only conjecture on my part. But the Amber Room left Königsberg sometime between January and April 1945. No one knows for sure. The records are unclear. Erich Koch, the gauleiter of Prussia, evacuated the panels on Hitler's direct order. Koch, though, was a protégé of Hermann Göring, in reality more loyal to Göring than Hitler.

The rivalry between Hitler and Göring for art is well documented. Göring justified his collecting by wanting to create a museum of national art at Karinhall, his home. Hitler was supposed to have first choice on any spoils, but Göring beat him to many of the best pieces. As the war progressed, Hitler took more and more personal control of the fighting, which limited the time he could devote to other matters. Göring, though, stayed mobile and was ferocious in collecting."

"What the fuck has this got to do with anything?" McKoy said.

"Göring wanted the Amber Room to become part of his Karinhall collection. Some argue it was he, not Hitler, who ordered the evacuation of the amber from Königsberg. He wanted Koch to keep the amber panels safe from the Russians, the Americans, and Hitler. But it was believed Hitler discovered the plan and confiscated the treasure before Göring could secure them."

"Daddy was right," Rachel softly said.

Paul stared at her. "What do you mean?"

"He told me once about the Amber Room and interviewing Göring after the war. All Göring said was Hitler beat him to it." She then told them about Mauthausen and the four German soldiers that were frozen to death.

"Where did you learn all your information?" Paul asked Grumer. "My father-in-law had a lot of articles on the Amber Room and none mentioned any of what you've just said." He'd purposefully omitted the reference to *former* father-in-law, and Rachel did not correct him like she usually did.

"There would be no mention," Grumer said. "The Western media rarely deals with the Amber Room. Few people even know what it is. German and Russian scholars, though, have long researched the subject. I've heard this particular information on Göring repeated often, but never such a firsthand account as Frau Cutler relates."

McKoy said, "How does this fit into our dig?"

"One account states that three trucks eventually were loaded with the panels somewhere west of Königsberg, *after*

Hitler took control. Those trucks headed west and were never seen again. They would have been heavy transports—"

"Like Büssing NAGs," McKoy said.

Grumer nodded.

McKoy plopped on the edge of the bed. "The three trucks we found?" The harsh tone had softened.

"Too much of a coincidence, wouldn't you say?"

"But the trucks are empty," Paul said.

"Exactly," Grumer said. "Perhaps the Retrievers of Lost Antiquities know even more of the story. Maybe that explains two Acquisitors' rather intense interest."

"But you don't even know if Knoll and this woman have anything to do with that group," Rachel said.

"No, Frau Cutler, I do not. But Margarethe does not impress me as being an independent collector. You were around Herr Knoll. Would you say the same?"

"Knoll refused to say who he worked for."

"Which makes him even more suspect," McKoy said.

Paul slipped the wallet found at the site from his jacket pocket and handed it to Grumer. "What about this?" He explained where it was found.

"You discovered what I was looking for," Grumer said. "The information Margarethe requested concerned any possible dating of the site beyond 1945. I searched all five skeletons, but found nothing. This proves the site was violated postwar."

"There's some writing on a scrap of paper inside. What is it?"

Grumer looked close. "Appears to be some sort of permit or license. Issued March 15, 1951. Expires March 15, 1955."

"And this Margarethe wanted to know this?" McKoy asked.

Grumer nodded. "She was willing to pay handsomely for the information."

McKoy ran a hand through his hair. The big man looked worn out. Grumer took the moment to explain. "Herr McKoy, I had no idea the site was dry. I was as excited as you when we broke through. The signals, though, were becoming clearer. No explosives or even remnants. Narrow passage in. Lack of any door or steel reinforcement for the shaft or the chamber. And the trucks. Heavy transports should not be there."

"Unless the goddamned Amber Room *used* to be there."

"That is correct."

"Tell us more about what happened," Paul said to Grumer.

"There is little to tell. Stories attest that the Amber Room was placed in crates, then loaded onto three trucks. The trucks were supposedly heading south to Berchtesgaden and the safety of the Alps. But the Soviet and American armies were all over Germany. There was nowhere to go. Supposedly, the trucks were hidden. But there is no record where. Perhaps their hiding place was the Harz mines."

"You figure since this Margarethe was so interested in Borya's letters and is here, the Amber Room must have something to do with all this," McKoy asked.

"It would seem a logical conclusion."

Paul asked, "Why do you think Loring is her employer?"

"Only a guess based on what I've read and heard through the years. The Loring family was, and is, interested in the Amber Room."

Rachel had a question. "Why erase the letters? Did Margarethe pay you to do that?"

"Not really. She only made clear that nothing should remain that dates the chamber past 1945."

"Why was that a concern?" Rachel asked.

"I truly have no idea."

"What does she look like?" Paul asked.

"She's the same woman as you described this afternoon."

"You realize that she could have killed Chapaev and Rachel's father."

"And you didn't say a damn word?" McKoy said to Grumer. "I ought to beat the livin' fuck out of you. You understand how much shit I'm in with a dry site. Now this." The big man rubbed his eyes, seemingly trying to calm himself, then quietly asked, "When's the next contact, Grumer?"

"She indicated that she would call me."

"I want to know the second that bitch does. I've had enough. Am I clear?"

"Perfectly," Grumer said.

McKoy stood and headed for the door. "You better, Grumer. Let me know the second you hear from that woman."

"Of course. Anything you say."

⚷

THE PHONE WAS RINGING IN THEIR ROOM WHEN PAUL OPENED the door. Rachel followed him inside as he answered. It was Fritz Pannik. He quickly recounted to Pannik what happened earlier, telling the inspector that the woman and Knoll were nearby, or at least had been a few hours ago.

"I will dispatch someone from the local police to take a statement from everyone first thing in the morning."

"You think those two are still here?"

"If what Alfred Grumer says is true, I would say yes. Sleep light, Herr Cutler, and I will see you tomorrow."

Paul hung up and sat on the bed.

"What do you think?" Rachel asked, sitting beside him.

"You're the judge. Did Grumer seem credible?"

"Not to me. But McKoy seemed to buy what he was saying."

"I don't know about that. I get the feeling McKoy's holding something back, too. I can't put my finger on it, but there's something he's not saying. He was listening closely to Grumer on the Amber Room. But we can't worry about that now. I'm concerned about Knoll and the woman. They're roaming around here, and I don't like it."

His eyes caught the swell of her breasts through the tight-fitting turtleneck sweater. Ice Queen? Not to him. He'd felt her body all last night, unnerved by the closeness. Periodically he'd taken in her scent as she slept. At one point, he tried to imagine himself three years back, still married to her, still able to physically love her. Everything was surreal. Lost treasure. Killers wandering about. His ex-wife in bed with him.

"Maybe you were right to begin with," Rachel said. "We're in way over our heads and should just get out of here. There's Marla and Brent to think about." She looked at him. "And there's us." Her hand came to his.

"What do you mean?"

She softly kissed him on the lips. He sat perfectly still. She then wrapped her arms around him and kissed him hard.

"Are you sure about this, Rachel?" he asked as they parted.

"I don't know why I'm so hostile sometimes. You're a good man, Paul. You don't deserve the hurt I caused."

"It wasn't all your fault."

"There you go again. Always shouldering blame. Can't you let me take the blame just once?"

"Sure. You're welcome to it."

"I want it. And there's something else I want."

He saw the look in her eye, understood, and instantly rose from the bed. "This is really weird. We haven't been together in three years. I've grown accustomed to that. I thought we were through . . . in that way."

"Paul, for once go with your instincts. Everything doesn't have to be planned. What's wrong with good old-fashioned lust?"

He held her gaze with his. "I want more than that, Rachel."

"So do I."

He moved toward the window, putting distance between them, and parted the sheers, anything to buy a little time. This was too much too fast. He stared down at the street, thinking about how long he'd dreamed of hearing those words. He'd not gone to court for the divorce hearing. Hours later, the final judgment had rolled out of the fax machine, his secretary laying it on his desk without a word. He'd refused to look at it, shoveling the paper, unread, into the trash. How could a judge's signature silence what his heart knew to be right?

He turned back.

Rachel looked lovely, even with Sunday's cuts and scrapes.

They truly were an odd couple from the beginning. But he'd loved her and she'd loved him. Together they'd produced two children, whom they both worshiped. Did they now have a second chance?

He turned back to the window and tried to find answers in the night. He was about to step toward the bed and surrender when he noticed someone appear on the street.

Alfred Grumer.

The *Doktor* walked with a firm, determined gait, apparently having just exited the Garni's front entrance two stories below.

"Grumer's leaving," he said.

Rachel jumped up and pushed close for a look. "He didn't say anything about leaving."

He grabbed his jacket and shot for the door. "Maybe he got the call from Margarethe. I knew he was lying."

"Where are you going?"

"You have to ask?"

FORTY-FIVE

PAUL LED RACHEL OUT THROUGH THE HOTEL ENTRANCE AND turned in Grumer's direction. The German was a hundred yards ahead, briskly negotiating the cobbled street between the dark shops and busy cafés that were still luring customers with beer, food, and music. Streetlights periodically lit the way with a mustard glow.

"What are we doing?" Rachel asked.

"Finding out what he's up to."

"Is this a good idea?"

"Maybe not. But we're doing it anyway."

He didn't say that it also relieved him of a difficult decision. He wondered if Rachel was merely lonely or scared. It bothered him what she'd said in Warthberg, defending Knoll even though the bastard had left her to die. He didn't like being second choice.

"Paul, there's something you need to know."

Grumer was ahead, still moving fast. He didn't break stride. "What?"

"Right before the explosion in the mine, I turned around and Knoll had a knife."

He stopped and stared at her.

"He had a knife in his hand. Then the shaft's ceiling gave way."

"And you're just now telling me this?"

"I know. I should have. But I was afraid you wouldn't stay or that you'd tell Pannik and he'd interfere."

"Rachel, are you nuts? This shit is serious. And you're right, I wouldn't have stayed, nor would I have let you. And don't tell me that you can do what the hell you want." His attention shot to the right. Grumer disappeared around a corner. "Damn. Come on."

He started to trot, his jacket flapping. Rachel kept pace. The street began to incline. He reached the corner where Grumer had just been and stopped. A closed *konditorei* stood to the left with an awning that skirted the corner. He cautiously glanced around. Grumer was still walking fast, seemingly unconcerned if anybody was behind him. The *Doktor* bisected a small square centered by a fountain bowered in geraniums. Everything—the streets, shops, and plants—reflected the maniacal cleanliness of German civic pride.

"We need to stay back," Paul said. "But it's darker here, and that'll help."

"Where are we going?"

"It looks like we're headed up toward the abbey." He glanced at his watch—10:25 P.M.

Ahead, Grumer suddenly disappeared left into a row of black hedges. They scampered up and saw a concrete walk dissolve into the blackness. A posted sign announced, ABBEY

OF THE SEVEN SORROWS OF THE VIRGIN. The arrow pointed forward.

"You're right. He is going to the abbey," Rachel said.

They started up the four-person-wide stone path. It wound
a steep course through the night to the rock-strewn bluff.
Halfway, they passed a couple strolling arm in arm. They
reached a sharp turn. Paul stopped. Grumer was ahead, still
climbing fast.

"Come here," he said to Rachel, wrapping an arm around
her shoulder, cradling her close. "If he looks back, all he'll
see are two lovers walking. He'll never see our faces at this
distance."

They walked slowly.

"You're not going to get away this easy," Rachel said.

"What do you mean?"

"In the room. You know where we were headed."

"I don't plan to get away."

"You just needed time to think, and this little jog gives
you that."

He didn't argue. She was right. He did need to think, but
not now. Grumer was his main concern at the moment. The
climb was winding him, his calves and thighs tightening. He
thought he was in shape, but his three-mile runs in Atlanta
were usually on flat earth, nothing like this murderous incline.

The path crested ahead and Grumer disappeared over the
top.

The abbey was no longer a distant edifice. Here the facade
spanned two football fields, rising sharply from the cliff
shoulder, the walls elevated by a vaulted stone foundation.
Bright sodium vapor lights hidden in the forested base
flooded the colored stone. Rows of tall mullioned windows
glistened up three stories.

A lighted gateway rose ahead, buildings stacked on either
side and above. Two bastions flanked the main portal. A
semidarkened forecourt lay beyond. Fifty yards ahead,
Grumer disappeared through the open portal. The bright

lights surrounding the gate worried him. Pigeons cooed from somewhere beyond the glare. No one else was in sight.

He led Rachel forward and glanced up at sculptures of the apostles Peter and Paul resting on blackened stone pedestals. On either side saints and angels vied with fish and mermaids. A coat of arms framed the portal's center, two golden keys on a royal blue background. A huge cross towered over the gable, the inscription clear under the floodlights. ABSIT GLORIARI NISI IN CRUCE.

"Glory only in the cross," he muttered.

"What?"

He pointed up. "The inscription. 'Glory only in the cross.' From Galatians, 6:14."

They passed through the portal. A freestanding sign identified the space beyond as GATEKEEPER'S COURT. Thankfully, the courtyard was unlit. Grumer was now at the far end, rushing up a wide set of stone steps, entering what looked like a church.

"We can't go in after him," Rachel said. "How many people could be in there at this hour?"

"I agree. Let's find another way in."

He studied the courtyard and surrounding buildings. Three-story structures rose on all sides, the facades baroque and adorned with Roman arches, elaborate cornices, and statues that added the required religious tone. The majority of windows were dark. Shadows danced behind drawn sheers in the few that were lit.

The church Grumer entered jutted forward from the opposite end of the dark courtyard, its symmetrical twin towers flanked by a brightly lit octagonal dome. It seemed an appendage of the farthest building, which would actually be the front of the abbey, the side facing Stod and the river, overlooking the highest point of the bluff.

He pointed to the far side of the courtyard, beyond the church, at a set of double oak doors. "Maybe those lead to another way."

They hustled across the cobbled courtyard, past islands of trees and shrubs. A cool wind eased by, leaving a chill. He

tried the lock. It opened. He pushed the leaden door inward—
slowly, to minimize the squeaks. An alleylike passageway
spanned out before them, four dim incandescent fixtures
glowed at the far end. They stepped inside. Halfway down
the corridor, a staircase rose up with wooden balustrades. Oil
paintings of kings and emperors lined the way up. Beyond
the staircase, farther down the musty corridor, another closed
door waited.

"The church would be on this level. That door ought to
lead inside," he whispered.

The latch opened on the first try. He inched the door open,
toward him. Warm air flooded the cool corridor. A heavy
velvet curtain extended in both directions, a narrow passageway spanning left and right. Light flitted through periodic
slits in the curtain and from the bottom. He gestured for quiet
and led Rachel into the church.

Through one of the curtain slits he spied the interior. Scattered pools of orange light lit the huge nave. The explosive
architecture, ceiling frescoes, and rich colored stucco combined into a visual symphony, nearly overpowering in depth
and form. Brownish red, gray, and gold predominated.
Fluted marble pilasters reached toward a vaulted ceiling,
each one adorned in elaborate gilt moldings supporting an
array of statuary.

His gaze drifted to the right.

A gilded crown framed the center of an oversize high
altar. A huge medallion bore the inscription, NON CORON-
ABITUR, NISI LEGITIME CERTAVERIT. *Without a just fight, there
is no victory,* he silently translated. The Bible again. Timo-
thy 2:5.

Two people stood off to the left—Grumer and the blonde
from this morning. He glanced back over his shoulder and
mouthed to Rachel. "She's here. Grumer's talking to her
again."

"Can you hear?" Rachel whispered in his ear.

He shook his head, then pointed left. The narrow corridor
ahead would lead them closer to where the two stood, the
velvet draping down to the stone floor enough to protect

them from sight. A small wooden staircase rose at the far end, ascending to what was most likely the choir. He concluded the curtained passage was probably used by acolytes who served Mass. They tiptoed forward. Another slit allowed him a view. He cautiously peered out, standing perfectly rigid before the velvet. Grumer and the woman stood near a forward people's altar. He'd read about this addition made to many European churches. The baroque Catholic of the Middle Ages sat far from the high altar, only passively experiencing God's closeness. Contemporary worshipers, thanks to liturgical reforms, demanded more active participation. So people's altars were added to ancient churches, the walnut of the podium and altar matching the rows of empty pews beyond.

He and Rachel were now about twenty meters from Grumer and the woman, whose whispers were difficult to hear in the hushed emptiness.

SUZANNE GLARED AT ALFRED GRUMER, WHO WAS TAKING A SURprisingly gruff attitude with her.

"What happened today at the excavation site?" Grumer asked in English.

"One of my colleagues appeared and became impatient."

"You are drawing a lot of attention to the situation."

She disliked the German's tone. "It was not my choosing. I had to deal with the matter, as it presented itself."

"Do you have my money?"

"You have my information?"

"Herr Cutler found a wallet at the site. It dates from 1951. The chamber was breached postwar. Is that not what you wanted?"

"Where is this wallet?"

"I could not retrieve it. Perhaps tomorrow."

"And Borya's letters?"

"There is no way I could secure them. After what happened this afternoon, everyone is on edge."

"Two failures and you want five million euros?"

"You wanted information on the site and the dating. I supplied that. I also eliminated the evidence in the sand."

"That was your own concoction. A way to up the price of your services. The reality is that I have no proof of anything you've said."

"Let's talk reality, Margarethe. And that reality is the Amber Room, correct?"

She said nothing.

"Three German heavy transports, empty. A sealed underground chamber. Five bodies, all shot in the head. A 1951 to 1955 dating. This is the chamber where Hitler hid the room, and somebody robbed it. I would guess that somebody was your employer. Otherwise, why all the concern?"

"Speculation, *Herr Doktor.*"

"You did not blink at my insistence on five million euros." Grumer's voice carried a smug tone she was liking less and less.

"Is there more?" she asked.

"If I recall correctly, a pervasive story circulated during the 1960s concerning Josef Loring being a Nazi collaborator. But, after the war, he managed to become well connected with the Czechoslovakian Communists. Quite a trick, actually. His factories and foundries, I assume, were powerful inducements for lasting friendships. The talk, I believe, was that Loring found Hitler's hiding place for the Amber Room. The locals in this area swore Loring came several times with crews and quietly excavated the mines before the government took control. In one, I would imagine, he found the amber panels and Florentine mosaics. Was it our chamber, Margarethe?"

"*Herr Doktor,* I neither admit nor deny any of what you are saying, though the history lesson does carry some fascination. What of Wayland McKoy? Is this current venture over?"

"He intends to excavate the other opening, but there will be nothing to find. Something you already know, correct? I would say the dig is over. Now, did you bring the payment we discussed?"

She was tired of Grumer. Loring was right. He was a greedy bastard. Another loose end. One that needed immediate attention.

"I have your money, Herr Grumer."

She reached into her jacket pocket and wrapped her right hand around the Sauer's checkered stock, a sound suppressor already screwed to the short barrel. Something suddenly swept past her left shoulder and thudded into Grumer's chest. The German gasped, heaved back, and then crumpled to the floor. In the dim altar light she immediately noticed the lavender-jade handle with an amethyst set in the pommel.

Christian Knoll leaped from the choir to the nave's stone floor, a gun in hand. She withdrew her own weapon and dived behind the podium, hoping the walnut was more wood than veneer.

She risked a quick look.

Knoll fired a muffled shot, the bullet ricocheting off the podium centimeters from her face. She reeled back and scrunched tight behind the podium.

"Very inventive in that mine, Suzanne," Knoll said.

Her heart raced. "Just doing my job, Christian."

"Why was it necessary to kill Chapaev?"

"Sorry, my friend, can't go into it."

"That is a shame. I did hope to learn your motives before killing you."

"I'm not dead yet."

She could hear Knoll chuckling. A sick laugh that echoed through the stillness.

"This time I'm armed," Knoll said. "Herr Loring's gift to me, in fact. A very accurate weapon."

The CZ-75B. Fifteen-shot magazine. And Knoll had used only one bullet. Fourteen chances left to kill her. Too damn many.

"No light bars to shoot out here, Suzanne. In fact, there is nowhere to go."

With a sickening dread, she realized he was right.

PAUL HAD HEARD ONLY SCATTERED BITS OF THE CONVERSATION.
Obviously his initial doubts about Grumer had been proved
right. The *Doktor* was apparently playing both ends against
the middle and had just discovered the price that deceit
sometimes elicited.

He'd watched in horror as Grumer died and the two combatants squared off, muffled shots popping through the
church like pillows fluffing. Rachel stood behind him, staring over his shoulder. They stood rigid, neither moving for
fear of revealing their presence. He knew they had to get out
of the church, but their exit needed to be absolutely silent.
Unlike the two in the nave, they were unarmed.

"That's Knoll," Rachel whispered in his ear.

He'd figured that. And the woman was definitely Jo
Myers, or Suzanne, as Knoll called her. He'd instantly recognized the voice. No doubt now that she'd killed Chapaev,
since she'd not denied the allegation when Knoll asked
about it. Rachel pressed tight against him. She was shaking.
He reached back and squeezed her leg, pressing her close,
trying to calm her down, but his hand shook, too.

KNOLL HUNCHED LOW IN THE SECOND ROW OF PEWS. HE LIKED
the situation. Though his opponent was unfamiliar with the
church's layout, it was clear Danzer had nowhere to go without him having at least a few seconds to shoot.

"Tell me something, Suzanne, why the mine explosion?
We've never crossed that line before."

"What did I do, cramp your style with the Cutler woman?
You were probably going to fuck her, then kill her, right?"

"Both thoughts crossed my mind. In fact, I was just getting ready to do the first when you so rudely interrupted."

"Sorry, Christian. Actually, the Cutler woman should
thank me. I saw she survived the explosion. I don't think she
would have been as lucky with your knife. Kind of like
Grumer over there, right?"

"As you say, Suzanne, only doing my job."

"Look, Christian, maybe we don't have to take this to the

extreme. How about a truce? We can go back to your hotel and sweat out our frustrations. How about it?"

Tempting. But this was serious business, and Danzer was only buying time.

"Come on, Christian, I guarantee it'll be better than what that spoiled bitch Monika puts out. You've never complained in the past."

"Before I consider that, I want some answers."

"I'll try."

"What is so important about that chamber?"

"Can't talk about that. Rules, you know."

"The trucks are empty. Nothing there. Why all the interest?"

"Same answer."

"The records clerk in St. Petersburg is on the payroll, right?"

"Of course."

"You knew I went to Georgia all along?"

"I thought I did a good job staying out of the way. Obviously not."

"Were you at Borya's house?"

"Of course."

"If I hadn't twisted that old man's neck, you would have?"

"You know me too well."

⚹——ᴅ

PAUL WAS PRESSED TO THE CURTAIN AS HE HEARD KNOLL ADMIT to killing Karol Borya. Rachel gasped and stepped back, bumping him forward, which rippled the velvet. He realized the movement and her sound would be more than enough to attract the attention of both combatants. In an instant, he shoved Rachel to the floor, rolling in mid-flight, absorbing most of the impact on his right shoulder.

⚹——ᴅ

KNOLL HEARD A GASP AND SAW THE CURTAIN MOVE. HE FIRED three shots into the velvet, chest high.

⚹——ᴅ

SUZANNE SAW THE CURTAIN MOVE, BUT HER INTEREST WAS IN getting out of the church. She used the moment of Knoll's three shots to send one of her own in his direction. The bullet splintered one of the pews. She saw Knoll duck for cover, so she bolted into the shadows of the high altar, leaping forward into a dark archway.

⚷——

"LET'S GO," PAUL MOUTHED. HE PULLED RACHEL TO HER FEET and they raced toward the door. The bullets had pierced the curtain and found stone. He hoped Knoll and the woman would be too preoccupied with each other to bother with them. Or maybe they'd team up against what might be deemed a common enemy. He wasn't going to stay around and find out which route they took.

They made it to the door.

His shoulder pounded with pain, but adrenaline streaking through his veins worked like anesthetic. Out in the corridor, beyond the church, he said, "We can't go back into the courtyard—we'll be sitting ducks."

He turned toward a stairway leading up.

"Come on," he said.

⚷——

KNOLL SAW DANZER LEAP INTO A DARK ARCHWAY, BUT THE PILlars, podium, and altar impeded a clear shot, the long shadows no help either. At the moment, though, he was more interested in who was behind the curtain. He'd entered the church that way himself, climbing the wooden stairway at the passage's end to the choir.

He cautiously approached the curtain and peered behind, gun ready.

Nobody was there.

He heard a door open, then close. He quickly stepped over to Grumer's body and withdrew the stiletto. He cleaned the blade and slipped the knife up his sleeve.

Then he parted the curtain and followed.

❦——

PAUL LED THE WAY UP THE STAIRCASE, GIVING THE HEAVILY framed ghostly images of kings and emperors that lined the way only a passing glance. Rachel hustled behind him.

"That bastard killed Daddy," she said.

"I know, Rachel. But right now we're in sort of a mess."

He turned on the landing and nearly leaped up the last flight. Another dark corridor waited at the top. He heard a door open behind them. He froze, stopping Rachel, covering her mouth with his hand. Footsteps came from below. Slow. Steady. Their way. He motioned for quiet, and they tiptoed to the left—the only way to go—toward a closed door at the far end.

He tried the latch handle.

It opened.

He inched the door inward and they slipped inside.

❦——

SUZANNE STOOD IN A DARK CUBICLE BEHIND THE HIGH ALTAR, the sweet scent of incense strong from two metal pots against the wall. Colorful priestly vestments hung in two rows on metal racks. She needed to finish what Knoll had started. The son of a bitch had certainly one-upped her. How he found her was of concern. She was careful leaving the hotel, checking her backside repeatedly on the way up to the abbey. No one had followed her, of that she was certain. No. Knoll was in the church, waiting. But how? Grumer? Possibly. It worried her that Knoll somehow knew her business so intimately. She'd wondered why there'd been no hot pursuit from the mine earlier, Knoll's show of disappointment as she sped away not nearly as satisfying as she'd expected.

She stared back out through the archway.

He was still in the church, and she needed to find him and settle this matter. Loring would want that. No more loose ends. None at all. She peered out and watched as Knoll disappeared through a curtain.

A door opened, then closed.

She heard footsteps climbing stairs.

Sauer in hand, she cautiously headed for the source of the sound.

❧———⚷

KNOLL HEARD FAINT STEPS ABOVE. WHOEVER IT WAS HAD GONE up the staircase.

He followed, gun ready.

❧———⚷

PAUL AND RACHEL STOOD INSIDE A CAVERNOUS SPACE, A FREE-standing sign proclaiming in German MARMOREN KAMMER, the English beneath reading MARBLE HALL. Pilastered marble columns, evenly spaced around the four walls, rose at least forty feet, each one decorated in gold leaf, the surrounding colors a soft peach and light gray. Magnificent frescoes of chariots, lions, and Hercules decorated the ceiling. A three-dimensional architectural painting framed the room, creating an illusion of depth to the walls. Incandescent light splashed across the ceiling. The motif might have been interesting if not for the fact that someone with a gun was probably coming after them.

He led the way as they scampered across checkerboard tile, bisecting a brass floor grille that rushed warm air up into the hall. Another ornate door waited at the opposite end. As far as he could see, it was the only other way out.

The door they entered through suddenly creaked inward.

Instantly, Paul opened the door in front of him and they slipped out onto a rounded terrace. Beyond a thick stone balustrade, blackness extended to the broad tangle of Stod below. The velvet bowl overhead was thick with stars. Behind them, the abbey's well-lit amber-and-white facade loomed stark against the night. Stone lions and dragons stared down and seemed to keep watch. A chilling breeze swept over them. The ten-person-wide terrace rounded in a horseshoe to another door at the opposite end.

He led Rachel around the loop to the far door.

It was locked.

Back across, the door they'd just come through began to open. He quickly looked around and saw there was nowhere to go. Over the railing was nothing but a sheer drop hundreds of meters down to the river.

Rachel seemed to sense their quandary, too, and she looked at him, fear filling her eyes, surely thinking the same thing he was.

Were they going to die?

FORTY-SIX

KNOLL OPENED THE DOOR AND SAW THAT IT LED OUT TO AN open terrace. He stood still. Danzer was still lurking somewhere behind him. But maybe she'd fled the abbey. No matter. As soon as he determined who else had been in the church, he'd head straight to her hotel. If he didn't find her there, he'd find her somewhere else. She would not be disappearing this time.

He peered around the edge of the thick oak door and surveyed the terrace. No one was there. He stepped out and closed the door, then crossed the wide loop. Halfway, he stole a quick glance over the side. Stod blazed to the left, the river ahead, a long drop down. He reached the other door and determined it was locked.

Suddenly, the door from the Marble Hall, at the other end of the loop, swung open and Danzer leaped out into the night. He lunged behind the stone rail and thick spindles.

Two muffled shots streaked his way.

The bullets missed.

He returned fire.

Danzer sent another round his way. Stone splinters from

the ricochet momentarily blinded him. He crawled to the door nearest him. The iron lock was furred in rust. He fired two shots into the handle and the latch gave way.

He yanked open the door and quickly crawled inside.

SUZANNE DECIDED ENOUGH. SHE SAW THE DOOR AT THE OTHER end of the horseshoe open. No one walked inside, so Knoll must have crawled. The confines were tightening, and Knoll was far too dangerous to keep openly pursuing him. She now knew that he was on the abbey's upper stories, so the smart move was to backtrack and head down to town before he had a chance to find his way out. She needed to get out of Germany, preferably back to Castle Loukov and the safety of Ernst Loring. Her business here was finished. Grumer was dead, and, as with Karol Borya, Knoll had saved her the trouble. The excavation site seemed secure. So what she was now doing seemed foolish.

She turned and raced back through the Marble Hall.

RACHEL CLUNG TO THE COLD STONE SPINDLE. PAUL DANGLED beside her, desperately gripping his own spindle. It had been her idea to leap over the railing and hang on just as someone exited the far door. Below her boots was a cascading blackness. A strong wind buffeted their bodies. Her grip was weakening by the second.

They'd listened in horror as bullets careened off the terrace and out into the chilly night, hoping that whoever was following them did not glance over the side. Paul had managed a look as the near door's lock was shot through and someone crawled inside. "Knoll," he'd mouthed. But for the last minute—silence. Not one sound.

Her arms ached. "I can't hold on much longer," she whispered.

Paul ventured another look. "There's nobody there. Climb." He swung his right leg out, then pulled himself up and over the railing. He reached down and helped her up.

Once on firm ground, they both leaned against the cold stone and stared down at the river below.

"I can't believe we did that," she said.

"I've got to be out of my damn mind to be in the middle of this."

"As I remember, you're the one who dragged me up here."

"Don't remind me."

Paul inched the half-closed door open and she followed him inside. The room was an elegant library lined floor to ceiling with inlaid bookshelves of shiny walnut, everything gilded in baroque style. They passed through a wrought-iron gate and quickly crossed a slick parquet floor. Two huge wooden globes flanked either side, set in recesses between the shelves. The warm air smelled of musty leather. A yellow rectangle of light extended from a doorway at the far end where the top of another staircase was visible.

Paul motioned ahead. "That way."

"Knoll came in here," she reminded.

"I know. But he had to have taken off after that shootout."

She followed Paul out of the library and down the staircase. A darkened corridor below immediately wound to the right. She hoped there was a door somewhere that led back to the inner courtyard. At the bottom she saw Paul turn, then a black shadow shot from the darkness and Paul's body folded to the floor.

A gloved hand encircled her neck.

She was lifted from the last step and slammed against the wall. Her vision blurred, then refocused, and she was staring straight into the feral eyes of Christian Knoll, a knife blade pinched into the bottom of her chin.

"That your ex-husband?" His words came in a throaty whisper, his breath warm. "Come to your rescue?"

Her eyes stole a look at Paul sprawled across the stone. He wasn't moving. She looked back at Knoll.

"You may find this hard to believe, but I have no complaint with you, Frau Cutler. Killing you would certainly be the most efficient thing to do, but not necessarily the smartest.

First your father dies, then you. And so close together. No. As
much as I might want to rid myself of a nuisance, I cannot kill
you. So, please. Go home."

"You killed . . . my father."

"Your father understood the risks he took in life. Even
seemed to appreciate them. You should have taken the advice he offered. I am quite familiar with Phaëthon's story. A
fascinating tale about impulsive ways. The helplessness of
the elder generation trying to teach the younger. What did
the Sun God tell Phaëthon? 'Look in my face and if you
could, look in my heart, see there a father's anxious blood
and passion.' Heed the warning, Frau Cutler. My mind can
easily change. Would you want those precious children of
yours to cry tears of amber if a lightning bolt struck you
dead?"

She suddenly visualized her father lying in the casket.
She'd buried him in his tweed jacket, the same one he'd
worn to court the day she changed his name. She'd never believed that he merely fell down the stairs. Now his killer was
here, pressed against her. She shifted and tried to knee Knoll
in the crotch, but the hand around her neck tightened, and the
knife tip broke the skin.

She gasped and sucked in a deep breath.

"Now, now, Frau Cutler. None of that."

Knoll released his right hand from her throat, but kept the
blade firm to her chin. He let his palm travel the length of her
body to her crotch, and he cupped her in a tight clasp. "I
could tell that you found me intriguing." His hand drifted up
and massaged her breasts through the sweater. "A shame I
don't have more time." He suddenly clamped tight on her
right breast and twisted.

The pain stiffened her.

"Take my advice, Frau Cutler. Go home. Have a happy
life. Raise your kids." His head motioned to Paul. "Please
your ex-husband and forget about all this. It does not concern you."

She managed through the pain to say again, "You . . .
killed my . . . father."

His right hand released her breast and throttled her neck. "The next time we meet, I will slit your throat. Do you understand?"

She said nothing. The knife tip moved deeper. She wanted to scream but couldn't.

"Do you understand?" Knoll slowly asked.

"Yes," she mouthed.

He withdrew the blade. Blood trickled from the wound in her neck. She stood rigid against the wall. She was concerned about Paul. He still hadn't moved.

"Do as I say, Frau Cutler."

He turned to leave.

She lunged at him.

Knoll's right hand arched up and the knife handle caught her square below the right temple. Her eyes flashed white. The corridor spun. Bile erupted in her throat. Then she saw Marla and Brent rushing toward her, arms outstretched, their mouths moving but the words inaudible as blackness overtook them.

PART FOUR

FORTY-SEVEN

SUZANNE RACED DOWN THE INCLINE BACK TO STOD. ALONG THE way she passed three late-night strollers to whom she paid no attention. Her only concern at the moment was to get back to the Gebler, grab her belongings, and disappear. She needed the safety of the Czech border and Castle Loukov, at least until Loring and Fellner could resolve this matter, member to member.

Knoll's sudden appearance had again caught her off guard. The bastard was determined, she'd give him that. She decided not to underestimate him a third time. If Knoll was in Stod, she needed to get out of the country.

She found the street below and trotted toward her hotel.

Thank god she'd packed. Everything was ready to go, her plan all along had been to leave after tending to Alfred Grumer. Fewer streetlamps illuminated the way than earlier, but the Gebler's entrance was well lit. She entered the lobby. A night clerk behind the front desk was pounding a keyboard and never looked up. Upstairs, she shouldered her travel bag and threw some euros on the bed, more than enough to cover the bill. No time for any formal checkout.

She took a moment and caught her breath. Maybe Knoll didn't know where she was staying. Stod was a big town with lots of inns. No, she decided. He knew and was probably headed here right now. She thought back to the abbey's terrace. Knoll was after whoever else had been in the church. And that other presence was likewise of concern to her. But she wasn't the one who tossed a knife into Grumer's chest.

Whatever he or she saw was more Knoll's problem than hers.

In her travel bag she found a fresh clip for the Sauer and popped it into place. She then pocketed the gun. Downstairs, she stepped quickly through the lobby and out the front door. She looked right, then left. Knoll was a hundred yards away, moving straight in her direction. When he spotted her, he started to run. She bolted ahead, down a deserted side street, and rounded a corner. She kept running and quickly turned two more corners. Maybe she could lose Knoll in the maze of venerable buildings that all looked alike.

She stopped. Her breathing came hard.

Footsteps echoed from behind.

Coming closer.

In her direction.

⚷——

KNOLL'S BREATH CONDENSED IN THE DRY AIR. HIS TIMING HAD been nearly perfect. A few moments more and he would have caught the bitch.

He turned a corner and halted.

Only silence.

Interesting.

He gripped the CZ and stepped cautiously forward. He'd studied the layout of the old part of town yesterday from a map obtained at the tourist bureau. The buildings covered blocks interrupted by narrow cobbled streets and even tighter alleys. Steep roofs, dormer windows, and arcades adorned with mythological creatures loomed everywhere. It would be easy to get lost in the warren of sameness. But he knew exactly where Danzer's slate-gray Porsche was parked. He'd found it yesterday on a reconnaissance mission, knowing that she would certainly have a quick means of transportation nearby.

So he started in that direction, the same direction the running footsteps had initially been headed.

He stopped fast.

Still, only silence.

No more soles slapping cobblestone in the distance.

He inched forward and turned a corner. The street ahead was a straight line, the only glow breaking the darkness loomed at the far end. Halfway, an intersection appeared. The lane to the right stretched about thirty meters, dead-ending into what looked like the back of a shop. A small black Dumpster rested just to the right, a parked BMW to its left. It was more an alley than a street. He stepped to the end and checked the car. Locked. He lifted the Dumpster lid. Empty except for newspapers and a few trash bags that smelled of rotting fish. He tried the doorknobs for the building. Locked.

He stepped back to the main street, gun in hand, and turned right.

SUZANNE WAITED A FULL FIVE MINUTES BEFORE SLITHERING OUT from under the BMW. She'd wiggled beneath, thankful for her petite size. Just in case, though, the 9mm was ready. But Knoll had not looked underneath, seemingly satisfied the car doors were locked, the alley apparently empty.

She retrieved her travel bag from the Dumpster where she'd stashed it under some newspapers. A lingering odor of fish accompanied the leather bag. She pocketed the Sauer and decided to use another route to her car, perhaps even leaving the damn thing and renting another in the morning. She could always come back later and retrieve the Porsche after this was settled. An Acquisitor's job was to do what his or her employer desired. Even though Loring had told her to handle things at her discretion, the situation with Knoll and the risk of drawing attention was escalating. Also, killing her opponent was proving far more difficult than she'd first imagined.

She stopped in the alley before the intersection and listened a few seconds more.

No footsteps could be heard.

She scooted out and instead of turning right as Knoll had done, she went left.

From a darkened doorway, a fist slammed her forehead. Her neck whipped back, then recoiled. The pain momentarily froze her, and a hand encircled her throat. Her body was lifted, then pounded into a damp stone wall. A sickening smile filled Christian Knoll's Nordic face.

"How stupid do you take me for?" Knoll said, inches from her.

"Come on, Christian. Can't we settle this? I meant what I said back at the abbey. Let's go back to your room. Remember France? That was fun."

"What's so important that you have to kill me?" His grip tightened.

"If I say, you'll let me go?"

"I am in no mood, Suzanne. My orders are to do as I please, and I believe you know what pleases me."

Buy some time, she thought. "Who else was in the church?"

"The Cutlers. It seems they have a continuing interest. Care to enlighten me?"

"How would I know?"

"I believe you know a lot more than you are willing to state." He squeezed harder.

"Okay. Okay, Christian. It's the Amber Room."

"What of it?"

"That chamber was where Hitler hid it. I had to be sure, that's why I'm here."

"Sure of what?"

"You know Loring's interest. He's looking for it, just like Fellner. We're just privileged to information you don't have."

"Such as?"

"You know I can't say. This isn't fair."

"And blowing me up is? What is going on, Suzanne? This is no ordinary quest."

"I'll make you a deal. Let's go back to your room. We'll talk after. Promise."

"I'm not feeling amorous right now."

But the words had the desired effect. The hand around her throat relaxed just enough for her to pivot off the wall and knee him solidly in the groin.

Knoll crumpled in pain.

She kicked him once more between the legs, driving the toe of her boot into his cupped hands. Her adversary crashed to the cobbles and she rushed away.

Blinding pain racked Knoll's groin. Tears welled in his eyes. The bitch had done it again. Quick as a cat. He'd relaxed only a second to readjust his grip. But enough for her to strike.

Damn.

He stared up to see Danzer disappearing down the street. His groin ached. He was having trouble breathing, but he could probably still take a shot at her. He reached for the pistol in his pocket, then stopped.

No need.

He'd tend to her tomorrow.

FORTY-EIGHT

WEDNESDAY, MAY 21, 1:30 A.M.

RACHEL OPENED HER EYES. HER HEAD POUNDED. HER STOMACH churned as if from seasickness. The stench of vomit rose from her sweater. Her chin ached. She gently traced the outline of a blood pimple, then remembered the knifepoint boring in.

Hovering over her was a man dressed in the brown cassock of a monk. His face was old and withered, and he watched her intently with anxious watery eyes. She was propped against the wall, in the corridor where Knoll had attacked her.

"What happened?" she asked.

"You tell us," said Wayland McKoy.

She looked beyond the monk and tried to focus. "I can't see you, McKoy."

The big man stepped closer.

"Where's Paul?" she asked.

"Over there, still out. Got a nasty blow to the head. You okay?"

"Yeah. Just have one monster headache."

"I bet you do. The monks heard some shots from the church. They found Grumer, then you two. Your room keys led them to the Garni and I hustled up here."

"We need a doctor."

"That monk is a doctor. He says your head's fine. No cracks."

"How about Grumer?" she asked.

"Aggravatin' the devil, probably."

"It was Knoll and the woman. Grumer came up here to meet with her again and Knoll killed him."

"Fuckin' bastard got what he deserved. Any reason why you two didn't invite me?"

She massaged her head. "You're lucky we didn't."

Paul groaned a few feet away. She pulled herself across the stone floor. Her stomach started to calm down. "Paul, you all right?"

He was rubbing the left side of his head. "What happened?"

"Knoll was waiting for us."

She slid close and checked his head.

"How did your chin get cut?" McKoy asked her.

"Not important."

"Look, Your Honor, I've got a dead German upstairs and police askin' a thousand questions. You two are found sprawled out cold, and you tell me it's not important. What the fuck's goin' on?"

"We need to call Inspector Pannik," Paul said to her.

"I agree."

"Excuse me. Hello? Remember me?" McKoy said.

The monk handed her a wet rag. She dabbed it to the side of Paul's head. Blood stained the cloth.

"I think he cut you," she said.

Paul reached up to her chin. "What did happen there?"

She decided to be honest. "A warning. Knoll told us to go home and stay out of this."

McKoy bent close. "Stay out of what?"

"We don't know," she said. "All we're sure of is the woman killed Chapaev and Knoll killed my father."

"How do you know that?"

She told him what happened.

"I couldn't hear all of what Grumer and the woman were saying in the church," Paul said. "Only little bits and pieces. But I think one of them—Grumer, maybe—mentioned the Amber Room."

McKoy shook his head. "I never dreamed things would go this far. What the crap have I done?"

Paul said, "What do you mean, *done*?"

McKoy said nothing.

"Answer him," Rachel said.

But McKoy stayed silent.

❧━━♂

MCKOY STOOD IN THE UNDERGROUND CHAMBER, HIS MIND A swirling montage of apprehension, and stared at the three rusted transports. He turned his gaze slowly to the ancient rock face, searching for a message. An old cliché, *if the walls could talk,* kept racing through his mind. Could these walls tell him more than he already knew? Or more than he already suspected? Would they explain why the Germans drove three valuable trucks deep into a mountain and then dynamited the only exit? Or was it even the Germans who sealed the exit? Could they describe how a Czech industrialist breached the cavern years later, stole what was there, and then blasted the entrance shut? Or maybe they knew nothing at all. As silent as the voices that had tried through the years to forge a trail, only to find a path leading to death.

Behind him, footsteps approached through the opening from the outer gallery. The other exit from the chamber was still stuffed tight with rock and rubble, his crews yet to start any excavation. They wouldn't until tomorrow at the earliest. He glanced at his watch and saw that it was nearly 11:00 A.M. He turned to see Paul and Rachel Cutler emerge through the shadows. "I didn't expect you two this early. How're your heads?"

"We want answers, McKoy, and no more stalling," Paul said. "We're in this whether we, or you, like it or not. You kept wondering last night what you'd done. What did you mean?"

"You don't plan to take Knoll's advice and go home?"

"Should we?" Rachel asked.

"You tell me, Judge."

"Quit delaying," Paul said. "What's going on?"

"Come over here." He led them across the chamber to one of the skeletons embedded in the sand. "There isn't much left of what these guys were wearin', but from the scraps the uniforms appear World War Two vintage. The camouflage pattern is definitely U.S. Marine." He bent down and pointed. "That sheath is for an M4 bayonet, U.S. issue from the war. I'm not certain, but the pistol holster is probably French. The Germans didn't wear American issue or use French equipment. After the war, though, all sorts of European military and paramilitary used American-issue stuff. The French Foreign Legion. Greek National Army. Dutch Infantry." He motioned across the chamber. "One of the skeletons over there is wearing breeches and boots with no pockets. Hungarian Soviets dressed like that *after* the war. The clothing. The empty trucks. And the wallet you found cinches things."

"Cinches what?" Paul asked.

"This place was robbed."

"How do you know about what these guys were wearing?" Rachel asked.

"Contrary to what you might think, I'm not some dumbass North Carolina redneck. Military history is my passion. It's also part of my preparation on these digs. I know I'm right. I felt it Monday. This chamber was breached *post* war. No doubt about it. These poor slobs were either ex-military, current military, or workers dressed in surplus. They were shot when the job was finished."

"Then all that you did with Grumer was an act?" Rachel asked.

"Shit, no. I wanted this place to be full of art, but after that first look Monday, I knew we had a violated site. I just didn't realize how violated till now."

Paul pointed to the sand. "That's the corpse with the letters." He bent down and retraced *O, I,* and *C* in the sand, spacing the letters as he remembered. "They were like that."

McKoy retrieved Grumer's photographs from his pocket.

Paul then added three additional letters—*L, R, N*—filling in the blank spaces—and changed the *C* to a *G.* The word now read LORING.

"Son of a bitch," McKoy said, comparing the photo to the ground. "I think you're right, Cutler."

"What made you think of that?" Rachel asked Paul.

"It was hard to see clear. It could have been a half *G.* Anyway, the name keeps coming up. Your father even mentioned it in one of his letters." Paul reached in his pocket and withdrew a folded sheet. "I read it again a while ago."

McKoy studied the handwritten paragraph. Halfway down, the Loring name caught his eye:

> *Yancy telephoned the night before the crash. He was able to locate the old man you mentioned whose brother worked at Loring's estate. You were right. I should never have asked Yancy to inquire again while in Italy.*

McKoy grabbed Paul's gaze with his own. "You believe your parents were the target of that bomb?"

"I don't know what to think anymore." Paul motioned to the sand. "Grumer talked last night about Loring. Karol talked about him. My father may have talked about him. Maybe even this guy here in the sand was talking about him. All I know is Knoll killed Rachel's father and the woman killed Chapaev."

"Let me show you somethin' else," McKoy said. He led them to a map lying flat near one of the light bars. "I took some compass readings this morning. The other shaft that's sealed goes northeast." He bent and pointed. "This is a map of the area from 1943. There used to be a paved road that paralleled the base of the mountain to the northeast."

Paul and Rachel squatted close to the map.

"I'd wager these trucks were driven in here through the other sealed entrance, over this road. They would have needed a compact surface. They're too heavy for mud and sand."

"You believe what Grumer said last night?" Rachel asked.

"That the Amber Room was here? No doubt about it."

"How can you be so sure?" Paul asked.

"My guess is this chamber wasn't sealed by the Nazis, but by whoever looted it after the war. The Germans would have needed to get the amber panels back after they were stashed. It makes no sense to blast the entrance shut. But the guy who came in here in the 1950s, now that bastard wouldn't want anyone to know what he'd found. So he murdered the help and collapsed the shaft. Our findin' this was a fluke, thanks to ground radar. The fact that we gained entrance, just another fluke."

Rachel seemed to understand. "Always pays to be lucky."

"The Germans and the looter probably didn't even know that another shaft passed this close to the chamber. Like you say, just dumb luck on our part, lookin' for railroad cars full of art."

"They had rail lines going into these mountains?" Paul asked.

"Damn right. That's how they moved munitions in and out."

Rachel stood and gazed at the trucks. "Then this could be the place Daddy talked about going to see?"

"It well could," McKoy said.

"Back to the original question, McKoy. What did you mean about what you'd done?" Paul asked.

McKoy stood. "You two I don't know from shit to shineola. But for some reason I trust you. Let's walk back outside to the shed, and I'll tell you all about it."

PAUL NOTICED THE MIDMORNING SUN AS IT CAST A DUSTY HUE through the shed's dingy panes.

"How much do you know about Hermann Göring?" McKoy asked.

"Just what's on the History Channel," Paul said.

McKoy smiled. "He was the number-two Nazi. But Hitler finally ordered his arrest in April 1945, thanks to Martin Bormann. He convinced the Führer that Göring intended to mount a coup for power. Bormann and Göring never got along. So Hitler branded him a traitor, stripped him of his titles, and arrested him. The Americans found him just as the war ended, when they took control of southern Germany.

"While he was imprisoned, awaitin' trial on war crimes, Göring was heavily interrogated. The conversations were eventually memorialized in what came to be called Consolidated Interrogation Reports. These were considered secret documents for years."

"Why?" Rachel asked. "Seems like they would be more historical than secret. The war was over."

McKoy explained that there were two good reasons why the Allies suppressed the reports. The first was because of the avalanche of art restitution requests that came after the war. Many were speculative and spurious. No government had the time or money to fully investigate and process hundreds of thousands of claims. And the CIRs would have done nothing but amplify those claims. The second reason was more prag-

matic. The general assumption was that everyone—apart
from a handful of corrupt people—nobly resisted Nazi terror.
But the CIRs revealed how French, Dutch, and Belgian art
dealers profited from the invaders by supplying art for the
Sonderauftrag Linz project, Hitler's Museum of World Art.
Suppression of the reports eased the embarrassment that fact
would have caused a great many.

"Göring tried to have his pick of the art spoils before
Hitler's thieves arrived in any conquered country. Hitler
wanted to purge the world of what he considered decadent
art. Picasso, van Gogh, Matisse, Nolde, Gauguin, and Grosz.
Göring recognized value in these masterpieces."

"What does any of that have to do with the Amber
Room?" Paul asked.

"Göring's first wife was a Swedish countess, Karin von
Kantzow. She visited the Catherine Palace in Leningrad before the war and loved the Amber Room. When she died in
1931 Göring buried her in Sweden, but the Communists des-
ecrated her grave, so he built an estate he called Karinhall
north of Berlin and encased her body there in an immense
mausoleum. The whole place was gaudy and vulgar. A hundred thousand acres, stretching north to the Baltic Sea and
east to Poland. Göring wanted to duplicate the Amber Room
in her memory so he constructed an exact ten-by-ten-meter
chamber ready to accept the panels."

"How do you know that?" Rachel asked.

"The CIRs contain interviews with Alfred Rosenberg, head
of the ERR, the department Hitler created to oversee the looting of Europe. Rosenberg talked repeatedly of Göring's obsession with the Amber Room."

McKoy then described the fierce competition between
Göring and Hitler for art. Hitler's taste reflected Nazi phi-
losophy. The farther east the origin of a work, the less valuable. "Hitler possessed no interest in Russian art. He
considered the entire nation subhuman. But Hitler didn't regard the Amber Room as Russian. Frederick William I, King
of Prussia, had given the amber to Peter the Great. So the

relic was German, and its return to German soil was considered culturally important.

"Hitler himself ordered the panels evacuated from Königsberg in 1945. But Erich Koch, the Prussian provincial governor, was loyal to Göring. Now here's the rub. Josef Loring and Koch were connected. Koch desperately needed raw materials and efficient factories to deliver the quotas Berlin imposed on all provincial governors. Loring worked with the Nazis, opening family mines, foundries, and factories to the German war effort. Hedgin' his bets, though, Loring also worked with Soviet intelligence. This may explain why it was so easy for him to prosper under Soviet rule in Czechoslovakia after the war."

"How do you know all this?" Paul asked.

McKoy stepped over to a leather briefcase angled from the top of a survey table. He retrieved a sheaf of stapled papers and handed them to Paul. "Go to the fourth page. I marked the paragraphs. Read 'em."

Paul flipped the sheets and found the marked sections:

Interviews with several contemporaries of Koch and Josef Loring confirm the two met often. Loring was a major financial contributor to Koch and maintained the German governor in a lavish lifestyle. Did this relationship lead to information about, or perhaps the actual acquisition of the Amber Room? The answer is hard to say. If Loring possessed either knowledge of the panels or the panels themselves, the Soviets apparently knew nothing.

Quickly after the war, in May 1945, the Soviet government mounted a search for the amber panels. Alfred Rohde, the director of the Königsberg art collections for Hitler, became the Soviets' initial information source. Rohde was passionately fond of amber, and he told Soviet investigators that

crates with the panels were still in the
Königsberg palace when he left the building
on April 5, 1945. Rohde showed investigators the burned-out room where he said the
crates were stored. Bits of gilded wood and
copper hinges (that were believed part of
the original Amber Room doors) still remained. The conclusion of destruction became
inescapable, and the matter was considered
closed. Then, in March 1946, Anatoly Kuchumov, curator of the palaces at Pushkin,
visited Königsberg. There, in the same
ruins, he found crumbled remains of the
Florentine mosaics from the Amber Room.
Kuchumov firmly believed that while other
parts of the room may have burned, the amber
did not, and he ordered a new search.

By then, Rohde was dead, he and his wife
having died on the same day they were ordered to reappear for a new round of Soviet
interrogations. Interestingly, the physi-
cian that signed the Rohdes' death certifi-
cate also disappeared the same day. At that
point, the Soviet Ministry of State Security took over the investigation along with
the Extraordinary State Commission, which
continued to search until nearly 1960.

Few have accepted the conclusion that the
amber panels were lost at Königsberg. Many
experts question if the mosaics were actually destroyed. The Germans were very clever
when necessary and, given the prize and personalities involved, anything is possible.
In addition, given Josef Loring's intense
postwar efforts in the Harz region, his
passion for amber, and the unlimited amount
of money and resources available to him,
perhaps Loring did find the amber. Inter-

views with heirs of local residents confirm
that Loring visited the Harz region often,
searching the mines, all with the knowledge
and approval of the Soviet government. One
man even stated Loring was working on the
assumption that the panels were trucked from
Königsberg west into Germany, their ultimate
destination south to the Austrian mines or
the Alps, but the trucks were diverted by
the impending approach of the Soviet and
American armies. Best estimates state three
trucks were involved. Nothing can be confirmed, however.

Josef Loring died in 1967. His son, Ernst,
inherited the family fortune. Neither has
ever spoken publicly on the subject of the
Amber Room.

"You knew?" Paul said. "All that Monday and yesterday
was an act? You've been after the Amber Room all along?"

"Why'd you think I let you hang around? Two strangers
appear out of nowhere. You think I'd have wasted two seconds with you if the first things out of your mouth weren't
'We're looking for the Amber Room,' and 'Who the hell's
Loring?' "

"Fuck you, McKoy," Paul said, surprised at his own language. He couldn't recall cursing so crudely, or as much as
he had the past few days. Apparently, this North Carolina
redneck was wearing off on him.

"Who wrote this?" Rachel asked, motioning to the paper.

"Rafal Dolinski, a Polish reporter. He did a lot of work on
the Amber Room. Kind of obsessed with the subject, if you
ask me. When I was over here three years ago, he approached me. He's the one who got me all hyped up over
amber. He'd done a lot of research and was writin' an article
for some European magazine. He was hopin' for an interview with Loring to cinch some interest by a publisher. He

sent a copy of this entire thing to Loring, along with a request to talk. The Czech never responded, but a month later Dolinski was dead." McKoy paused, then looked straight at Rachel. "Blown up in a mine near Warthberg."

Paul said, "Goddammit, McKoy. You knew all this and didn't tell us. Now Grumer's dead."

"Shit on Grumer. He was a greedy, lyin' bastard. He got himself killed by sellin' out. That's not my problem. I didn't tell him any of this on purpose. But somethin' was tellin' me this was the right chamber. Ever since the radar soundings. Could be a rail car, but if not, it could be three trucks with the Amber Room inside. When I saw those damn things Monday, waitin' in the dark, I thought I'd hit the mother lode."

"So you bilked investors for the opportunity to find out if you're right," Paul said.

"I figured either way, they'd win. Paintings or amber. What do they care?"

"You're a damn good actor," Rachel said. "Fooled me."

"My reaction when I saw the trucks empty wasn't an act. I was hopin' my gamble had paid off and the investors wouldn't mind a little change in booty. I was bankin' that Dolinski was wrong and the panels were never found by Loring, or anyone else. But when I saw that other sealed entrance and the empty beds, I knew I was in deep shit."

"You're still in deep shit," Paul said.

McKoy shook his head. "Think about it, Cutler. Somethin's happenin' here. This isn't some dry hole. That chamber back there was not meant to be found. We just stumbled onto it, thanks to good ole modern technology. Now, all at once, somebody is awfully interested in what we're doin', and they're awfully interested in what Karol Borya and Chapaev knew. Interested enough to kill 'em. Maybe they were interested enough to kill your parents."

Paul stared hard at McKoy.

"Dolinski told me about a lot of folks who ended up dead searchin' for the amber. Stretches all the way back to just after the war. Spooky as hell. Now he may well be one of 'em."

Paul did not argue the point. McKoy was right. Something definitely was going on and it involved the Amber Room. What else could it be? There were simply too many coincidences.

"Assuming you're right, what do we do now?" Rachel finally asked in a voice that signaled resignation.

McKoy's response was quick. "I'm going to the Czech Republic and talk to Ernst Loring. I think it's about time somebody did."

"We're going, too," Paul said.

"We are?" Rachel asked.

"You're damn right. Your father and my parents may have died over this. I've come this far. I plan to finish."

Rachel's look was curious. Was she discovering something about him? Something she may never have noticed before. A determination that hid beneath a deep veneer of controlled calm. Maybe she was. He was certainly discovering something about himself. The experience last night had jolted him. The rush when he and Rachel fled from Knoll. The terror in dangling from a balcony hundreds of feet above a blackened German river. They'd been lucky to escape with only a couple knots on their heads. But he was determined now to learn what had happened to Karol Borya, his parents, and Chapaev.

"Paul," Rachel said, "I don't want something like last night to happen again. This is foolish. We have two children. Remember what you tried to tell me last week and in Warthberg. I agree with you now. Let's go home."

His gaze bored into her. "Go. I'm not stopping you."

The sharpness of his tone and quickness of his response unnerved him. He recalled mouthing similar words to her three years ago when she told him she was filing for divorce. Bravado at the time. Words said only for her benefit. Proof that he could handle the situation. This time the words were more. He was going to Czech, and she could go with him or go home. He really didn't care which.

"Ever thought about somethin', Your Honor?" McKoy suddenly said.

Rachel looked at him.

"Your father kept Chapaev's letters and copied the ones he sent back. Why? And why leave 'em for you to find? If he really didn't want you involved, he would have burned the damn things and taken the secret to his grave. I didn't know that old man, but I can think like him. He was a treasure hunter once. He'd want the amber found, if there was any way possible. And you're the only one he trusted with the information. Granted, he went through his asshole to get to his appetite in sendin' the message, but the message is still loud and clear. 'Go find it, Rachel.' "

He was right, Paul thought. That's exactly what Borya had done. He'd never really considered it before now.

Rachel grinned. "I think my daddy would have liked you, McKoy. When do we leave?"

"Tomorrow. Right now, I've got to handhold the partners to buy us a little more time."

FORTY-NINE

NEBRA, GERMANY
2:10 P.M.

KNOLL SAT IN THE SILENCE OF A TINY HOTEL ROOM AND THOUGHT about *die Retter der Verlorenen Antiquitäten,* the Retrievers of Lost Antiquities. They were nine of the wealthiest men in Europe. Most were industrialists, but there were two financiers, a land baron, and one doctor among its current membership. Men with little to do except search the world for stolen treasure. Most of them were well-known private collectors, and their interests varied: old Masters. Contemporary. Impressionist. African. Victorian. Surrealist. Neo-lithic. Diversity was what made the club interesting. It also defined specific territories where a member's Acquisitor concentrated his or her collecting. Most times, those territorial lines were not crossed. Occasionally, members vied with one another to see who could locate the same object faster. A race for acquisition, the challenge lying in finding what was thought lost forever. In short, the club was an outlet. A way for rich men to dispense a competitive spirit that rarely knew any bounds.

But that was okay. He knew no bounds either and liked it that way.

He thought back to last month's gathering.

Club meetings rotated between members' estates, the locales varying from Copenhagen south to Naples. It was customary that an unveiling occur at each gathering, preferably a find by the host's Acquisitor. Sometimes that wasn't possible and other members would volunteer an unveiling, but Knoll knew how each member longed to show off something new when it was their turn to entertain. Fellner particularly liked the attention. As did Loring. Just another facet of their intense competition.

Last month had been Fellner's turn. All nine members had gathered at Burg Herz, but only six Acquisitors had been free to attend. That was not unusual, since quests took precedence over the courtesy of appearing at another Acquisitor's unveiling. But jealousy could also account for an absence. Exactly, he assumed, why Suzanne Danzer had skipped the affair. Next month was Loring's turn in the rotation and Knoll had planned to return the courtesy, boycotting Castle Loukov. That was a shame, since he and Loring got along well. Loring had several times rewarded him with gifts for acquisitions that ultimately ended up in the Czech's private collection. Club members routinely stroked another's Acquisitor, thereby multiplying by nine the pairs of eyes scouring the world in search of treasure they found particularly enticing. Members routinely traded or sold among themselves. Auctions were common. Items of collective interest were bidded out at the monthly gathering, a way for a member to raise funds from acquisitions of no particular personal interest while keeping the treasures within the group.

It was all so orderly, so civilized.

So why was Suzanne Danzer so eager to change the rules? Why was she trying to kill him?

A knock on the door interrupted his thoughts. He'd been waiting nearly two hours after driving west from Stod to Nebra, a tiny hamlet halfway to Burg Herz. He stood and opened the door. Monika immediately stepped inside. The scent of sweet lemons accompanied her entrance. He closed and locked the door behind her.

She surveyed him up and down. "Rough night, Christian?"

"I'm not in the mood."

She plopped on the bed, cocking one leg in the air, the crotch of her jeans exposed.

"For that, either," he said. His groin still ached from Danzer's kicks, though he was not about to tell her that.

"Why was it necessary that I drive here to meet you?" she asked. "And why can't Father be involved?"

He told Monika what happened in the abbey, about Grumer, and the chase through Stod. He left out the final street confrontation and said, "Danzer got away before I could reach her, but she mentioned the Amber Room. She said the chamber in that mountain was where Hitler hid the panels in 1945."

"You believe her?"

He'd considered that point all day. "I do."

"Why didn't you go after her?"

"No need. She's headed back to Castle Loukov."

"How do you know that?"

"Years of sparring."

"Loring called again yesterday morning. Father did as you asked and told him we hadn't heard from you."

"Which explains why Danzer so openly traipsed around Stod."

She was studying him closely. "What are you thinking of doing?"

"I want permission to invade Castle Loukov. I want to go into Loring's preserve."

"You know what Father would say."

Yes, he did. Club rules expressly forbade one member from invading the privacy of another. After an unveiling, the whereabouts of any acquisition was nobody's business. The glue that bound their collective secrecy was the mere knowledge of acquisition that all nine possessed on each other. Club rules also forbade revelations of sources unless the acquiring member desired to say. That secrecy protected not only the member but the Acquisitor, as well, assuring that cultivated information could be harvested again without interference. Privacy was the key to their entire union, a way for similar men of similar interests to exact similar pleasure. The sanctity of their individual estates was an inviolate rule, any breach of which required instant expulsion.

"What's the matter?" he said. "No nerve? Are you not now in charge?"

"I have to know why, Christian."

"This is way beyond a simple acquisition. Loring has already violated club rules by having Danzer try to kill me. More than once, I might add. I want to know why, and I believe the answer is in Volary."

He hoped he'd gauged her correctly. Monika was proud and arrogant. She'd clearly resented her father's usurpation yesterday. That anger should cloud her better judgment, and she didn't disappoint him.

"Fucking right. I want to know what that bitch and old fart are doing, too. Father thinks we're imagining all this, that there was some sort of misunderstanding. He wanted to talk to Loring, tell him the truth, but I talked him out of it. I agree. Do it."

He saw the hungry look in her eye. To her, competition
was an aphrodisiac.

"I'm heading there today. I suggest no more contact until
I'm in and out. I'm even willing to accept the blame, if
caught. I was acting on my own, and you know nothing."

Monika grinned. "How noble, my knight. Now come over
here and show me how much you missed me."

⚷———▪

PAUL WATCHED FRITZ PANNIK STROLL INTO THE GARNI'S DINING
room and walk straight to the table he and Rachel occupied.
The inspector sat down and told them what he knew so far.

"We have checked the hotels and learned that a man
matching Knoll's description was registered across the street
in the Christinenhof. A woman matching the description of
this Suzanne was registered a few doors down at the
Gebler."

"You know anything more about Knoll?" Paul asked.

Pannik shook his head. "Unfortunately, he is an enigma.
Interpol has nothing in their files, and without fingerprint
identification there is no realistic way to learn more. We
know nothing of his background, or even where he resides.
The mention of an apartment in Vienna to Frau Cutler was
certainly false. To be safe, I checked the information. But
nothing suggests Knoll lives in Austria."

"He must have a passport," Rachel said.

"Several probably, and all under assumed names. A man
such as this would not register his true identity with any government."

"And the woman?" Rachel asked.

"We know even less about her. The crime scene for Chapaev was clean. He died of nine-millimeter wounds from
close range. That suggests a certain callousness."

Paul told Pannik about the Retrievers of Lost Antiquities
and Grumer's theory about Knoll and the woman.

"I have never heard of such an organization, but will make
inquiries. The name Loring, though, is familiar. His foundries

produce the best small arms in Europe. He also is a major steel producer. One of the leading industrialists in Eastern Europe."

"We're going to see Ernst Loring," Rachel said.

Pannik cocked his head in her direction. "And the purpose of the visit?"

She told him what McKoy said about Rafal Dolinski and the Amber Room. "McKoy thinks he knows something about the panels, maybe about my father, Chapaev, and—"

"Herr Cutler's parents?" Pannik asked.

"Maybe," Paul said.

"Forgive me, but don't you believe that this matter should be handled by the proper authorities? The risks appear to be escalating."

"Life's full of risks," Paul said.

"Some are worth taking. Some are foolish."

"We think it's worth taking," Rachel said.

"The Czech police are not the most cooperative," Pannik said. "I would assume that Loring has enough contacts in the Justice Ministry to make any official inquiry difficult at the least. Though the Czech Republic is no longer Communist, remnants of secrecy remain. Our department finds official information requests are many times delayed beyond what we consider reasonable."

"You want us to be your eyes and ears?" Rachel said.

"The thought did occur to me. You are private citizens on a purely personal mission. If you happen to learn enough for me to institute official action, then so much the better."

Paul had to say, "I thought we were taking too many risks."

Pannik's eyes were cold. "You are, Herr Cutler."

SUZANNE STOOD ON THE BALCONY THAT JUTTED FROM HER BED-chamber. A late afternoon sun burned blood orange and gently warmed her skin. She felt safe and alive at Castle Loukov. The estate spread for miles, once the domain of Bohemian princes, the surrounding woods game preserves, all the deer and boar exclusively for the ruling class. Villages also once dotted the forests, places where quarrymen, masons, carpenters, and blacksmiths lived while working on the castle. It took two hundred years to finish the walls and less than an hour for the Allies to bomb them to rubble. But the Loring family rebuilt, this latest incarnation every bit as magnificent as the original.

She stared out over the rustling treetops, her lofty perch facing southeast, a light breeze refreshing her. The villages were all gone, replaced by isolated houses and cottages, residences where generations of Loring's staff had lived. Housing had always been provided for stewards, gardeners, maids, cooks, and chauffeurs. About fifty all total, the families perpetually residing on the estate, their children simply inheriting the jobs. The Lorings were generous and loyal to their help—the life beyond Castle Loukov was generally brutal—so it was easy to see why employees served for life.

Her father had been one of those people, a dedicated art historian with an untamable streak. He became Ernst Loring's second Acquisitor a year before she was born. Her mother died suddenly when she was three. Both Loring and her father spoke of her mother often, and always in glowing terms. She'd apparently been a lovely lady. While her father traveled the world acquiring, her mother tutored Loring's two sons. They were much older, she'd never really been close with either, and by the time she was a teenager they were gone to university. Neither returned to Castle Loukov much. Neither knew anything of the club, or of what their father did. That was a secret only she and her benefactor shared.

Her love of art had always endeared her to Loring. His offer to succeed her father came the day after he was buried. She'd been surprised. Shocked. Unsure. But Loring harbored no doubts on either her intelligence or resolve, and his unfettered confidence was what constantly inspired her to succeed. But now, standing alone in the sun, she realized that she'd chanced far too many risks over the past few days.

Christian Knoll was not a man to take lightly. He was well aware of her attempts on his life. She'd twice made a fool of him. Once in the mine, the other with the kick in the groin. Never before had their quests risen to this level. She was uncomfortable with the escalation, but understood its need. Still, this matter required resolution. Loring needed to talk with Franz Fellner and reach some accommodation.

A light knock came from inside.

She reentered her bedchamber and answered the door. One of the house stewards said, *"Pan Loring si přeje vás vidêt. Ve studovnê."*

Loring wanted to see her in his study.

Good, she needed to talk with him, as well.

The study was two floors down at the northwest end of the castle's ground floor. Suzanne had always considered it a hunter's room, since the walls were lined with antlers and horns, the ceiling decorated with the heraldic animals of Bohemian kings. A huge seventeenth-century oil painting dominated one wall and depicted muskets, game bags, hog spears, and powder horns in astonishingly realistic terms.

Loring was already comfortable on the sofa when she walked in. "Come here, my child," he said in Czech.

She sat beside him.

"I have thought long and hard about what you reported earlier, and you are right, something needs to be done. The cavern in Stod is most certainly the place. I thought it would never be found, but it now apparently has."

"How can you be sure?"

"I cannot. But from the few things Father told me before he died, the location certainly appears genuine. The trucks, bodies, the sealed entrance."

"That trail is cold again," she made clear.

"Is it, my dear?"

Her analytical mind took over. "Grumer, Borya, and Chapaev are dead. The Cutlers are amateurs. Even though Rachel Cutler survived the mine, what does it matter? She knows nothing other than what was in her father's letters, and that isn't much. Fleeting references, easily discounted."

"You said her husband was in Stod, at the hotel, with McKoy's group."

"But, again, there is no trail leading here. Amateurs will make little progress, as in the past."

"Fellner, Monika, and Christian are not amateurs. I'm afraid we have tickled their curiosity a bit too much."

She knew of Loring's conversations with Fellner over the past few days, conversations where Fellner had apparently lied and said he knew nothing of Knoll's whereabouts. "I agree. Those three are certainly planning something. But you can handle the matter with *Pan* Fellner, face-to-face."

Loring pushed himself up from the couch. "This is so difficult, *drahá*. I have so few years left—"

"I won't hear talk like that," she said quickly. "You are in good health. Many productive years to go."

"I'm seventy-seven. Be realistic."

The thought of him dying bothered her. Her mother died when she was too young to feel the loss. The pain from when her father died was still quite real, the memories vivid. Losing the other father in her life would be more than difficult.

"My two sons are good men. They run the family businesses well. And when I am gone, all that will belong to them. It is their birthright." Loring faced her. "Money is so transparent. There is a certain thrill from the making of it. But it simply remakes itself if invested and managed wisely. Little skill is needed to perpetuate billions in hard currency. This family is proof of that. The bulk of our fortune was made two hundred years ago and simply passed down."

"I think you underestimate the value of your and your father's careful steerage through two world wars."

"Politics does sometimes interfere, but there will always be refuges where currency can be safely invested. For us, it was America."

Loring came back and sat on the edge of the couch. He smelled of bitter tobacco, as did the entire room. "Art, though, *drahá,* is much more fluid. It changes as we change, adapts as we do. A masterpiece of five hundred years ago might be frowned upon today.

"Yet, amazingly, some art forms can and do last the millennia. That, my dear, is what excites me. You understand that excitement. You appreciate it. And because of that, you have brought great joy to my life. Though my blood does not course through your veins, my spirit does. There is no doubt that you are my daughter in spirit."

She'd always felt that way. Loring's wife had died nearly twenty years ago. Nothing sudden or unexpected. A painful bout with cancer that slowly claimed her. His sons left decades ago. He had few pleasures, other than his art, gardening, and woodworking. But his tired joints and atrophied muscles severely restricted those activities. Though he was a billionaire, residing in a castle fortress and possessed of a name known throughout Europe, she was, in many ways, all this old man had left.

"I've always thought of myself as your daughter."

"When I am gone, I want you to have Castle Loukov."

She said nothing.

"I am also bequeathing you a hundred and fifty million euros so you can maintain the estate, along with my entire art collection, public and private. Of course, only you and I know the extent of the private collection. I have also left instructions that you are to inherit my club membership. It is mine to do with as I please. I want you to succeed in my place."

His words were too much. She struggled to speak. "What of your sons? They are your rightful heirs."

"And they will receive the bulk of my wealth. This estate, my art, and the money are nowhere near what I possess. I have discussed this with both of them, and neither offered any objection."

"I don't know what to say."

"Say you will do me proud and let all this live on."

"There is no doubt."

He smiled and lightly squeezed her hand. "You have always done me proud. Such a good daughter." He paused. "Now, though, we must do one final thing to ensure the safety of what we have worked so hard to achieve."

She understood. She'd understood all day. There really was only one way to solve their problem.

Loring stood, walked to the desk, and calmly dialed the phone. When the connection was made with Burg Herz he said, "Franz, how are you this evening?"

A pause while Fellner spoke on the other end. Loring's face was knotted. She knew this was difficult for him. Fellner was not only a competitor, but also a longtime friend.

Yet it had to be done.

"I very much need to talk with you, Franz. It is vitally important. . . . No, I would like to send my plane for you and talk this evening. Unfortunately, there is no way I can leave the Republic. I can have the jet there within the hour and have you back home by midnight. . . . Yes, please bring Monika—this concerns her, as well—and Christian, too. . . . Oh, still have not heard from him? A shame. I'll have the plane at your landing field by five-thirty. I'll see you soon."

Loring hung up and sighed. "Such a pity. To the end, Franz continues to maintain the charade."

FIFTY

PRAGUE, CZECH REPUBLIC
6:50 P.M.

THE SLEEK GOLD-AND-GRAY CORPORATE JET ROLLED ACROSS the tarmac and settled to a stop. The engines whined down. Suzanne stood with Loring in the dim light of late evening as workers nestled metal stairs close to the open hatch. Franz

Fellner exited first, dressed in a dark suit and tie. Monika followed, sporting a white turtleneck, navy blue silhouette blazer, and tight-fitting jeans. Typical, Suzanne thought. A vile mix of breeding and sexuality. And though Monika Fellner had just stepped off a multimillion-dollar private jet at one of Europe's premier metropolitan airports, her face reflected the disdain of someone clearly slumming.

Only two years separated them, with Monika the elder. Monika started attending club functions a couple of years back, making no secret of the fact that she would someday succeed her father. Everything had come so easily to her. Suzanne's life had been so radically different. Though she'd grown up at the Loring estate, she was always expected to work hard, study hard, acquire hard. She'd wondered many times if Knoll was a divisive factor between them. Monika had made it clear more than once that she considered Christian *her* property. Until a few hours ago, when Loring told her Castle Loukov would one day be hers, she'd never considered a life like Monika Fellner's. But that reality was now at hand, and she couldn't help but wonder what dear Monika would think if she knew they would soon be equals.

Loring stepped forward and briskly shook Fellner's hand. He then hugged and kissed Monika lightly on the cheek. Fellner acknowledged Suzanne with a smile and a polite nod, club member to Acquisitor.

The drive to Castle Loukov in Loring's touring Mercedes was pleasant and relatively quiet, the talk of politics and business. Dinner was waiting in the dining hall when they arrived. As the main course was served, Fellner asked in German, "What is so urgent, Ernst, that we need to speak this evening?"

Suzanne noticed that, so far, Loring had kept the mood friendly, using light conversation to put his guests at ease. Her employer sighed. "It is the matter of Christian and Suzanne."

Monika cut Suzanne a look, one she'd seen before and grown to hate.

"I know," Loring said, "that Christian was unharmed in the mine explosion. As I am sure you know, Suzanne caused the explosion."

Fellner set his knife and fork on the table and faced his host. "We are aware of both."

"Yet you continued to tell me the past two days you knew nothing of Christian's whereabouts."

"Frankly, I did not consider the information any of your business. At the same time I kept wondering, why all the interest?" Fellner's tone had harshened, the need for appearances seemingly gone.

"I know of Christian's visit to St. Petersburg two weeks ago. In fact, that is what started all this."

"We assumed you were paying the clerk." Monika's tone was brusque, more so than her father's.

"Again, Ernst, what is this visit about?" Fellner asked.

"The Amber Room," Loring slowly said.

"What of it?"

"Finish your dinner. Then we will talk."

"Truthfully, I am not hungry. You fly me three hundred kilometers on short notice to talk, so let us talk."

Loring folded his napkin. "Very well, Franz. You and Monika come with me."

Suzanne followed as Loring led their guests through the castle's ground-floor maze. The wide corridors wound past rooms adorned with priceless art and antiques. This was Loring's public collection, the result of six decades of personal acquiring and another ten decades before that by his father, grandfather, and great-grandfather. Some of the most valuable objects in the world rested in the surrounding chambers—the full extent of Loring's public collection was known only to her and her employer, all protected behind thick stone walls and the anonymity a rural estate in a former Communist-bloc country provided.

And soon it would all be hers.

"I am about to breach one of our sacred rules," Loring

said. "As a demonstration of my good faith, I intend to show you my private collection."

"Is that necessary?" Fellner asked.

"I believe it is."

They passed Loring's study and continued down a long hall to a solitary room at the end. It was a tight rectangle, topped by a groined vault ceiling with murals that depicted the zodiac and portraits of the Apostles. A massive delft tile stove consumed one corner. Walnut display cases lined the walls, their seventeenth-century wood inlaid with African ivory. The glass shelves brimmed with sixteenth- and seventeenth-century porcelain. Fellner and Monika took a moment and admired some of the pieces.

"The Romanesque Room," Loring said. "I don't know if you two have been here before."

"I haven't," Fellner said.

"Neither have I," Monika said.

"I keep most of my precious glass here." Loring gestured to the tiled stove. "Merely for looks, the air comes from there." He pointed to a floor grate. "Special air handlers, as I am sure you utilize."

Fellner nodded.

"Suzanne," Loring said.

She stepped before one of the wooden cases, fourth in a line of six, and slowly said in a low voice, "A common experience resulting in a common confusion." The cabinet and a section of the stone wall rotated on a center axis, stopping halfway, creating an entrance to either side.

"Voice activated to my tone and Suzanne's. Some members of the staff know of this room. It, of course, has to be cleaned from time to time. But, as I am sure with your people, Franz, mine are absolutely loyal and have never spoken of this outside the estate. To be safe, though, we change the password weekly."

"This week's is interesting," Fellner said. "Kafka, I believe. The opening line to *A Common Confusion*. How fitting."

Loring grinned. "We must be loyal to our Bohemian writers."

Suzanne stepped aside and allowed Fellner and Monika to enter first. Monika brushed past, casting her a look of cool disgust. She then followed Loring inside. The spacious chamber beyond was dotted with more display cases, paintings and tapestries.

"I am sure you have a similar place," Loring said to Fellner. "This is from over two hundred years of collecting. The past forty with the club."

Fellner and Monika weaved through the individual cases.

"Marvelous things," Fellner said. "Very impressive. I recall many from unveilings. But, Ernst, you have been holding back." Fellner stood in front of a blackened skull encased in glass. "Peking Man?"

"Our family has possessed it since the war."

"As I recall, it was lost in China during transport to the United States."

Loring nodded. "Father acquired it from the thief who stole it from the marines in charge."

"Amazing. This dates our ancestry back a half million years. The Chinese and Americans would kill to have it returned. Yet here it rests, in the middle of Bohemia. We live in odd times, don't we?"

"Quite right, old friend. Quite right." Loring motioned to the double doors at the far end of the long chamber. "There, Franz."

Fellner walked toward a set of tall enameled doors. They were painted white and veined in gilded molding. Monika followed her father.

"Go ahead. Open them," Loring said.

Suzanne noticed that, for once, Monika kept her mouth shut. Fellner reached for the brass handles, twisted them, and pushed the doors inward.

"Mother of God," Fellner said, stepping inside the brightly lit chamber.

The room was a perfect square, its ceiling high and arched

and covered in a colorful mural. Mosaic pieces of whiskey-colored amber divided three of the four walls into clearly defined panels. Mirrored pilasters separated each panel. Amber molding created a wainscoting effect between tall, slender upper panels and short, rectangular lower ones. Tulips, roses, sculpted heads, figurines, seashells, flowers, monograms, rocaille, scrollwork, and floral garlands—all forged in amber—sprang from the walls. The Romanov crest, an amber bas-relief of the two-headed eagle of the Russian tsars, emblazoned many of the lower panels. More gilded molding spread like vines across the uppermost fringes and above three sets of white double doors. Cherub carvings and feminine busts dotted the spaces in between and above the upper panels, and likewise framed the doors and windows. The mirrored pilasters were dotted with gilded candelabra that sprouted electric candles, all burning bright. The floor was a shiny parquet, the woodwork as intricate as the amber walls, the polished surface reflecting the bulbs like distant suns.

Loring stepped inside. "It is exactly as in the Catherine Palace. Ten meters square with the ceiling seven and a half meters tall."

Monika had maintained better control than her father. "Is this why all the games with Christian?"

"You were coming a bit close. This has been a secret for over fifty years. I could not let things continue to escalate and risk exposure to the Russians or Germans. I do not have to tell you what their reaction would be."

Fellner crossed the room to the far corner, admiring the marvelous amber table fitted tight at the junction of two lower panels. He then moved to one of the Florentine mosaics, the colored stone polished and framed in gilded bronze. "I never believed the stories. One swore the Soviets had saved the mosaics before the Nazis arrived at the Catherine Palace. Another said remnants were found in the Königsberg ruins after the bombing in 1945 crumbled it to dust."

"The first story is false. The Soviets were not able to spirit the four mosaics away. They did try to dismantle one of the upper amber panels, but it fell apart. They decided to leave the rest, including the mosaics. The second story, though, is true. An illusion staged by Hitler."

"What do you mean?"

"Hitler knew Göring wanted the amber panels. He also knew of Erich Koch's loyalty to Göring. That is why the Führer personally ordered the panels moved from Königsberg and sent a special SS detachment to make the transfer, just in case Göring became difficult. Such a strange relationship between Hitler and Göring. Complete distrust of one another, yet total dependency. Only in the end, when Bormann was finally able to undermine Göring, did Hitler turn on him."

Monika drifted to the windows, which consisted of three sets of twenty-pane casements from floor to midway up, each topped by half-moons, three sets of eight-paned, arched windows overhead. The lower casements were actually double doors shaped to look like windows. Beyond the panes came light and what appeared to be a garden scene.

Loring noticed her interest.

"This room is entirely enclosed within stone walls, the space not even noticeable from the outside. I commissioned a mural to be painted and the lighting perfected to provide an illusion of outside. The original room opened to the Catherine Palace's grand courtyard, so I chose a nineteenth-century setting at a time after the courtyard had been enlarged and enclosed with fencing." Loring stepped close to Monika. "The ironworks of the gates there in the distance are exact. The grass, shrubs, and flowers are from contemporary pencil drawings used as models. Quite remarkable, actually. It appears as if we are standing on the second floor of the palace. Can you imagine the military parades that regularly occurred, or watching the nobles taking their evening promenade while a band played in the distance?"

"Ingenious." Monika turned back toward the Amber Room. "How were you able to reproduce the panels so exactly? I visited St. Petersburg last summer and toured the Catherine Palace. The restored Amber Room was nearly complete. They have the moldings, gild, windows, and doors replaced and many of the panels. Quite good work, but not like this."

Loring stepped to the center of the room. "It is quite simple, my dear. The vast majority of what you see is original, not a reproduction. Do you know the history?"

"Some," Monika said.

"Then you surely know that the panels were in a deplorable condition when the Nazis stole them in 1941. The original Prussian craftsmen fastened the amber to solid oak slabs with a crude mastic of beeswax and tree sap. Keeping amber intact in such a situation is akin to preserving a glass of water for two hundred years. No matter how careful one is, eventually the water will either spill or evaporate." He motioned around. "The same is true here. Over two centuries the oak expanded and contracted, and in some places rotted. Dry stove heating, bad ventilation, and the humid climate in and around Tsarskoe Selo only made things worse. The oak pulsed with the seasons, the mastic eventually cracked and pieces of amber dropped off. Nearly thirty percent was gone by the time the Nazis arrived. Another ten percent was lost during the theft. When Father found the panels, they were in a sorry state."

"I always believed Josef knew more than he acknowledged," Fellner said.

"You cannot imagine how disappointed Father was when he finally found them. He'd searched for seven years, imagined their beauty, recalled their majesty when he'd seen them in St. Petersburg before the Russian Revolution."

"They were in that cavern outside Stod, right?" Monika asked.

"Correct, my dear. Those three German transports contained the crates. Father found them during the summer of 1952."

"But how?" Fellner asked. "The Russians were looking in

earnest, as were private collectors. Back then, everyone wanted the Amber Room and no one believed it had been destroyed. Josef was under the yoke of the Communists. How did he manage such a feat? And, even more important, how did he manage to keep it?"

"Father was close with Erich Koch. The Prussian gauleiter confided in him that Hitler wanted the panels transported south out of the occupied Soviet Union before the Red Army arrived. Koch was loyal to Göring, but he was no fool. When Hitler ordered the evacuation, he complied, and initially told Göring nothing. But the panels made it only as far as the Harz region, where they were hidden in the mountains. Koch eventually told Göring, but even Koch did not know where precisely they were hidden. Göring located four soldiers from the evacuation detail. Rumor was he tortured them, but they told him nothing of the panels' whereabouts." Loring shook his head. "Göring was fairly insane by the end of the war. Koch was scared to death of him, which was one reason he scattered pieces from the Amber Room—door hinges, brass knobs, stones from the mosaics—at Königsberg. To telegraph a false message of destruction not only to the Soviets, but to Göring, as well. But those mosaics were reproductions the Germans had been working on since 1941."

"I never accepted the story that the amber burned in the Königsberg bombings," Fellner said. "The whole town would have smelled like an incense pot."

Loring chuckled. "That is true. I never understood why no one noted that. There was never a mention of an odor in any report of the bombing. Imagine twenty tons of amber slowly smoldering away. The scent would have drifted for miles, and lingered for days."

Monika lightly stroked one of the polished walls. "None of the cold pomposity of stone. Almost warm to the touch. And much darker than I imagined. Certainly darker than the restored panels in the Catherine Palace."

"Amber darkens with time," her father said. "Though sliced into pieces, polished, and glued together, amber will continue to age. The Amber Room of the eighteenth century would have been a much brighter place than this room is today."

Loring nodded. "And though the pieces in these panels are millions of years old, they are as fragile as crystal and equally finicky. That is what makes this treasure even more amazing."

"It sparkles," Fellner said. "It is like standing in the sun. Radiance, but no heat."

"Like the original, the amber here is backed with silver foil. Light simply comes back."

"What do you mean *like* the original panels?" Fellner asked.

"As I mentioned, Father was disappointed when he breached the chamber and found the amber. The oak had rotted, nearly all the pieces had fallen off. He carefully recovered everything and obtained copies of photographs the Soviets had made of the room before the war. Like the current restorers at Tsarskoe Selo, Father used those pictures to rebuild the panels. The only difference—he possessed the original amber."

"Where did he find the craftsmen?" Monika asked. "My recollection is that the knowledge of how to fashion the amber was lost in the war. Most of the old masters were killed."

Loring nodded. "Some survived, thanks to Koch. Göring intended to create a room identical to the original and instructed Koch to jail the craftsmen for safekeeping. Father was able to locate many before the war ended. After, he offered them a good life for themselves and whatever remained of their family. Most accepted his offer and lived here in seclusion, rebuilding this masterpiece slowly, piece by piece. Several of their descendants still live here and maintain this room."

"Is that not risky?" Fellner asked.

"Not at all. These men and their families are loyal. Life in the old Czechoslovakia was difficult. Very brutal. To a man, they were grateful for the generosity the Lorings showed them. All we ever asked was their best work and secrecy. It took nearly ten years to complete what you see here. Thankfully, the Soviets insisted on training their artists as realists, so the restorers were competent."

Fellner waved his hands at the walls. "Still, this must have cost a fortune to complete."

Loring nodded. "Father purchased the amber needed for replacement pieces on the open market, which was expensive, even in the 1950s. He also employed some modern techniques while rebuilding. The new panels are not oak. Instead, pieces of pine, ash, and oak were fused together. Separate pieces allow for expansion, and a moisture barrier was added between the amber and the wood. The Amber Room is not only fully restored, it will also last."

Suzanne stood quiet near the doors and carefully watched Fellner. The old German was openly stunned. She marveled at what it took to astonish a man like Franz Fellner, a billionaire with an art collection to rival any museum in the world. But she understood his shock, recalling how she felt the first time Loring showed her.

Fellner pointed. "Where do the two other sets of doors lead?"

"This room is actually in the center of my private gallery. We walled the sides and placed the doors and windows exactly as in the original. Instead of rooms in the Catherine Palace, these doors flow to other private collection areas."

"How long has the room been here?" Fellner asked.

"Fifty years."

"Amazing you have been able to conceal it," Monika said. "The Soviets are difficult to deceive."

"Father fostered good relations with both the Soviets and the Germans during the war. Czechoslovakia provided a convenient route for the Nazis to funnel currency and gold to Switzerland. Our family aided many such transfers. The Soviets, after the war, enjoyed the same courtesy. The price of that favor was the freedom to do as we pleased."

Fellner grinned. "I can imagine. The Soviets could ill afford you to inform the Americans or the British about what was transpiring."

"There is an old Russian saying, 'But for the bad, it would not be good.' It refers to the ironic tendency of how Russian art seems to spring from turmoil. But it likewise explains how this was made possible."

Suzanne watched Fellner and Monika approach the chest-high cases lining two of the amber walls. Inside were an assortment of objects. A seventeenth-century chessboard with pieces, an eighteenth-century samovar and flask, a woman's toilet case, a sand glass, spoons, medallions, and ornate boxes. All of amber, crafted, as Loring explained, by either Königsberg or Gdańsk artisans.

"The pieces are lovely," Monika said.

"Like the *kunstkammer* of Peter the Great's time, I keep my amber objects in my room of curiosity. Most were collected by Suzanne or her father. Not for public display. War loot."

The old man turned toward Suzanne and smiled. He then looked back toward their guests.

"Shall we retire to my study, where we can sit and talk a bit more?"

FIFTY-ONE

SUZANNE TOOK A SEAT BEYOND MONIKA, FELLNER, AND LORING. She preferred to watch from the side, allowing her boss this moment of triumph. A steward had just withdrawn after serving coffee, brandy, and cake.

"I always wondered about Josef's loyalties," Fellner said. "He survived the war remarkably well."

"Father hated the Nazis," Loring said. "His foundries and factories were placed at their disposal, but it was an easy matter to forge weak metal, or produce bullets that rusted, or guns that did not like the cold. It was a dangerous game— Nazis were fanatical about quality, but his relationship with Koch helped. Rarely was he questioned about anything. He knew the Germans would lose the war, and he foretold the Soviet takeover of Eastern Europe, so he worked covertly with Soviet intelligence throughout."

"I never realized," Fellner said.

Loring nodded. "He was a Bohemian patriot. He simply operated in his own way. After the war, the Soviets were grateful. They needed him, too, so he was left alone. I was able to continue that relationship. This family has worked closely with every Czechoslovakian regime since 1945. Father was right about the Soviets. And so, I might add, was Hitler."

"What do you mean?" Monika asked.

Loring brought the fingers of both hands together in his lap. "Hitler always believed the Americans and British would join him in a war against Stalin. The Soviets were Germany's real enemy, and he believed Churchill and Roosevelt felt the same way. That's why he hid so much money and art. He intended to retrieve it all, once the Allies joined him in a new alliance to defeat the USSR. A madman for sure, but history has proved a lot of Hitler's vision correct. When Berlin was blockaded by the Soviets in 1948, America, England, and Germany immediately joined against the Soviets."

"Stalin scared everybody," Fellner said. "More so than Hitler. He murdered sixty million to Hitler's ten. When he died in 1953, we all felt safer."

After a moment Loring said, "I assume Christian reported the skeletons found in the cavern at Stod?"

Fellner nodded.

"They worked the site, foreigners hired in Egypt. There was a huge shaft then, only the outer entrance dynamited shut. Father found it, cleared the opening, and removed the crumbled panels. He then sealed the chamber with the bodies inside."

"Josef killed them?"

"Personally. While they slept."

"And you've been killing people ever since," Monika said.

Loring faced her. "Our Acquisitors assured that the secret remained safe. I do have to say, the ferocity and determination with which people have searched surprised us. Many became obsessed with finding the amber panels. Periodically, we would leak false leads, rumors to keep searchers moving in a different direction. You might recall an article in *Rabochaya Tribuna* from a few years back. They reported Soviet military intelligence had located the panels in a mine near an old tank base in East Germany, about two hundred fifty kilometers southeast of Berlin."

"I have that article," Fellner said.

"All false. Suzanne arranged a leak to the appropriate people. Our hope was that most people would use common sense and give up the search."

Fellner shook his head. "Too valuable. Too intriguing. The lure is almost intoxicating."

"I understand completely. Many times I venture into the room to simply sit and stare. The amber is almost therapeutic."

"And priceless," Monika said.

"True, my dear. I read something once about war loot— artifacts made of precious stones and metals—the writer postulated that they would never have survived the war intact, the sum of their individual parts being far greater than the whole. One commentator, I believe in the *London Times,* wrote that the fate of the Amber Room could be gauged similarly. He concluded only objects like books and paintings, whose total configuration, as opposed to the actual raw material used in their composition, would survive a war."

"Did you help with that postulation?" Fellner asked.

Loring lifted his coffee from the side table and smiled. "The writer conceived that on his own. But we did make sure the article received wide circulation."

"So what happened?" Monika asked. "Why was it necessary to kill all those people?"

"In the beginning, we had no choice. Alfred Rohde supervised the loading of the crates in Königsberg and was aware of their ultimate destination. The fool told his wife, so Father eliminated both before they told the Soviets. By then, Stalin had empaneled a commission to investigate. The Nazi ruse at Königsberg Palace did not deter the Soviets at all. They believed the panels still existed and they searched with a vengeance."

"But Koch survived the war and talked to the Soviets," Fellner said.

"That's true. But we funded his legal defense until the day he died. After the Poles convicted him of war crimes, the only thing that kept him from the gallows was a Soviet veto. They thought he knew where the Amber Room was hidden. The reality was that Koch knew only the trucks left Königsberg headed west, then south. He knew nothing of what happened later. It was our suggestion that he tantalize the Soviets with the prospects of finding the panels. Not until the 1960s did they finally agree to terms. His life was spared in return for the information, but it was an easy matter then to blame everything on time. The Königsberg of today is far different from the one that existed during the war."

"So, by funding Koch's legal defense, you assured his loyalty. He'd never betray his only revenue source, nor would he ever play the trump card, since there would be no reason to trust the Soviets to keep their word."

Loring smiled. "Exactly, old friend. The gesture also kept us in constant contact with the only living person we knew of who could provide any meaningful information on the panels' location."

"One also that would be difficult to kill without drawing undue attention."

Loring nodded. "Thankfully, Koch cooperated and never revealed anything."

"And the others?" Monika asked.

"Occasionally some ventured close, and it became necessary for accidents to be arranged. Sometimes we dispensed with caution and simply killed them, particularly when time was of the essence. Father conceived the 'curse of the Amber Room' and fed the story to a reporter. Typical of the press, and please forgive my insolence, Franz, but the phrase caught on quickly. Made good headlines, I presume."

"And Karol Borya and Danya Chapaev?" Monika asked.

"These two were the most troublesome of all, though I did not fully realize until just recently. They were close to the truth. In fact, they may well have stumbled onto the same information we found after the war. For some reason they kept the information to themselves, guarding what they considered to be secret. It appears hatred for the Soviet system may have contributed to their attitude.

"We knew about Borya from his work with the Soviet's Extraordinary Commission. He eventually immigrated to the United States and disappeared. Chapaev's name was familiar, too. But he melted into Europe. Since there was no apparent danger from either, we left them alone. Until, of course, Christian's recent intervention."

"Now they are silenced forever," Monika said.

"The same thing you would have done, my dear."

Suzanne watched Monika bristle at Loring's rebuke. But he was right. The bitch would surely kill her own father to protect her vested interests.

Loring broke the moment and said, "We learned of Borya's whereabouts about seven years ago quite by accident. His daughter was married to a man named Paul Cutler. Cutler's father was an American art enthusiast. Over the course of several years, the senior Cutler made inquires across Europe about the Amber Room. Somehow he tracked down a relative of one of the men who worked here at the estate on the duplicate. We now know that Chapaev provided Borya with the name, and Borya asked Cutler to make inquiries. Six years ago those inquiries reached a point that forced us to act. So a plane was exploded. Thanks to lax Italian police authorities, and some well-placed contributions, the crash was attributed to terrorists."

"Suzanne's handiwork?" Monika asked.

Loring nodded. "She's quite gifted in that regard."

"Does the clerk in St. Petersburg work for you?" Fellner asked.

"Of course. The Soviets, for all their inefficiency, had a nasty tendency to write everything down. There are literally millions of pages of records, no telling what is in them, and no way to efficiently scan them all. The only way to ensure against curious minds stumbling across something interesting was to pay the clerks for attentiveness."

Loring finished his coffee, then set the porcelain cup and saucer aside. He looked straight at Fellner. "Franz, I am telling you all this as a show of good faith. Regretfully, I let the present situation get out of hand. Suzanne's attempt on Christian's life and their joust yesterday in Stod is evidence of how this could continue to escalate. That might eventually bring unwanted attention to both of us, not to mention the club. I thought that if you knew the truth we could stop the battling. There is nothing to find regarding the Amber Room. I am sorry about what happened to Christian. I know Suzanne did not want to do it—she acted on my orders—what I thought necessary at the time."

"I, too, regret what has happened, Ernst. I will not lie and say that I am glad you have the panels. I wanted them. But a part of me is joyous they are safe and intact. I always feared the Soviets would locate them. They are no better than Gypsies when it comes to preserving treasure."

"Father and I both felt the same. The Soviets allowed such a deterioration of the amber that it is almost a blessing the Germans stole it. Who knows what would have happened

if the Amber Room's future had been left to Stalin or
Khrushchev? The Communists were far more concerned
with building bombs than preserving heritage."

"You propose some sort of truce?" Monika asked.

Suzanne almost smiled at the bitch's impatience. Poor
darling. No unveiling of the Amber Room lay in her future.

"That is exactly what I desire." Loring turned. "Suzanne,
if you please."

She stood and walked to the study's far corner. Two pine
cases rested on the parquet floor. She carried them by rope
handles to where Franz Fellner sat.

"The two bronzes you have admired so greatly all these
years," Loring said.

Suzanne lifted the lid to one of the crates. Fellner fished
the vessel from a bed of shredded cedar and admired it in the
light. Suzanne knew the piece well. Tenth century. Liberated
by her from a man in New Delhi who stole both from a village in southern India. They remained among India's most
coveted lost objects, but had safely rested in Castle Loukov
the past five years.

"Suzanne and Christian battled hard for those," Loring
said.

Fellner nodded. "Another fight we lost."

"They are yours now. As an apology for what has happened."

"Herr Loring, forgive me," Monika said quietly. "But I
make the decisions relative to the club now. Ancient bronzes
are intriguing, but they do not hold the same interest for me.
I'm wondering how this matter needs to be handled. The
Amber Room has long been one of the most sought-after
prizes. Are the other members to be told?"

Loring frowned. "I would prefer the issue remain among
us. The secret has stayed safe a long time, and the fewer who
know the better. But, under the circumstances, I will defer
to your decision, my dear. I trust the remaining members
to keep the information confidential, as with all acquisitions."

Monika sat back in her chair and smiled, apparently pleased with the concession.

"There is one other item I want to address," Loring said, this time specifically to Monika. "As with you and your father, things will eventually change here, as well. I have left instructions in my will that Suzanne shall take over this estate, my collections, and my club membership, once I am gone. I have also left her enough cash to adequately handle any need."

Suzanne enjoyed the look of shock and defeat that invaded Monika's face.

"She will be the first Acquisitor ever elevated to club membership. Quite an accomplishment, would you not say?"

Neither Fellner nor Monika said anything. Fellner seemed enraptured with the bronze. Monika sat silent.

Fellner laid the bronze gingerly back into the crate. "Ernst, I consider this matter closed. It is unfortunate things deteriorated as they did. But I understand now. I believe I would have done the same under the circumstances. To you, Suzanne, congratulations."

She nodded at the gesture.

"On telling the members, let me consider the situation," Monika said. "I'll have an answer for you by June's meeting on how to proceed."

"That is all an old man can ask, my dear. I will await your decision." Loring looked at Fellner. "Now, would you like to stay the night?"

"I think we should return to Burg Herz. I have business in the morning. But I assure you, the trip was worth the trouble. Before we go, though, may I see the Amber Room one last time?"

"Certainly, old friend. Certainly."

The ride back to Prague's Ruzynè airport was quiet. Fellner and Monika sat in the Mercedes's backseat, Loring in the passenger seat next to Suzanne. Several times Suzanne glanced at Monika in the rearview mirror. The bitch's face stayed tight. She was obviously not pleased by the two elder men dominating the earlier conversation. Clearly Franz Fellner was not a man to let go easily and Monika was not the type to share.

About halfway Monika said, "I must ask your forgiveness, Herr Loring."

He turned to face her. "For what, my dear?"

"My abruptness."

"Not at all. I recall when my father turned over membership to me. I was much older than you and equally determined. He, like your father, found it difficult to let go. But if it is any conciliation, eventually he fully retired."

"My daughter is impatient. Much like her mother was," Fellner said.

"More like you, Franz."

Fellner chuckled. "Perhaps."

"I assume Christian will be told of all this?" Loring said to Fellner.

"Immediately."

"Where is he?"

"I really do not know." Fellner turned to Monika. "Do you, *liebling*?"

"No, Father. I haven't heard from him."

They arrived at the airport a little before midnight. Loring's jet waited on the oily tarmac, fueled, ready to go. Suzanne parked beside the aircraft. All four of them climbed out and Suzanne popped the trunk. The plane's pilot clambered down the jet's metal stairs. Suzanne pointed to the two pine cases. The pilot lifted each and moved to an open cargo bay door.

"I had the bronzes packed tight," Loring said over the whine of the engines. "They should make the trip with no problem."

Suzanne handed Loring an envelope.

"Here are some registration papers I prepared and had certified by the ministry in Prague. They should be of assistance if any customs officials make an inquiry at the landing strip."

Fellner pocketed the envelope. "I rarely have inquiries."

Loring smiled. "I assumed as much." He turned to Monika and embraced her. "Lovely to see you, my dear. I look forward to our battles in the future, as I am sure Suzanne does."

Monika smiled and kissed the air above Loring's cheeks. Suzanne said nothing. She knew her role well. An Acquisitor's place was to act, not speak. One day she'd be a club member and could only hope her own Acquisitor conducted himself or herself similarly. Monika gave her a quick disconcerting glance before climbing the stairs. Fellner and Loring shook hands, then Fellner disappeared into the jet. The pilot slammed the cargo doors shut and hopped up the stairs, closing the hatch behind him.

Suzanne and Loring stood as the jet taxied toward the runway, the warm air from its engines rushing past. They then climbed into the Mercedes and left. Just outside the airport, Suzanne stopped the car on the side of the road.

The sleek jet shot down the darkened runway and arched into the clear night sky. Distance masked any sound. Three commercial jets rolled across the tarmac, two arriving, one leaving. They sat in the car, necks cocked to the right and up.

"Such a shame, *drahá,*" Loring whispered.

"At least their evening was pleasant. Herr Fellner was in awe of the Amber Room."

"I am pleased he was able to see it."

The jet vanished into the western sky, its running lights fading with altitude.

"The bronzes were returned to the glass cases?" Loring asked.

She nodded.

"Pine containers packed tight?"

"Of course."

"How does the device work?"

"A pressure switch, sensitive to altitude."

"And the compound?"

"Potent."

"When?"

She glanced at her watch and calculated velocity against the time. Based on what she believed to be the jet's ascent rate, five thousand feet would be just about—

In the distance a brilliant yellow flash filled the sky for an instant, like a star going nova, as the explosives she'd placed in the two pine crates ignited the jet fuel and obliterated any trace of Fellner, Monika, and the two pilots.

The light faded.

Loring's eyes stayed off in the distance, where the explosion occurred. "Such a shame. A six-million-dollar jet gone." He slowly turned toward her. "But the price to be paid for your future."

FIFTY-TWO

THURSDAY, MAY 22, 8:50 A.M.

KNOLL PARKED IN THE WOODS ABOUT A HALF KILOMETER OFF the highway. The black Peugeot was a rental, obtained in Nürnberg yesterday. He'd spent the night a few kilometers to the west in a picturesque Czech village, making a point to get a good night's sleep, knowing today and tonight were going to be arduous. He'd eaten a light breakfast at a small café, then left quickly so no one would recall anything about him. Loring surely possessed eyes and ears everywhere in this part of Bohemia.

He knew the local geography. He was actually already on Loring land, the ancient family estate spanning for miles in all directions. The castle was situated toward the northwest corner, surrounded by dense forests of birch, beech, and poplar. The Šumava region of southwest Czechoslovakia was an important timber source, but the Lorings had never needed to market their lumber.

He retrieved his backpack from the trunk and started the hike north. Twenty minutes later Castle Loukov appeared. The fortification was perched on a rocky mount, high above the treetops less than a kilometer away. To the west, the muddy Orlík Stream inched a path south. His vantage point offered a clear view of the compound's east entrance—the one used by motor vehicles—and the west postern gate used exclusively by staff and delivery trucks.

The castle was an impressive sight. A varied array of towers and buildings rose skyward behind rectangular walls. He knew the layout well. The lower floors were mainly ceremonial halls and exquisitely decorated public rooms, the upper stories littered with bedrooms and living quarters. Somewhere, hidden among the rambling stone structures, was a private collection chamber similar to what Fellner and the other seven members possessed. The trick would be finding it and determining how to get inside. He had a pretty good idea where the space might be, a conclusion he'd made at one of the club meetings based on the architecture, but he still was going to have to search. And fast. Before morning.

Monika's decision to allow the invasion was not surprising. She'd do anything to assert control. Fellner had been good to him, but Monika was going to be better. The old man would not live forever. And though he'd miss him, the possibilities Monika presented were nearly intoxicating. She was tough, but vulnerable. He could master her, of that he was sure. And by doing that he could master the fortune she'd inherit. A dangerous game, granted, but one worth the risks. It helped that Monika was incapable of love. But so was he. They were a perfect match, lust and power all the mastic they would need to bind them permanently.

He slipped off the backpack and found his binoculars. From the safety of a thick stand of poplar trees, he studied the castle's entire length. Blue sky backclothed its silhouette. His gaze angled off to the east. Two cars appeared on the paved road, both winding up the steep incline.

Police cars.

Interesting.

※———※

SUZANNE DROPPED A FRESHLY BAKED CINNAMON BUN ON THE china plate and added a dab of raspberry jam. She took a seat at the table, Loring already perched at the far end. The room was one of the castle's smaller dining spaces, reserved for the family. Oak cases filled with Renaissance goblets lined one of the alabaster walls. Another wall was encrusted with Bohemian semiprecious stones that outlined gilded icons of Czech patrons. She and Loring were eating alone, as they did every morning when she was there.

"The Prague newspaper is headlined with the explosion," Loring said. He folded the newspaper and set it on the table. "The reporter proposes no theories. Merely states the plane exploded shortly after takeoff, all aboard killed. They do name Fellner, Monika, and the pilots."

She sipped her coffee. "I am sorry about *Pan* Fellner. He was a respectable man. But good riddance to Monika. She would have been a blight to us all, eventually. Her reckless ways would have developed into a problem."

"I believe you are right, *drahá.*"

She savored a bite of warm bun. "Perhaps the killing may now end?"

"I certainly hope so."

"It is a part of my job I do not relish."

"I would not expect you to."

"Did my father enjoy it?"

Loring stared at her. "Where did that come from?"

"I was thinking about him last night. He was so gentle with me. I never knew he possessed such capabilities."

"Dear, your father did what was necessary. As you do. You are so much like him. He would be proud."

But she wasn't particularly proud of herself at the moment. Murdering Chapaev and all the others. Would their images linger in her mind forever? She feared they might. And what about her own motherhood? She'd once thought that a part of her future. But after yesterday that ambition might need adjustment. The possibilities now were both endless and exciting. The fact that people died to make it all possible was regrettable, but she could not dwell on it. Not anymore. It was time to move forward and her conscience be damned.

A steward appeared and crossed the terrazzo floor, stopping at the table. Loring glanced up.

"Sir, the police are here and wish to speak with you."

She glanced at her employer and smiled. "I owe you a hundred crowns."

He'd wagered her last evening, on the drive back from Prague, that the police would appear at the castle before ten. It was 9:40.

"Show them in," Loring said.

A few moments later, four uniformed men strolled briskly into the dining hall.

"*Pan* Loring," the lead man said in Czech, "we are so happy to learn you are well. The tragedy with your jet was awful."

Loring rose from the table and stepped toward the police. "We are all in shock. Herr Fellner and his daughter were guests here last evening for dinner. The two pilots have been in my employ many years. Their families live on the estate. I am about to visit their widows. It is tragic."

"Forgive this intrusion. But we need to ask some questions. Particularly, why this might have happened."

Loring shrugged. "I cannot say. Only that my offices reported several threats made against me during the past few weeks. One of my manufacturing concerns is considering an expansion into the Middle East. We have been involved in some public negotiations there. The callers apparently did not desire my corporate presence in the country. We reported the threats to the Saudis and I can only assume this may be related. Beyond that I cannot say. I never realized I had so violent an enemy."

"Do you have any information on these calls?"

Loring nodded. "My personal secretary is familiar with them. I have instructed him to be available today in Prague."

"My superiors wanted me to assure you that we will get to the bottom of what happened. In the meantime, do you think it wise to reside here without protection?"

"These walls afford me ample security, and the staff has now been alerted. I will be fine."

"Very·well, *Pan* Loring. Please be aware that we are here if you need us."

The policemen withdrew. Loring stepped back to the table. "Your impressions?"

"No reason not to accept what was said. Your connections in the justice ministry should also help."

"I will place a call later, thanking them for the visit, and pledge full cooperation."

"The club members should be called personally. Your sorrow clear."

"Quite right, I'll tend to that now."

⚔——🗝

PAUL DROVE THE LAND ROVER. RACHEL SAT IN THE FRONT SEAT, McKoy in the back. The big man had stayed silent most of the way east from Stod. The autobahn had taken them as far as Nürnberg, then a series of two-lane highways wound across the German border into southwestern Czechoslovakia.

The terrain had become progressively hilly and forested, alternating grain fields and lakes dotting the rolling countryside. Earlier, when he reviewed the road map to determine the fastest route east, he'd noticed České Budějovice, the region's largest town, and recalled a CNN report on its Budvar beer, better known by its German name, *Budweiser.* The American company by the same name had tried in vain to purchase the namesake, but the townspeople had steadfastly refused the millions offered, proudly noting that they were producing beer centuries before America even existed.

The route into Czechoslovakia led them through a series of quaint medieval towns, most adorned with either an overlooking castle or battlements with thick stone walls. Directions from a friendly shopkeeper adjusted the route, and it was a little before two o'clock when Rachel spotted Castle Loukov.

The aristocratic fortress was perched on a craggy height above a dense forest. Two polygonal towers and three rounded ones rose high above an outer stone curtain encrusted with shiny mullion windows and dark arrow slits. Casements and semicircular bastions wrapped the gray-white silhouette, and chimneys rose all around. A red, white, and blue flag flapped in the light afternoon breeze. Two wide bars and a triangle. Paul recognized it as the Czech national emblem.

"You almost expect armored knights to come storming out on horseback," Rachel said.

"Son of a bitch knows how to live," McKoy said. "I like this Loring already."

Paul navigated the Rover up a steep road to what appeared to be the main gate. Huge oak doors reinforced with iron straps were swung open, revealing a paved courtyard. Colorful rosebushes and spring flowers lined the buildings. Paul parked and they climbed out. A gray metallic Porsche sat beside a cream-colored Mercedes.

"Sucker drives good, too," McKoy said.

"Wonder where the front door is?" Paul asked.

Six separate doors opened to the courtyard from the various buildings. Paul took a moment and studied the dormers, crested gables, and richly patterned half-timbering. An interesting architectural combination of Gothic and baroque, proof, he assumed, of a prolonged construction and multiple human influences.

McKoy pointed and said, "My guess is that door there."

The arched oak door was surrounded by pillared ashlars, an elaborate coat of arms etched into the gable surmount.

McKoy approached and banged a burnished metal knocker. A steward answered and McKoy politely explained who they were and why they were there. Five minutes later they were seated in a lavish hall. Stag heads, boars, and antlers sprouted from the walls. A fire raged in a huge granite hearth, the long space softly illuminated by stained-glass lamps. Massive wooden pillars supported an ornate stuccoed ceiling, and part of the walls were adorned with heavy oil paintings. Paul surveyed the canvases. Two Rubens, a Dürer, and a Van Dyck. Incredible. What the High Museum would give to display just one of them.

The man who quietly entered through the double doors was nearing eighty. He was tall, his hair a lusterless gray, the faded goatee covering his neck and chin withdrawn with age. He possessed a handsome face that, for someone of such obvious wealth and stature, made little impression. Maybe, Paul thought, the mask was intentionally kept free of emotion.

"Good afternoon. I am Ernst Loring. Ordinarily I do not accept uninvited visitors, particularly those who just drive through the gate, but my steward explained your situation, and I have to say, I am intrigued." The older man spoke clear English.

McKoy introduced himself and offered his hand, which Loring shook. "Glad to finally meet you. I've read about you for years."

Loring smiled. The gesture seemed gracious and expected. "You must not believe any of what you read or hear. I am afraid the press likes to make me far more interesting than I truly am."

Paul stepped forward and introduced himself and Rachel.

"A pleasure to meet you both," Loring said. "Why don't we sit? Some refreshments are on the way."

They all took a seat in the neo-Gothic armchairs and sofa that faced the hearth. Loring turned toward McKoy.

"The steward mentioned a dig in Germany. I read a piece on that the other day, I believe. Surely that requires your constant attention. Why are you here and not there?"

"Not a damn thing there to find."

Loring's face showed curiosity, nothing more. McKoy told their host about the dig, the three transports, five bodies, and letters in the sand. He showed Loring the photographs Alfred Grumer had taken along with one more snapped yesterday morning after Paul traced the remaining letters to form LORING.

"Any explanation why the dead guy scrawled your name in that sand?" McKoy asked.

"There is no indication that he did. As you say, this is speculation on your part."

Paul sat silent, content to let McKoy lead the charge, and gauged the Czech's reaction. Rachel seemed to be appraising the older man, too, her look similar to when she watched a jury during a trial.

"However," Loring said, "I can see why you might think that. The original few letters are somewhat consistent."

McKoy grabbed Loring's gaze with his own. "*Pan* Loring, let me get to the point. The Amber Room was in that chamber, and I think you or your father were there. Whether you still have the panels, who knows? But I think you once did."

"Even if I possessed such a treasure, why would I openly admit that to you?"

"You wouldn't. But you might not want me to release all this information to the press. I signed several production agreements with news agencies around the world. The dig is a definite bust, but this stuff is the kind of dynamite that could allow me to recoup at least some of what my investors are out. I figure the Russians will be really interested. From what I hear they can be, shall we say, *persistent* in recoverin' their lost booty?"

"And you thought I might be willing to pay for silence?"

Paul couldn't believe what he was hearing. A shakedown? He had no idea McKoy had come to Czechoslovakia to blackmail Loring. Neither, apparently, did Rachel.

"Hold on, McKoy," Rachel said, her voice rising. "You never said a word about extortion."

Paul echoed her sentiment. "We want no part of this."

McKoy was undeterred. "You two need to get with the program. I thought about it on the way over. This guy isn't goin' to take us on a tour of the Amber Room, even if he does have it. But Grumer's dead. Five other men are dead back in Stod. Your father, your parents, Chapaev, they're all dead. Bodies littered everywhere." McKoy glared at Loring. "And I think this son of a bitch knows a shitload more than he wants us to believe."

A vein pulsed in the old man's temple. "Extraordinary rudeness from a guest, *Pan* McKoy. You come to my home and accuse me of murder and thievery?" The voice was firm but calm.

"I haven't accused you. But you know more than you're willin' to say. Your name has been mentioned with the Amber Room for years."

"Rumors."

"Rafal Dolinski," McKoy said.

Loring said nothing.

"He was a Polish reporter who contacted you three years back. He sent a narrative of an article he was working on. Nice fellow. Real likable. Very determined. Got blown up in a mine a few weeks later. You recall?"

"I know nothing of that."

"A mine near the one that Judge Cutler here got a real close look at. Maybe even the same one."

"I read about that explosion a few days ago. I did not realize the connection to this moment."

"I bet," McKoy said. "I think the press will love this speculation. Think about it, Loring. It's got all the aroma of a great story. International financier, lost treasure, Nazis, murder. Not to mention the Germans. If you found the amber in their territory, they're goin' to want it back, too. Would make an excellent bargainin' chip with the Russians."

Paul felt he had to say, "Mr. Loring, I want you to know Rachel and I knew nothing of this when we agreed to come here. Our concern is finding out about the Amber Room, to satisfy some curiosity Rachel's father generated, nothing more. I'm a lawyer. Rachel is a judge. We would never be a party to blackmail."

"No need for explanation," Loring said. He turned to McKoy. "Perhaps you are correct. Speculation may be a problem. We live in a world where perception is far more important than reality. I will take this urging more as a form of insurance than blackmail." A smile curled on the old man's thin lips.

"Take it any way you want. All I want is to get paid. I've got a serious cash-flow problem, and a whole lot of things to say to a whole lot of people. The price of silence is risin' by the minute."

Rachel's face tightened. Paul figured she was about to explode. She hadn't liked McKoy from the start. She'd been suspicious of his overbearing ways, concerned about their getting intertwined with his activities. He could hear her now. *His* doing they were in as deep as they were. *His* problem to get them out.

"Might I make a suggestion?" Loring offered.

"Please," Paul said, hoping for some sanity.

"I would like time to think about this situation. Surely, you do not plan to travel all the way back to Stod. Stay the night. We'll have dinner and talk more later."

"That would be marvelous," McKoy quickly said. "We were plannin' to find a room somewhere anyway."

"Excellent, I will have the stewards bring your things inside."

FIFTY-THREE

SUZANNE OPENED THE BEDCHAMBER DOOR. A STEWARD SAID IN Czech, "*Pan* Loring wants to see you in the Ancestors' Room. He said to take the back passages. Stay out of the main halls."

"He say why?"

"We have guests for the night. It may be related to them."

"Thank you. I'll head downstairs immediately."

She closed the door. Strange. *Take the back passages.* The castle was reamed with a series of secret corridors once used by aristocracy as a means of escape, now utilized by staff who maintained the castle's infrastructure. Her room was toward the rear of the complex, beyond the main halls and family quarters, halfway to the kitchen and work areas, past the point where the covert passages started.

She left the bedchamber and descended two floors. The nearest entry into the hidden corridors was a small sitting room on the ground floor. She stepped close to a paneled wall. Intricate moldings framed richly stained slabs of grain-free walnut. Above the Gothic fireplace she found a release switch camouflaged as part of the scrollwork. A section of wall beside the fireplace sprang open. She stepped into the passage and pulled the panel shut.

The mazelike route wound in right angles down a narrow, single-person corridor. Outlines of doors in the stone appeared periodically, leading out into either hallways or rooms. She'd played here as a child, imagining herself a Bohemian princess darting for freedom from infidel invaders

breaching the castle walls, and so she was familiar with their
path.

The Ancestors' Room possessed no entrance into the
maze, the Blue Room being the closest point of egress. Loring named the space for its gold-embossed blue leather wall
hangings. She exited and listened at the door for any sounds
emanating from the corridor outside. Hearing none, she
quickly slipped down the hall and stepped into the Ancestors' Room, closing the door behind her.

Loring was standing in an oriel-like semicircular bay before leaded glass windows. On the wall, above two lions
carved in stone, was the family coat of arms. Portraits of
Josef Loring and the rest of the ancestors adorned the walls.

"It seems providence has delivered us a gift," he said. Loring told her about Wayland McKoy and the Cutlers.

She raised and eyebrow. "This McKoy has nerve."

"More than you realize. He does not intend any extortion.
I would imagine he was testing to see my reaction. He is
more astute than he wants his listener to perceive. He did not
come for money. He came to find the Amber Room, probably wanting me to invite them to stay."

"Then why did you?"

Loring clasped his hands behind his back and stepped
close to the oil painting of his father. The quiet, involuted
stare of the elder Loring glared down. In the image, shocks
of white hair drooped across the furrowed brow, the stare
one of an enigmatic man who dominated his era, and somehow expected the same of his children. "My sisters and
brother did not survive the war," Loring quietly said. "I always thought that a sign. I was not the firstborn. None of this
was meant to be mine."

She knew that, so she wondered if Loring was talking to
the painting, perhaps finishing a conversation he and his father had started decades ago. Her father had told her about
old Josef. How demanding, uncompromising, and difficult
he could be. He'd expected a lot from his last surviving
child.

"My brother was to inherit. Instead I was given the responsibility. The past thirty years have been difficult. Very difficult, indeed."

"But you survived. Prospered, in fact."

He turned to face her. "Another sign from providence, perhaps?" He stepped close to her. "Father left me with a dilemma. On the one hand, he bestowed a treasure of unimaginable beauty. The Amber Room. On the other, I am forced to constantly fend off challenges to ownership. Things were so different in his day. Living behind the Iron Curtain came with the advantage of being able to kill whomever you wanted." Loring paused. "Father's sole wish was that all this be kept in the family. He was particularly emphatic about that. You are family, *drahá*, as much as my own flesh and blood. Truly, my daughter in spirit."

The old man stared at her for a few seconds and then lightly brushed her cheek with his hand.

"Between now and this evening, stay in your room, out of sight. Later, you know what we must do."

⚷

KNOLL CREPT THROUGH THE WOODS, THE FOREST THICK BUT NOT impassable. He minimized his approach by choosing an open route under the enveloping canopy, following defined trails, detouring only at the end to make his final assault unnoticed.

The early evening loomed cool and dry, the night ahead surely to be outright cold. The setting sun angled to the west, its rays piercing the spring leaves and leaving only a muted glow. Sparrows squawked overhead. He thought about Italy, two weeks ago, traversing another forest, toward another castle, on another quest. That journey had ended in two deaths. He wondered what tonight's sojourn would bring.

His path led him up a steady incline, the rocky spur ending at the base of the castle walls. He'd been patient all afternoon, waiting in a grove of beech trees about a kilometer south. He'd watched the two police cars come and go early

in the morning, wondering what business they'd had with
Loring. Then, midafternoon, a Land Rover entered the main
gate and had not left. Perhaps the vehicle brought guests.
Distractions that could occupy Loring and Suzanne long
enough to mask his brief visit, like he'd hoped for from the
Italian whore who'd visited Pietro Caproni. As yet he did not
know if Danzer was even in residence, her Porsche had neither entered nor left, but he assumed she was there.

Where else would she be?

He stopped his advance thirty meters from the west entrance. A door appeared below a massive round tower. The
rough stone curtain rose twenty meters, smooth and devoid
of openings except for an occasional arrow slit. Batters at the
base sloped outward, a medieval innovation for strength and
a way for stones and missiles dropped from above to bounce
toward attackers. He mused at their usefulness to modern invaders. Much had changed in four hundred years.

He traced the walls skyward. Rectangular windows with
iron grilles lined the upper stories. Surely, in medieval days,
the tower's job had been to defend the postern entrance. But
its height and size seemed also to provide a ready transition
between the varying roofline of the adjacent wings. He was
familiar with the entrance from club meetings. It was used
mainly by the staff, a paved cul-de-sac outside the walls allowed vehicles to turn around.

He needed to slip inside quickly and quietly. He studied
the heavy wood door reinforced with blackened iron. Almost
certainly it would be locked, but not protected by an alarm.
He knew Loring, like Fellner, maintained loose security. The
vastness of the castle, along with its remote location, was
much more effective than any overt system. Besides, nobody
outside of club members and Acquisitors knew any of what
was really stashed within the confines of each member's
residence.

He peered through thick brush and noticed a black slit at
the edge of the door. Quickly, he trotted over and saw that
the door was indeed open. He pushed through into a wide,

barrel-vaulted passage. Three hundred years ago the entrance would have been used to haul cannons inside or allow castle defenders to sweep outside. Now the route was lined with tread marks from rubber tires. The dark passage twisted twice. One left, the other right. He knew that to be a defense mechanism to slow down invaders. Two portcullises, one halfway up the incline, the other near the end, could be used to lead invaders astray.

Another obligation of the monthly host for a club function was to provide overnight accommodations for members and Acquisitors, if requested. Loring's estate contained more than enough beds to sleep everyone. Historic ambience was probably why most members accepted Loring's hospitality. Knoll had stayed many times at the estate and recalled Loring once explaining the castle's history, how his family defended the walls for nearly five hundred years. Battles to the death fought within this very passage. He also remembered discussions about the array of secret corridors. After the bombing, during rebuilding, back passages allowed a ready way to heat and cool the many rooms, along with providing running water and electricity to chambers once warmed only by flames. He particularly recalled one of the secret doors that opened from Loring's study. The old man had showed his guests the novelty one night. The castle was littered with a maze of such passages. Fellner's Burg Herz was similar, the innovation a common architectural addition for fifteenth and sixteenth century fortresses.

He crept up the dim path, stopping at the end of an inclined entrance. A small inner ward lay ahead. Buildings from five epochs surrounded him. One of the castle's circular keeps towered at the far end. Sounds of pots clanging and voices spilled from the ground floor. The aroma of meat grilling mixed with a potent miasma from garbage containers off to one side. Tattered vegetable and fruit crates, along with wet cardboard boxes, were stacked like building blocks. The courtyard was clean, but was definitely the working bowels of this immense showpiece—the kitchens, stables, garrison hall, buttery, and salting house from ancient days—now where the hired help toiled to ensure the rest of the place stayed immaculate.

He lingered in the shadows.

Windows abounded in the upper stories, any one of which could allow a pair of eyes to spot him and raise an alarm. He needed to get inside without arousing suspicion. The stiletto was snug against his right arm under a cotton jacket. Loring's gift, the CZ-75B, was strapped in a shoulder harness, two spare ammunition clips in his pocket. Forty-five rounds in all. But the last thing he wanted was that kind of trouble.

He crouched low and crept up the final few feet, hugging a stone wall. He slipped over the wall's edge onto a narrow walk and darted for a door ten meters away. He tried the lock. It was open. He stepped inside. Smells of fresh produce and dank air immediately greeted him.

He stood in a short hall that spilled into a darkened room. A massive, octagonal oak support held up a low beamed ceiling. A blackened hearth dominated one wall. The air was chilled, boxes and crates stacked high. It was apparently an old pantry now used for storage. Two doors led out. One directly ahead, the other to the left. Recalling the sounds and smells outside, he concluded the left exit surely led to the kitchen. He needed to head east, so he chose the door ahead and stepped into another hall.

He was just about to start forward when he heard voices and movement from around the corner ahead. He quickly backtracked into the storage room. He decided, instead of leaving, to take up a position behind one of the walls of crates. The only artificial light was a bare bulb suspended from the center rafter. He hoped the approaching voices were merely passing through. He did not want to kill or even maim any member of the staff. Bad enough he was doing what he was, he didn't need to compound Fellner's embarrassment with violence.

But he'd do what he had to.

He squeezed behind a crate stack, his back rigid against

the rough stone wall. He was able to peer out, thanks to the pile's unevenness. The silence was broken only by a trapped fly that buzzed at the dingy windows.

The door opened.

"We need cucumbers and parsley. And see if the canned peaches are there, too," a male voice said in Czech.

Luckily, neither man pulled the chain for the overhead light, relying instead on the afternoon sun filtered by the nasty leaded panes.

"Here," the other male said.

Both men moved to the other side of the room. A cardboard box was dropped to the floor, a lid jerked open.

"Is *Pan* Loring still upset?"

Knoll peered out. One man wore the uniform required of all Loring's staff. Maroon trousers, white shirt, thin black tie. The other sported the jacketed butler's ensemble of the serving staff. Loring often bragged about designing the uniforms himself.

"He and *Pani* Danzer have been quiet all day. The police came this morning to ask questions and express condolences. Poor *Pan* Fellner and his daughter. Did you see her last night? Quite a beauty."

"I served drinks and cake in the study after dinner. She was exquisite. Rich, too. What a waste. The police have any idea what happened?"

"*Ne.* The plane simply exploded on the way back to Germany, all aboard killed."

The words slapped Knoll hard across the face. Did he hear right? Fellner and Monika dead?

Rage surged through him.

A plane had blown up with Monika and Fellner on board. Only one explanation made any sense. Ernst Loring had ordered the action, with Suzanne as his mechanism. Danzer and Loring had gone after him and failed. So they killed the old man and Monika. But why? What was going on? He wanted to palm the stiletto, push the crates aside, and slash the two staffers to pieces, their blood avenging the blood of his former employers. But what good would that do? He told himself to stay calm. Breathe slow. He needed answers. He needed to know why. He was glad now that he'd come. The source of all that happened, all that may happen, was somewhere within the ancient walls that encompassed him.

"Bring the boxes and let's go," one of the men said.

The two men left through the door toward the kitchen. The room again went quiet. He stepped from behind the crates. His arms were tense, his legs tingling. Was that emotion? Sorrow? He didn't think himself capable. Or was it more the lost opportunity with Monika? Or the fact that he was suddenly unemployed, his once orderly life now disrupted? He willed the feeling from his brain and left the storage room, reentering the inner corridor. He twisted left and right until he found a spiral staircase. His knowledge of the castle's geography told him that he needed to ascend at least two floors before reaching what was regarded as the main level.

At the top of the staircase he stopped. A row of leaded glass windows opened to another courtyard. Across the bailey, on the upper story of the far rectangular keep, through a set of windows apparently opened to the evening, he saw a woman. Her body darted back and forth. The room's location was not dissimilar from the location of his own room at Burg Herz. Quiet. Out of the way. But safe. Suddenly the woman settled in the open rectangle, her arms reaching out to swing the double panes inward.

He saw the girlish face and wicked eyes.

Suzanne Danzer.

Good.

FIFTY-FOUR

KNOLL GAINED ENTRANCE TO THE BACK PASSAGES MORE EASILY
than he expected, watching from a cracked-open door while
a maid released a hidden panel in one of the ground-floor
corridors. He figured he was in the south wing of the west
building. He needed to cross to the far bastion and move
northeast to where he knew the public rooms were located.

He entered the passage and stepped lightly, hoping not to
encounter any of the staff. The lateness of the day seemed to
lessen the chances of that happening. The only people drifting about now would be chambermaids making sure any
guests' needs were taken care of for the night. The dank corridor was lined overhead with air ducts, water pipes, and an
electrical conduit. Bare bulbs lit the way.

He negotiated three spiral staircases and found what he
thought was the north wing. Tiny Judas holes dotted the
walls, set in recessed niches and shielded by rusty lead covers. Along the way, he slid a few open and spied a view into
various rooms. The peepholes were another holdover from
the past, an anachronism when eyes and ears were the only
way to learn information. Now they were nothing but ready
navigation markers, or a delicious opportunity for a voyeur.

He stopped at another viewpoint and twisted open a lead
cover. He recognized the Carolotta Room from the handsome bed and escritoire. Loring had named the space for the
mistress of King Ludwig I of Bavaria, and her portrait
adorned the far wall. He wondered what decoration disguised the peephole. Probably the wood carvings he recalled
from having been assigned the chamber one night.

He moved on.

Suddenly, he heard voices vibrating through the stone. He searched for a look. Finding a Judas hole, he peered inside and saw the figure of Rachel Cutler standing in the middle of a brightly lit room, maroon towels wrapped around her naked frame and wet hair.

He stopped his advance.

"I TOLD YOU MCKOY WAS UP TO SOMETHING," RACHEL SAID.

Paul was sitting before a polished rosewood escritoire. He and Rachel were sharing a room on the castle's fourth floor. McKoy had been given another room farther down. The steward who brought their bag upstairs had explained that the space was known as the Wedding Chamber, in honor of the seventeenth-century portrait of a couple in allegorical costume that hung over the sleigh bed. The room was spacious and equipped with a private bath, and Rachel had taken the opportunity to soak in the tub for a few minutes, cleaning up for dinner that Loring informed them would be at six.

"I'm uncomfortable with this," he said. "I imagine Loring is not a man to take lightly. Especially to blackmail."

Rachel slipped the towel from her head and stepped back into the bathroom, dabbing her locks dry. A hair dryer came on.

He studied a painting on the far wall. It was a half-figure of a penitent St. Peter. A da Cortona or maybe a Reni. Seventeenth-century Italian, if he remembered correctly. Expensive, provided one could even be found outside a museum. The canvas appeared original. From what little he knew about porcelain, the figurines resting on corbels attached to the wall on either side of the painting were Riemenschneider. Fifteenth-century German and priceless. On the way up the staircase to the bedroom they'd passed more paintings, tapestries, and sculptures. What the museum staff in Atlanta would give to display just a fraction of the items.

The hair dryer clicked off. Rachel stepped out of the bathroom, fingers teasing her auburn hair. "Like a hotel room," she said. "Soap, shampoo, and hair dryer."

"Except that the room is decorated with fine art worth millions."

"This stuff's original?"

"From what I can see."

"Paul, we have to do something about McKoy. This is going too far."

"I agree. But Loring bothers me. He's not at all what I expected."

"You've been watching too many James Bond movies. He's just a rich old man who loves art."

"He took McKoy's threat too calmly for me."

"Should we call Pannik and let him know we're staying over?"

"I don't think so. Let's just play it by ear right now. But I vote to get out of here tomorrow."

"You won't get any grief from me on that."

Rachel undraped the towel and slipped on a pair of panties. He watched from the chair, trying to remain impassive.

"It's not fair," he said.

"What's not?"

"You dancing around naked."

She snapped her bra in place, then walked over and climbed in his lap. "I meant what I said Tuesday night. I want to try again."

He stared at the Ice Queen, seminaked in his arms.

"I never stopped loving you, Paul. I don't know what happened. I think my pride and anger just took hold. There came a point when I felt stifled. It's nothing you did. It was me. After I went on the bench, something happened. I can't really explain."

She was right. Their problems had escalated after she was sworn in. Perhaps the mollification from everyone saying "Yes, ma'am" and "Her Honor" all day was hard to leave behind at the office. But to him she was Rachel Bates, a woman he loved, not an item of respect or a conduit to the wisdom of Solomon. He argued with her, told her what to do, and complained when she didn't do it. Perhaps, after a while, the startling contrast between their two worlds became difficult to delineate. So difficult that she'd ultimately rid herself of one side of the conflict.

"Daddy's death and all this has brought things home to me. All of Mama's and Daddy's family were killed in the war. I have no one other than Marla and Brent . . . and you."

He stared at her.

"I mean that. You are my family, Paul. I made a big mistake three years ago. I was wrong."

He realized how hard it was for her to say those words. But he wanted to know, "How so?"

"Tuesday night when we were darting though that abbey, hanging from the balcony, that's enough to bring anything home. You came over here when you thought I was in danger and risked a lot for me. I shouldn't be so difficult. You don't deserve that. All you ever asked was a little peace and quiet and consistency. All I ever did was make things hard."

He thought of Christian Knoll. Though Rachel had never admitted anything, she'd been attracted to him. He could feel it. But Knoll had left her to die. Perhaps that act had served as a reminder to her analytical mind that not everything was as it appeared. Her ex-husband included. What the hell. He loved her. Wanted her back. Time to put up or shut up.

He kissed her.

KNOLL WATCHED AS THE CUTLERS EMBRACED, AROUSED BY THE sight of a half-dressed Rachel Cutler. He'd concluded during the car trip from Munich to Kehlheim that she still cared for her ex-husband. Which was most likely why she rebuked his advances in Warthberg. She was definitely attractive. Full bosom, thin waist, inviting crotch. He'd wanted her in the mine and fully intended to have her until Danzer intruded with the explosion. So why not rectify the situation tonight? What did it matter anymore? Fellner and Monika were dead. He was unemployed. And none of the other club members would hire him after what he was about to do.

A knock on the bedchamber door caught his attention.

He stared hard through the Judas hole.

⚬——⚋

"WHO IS IT?" PAUL ASKED.

"McKoy."

Rachel hopped up and grabbed her clothes, disappearing into the bathroom. Paul stood and opened the door. McKoy stepped in, dressed in a pair of evergreen corduroy pants and a striped crew shirt. Brown chukkas wrapped his big feet.

"Kind of casual, McKoy," he said.

"My tux is at the cleaners."

Paul slammed the door shut. "What were you doing with Loring?"

McKoy faced him. "Lighten up, counselor. I wasn't tryin' to shake the old fart down."

"Then what *were* you doing?"

"Yeah, McKoy, what was all that about?" Rachel asked, stepping from the bathroom, now dressed in pleated jeans and a tight-fitting turtleneck.

McKoy eyed her up and down. "You dress down well, Your Honor."

"Get to the point," she said.

"The point was to see if the old man would crack, and he did. I pushed to see what he was made of. Get real. If there was nothin' to Loring's involvement, he would have said sayonara, get the hell out of here. As it was he couldn't hardly wait for us to spend the night."

"You weren't serious?" Paul asked.

"Cutler, I know you two think I'm pond scum, but I do have morals. True, they're relatively loose most of the time. But I still have 'em. This Loring either knows somethin' or

wants to know somethin'. Either way, he's interested enough
to put us up for the night."

"You think he's part of that club Grumer rambled about?"
Paul asked.

"I hope not," Rachel said. "That could mean Knoll and
that woman are around."

McKoy was unconcerned. "That's a chance were goin' to
have to take. I got a feelin' about this. I've also got a bunch
of investors waitin' in Germany. So I need answers. My
guess is the old bastard downstairs has got 'em."

"How long can your people hold off the partners' curiosity?" Rachel asked.

"Couple of days. No more. They're goin' to start on that
other tunnel in the mornin', but I told 'em to take their time.
Personally, I think it's a total waste."

"How do we need to handle dinner?" Rachel asked.

"Easy. Eat the man's food, drink his liquor, and turn on the
information vacuum cleaner. We need to get more than we
give. Understand?"

Rachel smiled. "Yeah, I understand."

DINNER WAS CORDIAL, LORING LEADING HIS GUESTS IN PLEAS-
ant conversation about art and politics. Paul was fascinated
by the extent of the old man's art knowledge. McKoy stayed
on his best behavior, accepting Loring's hospitality, pro-
fusely complimenting their host on the meal. Paul watched it
all carefully, noting Rachel's intense interest in McKoy. It
seemed as if she was waiting for him to cross the line.

After dessert, Loring escorted them on a tour of the castle's expansive ground floor. The decor seemed a mixture of
Dutch furniture, French clocks, and Russian chandeliers.
Paul noticed an emphasis on classicism along with realistically clear images in all the carvings. There was a well-
balanced composition throughout, an almost plastic-perfect
shape and form. The craftsmen had certainly known their
trade.

Each space carried a name. The Walderdorff Chamber. Molsberg Room. Green Room. Witches' Room. All were decorated with antique furniture—most originals, Loring explained—and art, so much that Paul was having trouble taking it all in, and he wished a couple of the museum's curators were there to explain. In what Loring called the Ancestors' Room the old man lingered before an oil painting of his father.

"My father was descended from a long line. Amazingly, all from the paternal side. So there have always been Loring males to inherit. It is one reason we have dominated this site for nearly five hundred years."

"What about when the Communists ruled?" Rachel asked.

"Even then, my dear. My family learned to adapt. There was no choice. Either change or perish."

"Meanin' you worked for the Communists," McKoy said.

"What else was there to do, *Pan* McKoy?"

McKoy did not reply and simply returned his attention to the painting of Josef Loring. "Was your father interested in the Amber Room?"

"Very much."

"Did he see the original in Leningrad before the war?"

"Actually, Father saw the room prior to the Russian Revolution. He was a great admirer of amber, as I am sure you already know."

"Why don't we cut the crap, Loring."

Paul cringed at the sudden intensity of McKoy's voice. Was it genuine or more games?

"I got a hole in a mountain a hundred fifty kilometers west of here that cost a million dollars to dig. All I got for the trouble are three trucks and five skeletons. Let me tell you what I think."

Loring sank into one of the leather chairs. "By all means."

McKoy accepted a glass of claret from a steward balancing a tray. "There's a story Dolinski told me, about a train leavin' occupied Russia sometime around May 1, 1945. The crated Amber Room was supposedly on board. Witnesses

said the crates were offloaded in Czechoslovakia, near
Týnec-nad-Sázavou. From there the crates were supposedly
trucked south. One version says they were stored in an underground bunker used by Field Marshal von Schörner,
commander of the German army. Another version says they
headed west to Germany. A third version says east to Poland.
Which one's right?"

"I, too, have heard such stories. But if I recall, that bunker
was extensively excavated by the Soviets. Nothing there, so
that eliminates one choice. As to the version east to Poland,
I doubt it."

"Why's that?" McKoy said, sitting, too.

Paul remained standing, Rachel beside him. It was interesting watching the two men spar. McKoy had handled the
partners expertly, and was doing equally well now, apparently intuitive enough to know when to push and when to
pull.

"The Poles have not the brains or the resources to harbor
such a treasure," Loring said. "Somebody would surely have
discovered it by now."

"Sounds like prejudice to me," McKoy said.

"Not at all. Just a fact. Throughout history Poles have
never been able to collate themselves into a unified country
for long. They are the led, not the leaders."

"So you say west to Germany?"

"I say nothing, *Pan* McKoy. Only that of the three choices
you offered, west seems the most likely."

Rachel sat down. "Mr. Loring—"

"Please, my dear. Call me Ernst."

"Okay . . . Ernst. Grumer was convinced that Knoll and
the woman who killed Chapaev were working for members
of a club. He called it the Retrievers of Lost Antiquities.
Knoll and the woman were supposedly Acquisitors. They
steal works of art that have already been stolen, members
competing with one another on what can be found."

"Sounds intriguing. But I can assure you I am not a member of such an organization. As you can see, my home is

filled with art. I am a public collector and openly display my treasures."

"How about amber? Haven't seen much of that," McKoy said.

"I have several beautiful pieces. Would you like to see?"

"Damn right."

Loring led the way out of the Ancestors' Room and down a twisting corridor deeper into the castle. The room they finally entered was a tight square with no windows. Loring flicked a switch embedded in the stone that lighted wooden display cases lining the walls. Paul paraded down the cases, immediately recognizing Vermeyen vessels, Bohemian glass, and Mair goldsmithing. Each piece was three-hundred-plus years old and in mint condition. Two cases were filled entirely with amber. Among the collection was a casket case, chessboard and pieces, a two-tiered chest, snuffbox, shaving basin, soap dish, and lather brush.

"Most are eighteenth century," Loring said. "All from the Tsarskoe Selo workshops. The masters who crafted these beauties worked on the Amber Room panels."

"They are the best I've ever seen," Paul said.

"I am quite proud of this collection. They each cost me a fortune. But, alas, I have no Amber Room to go with them, as much as I would like to."

"Why don't I believe you?" McKoy asked.

"Frankly, *Pan* McKoy, it matters not whether you believe me. The more important question is how are you to prove otherwise. You come into my home and make wild accusations—threaten me with exposure in the world media—yet have nothing to substantiate your allegations except a manufactured picture of letters in the sand and the ramblings of a greedy academician."

"I don't recall saying anythin' about Grumer being an academic," McKoy said.

"No, you did not. But I am familiar with the *Herr Doktor.* He was possessed of a reputation that I would not consider enviable."

Paul noticed the shift in Loring's tone. No longer conge-
nial and conciliatory. Now the words came slow and deliberate, the meaning clear. The man's patience was apparently
running thin.

McKoy seemed unimpressed. "I'd think, *Pan* Loring, a
man of your experience and breedin' could handle a rough-
by-the-edges sort like me."

Loring smiled. "I do find your frankness refreshing. It is
not often a man speaks to me as you have."

"Given any more thought to my offer from this afternoon?"

"As a matter of fact, I have. Would a million dollars U.S.
solve your investment problem?"

"Three million would be better."

"Then I assume you will settle for two without the need
for haggling?"

"I will."

Loring chuckled. "*Pan* McKoy, you are a man after my
own heart."

FIFTY-FIVE

FRIDAY, MAY 23, 2:15 A.M.

PAUL AWAKENED. HE'D HAD TROUBLE SLEEPING, EVER SINCE HE
and Rachel turned in a little before midnight. Rachel was
sound asleep beside him in the sleigh bed, not snoring, but
breathing heavily like she used to. He thought again about
Loring and McKoy. The old man had willingly coughed up
two million dollars. Maybe McKoy was right. Loring was
hiding something two million dollars was a bargain to protect. But what? The Amber Room? That prospect was a bit

far-fetched. He imagined Nazis ripping the amber panels off the palace walls, then trucking them across the Soviet Union, only to dismantle them again and truck them into Germany four years later. What kind of shape would they even be in? Would they be worth anything other than as raw material to be fashioned into other works of art? What had he read in Borya's articles? The panels comprised a hundred thousand pieces of amber. Certainly that was worth something on the open market. Maybe that was it. Loring found the amber and sold it, garnering enough that two million dollars was a bargain to silence.

He rose from the bed and crept toward his shirt and pants draped over a chair. He slipped them on but passed on his shoes—bare feet would make less noise. Sleep was not coming easily, and he'd very much like to investigate the ground-floor display rooms again. The array of art earlier had been nearly overpowering, difficult to take in. He hoped Loring wouldn't mind a little private viewing.

He stole a glance at Rachel. She was curled under the down comforter, her naked body covered only by one of his twill shirts. She'd made love to him two hours ago for the first time in nearly four years. He could still feel the intensity between them, his body drained from a release of emotions he thought never again possible. Could they make things right? God knows he wanted to. The past couple weeks had certainly been bittersweet. Her father was gone, but perhaps the Cutler family could be restored. He hoped he wasn't simply something with which to fill a void. Rachel's words earlier about him being all the family she had left still rang in his ears. He wondered why he was so suspicious. Perhaps it was the kick in the gut he'd experienced three years ago—caution shielding his heart from another crushing break.

He inched the door open and quietly slipped into the hall. Incandescent wall sconces burned softly. Not a sound drifted in the air. He crossed to a thick stone railing and glanced down at a foyer four stories below, the marbled space illuminated by a series of table lamps. A massive, unlit crystal chandelier hung down to the third-floor level.

He followed a carpet runner down a right-angled stone staircase to the ground floor. Barefoot and silent he moved deeper into the castle, negotiating wide corridors past the dining hall toward a series of spacious rooms where art was displayed. None of the doors to any room was shut.

He stepped into the Witches' Room, which, as Loring explained earlier, was where a local witches' court was once held. He approached a series of ebony cabinets and switched on tiny halogen lights. Roman Age artifacts lined the shelves. Statuettes, standards, plates, vessels, lamps, bells, tools. A few exquisitely carved goddesses, as well. He recognized Victoria, the Roman symbol for victory, a crown and palm leaf in her outstretched hands beckoning a choice.

A sound suddenly came from the hall. Not much. Like a scuff on carpet. But in the silence it rang loud.

His head whipped left to the open doorway and he froze, barely breathing. Was it a footstep or just a centuries-old building settling down for the night? He reached up and gently flicked off the cabinet lights. The cases went dark. He crept to a sofa and crouched down behind.

Another sound slipped past him. A footstep. Definitely. Somebody was in the hall. He shrank farther behind the couch and waited, hoping whoever it was moved on. Perhaps it was simply one of the staff making required rounds.

A shadow spread across the lit doorway. He peered over the sofa.

Wayland McKoy walked past.

He should have known.

He tiptoed to the doorway. McKoy was a few feet away, headed in the direction of a room at the far end. Earlier, Loring had merely pointed out the darkened space, calling it the Romanesque Room, but had not offered a tour.

"Couldn't sleep?" he whispered.

McKoy reeled back with a start and whirled around. "Goddammit, Cutler," he mouthed. "You scared the fuck out of me." The big man wore a pair of jeans and a pullover sweater.

He pointed to McKoy's bare feet. "We're starting to think alike. That's scary."

"A little redneck wouldn't hurt you a bit, city lawyer."

They stepped into the shadow of the Witches' Room and spoke in hushed whispers.

"You curious, too?" Paul asked.

"Damn right. Two fuckin' million. Loring jumped on that like flies on shit."

"Wonder what he knows?"

"I don't know. But it's somethin'. Trouble is, this Bohemian Louvre is so full of crap, we may never find out."

"We could get lost in this maze."

Suddenly, something clattered down the hall. Like metal to stone. He and McKoy leaned their heads out and glanced left. A dim yellow rectangle of light spilled from the Romanesque Room at the far end.

"I vote we go see," McKoy said.

"Why not? We've come this far."

McKoy led the way down the carpet runner. At the open door of the Romanesque Room they both froze.

"Oh, shit," Paul said.

KNOLL HAD WATCHED THROUGH THE JUDAS HOLE AS PAUL CUTler donned his clothes and crept out. Rachel Cutler had never heard her ex-husband leave and was still asleep under the covers. He'd been waiting for hours before making his move, allowing ample time for everyone to retire for the night. He planned to start with the Cutlers, move to McKoy, then Loring and Danzer, particularly enjoying the last two—savoring the moment of their deaths—exacting compensation for the murders of Fellner and Monika. But Paul Cutler's unexpected leaving had raised a problem. From what Rachel described, her ex-husband wasn't the adventurous type. Yet here he was, venturing off barefoot in the middle of the night. Certainly not heading for the kitchen and a midnight snack. He was most likely snooping. He'd have to tend to him later.

After Rachel.

He crept down the passage, following a trail of bare bulbs. He found the first exit and tripped the spring-loaded switch. A slab of stone swung open and he stepped into one of the empty fourth-floor bedrooms. He crossed to the hall door and hustled back to the room where Rachel Cutler slept.

He entered and locked the door behind him.

Approaching the Renaissance fireplace, he located the switch disguised as a piece of gilded molding. He'd not entered from the secret passages for fear of making too much noise, but he might need to make a hasty exit. He tripped the switch and left the concealed door half open.

He inched over to the bed.

Rachel Cutler still slept peacefully.

He twisted his right arm and waited for the stiletto to slither down into his palm.

<hr />

"IT'S A FRIGGIN' SECRET DOOR," MCKOY SAID.

Paul had never seen one before. Old movies and novels proclaimed their existence, but right before his eyes, thirty feet away, a section of stone wall was swung open on a center pivot. One of the wooden display cases was firmly affixed to it, three feet on either side allowing entrance into a lit room beyond.

McKoy stepped forward.

Paul grabbed him. "You crazy?"

"Do the math, Cutler. We're supposed to go."

"What do you mean?"

"I mean our host didn't leave this open by accident. Let's not disappoint him."

Paul believed going any farther was foolish. He'd pushed things coming downstairs to start with, but now he wasn't sure about following the situation to its conclusion. Maybe he should just go back upstairs to Rachel. But his curiosity told him to go on.

So he followed McKoy.

In the room beyond, more lighted cases lined the walls and center. Paul strolled through the maze in awe. Antico statues and busts. Egyptian and Near East carvings. Mayan etchings. Antique jewelry. A couple of paintings caught his eye. A seventeenth-century Rembrandt he knew was stolen from a German museum thirty years ago and a Bellini taken from Italy about the same time. Both were among the world's most sought-after art treasures. He recalled a seminar at the High Museum on the topic.

"McKoy, this stuff is all stolen."

"How do you know?"

He stopped in front of one chest-high case that displayed a blackened skull resting on a glass pedestal. "This is Peking Man. Nobody has seen it since World War Two. And those two paintings over there are definitely stolen. Shit. What Grumer said was right. Loring is part of that club."

"Calm down, Cutler. We don't know that. This guy may just have a little private stash he keeps to himself. Let's not go off half-cocked."

He stared ahead at a set of open, white-enameled double doors. He noticed the whiskey-colored mosaic walls beyond. He stepped forward. McKoy followed. In the doorway they both went motionless.

"Oh, fuck," McKoy whispered.

Paul gazed at the Amber Room. "You got that right."

The visual spectacle was broken by two people who entered through another set of open double doors to the right. One was Loring. The other, the blond woman from Stod. Suzanne. Both held pistols.

"I see you accepted my invitation," Loring said.

McKoy stiffened. "Didn't want to disappoint you."

Loring motioned with the gun. "What do you think of my treasure?"

McKoy stepped farther inside. The woman's grip on her gun tightened, barrel jutted forward. "Stay cool, little lady. Just goin' to admire the handiwork." McKoy approached one of the amber walls.

Paul turned to the woman Knoll had called Suzanne. "You found Chapaev through me, didn't you?"

"Yes, Mr. Cutler. The information was most helpful."

"You killed that old man for this?"

"No, *Pan* Cutler," Loring said. "She killed for me."

Loring and the woman stayed to the far side of the thirty-foot-square room. Double doors opened out of three walls, windows lined the fourth, but Paul assumed they were fake. This chamber was clearly an inside one. McKoy continued to admire the amber, massaging its smoothness. If not for the seriousness of their predicament, Paul would have been in awe, as well. But not too many probate lawyers found themselves in a Czech castle with two semiautomatic handguns pointed at them. Definitely not a course on this in law school.

"Tend to it," Loring softly said to Suzanne.

The woman left. Loring stayed across the room and kept his gun trained. McKoy moved close to Paul.

"We will wait here, gentlemen, until Suzanne fetches the other Cutler."

McKoy stepped close.

"What the shit we do now?" Paul whispered.

"Hell if I know."

KNOLL SLOWLY PEELED BACK THE COMFORTER AND CRAWLED onto the bed. He nestled close to Rachel and gently massaged her breasts. She responded to his touch, sighing gently, still half asleep. He let his hand roam down the length of her body and discovered she was naked beneath the shirt. She slid over and cuddled close.

"Paul," she whispered.

He wrapped his hand around her throat, rolled her over onto her back, and then slipped on top. Rachel's eyes went wide with fear. He brought the stiletto to her throat, gently probing the scab from Tuesday night's encounter with the tip. "You should have taken my advice."

"Where's Paul?" she managed to mouth.

"I have him."

She started to struggle. He pressed the blade flat against her throat. "Sit still, Frau Cutler, or I will twist the edge to your skin. Do you understand?"

She stopped moving.

He motioned with his head toward the open panel, relaxing his grip slightly to allow a look. "He's in there." He retightened the lock on her throat and moved the knife down her shirt, flicking off each button. Then he parted the folds. Her bare chest heaved. He lightly traced the outline of one nipple with the knifepoint. "I watched earlier from behind the wall. Your lovemaking is intense."

She spat on him.

He backhanded her face. "Insolent bitch. Your father did the same thing and you saw what happened to him."

He slugged her in the stomach and heard the breath leave her. He delivered another blow to her face, this time with his fist. His hand returned to her throat. Her eyes rolled in a daze. He pinched her cheeks and shook her head from side to side.

"You love him? Why risk his life? Pretend you are a whore, the price of my pleasure . . . a life. It will not be unpleasant."

"Where . . . is . . . Paul?"

He shook his head. "Such stubbornness. Channel all that anger into passion and your Paul will see morning."

His groin throbbed, ready for action. He returned the knife to her chin and pressed.

"Okay," she finally said.

He hesitated. "I am withdrawing the knife. But one millimeter of movement and I will kill you. Then him."

He slowly released his hand and the knife. He unbuckled his belt and was about to wiggle out of his pants when Rachel screamed.

⚷━━

"HOW'D YOU GET THE PANELS, LORING?" MCKOY ASKED.

"A gift from heaven."

McKoy chuckled. Paul was impressed with how cool the big man was staying. Glad somebody was calm. He was scared to death.

"I assume you plan to use that gun at some point. So humor a condemned man and answer a few questions."

"You were right earlier," Loring said. "Trucks left Königsberg in 1945 with the panels. They were eventually loaded onto a train. That train stopped in Czechoslovakia. My father tried then to secure the panels, but couldn't. Field Marshal von Schörner was loyal to Hitler and could not be bought. Von Schörner ordered the crates trucked west to Germany. They were to go to Bavaria, but only made it as far as Stod."

"My cavern?"

"Correct. Father found the panels seven years after the war."

"And shot the help?"

"A necessary business decision."

"Rafal Dolinski another necessary business decision?"

"Your reporter friend did contact me and provided a copy of his narrative. Too informative for his own good."

"What about Karol Borya and Chapaev?" Paul asked.

"Many have sought what you see before you, *Pan* Cutler. Would you not agree it is a treasure worth dying for?"

"My parents included?" Paul asked.

"We became aware of your father's inquiries across Europe, but finding that Italian was a bit too close. That was our first and only breach of secrecy. Suzanne dealt with both the Italian and your parents. Unfortunate, but another necessary business decision."

He lunged toward the old man. The gun jutted forward and took aim. McKoy grabbed him by the shoulder. "Calm down, Rocket Man. Gettin' yourself shot isn't going to solve a thing."

He struggled to get free. "Wringing his goddamned neck

would." Anger seethed through him. He never thought himself capable of such rage. He wanted to kill Loring, regardless of the consequences, and enjoy every second of the bastard's torment. McKoy forced him to the other side of the room. Loring inched to the opposite amber wall. McKoy's back was to Loring when the big man whispered, "Stay cool. Follow my lead."

SUZANNE SWITCHED ON AN OVERHEAD CHANDELIER AND flooded the foyer and staircase with light. There was no danger of the staff interfering with the night's activities; Loring had specifically instructed that no one reenter the main wing after midnight. She'd already thought about body disposal, deciding to bury all three in the woods beyond the castle before morning. She slowly climbed the stairs and reached the fourth-floor landing, gun in hand. A scream suddenly pierced the silence from the direction of the Wedding Chamber. She raced down the hall, past the open banister, to the oak door.

She tried the handle. Locked.

Another scream came from inside.

She fired two shots at the ancient latch. The wood splintered. She kicked the door. Once. Twice. Another shot. A third kick and the door flung inward. In the semidarkened chamber she saw Christian Knoll on the bed, Rachel Cutler struggling beneath him.

Knoll saw her, then slugged Rachel hard in the face. He then reached for something on the bed. She saw the stiletto come up in his hand. She aimed and fired, but Knoll rolled off the far side of the bed and her bullet missed. She noticed the open panel near the fireplace. The bastard was using the back passages. She dived to the floor, shielding herself behind a chair, knowing what was coming.

The stiletto zoomed across the darkness and ripped into the upholstery, mere inches away. She fired two more shots in Knoll's direction. Four muffled shots came back, obliterating the back of the chair. Knoll was armed. This was too

close. She sent another shot at Knoll, then crawled to the
open doorway and rolled out into the hall.

Two more shots from Knoll ricocheted off the doorjamb.

Outside, she stood and started running.

"I HAVE TO GET TO RACHEL," PAUL WHISPERED, STILL SEETHING.

McKoy's back remained to Loring. "Get out of here when
I make a move."

"He has a gun."

"I'm bettin' the bastard won't shoot in here. He's not goin'
to risk a hole in the amber."

"Don't count on it—"

Before he could question further what McKoy intended,
the big man turned to Loring. "I guess my two million is
gone, huh?"

"Unfortunately. But bold of you to try."

"Comes from my mother's side. She worked the cucum-
ber fields in eastern North Carolina. Didn't take shit off nobody."

"How charming."

McKoy inched closer. "What makes you think people
don't know we're here?"

Loring shrugged. "A risk I am prepared to take."

"My people know where I am."

Loring smiled. "I doubt that, *Pan* McKoy."

"How about a deal?"

"Not interested."

McKoy suddenly lunged at Loring, crossing the ten feet
that separated them as fast as his beefy frame allowed. As the
old man fired, McKoy winced, then screamed, "Go, Cutler!"

Paul darted for the double doors leading out of the Amber
Room, glancing back momentarily to see McKoy crumble to
the parquet and Loring readjust his aim. He leaped from the
room, rolled across the stone floor, then stood and raced
through the darkened gallery, out the opening into the Romanesque Room.

He expected Loring to be following, more shots on the way, but the old man certainly couldn't move fast.

McKoy had actually allowed himself to be shot so he could get away. He never knew people really did that. That was something that only happened in movies. Yet the last thing he saw before fleeing the room was the big man lying on the floor.

He flushed that thought from his mind and concentrated on Rachel as he ran down the corridor for the stairway.

KNOLL HEARD SUZANNE SCAMPER OUT INTO THE HALL. HE crossed the room and retrieved the knife. He marched to the open door and risked a glance. Danzer was bolting to the stairway twenty meters away. He anchored his feet and sent the perfectly balanced stiletto flying her way, piercing Danzer's left thigh, the sharp blade sucking into her flesh down to the handle.

She cried out and folded to the carpet runner in agony.

"Not this time, Suzanne," he calmly said.

He walked to her.

She was gripping the back of her thigh, blood oozing from the embedded blade. She tried to turn and level her gun, but he instantly kicked the CZ-75B from her grasp.

The gun clattered away.

He brought his shoe down across her neck and pinned her to the floor. He pointed his own weapon.

"Enough fun and games," he said.

Danzer reached back and tried to wrap her palm around the stiletto's handle, but he slammed the sole of his shoe into her face.

He then fired two shots into Danzer's head and she stopped moving.

"For Monika," he whispered.

He jerked the knife from her thigh and swiped the blade clean on her clothes. He found Danzer's gun and stepped back into the bedchamber, determined to finish what he'd started.

FIFTY-SIX

MCKOY TRIED TO RISE AND FOCUS BUT COULDN'T. THE AMBER Room spun around him. His legs were limp, his head woozy. Blood poured from a bullet wound to his shoulder. He was rapidly losing consciousness. Never had he imagined dying like this, surrounded by a treasure worth millions, powerless to do anything.

He'd been wrong about Loring. There'd been no risk to the amber. The bullet was simply planted in flesh. He hoped Paul Cutler had managed to escape. He started to pull himself up. Footsteps approached from the outer gallery, coming toward him. He fell back to the parquet and lay prone. He eased open his left eye and caught the blurred image of Ernst Loring reentering the Amber Room, the gun still in hand. He lay perfectly still, trying to maximize what little strength remained.

He took a deep breath and waited for Loring to draw close. The old man, with his shoe, cautiously nudged McKoy's left leg, apparently testing to see if death had taken hold. He held his breath and managed to keep his body rigid. His head started spinning from the lack of oxygen combined with the blood loss.

He needed the bastard closer.

Loring took two steps forward.

He suddenly clipped the old man's legs out from under him. Pain racked his right shoulder and chest. Blood spurted from his wound. But he tried to hang on long enough to finish.

Loring slammed to the floor, the impact jarring his grip on the gun. McKoy's right hand locked around the old man's neck. The image of Loring's shocked expression blinked in and out. He needed to hurry.

"Say hello to the devil for me," he whispered.

With his last bit of strength, he strangled Ernst Loring to death.

Then he surrendered to the darkness.

PAUL NEGOTIATED THE MAZE OF GROUND-FLOOR CORRIDORS and bolted for the staircase leading up to the fourth floor. Just before entering the brightly lit foyer, two shots popped from above.

He stopped.

This was foolish. The woman was armed. He wasn't. But who was she firing at? Rachel? McKoy had taken a bullet so he could get away. It now looked like it was his turn.

He loped up the stairs, two at a time.

KNOLL DROPPED HIS PANTS. KILLING DANZER HAD BEEN SATIS-fying foreplay. Rachel lay sprawled on the bed, still dazed from his fist. He tossed the gun on the floor and palmed the stiletto. He approached the bed, gently parted her legs, and ran his tongue up the length of her thigh. She did not resist. This was going to be nice. Rachel, apparently still groggy, lightly moaned and responded to his touch. He slipped the stiletto back into the sheath under his right sleeve. She was dazed and docile. There would be no need for the knife. He cupped her bare butt with his hands and returned his tongue to her crotch.

"Oh, Paul," she whispered.

"I told you it would not be unpleasant," he mouthed.

He raised up and prepared to mount her.

PAUL TURNED AT THE FOURTH-FLOOR LANDING AND DASHED UP
the last flight of stairs. He was winded, his legs ached, but
Rachel was up there and needed him. At the top he saw
Suzanne's body, her face obliterated by two bullet holes. The
sight was sickening, but he thought of Chapaev and his parents and felt nothing but satisfaction. Then a thought electri-
fied his brain.

Who the hell shot her?

Rachel?

Moaning resonated from down the hall.

Then his name.

He inched his way to the bedchamber. The door was flung
back, its top hinge splintered away. He gazed into the semi-
darkness. His eyes adjusted. A man was on the bed, and
Rachel was beneath him.

Christian Knoll.

Paul went berserk and rushed the length of the room, cat-
apulting himself onto Knoll. Momentum rolled them off the
bed and to the floor. He landed on his right shoulder, the
same one injured Tuesday night in Stod. Pain seared through
his right arm. He raised a fist and brought it down. Knoll was
bigger and more experienced, but he was mad as hell. He
swung his fist again and Knoll's nose gave way. Knoll
howled, but he pivoted and used his legs to send Paul flying
up and over him. Knoll curled himself forward and rolled
out of the way, then pounced, ramming a fist hard into Paul's
chest. He gagged on his own saliva and tried to catch a
breath.

Knoll stood and yanked him from the floor. A fist
slammed into his jaw, sending him reeling into the center of
the room. He was dazed, trying hard to focus on the spinning
furniture and the tall man approaching. Forty-one years old,
and this was his first fistfight. Odd, he thought, the sensation
of being slugged. Suddenly, the image of Knoll's naked ass
on top of Rachel flashed through his mind. He caught hold of
himself, grabbed a breath, and lunged, met only by another
fist to the stomach.

Damn. He was losing the fight.

Knoll caught him by the hair.

"You interrupted my pleasure, and I do not like being interrupted. Did you not notice Fräulein Danzer on the way in? She interrupted also."

"Fuck you, Knoll."

"So defiant. And brave. But weak."

Knoll released his grip and slugged him. Blood gushed from his nose. The momentum of the blow sent Paul tumbling through the open doorway, out into the hall. He was having trouble seeing out of his right eye.

He couldn't take much more.

RACHEL WAS VAGUELY AWARE THAT SOMETHING WAS HAPPENING, but it was all so confusing. One moment it seemed as if Paul were making love to her, and the next she heard fighting and bodies being flung across the room. Then a voice.

She raised up.

Paul's face came into view, then another.

Knoll.

Paul was clothed, but Knoll was naked from the waist down. She tried to assimilate the information, making sense of what at first seemed impossible.

She heard Knoll's voice.

"You interrupted my pleasure, and I do not like being interrupted. Did you not notice Fräulein Danzer on the way in? She interrupted also."

"Fuck you, Knoll."

"So defiant. And brave. But weak."

Then Knoll slugged Paul in the face. Blood splattered and Paul rolled out into the hall. Knoll followed. She tried to stand from the bed, but collapsed to the floor. She slowly pulled herself across the parquet toward the doorway. Along the way she crossed a pair of pants, some shoes, and something hard.

She reached down. There were two guns. She ignored

both and kept crawling. At the doorway she pulled herself up
to her feet.

Knoll was moving toward Paul.

PAUL REALIZED THIS WAS THE END. HE COULD HARDLY BREATHE
from the blows to his chest, his lungs were constricted, most
likely several ribs were broken. His face ached beyond belief
and he was having trouble seeing. Knoll was merely toying
with him. He was no match for this professional. He staggered to his feet, using the stone banister for support, not unlike the banister from Tuesday night at the abbey high above
Stod. He gazed down four stories and felt like vomiting. The
glow from the bright crystal chandelier burned his eyes, and
he squinted. His body was suddenly yanked back and twirled
around. Knoll's smiling face gleamed at him.

"Had enough, Cutler?"

All he could think to do was spit in Knoll's face. The German jumped back and then lunged at him, ramming a fist
into his stomach. Spit and blood coughed up as he gasped for
air. Knoll brought another blow down across the nape of his
neck, slamming him to the floor. Knoll reached down and
pulled him to his feet. His legs were rubber. He propped him
against the railing, then stepped back and twitched his right
arm.

A knife appeared.

RACHEL WATCHED THROUGH FOGGED EYES AS KNOLL BATTERED
Paul. She wanted to help but barely had the strength to stand.
Her face ached, the swelling on her right cheek beginning to
affect her vision. Her head pounded. Everything was blurred
and spinning. Her stomach tossed like a boat on a stormy
sea.

Paul's body crumbled to the floor. Knoll reached down
and yanked him to his feet. She suddenly thought of the two
guns and stumbled back to the center of the bedchamber. She

groped the floor until she found one of the pistols, then staggered back to the doorway.

Knoll had stepped away from Paul, his back to her. A knife appeared in the German's hand and she knew there'd be only a second to react. Knoll moved toward Paul, the blade rising. She pointed the gun and, for the first time in her life, pulled a trigger. The bullet left the barrel, not with a report, but with the muffled pop like when balloons burst at one of the kids' birthday parties.

The bullet plowed into Knoll's back.

He stumbled and turned, then moved toward her with the knife.

She fired again. The gun bucked in her hand, but she held tight.

Then again.

And again.

Bullets ripped through Knoll's chest. She thought of what must have happened in the bed and lowered her aim, firing three more shots at his exposed crotch. Knoll screamed, but somehow kept standing. He stared down at blood pouring from his wounds. He staggered toward the banister. She was about to fire again when Paul suddenly lunged forward, shoving the half-naked German over the top and out into the open air of the four-story foyer. She fell toward the railing and glanced over just as Knoll's body found the chandelier and ripped the massive crystal fixture from the ceiling. Blue sparks exploded, Knoll and glass free-falling to the marble below, a thud from the body accompanying the shattering of glass, the crystal flung about and then tinkling to the floor like the applause that lingered after a symphony's climax.

Then, silence. Not a sound.

Below, Knoll did not move.

She looked at Paul. "You okay?"

He said nothing, but wrapped his arm around her. She reached over and gently caressed his face. "Does it hurt as bad as it looks?" she asked.

"Damn right."

"Where's McKoy?"

Paul heaved a deep breath. "Took a bullet . . . so I could get to you. Last I saw he was . . . bleeding all over the Amber Room."

"The Amber Room?"

"Long story. Not now."

"I guess I'm going to have to take back all the nasty things I said about that big fool."

"I guess you are," a voice suddenly said from below.

She glanced over the rail. McKoy stumbled into the dim foyer, holding his bloodied right shoulder.

"Who's this?" he asked, pointing to the body.

"The bastard who killed my father," Rachel called down.

"Seems that score's settled. Where's the woman?"

"Dead," Paul said.

"Good fuckin' riddance."

"Where's Loring?" Paul asked.

"I strangled the motherfucker."

Paul winced from the pain. "Good fuckin' riddance. You okay?"

"Nothin' a good surgeon can't fix."

Paul managed a weak smile. He looked at Rachel. "I think I'm beginning to like that guy."

She smiled back, the first in a while. "Me, too."

EPILOGUE

PAUL AND RACHEL STOOD AT THE FRONT OF A SIDE CHAPEL. ITAL-ian marble surrounded them in elegant tones of sienese yellow with Russian malachite intermixed. Slanting rays from the morning sun cast a towering iconostasis beyond the priest in a glinting hue of sparkling gold.

Brent stood to the left of his father, Marla beside her mother. The patriarch pronounced the marriage vows in a solemn voice, the occasion enhanced by a chanting choir. St. Isaac's Cathedral was empty except for the wedding party and Wayland McKoy. Paul's eyes were drawn to a stained-glass window centered in a wall of icons. Christ standing tall after the Resurrection. A new beginning. How appropriate, he thought.

The priest finished the vows and bowed his head as the service ended.

He gently kissed Rachel and whispered, "I love you."

"And I you," she said.

"Ah, go ahead, Cutler, give her a good lip lock," McKoy said.

He smiled, then took the advice, kissing Rachel passionately.

"Daddy," Marla said, signaling enough.

"Leave 'em alone," Brent said.

McKoy stepped forward. "Smart kid. Which one of you he take after?"

Paul smiled. The big man looked strange in a suit and tie. The wound to McKoy's shoulder had apparently healed. He and Rachel had also recovered, the past three months something of a blinding whirlwind.

Within an hour of Knoll's death, Rachel had telephoned Fritz Pannik. It was the German inspector who arranged for the Czech police to immediately intervene, and Pannik himself arrived at Castle Loukov, with Europol, at daybreak. The Russian ambassador in Prague was summoned by mid-morning, and officials from the Catherine Palace and Hermitage flew in the next afternoon. A team from Tsarskoe Selo arrived the following morning, and the Russians wasted no time dismantling the amber panels and transporting them back to St. Petersburg, the Czech government offering no resistance after learning the details of Ernst Loring's sordid activities.

Europol investigators quickly established a link to Franz Fellner. Documents at both Castle Loukov and Burg Herz confirmed the activities of the Retrievers of Lost Antiquities. With no heirs left to assume control of the Fellner estate, the German government intervened. Fellner's private collection was eventually located, and it took only a few more days for investigators to learn the identity of the remaining club members. Their estates were raided under guidance from Europol's art theft division.

The cache was enormous.

Sculptures, carvings, jewelry, drawings, and paintings, particularly old Masters thought lost forever. Billions of dollars in stolen treasure were retrieved virtually overnight. But since Acquisitors looted only what had already been stolen, many claims of ownership were muddy at best, nonexistent at worst. The number of both governmental and private claims filed in courts scattered across Europe rose quickly into the thousands. So many that eventually a political solution was fashioned by the EC Parliament utilizing the World Court as final arbitrator. One journalist covering the spectacle observed that it would probably take decades before all the legal haggling was completed, "lawyers the only real winners in the end."

Interestingly, the Loring family's duplication of the

Amber Room was so precise that the reconstructed panels fit perfectly back into the lacunae at the Catherine Palace. The initial thought was to display the recovered amber elsewhere and allow the newly restored room to remain. But Russian purists strongly argued that the amber should be returned to its rightful home—the home Peter the Great would have intended—though in actuality Peter cared little for the panels, his daughter, Empress Elizabeth, being the one who actually commissioned the Russian version of the room. So within ninety days of its discovery, the original Amber Room panels once again adorned the first floor of the Catherine Palace.

The Russian government was so grateful that Paul, Rachel, the children, and McKoy were invited to the official unveiling and flown over at government expense. While there, Paul and Rachel decided to remarry in the Orthodox church. There'd been a little initial resistance, given they were divorced. But once the circumstances had been explained, and the fact that they were remarrying each other made clear, the Church agreed. It had been a lovely ceremony. One he would remember for the rest of his life.

Paul thanked the priest and stepped from the altar.

"That was nice," McKoy said. "A good way to end all this shi—I mean, crap."

Rachel smiled. "Children cramp your style?"

"Just my vocabulary."

They started walking toward the front of the cathedral.

"The Cutler family off to Minsk?" McKoy asked.

Paul nodded. "One last thing to do, then home."

Paul knew McKoy had come for the publicity, the Russian government grateful for the return of one of its most prized treasures. The big man had smiled and backslapped his way though the unveiling yesterday, enjoying the press attention. He'd even done the Larry King show live last evening by satellite, fielding questions from around the world. *National Geographic* was talking to him about a one-hour special on the Amber Room with a worldwide distribution, the money they'd mentioned enough to satisfy his investors and resolve any issue of litigation from the Stod dig.

They stopped at the main doors.

"You two take care of yourself," McKoy said. He motioned to the children. "And them."

Rachel kissed him on the cheek. "Did I ever thank you for what you did?"

"You'd have done the same for me."

"Probably not."

McKoy smiled. "Anytime, Your Honor."

Paul shook McKoy's hand. "Keep in touch, okay?"

"Oh, I'll probably need your services again before long."

"Not another dig?" Paul said.

McKoy shrugged. "Who knows? Still lots of shi—stuff—out there to find."

⸻

THE TRAIN LEFT ST. PETERSBURG TWO HOURS LATER, THE JOURney south to Belarus a five-hour ride through dense forests and sloping fields of blue flax. Autumn had arrived, and the leaves had surrendered to the chill in bursts of red, orange, and yellow.

Russian officials had intervened with Belarussian authorities to make everything possible. Karol and Maya Borya's caskets had arrived the day before, flown over by special arrangement. Rachel knew that her father wanted to be buried back in his homeland, but she wanted her parents together. Now they would be, in Belarussian soil, forever.

The caskets were waiting at the Minsk train station. They were then trucked to a lovely cemetery forty kilometers west of the capital, as near as possible to where Karol and Maya Borya had been born. The Cutler family followed the flatbed in a rental car, a United States envoy with them to make sure everything went smoothly.

The patriarch of Belarus himself presided at the private reburial, Rachel, Paul, Marla, and Brent standing together as solemn words were said. A light breeze eased across brown grass as the coffins were lowered into the ground.

"Say good-bye to your papa and nana," Rachel told the children.

She handed each a sliver of blue flax. The children stepped to the open graves and tossed down the buds. Paul came close and held her. Her eyes teared. She noticed that Paul's were watery, too. They'd never spoken about what happened that night in Castle Loukov. Thankfully, Knoll had never finished what he started. Paul risked his life to stop him. She loved her husband. The priest this morning cautioned them both that marriage was for life, something to be taken seriously, especially with children involved. And he was right. Of that she was sure.

She approached the graves. She'd said good-bye to her mother twenty years ago.

"Bye, Daddy."

Paul stood behind her. "Good-bye, Karol. Rest in peace."

They stood for a little while in silence, then thanked the patriarch and started for the car. A hawk soared overhead in the clear afternoon. A breeze rolled past them, neutralizing the sun. The children trotted ahead toward the gate.

"Back to work, huh?" she said to Paul.

"Time to get reacquainted with real life."

She'd won reelection in July, though she'd done almost no campaigning, the aftermath and attention from the recovery of the Amber Room springboarding a victory over two opponents. Marcus Nettles had been crushed, but she'd made a point to visit the cantankerous lawyer and make peace, part of her new attitude of reconciliation.

"You think I ought to stay on the bench?" she asked.

"That's your call, not mine."

"I was thinking maybe it's not such a good idea. It takes too much of my attention."

"You have to do what makes you happy," Paul said.

"I used to think being a judge made me happy. But I'm not so sure anymore."

"I know a firm that would love to have an ex–superior court judge in its litigation department."

"And that wouldn't be Pridgen and Woodworth, would it?"

"Maybe. I have some pull there, you know."

She wrapped her arm around his waist as they continued to walk. It felt good to be near him. For a few moments they strolled in silence and she savored her contentment. She thought about her future, the children, and Paul. Practicing law again might be just the thing for them all. Pridgen & Woodworth would be an excellent place to work. She looked over at Paul and heard again what he'd just said.

"I have some pull there, you know."

So she hugged him hard and, for once, didn't argue.

WRITER'S NOTE

IN RESEARCHING THIS NOVEL I TRAVELED THROUGHOUT GER-many, to Austria and Mauthausen concentration camp, then finally to Moscow and St. Petersburg where I spent several days at the Catherine Palace in Tsarskoe Selo. Of course, the primary goal of a novel is to entertain, but I also wanted to accurately inform. The subject of the Amber Room is relatively unexplored in this country, though the Internet has recently started to fill that void. In Europe, the artifact holds an endless fascination. Since I do not speak German or Russian, I was forced to rely on English-version accounts of what may or may not have happened. Unfortunately, a careful study of those reports reveals conflicts in the facts. The consistent points are presented within the course of the narrative. The inconsistent details were either disregarded or modified to suit my fictional needs.

A few specific items: Prisoners at Mauthausen were tortured in the manner depicted. However, Hermann Göring never appeared there. Göring and Hitler's personal competition for looted art is well documented, as is Göring's obsession with the Amber Room, though there is no evidence he ever attempted to actually possess it. The Soviet commission for which Karol Borya and Danya Chapaev supposedly worked was real and actively sought looted Russian art for years after the war, the Amber Room at the top of its wanted list. Some say there is, in fact, a curse of the Amber Room, as several have died (as detailed in chapter 41) in the search—whether by coincidence or conspiracy is unknown. The Harz Mountains were extensively used by the Nazis to hide plunder, and the information described in chapter 42 is accurate, including the tombs found. The town of Stod is fictional, but the location, along with the abbey that overlooks it, is based on Melk in Austria, a truly impressive place. All the stolen art detailed at various points in the story is real and remains among the missing. Finally, the speculation, history, and contradictions about what may have happened to the Amber Room noted in chapters 13, 14, 28, 41, 44, and 48, including a possible Czech connection, are based on actual reports, though my resolution of the mystery is fictional.

The Amber Room's disappearance in 1945 was a tremendous loss. At present, the room is being restored at the Catherine Palace by modern-day artisans who are laboring to re-create, panel by panel, magnificent walls crafted entirely of amber. I was fortunate to spend a few hours with the chief restorer, who showed me the difficulty of the endeavor. Luckily, the Soviets photographed the room in the late 1930s, planning on a restoration in the 1940s—but of course, war interfered. Those black-and-white images now act as a map for the re-creation of what was first fashioned more than 250 years ago.

The chief restorer also provided me with his insight into what may have happened to the original panels. He believed, as many others do (and as postulated in chapter 51), that the amber was either totally destroyed in the war or, like gold and other precious metals and jewels, the amber itself commanded the greatest market worth. It was simply found and sold off piece by piece, the sum of its parts far greater in value than the whole. Like gold, amber can be reshaped, leaving no trace of its former configuration, so it is possible that jewelry and other amber objects sold throughout the world today may contain amber from that original room.

But, who knows?

As Robert Browning was quoted saying in the narrative: *Suddenly, as rare things will, it vanished.*

How true.

And how sad.